I0761418

ALSO BY WILL WIGHT

THE LAST HORIZON

The Captain

The Engineer

CRADLE

Unsouled

Soulsmith

Blackflame

Skysworn

Ghostwater

Underlord

Uncrowned

Wintersteel

Bloodline

Reaper

Dreadgod

Waybound

Threshold: Stories from Cradle

THE TRAVELER'S GATE TRILOGY

House of Blades

The Crimson Vault

City of Light

THE ELDER EMPIRE

Of Sea & Shadow

Of Shadow & Sea

Of Dawn & Darkness

Of Darkness & Dawn

Of Kings & Killers

Of Killers & Kings

KINDLE-EXCLUSIVE COLLECTED EDITIONS

Cradle: Foundation

Cradle: Path of Gold

Cradle: Rise of Lords

The Traveler's Gate Chronicles

The Traveler's Gate Trilogy

For the most up-to-date bibliography, please visit **WillWight.com**

THE
KNIGHT
THE LAST HORIZON
BOOK THREE

WILL WIGHT

HIDDEN
GNOME
PUBLISHING

The Knight

Book and cover design by Patrick Foster
Cover painting by Simon Carr/scarrindustries.com

ISBN 978-1-959001-69-0 (trade hardcover)

ISBN 978-1-959001-70-6 (trade paperback)

www.WillWight.com

PRINTED IN CHINA

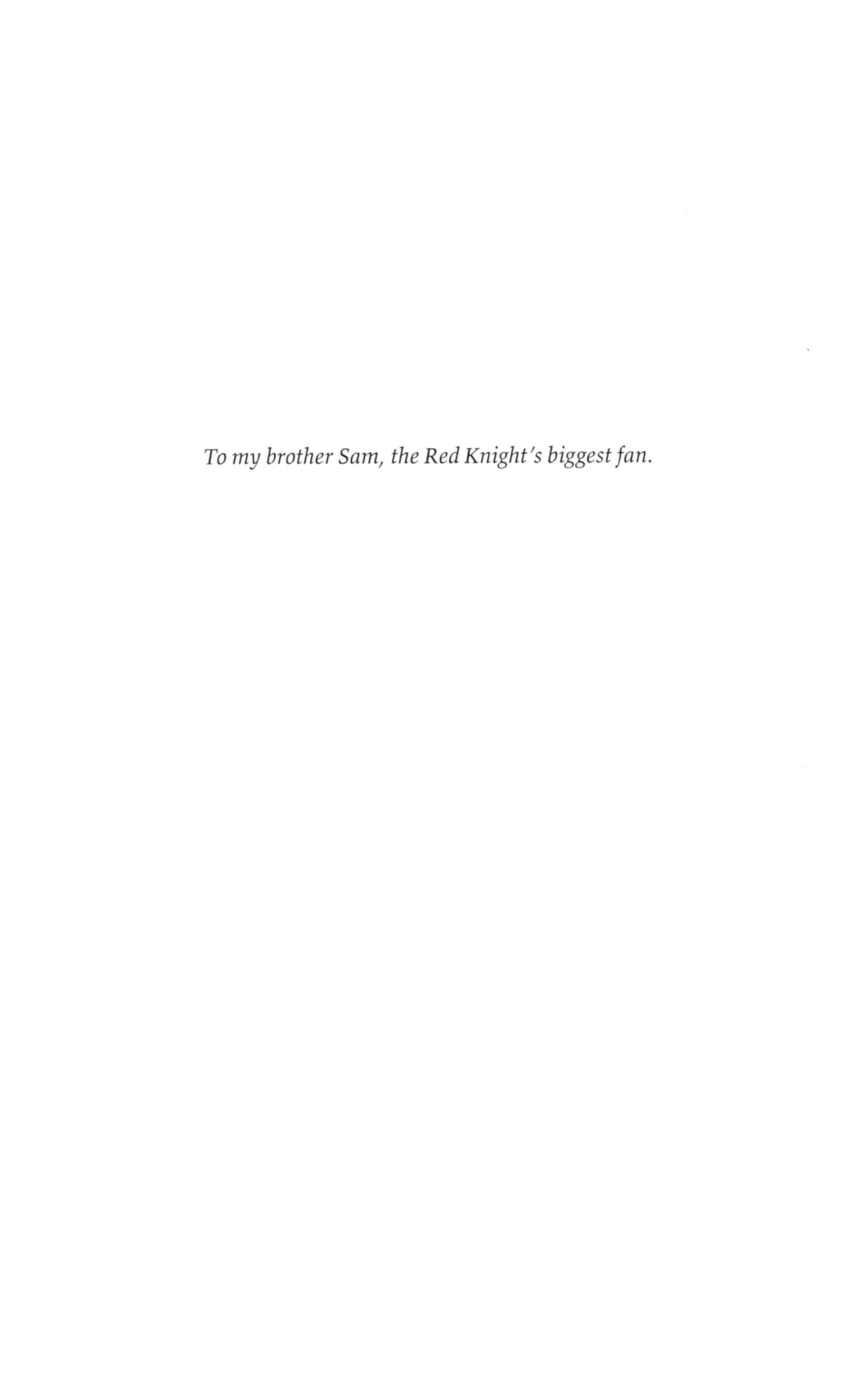

To my brother Sam, the Red Knight's biggest fan.

PROLOGUE

IN ANOTHER LIFE

THE PRIME COLISEUM on Visiria shook with the shouts of a hundred thousand people. Tens of millions more watched from all over the galaxy, thanks to the Subline feed. I felt the rubberized turf tremble in my knees and fingertips as I tried to push myself to my feet.

Blood dripped from my nose and I couldn't stop it. The best I could do was avoid falling over. My vision was nothing but a cloud, and I tried to focus on my blurry opponent.

She was off-balance too. I had come out worse in our last exchange, but she wasn't unscathed. That was my chance to strike again.

My wand came up, trembling, as I called water. With my concentration so shaky, the conjured liquid shook and dripped, barely holding together. I'd be lucky if I could hit her with the force of a garden hose.

My vision cleared enough to see her, and her back was turned to me. She was facing the crowds in the arena stands that towered into the sky. White hair was cut short, and she raised red hands to the audience.

They roared encouragement. Ships drifted lazily overhead as

more people watched from the clouds. Holographic text flashed in the sky over the arena: *'FINISH HIM!'*

It would have looked like a scene from a Subline game, but this was painfully real.

She wasn't in a hurry to turn around, so I forced out the last of my concentration. Stumbling to my feet, I shouted as I slashed my wand.

I outdid myself. A blade of water cut across the arena, white spray reaching the shield that protected the audience. It wasn't focused enough to cut through metal, or even a particularly thick tree, but it should do something to her. She didn't even have her energy deployed.

Only when the water cleared did I see her unharmed.

Without turning around, she had shifted her upper body to the right. The compressed wave cut right past her, doing nothing but giving the spectators in the first few rows a thrill.

She turned back to me and grinned. She was older, a veteran of the arena and the battlefield both. One arm had been lost to an Iron Legion ambush, replaced with an Aethertech prosthetic—only a low-grade one, for now, since nothing better was allowed in the arena.

"Not bad!" she called. "I needed a shower!"

With exaggerated movements, she combed her wet hair back with metal fingers and gave a sigh. Of course, it wasn't for me. The cameras caught everything.

And the laughter of the crowd shook the arena as much as their cheers had earlier.

Without enough time to gather more water, I shoved out at her with basic telekinesis, but she waded through without effort and planted her left fist in my stomach.

I doubt that was enough to knock me out, but the next thing I remember is being examined by doctors in one of the Prime Coliseum's prep rooms.

The Visiri medics finished scanning me and giving me my instructions—don't fight again for a week, don't dispel the healing spell, take three different pills twice a day each—before leaving me to peel my way out of my costume.

They'd bandaged me up where they needed to, but I was still half-dressed. My entire concept was based around being a wizard, so I had a mantle over a padded combat uniform. I winced as I pulled it away, wishing I had someone to help me.

While I slowly undressed and limped my way to the shower, a screen played in the corner of the room. I couldn't bother to turn it off as it announced that the next warm-up fight would begin soon.

I didn't look to see what anyone said about my loss. I didn't want to know, and more importantly, it's not like there would have been anything interesting. Most people wouldn't think anything at all.

Humans were rare on the Visirian duelist circuit, and wizards even rarer. If it weren't for those things, I would still be performing on out-worlds and colonies. My record wasn't good enough to fight in the Prime Coliseum.

Not that I could call what I'd done 'fighting.'

I stumbled in the shower as the room shook, and I wondered about an attack on the arena before I realized someone was knocking.

"Varic!" a woman's voice called through the door. "I'm coming in!"

I scrambled out of the shower. Fortunately, my bandages repelled water, so I'd been able to keep them on.

"I'm in the shower!"

"I'll give you ten seconds to get out!" she shouted. "Ten! Never mind, I'm not going to count. You count."

I muttered the seconds down from nine as I pulled on clean clothes without drying. My wounds brought tears to my eyes, but I managed to finish dressing before the door slammed open. It had been locked, but she had a key to every room in the Coliseum.

My opponent strode inside, beaming. Her third eye shone white. "You felt that pressure out there, didn't you? When you feel like you're going to die, the eyes of the galaxy are on you, and you *still* cast your spell? That's when you're ready."

Kyri Prest was a legend of the arena. Not only had she stayed active for twenty-three seasons and counting, but she was one of the few Visiri to have earned an Archmage title.

She was an Archmage of water elementalism. And my teacher.

"I did cast a spell," I said. "But it was sloppy. I could barely pull it together."

Kyri nodded. "Yeah, that was bad. By the time I'm done with you, you'll cast perfect spells in your sleep."

I sat down on a bench and rubbed my bandaged head. "I don't have much time left. My dad wants me back at the company next year."

"We'll have to show him some results, then." Kyri looked me up and down with her third eye and flicked a finger at me. Droplets of water fled from my skin and clothes, leaving me perfectly dry. "A lot of people saw that fight, so you'll get some calls. There are always newcomers looking to cut their teeth, pros who want an easy fight, fighters who hate wizards...Oh, anybody who hates humans, we'll see a few of those."

"At least I have options."

In that life, I hadn't given up on the Vallenar Corporation. It was more like my father had given up on me.

He'd determined I couldn't learn his Mirror of Silence—or maybe he'd decided he didn't want to trust me with it—so he'd arranged for my choice of the best tutors from all across the galaxy.

I had chosen Kyri because I had visions of myself following in her footsteps and setting records in an arena. She was not only a powerful water elementalist but a skilled Combat Artist, and if I could have lived up to her legend with only magic, I would have set a record for competitive duels.

After five years working at it, the truth became clear: I couldn't do it.

The superhuman speed, strength, and durability of a Visiri became trump cards that my human magic couldn't match.

My teacher hadn't given up on me, but I had. At the time, I was actually looking forward to returning to the Corporation. They could find work for an elementalist.

Though I had almost a year left, I already considered it over.

Kyri studied me, metal arm crossed beneath her natural one. The Visiri third eye is famous throughout the galaxy, but most people don't understand it. They think it can see flows of the Aether, like Aethril can, or even that it sees into infrared.

The truth is stranger, at least to humans. Visiri can see life energy.

Which isn't real, despite mythology on many planets and the Visiri's own pool of private energy. The "life energy" they see is a reflection of a person's power and vitality through the Aether.

But that means they can see living things more clearly than any other major sentient race, and can see details invisible to most. When she examined me with that third eye, I felt like she was staring into my soul.

"Why do you look like you lost?" she asked me.

"You beat me."

"Of course I did. But looking at you, you don't look like you lost a match. You look like you *lost.*"

My head, shoulder, knee, arm, and ribs were all pounding. I didn't want to have that, or any, conversation at the time. "Don't you have interviews?"

"Nah, I took care of those. Match was too easy, anyway. Nobody wanted to hear about it."

I wasn't sure what attitude she wanted to see from me after comments like that.

"*That's* why I lost," I said. "I'd still like to learn whatever I can from you, but clearly the arena isn't for me."

She scratched at her shoulder, where muscle met Aethertech. "You don't think you can get anything done in the Coliseum?"

"Apparently I can't."

"All right, then. Let's go somewhere else."

I rubbed my throbbing head again. "Now?"

"You want to use magic in a fight? That means we've got to practice while you feel like death. Get your shoes on, let's go."

We met at her ship, a sleek and flashy private cruiser that must have cost as much as a military warship. It was made for speed and comfort, not combat, so we made it into the Lesser Karoshan system in only a few hours.

At least I got to sleep during the dive.

Through the parts of the flight while I was conscious, I spent my time wallowing in pain and self-pity. But I snapped out of it when I saw the system as we arrived.

Lesser Karosha is next door to the primary Karoshan system, and as such it was choked with the blocky black constructions of Karoshan ships and colonies. Even more so this time. We came out of Subspace into a military blockade.

I tensed as we flew through a massive circle of gun platforms, all of which were pointed inwards. Clearly, the Karoshans had a chokehold on this Subspace entrance, but they didn't fire on us. Which meant Kyri had permission to be here.

A Karoshan voice crackled over the communicator. *"Lieutenant Prest, proceed to the provided coordinates and report to Captain Mershek."*

Only once we cleared the defensive emplacements did I realize why there were so many Karoshan starships here. On the far side of a blue planet, three small moons of metal and bone hung in orbit.

Iron Hives. They were surrounded by a swarm of lesser ships, and the void was lit by weapons streaking back and forth between the Karoshans and the Iron Legion.

My heart spiked like I was about to enter the arena again. "We're here to fight the Legion? I'm not—I mean, I can't. I can barely lift a wand."

Kyri was piloting the ship down to the surface of the planet, and only then did I see the flash of weapons from land. The Legion had made it down. "Don't worry, I'm starting you off light. We won't raid a Hive until you have a little experience under your belt."

I hadn't known Hive-raiding was on the table. I started to wonder if my father would take my call.

We landed minutes later, behind a huge, dark wall that the Karoshans had erected in haste. It cut across a city, having been raised in the center of what looked like a public park.

Karoshan soldiers bustled here and there, and it was like being a child in a world of adults. They hauled guns that weighed more than I did, shouted in voices that sounded like the roar of the entire Prime Coliseum, and their footsteps pounded the earth.

They were all dressed in black uniforms, and many of them had brightly colored hair-cables spilling from the backs of their helmets. Guns at the top of the wall thundered, shooting down at unseen creatures on the far side.

I wanted to *keep* those creatures unseen.

Kyri strode across the chaos as though she were used to it, and she might have been. Visiria is part of the Karoshan Alliance, and Kyri Prest had earned her Archmage title on the battlefield.

Before that, I'd never thought of her working with the Karoshan military, though. It surprised me. In that life, I had only heard legends of Karoshan soldiers. They were the horror stories that Galactic Union soldiers shared to scare newcomers and spoiled rich kids.

Seeing them in reality brought all those stories to life. It's hard not to be intimidated when you're surrounded by people whose head is three feet higher up than yours.

Kyri reported to Captain Mershek, a man with red hair-cables and a badge of office that were his only distinguishing characteristics as far as I could tell. She introduced me as her student and even joked about teaching me what a battlefield smelled like.

Captain Mershek didn't acknowledge me at all. "I'm assigning you to the Sixty-Fifth Mage Corps. You'll find the coordinates in your processor."

I received the message immediately and pulled up the coordinates in my ocular implant. An arrow pointed me to a nearby elevator, and from there to the top of the wall.

Only then did I see the mages up there, slinging spells to the side of a gun battery that dwarfed even the Karoshans. In the second I watched, a spell erupted from the Iron Legion side, washing over them.

It reduced the gun to a spray of molten metal. Most of the mages didn't make it either.

The arrow in my vision winked out.

Captain Mershek cursed in Karoshan and turned from us, shouting into his helmet. After only a few seconds, he turned back to us and pointed to the wall. "Get up there! You *are* the Sixty-Fifth Mage Corps. I'll get you reinforcements as soon as I—"

He cut off as he got another call, abruptly striding away.

Kyri was pulling me into a sprint, which for her was a light jog. She was totally serious now, focused on the top of the wall. "They'll be climbing. I'll keep them off us, you go for the heavy hits. Target the biggest thing you see."

One of the elevators remained intact and functional, though there were a few spots of cooling red metal splattered on its surface. It was an open platform, made to lift equipment, and it had started moving upward before we reached it.

Kyri grabbed me and we leaped fifteen feet in the air, landing on the platform. I groaned in pain, but I wasn't the only one. Several of the Karoshans who shared the platform were injured, but they carried weapons to the top anyway.

None of them reacted to us leaping onto the platform except to shoot us a quick glance.

Kyri had her wand out, a jagged spike of silver metal that looked like a steel icicle. "This is why you need to learn to play hurt," she said. "An enemy like the Iron Legion won't wait until you recover."

I had a lot to say to that.

For one thing, only hours ago I was fighting in a duel for entertainment. A sport. I wanted to cry about the unfairness of plunging straight from that into a war zone.

But it was hard to complain while surrounded by wounded soldiers.

"I've never fought the Legion before," I said instead. "I don't know—I don't know anything!"

Kyri pulled her arm off.

She didn't look at me as she tossed the low-grade one aside and pulled her best arm out of a magic storage pouch at her side. This limb was high-grade, silver and sleek, running with blue lights. She clipped the arm onto her shoulder and was moving it naturally in seconds, opening and closing metal fingers to test them.

She watched the arm, not me, but I felt her attention nonetheless. "Do you want to make a difference with your magic…or not?"

I swallowed the nausea that came from the combination of pain and nerves. I gripped my own wand, a creation of titanium and blue crystal that resembled the one I would use in a later life.

Then I called water.

CHAPTER ONE

IN THIS LIFE
FIVE YEARS AGO

Raion stood before the other four Titan Knights, his friends, and gave them a brilliant smile. "Tomorrow," he said, "we kill one of the Seven Calamities. The galaxy will be safe once again!"

Parryl, the Green Knight, raised her hand. She was a Lichborn girl who had grown up in the Titan Knights, though Raion still thought of her as the youngest of the group. "Do you have any new information to share?"

Raion put his fists on his hips. "I can share my resolve!"

The other four started to leave.

"Wait! We can't go into battle unless our hearts are as one!"

Kherius, the White Knight, sighed and turned back around. He was a large human, the tallest of the whole team, and he had the rough and grizzled look of an inner-sector asteroid miner. In fact, he was an accomplished Aether Technician, but he looked like he'd never seen the inside of a lab.

"Let's splatter the bugs!" Kherius shouted, and Raion beamed.

The Blue Knight shot a longing glance at the door, but she didn't leave. As an Aethril, Laraena's skin was powder blue and her pale hair glistened as though set with stars. Like many of her species, she was an adept wizard, an Archmage of ice elementalism.

"Let's get them," she said in a monotone. "Woo. We can do it."

Even if it was sarcastic, that was the most emotion Raion had ever heard Laraena express. He looked over her proudly and she blushed.

Javik Leed, the Yellow Knight, closed his eyes and visibly counted to three. Raion was proud of him too. His therapist had insisted he learn to control his temper, especially in team scenarios.

"I can't do it this time, Raion," he said. "I'll be ready, but I can't pretend to be excited."

Raion cocked his head. "You don't have to be excited. But isn't it better to focus on victory?"

"This is serious."

"Do you think it's better to imagine what will happen if we lose?"

Javik struggled with himself, and his lips even moved as he counted silently. Raion waited for him to come to a conclusion.

For the first year or so of working together, Javik had thought Raion didn't take his role seriously enough. He had learned better, but he still didn't understand Raion's attitude.

That was all right. Raion was happy enough that Javik had made an effort to understand him.

Finally, Javik clapped his hands together and looked around the circle, meeting all their eyes in turn. "No matter what happens tomorrow, we will face it together. And as long as one of us remains standing, the people will have someone to protect them."

That got a genuine cheer out of Raion, and even the Green and White Knights joined him. Laraena gave a polite clap.

"I never doubted your resolve," Raion said. "I never doubted any of you. I can feel your commitment, and the universe could have no better protectors. There is no one I would rather fight beside than you."

That improved their mood. He could feel it in the bond they shared.

They might not see friendship in the same way he did, but

they *were* his friends. They would fight together, and they would die together.

And, once the others had left and Raion was alone in his room, he stared into the darkness and tried not to think about how likely it was that they *would* all die together.

The D'Niss had been increasing their activity lately, and they weren't the only threat in the galaxy that required the Titan Force. Not only were the Knights stretched thin, but the D'Niss were only getting stronger.

The next day, they would face the most powerful foe yet, and their enemies were up to something. The Seven Calamities were trying to gather enough power to summon Esh'kinaar, the Swarm-Queen.

Even should they succeed, Raion wouldn't give up. The galaxy needed him.

But he didn't want his friends to die.

With no other option, Raion decided to get some sleep. The best thing he could do for the other Knights was to trust them. They could take care of each other, and only with the power of their unity could they hope to win.

Just when he had resolved to go to sleep, his console buzzed. His wrist-computer sat on the folded strap that usually held it to his arm, plugged into a socket on the wall next to his bunk.

He glanced at it and checked it with his processor. The feed streamed into his eyes directly. That hadn't been an emergency alert—nothing that required him to leap to his feet and go summon his Titan—but it was high-priority enough to get through some of his automatic filtering.

Most of the people who could call him with such urgency were the other Titan Knights, and they were in the same building.

It began with a video message from Doctor Janbell Cryce, inventor of the Divine Titans.

Raion's feed filled with Doctor Cryce's voice. She was an older Lichborn woman, and she looked like she was facing down the end of a long week in the lab. There were smudges he couldn't identify on her gray skin, her hair was a tangled mess of black that she'd halfheartedly tied back, and her coat was wrinkled and stained.

Exhausted as she must have been, she positively beamed with energy. She was perched at the edge of her chair, staring into the camera, and she began speaking as soon as the call started as though she could wait no longer.

"They're retreating!" the Doctor shouted. She rubbed her hands together eagerly. "We got word yesterday but we only confirmed it now, thanks to Subspace delays that—Well, that's not important. The D'Niss are *retreating,* Raion. We've done it."

Raion didn't remember getting out of bed, but he was standing, eyes wide.

"That last battle was too much for them. Every D'Niss you killed is irreplaceable, and the Seven Calamities have decided to cut their losses. At least three of them have returned to their universe, and most of the others took their swarms and headed back to Dark Space."

They'd fought for years to defeat the D'Niss, all in the hopes that they could make the alien incursion too costly. Their leaders, the Seven Calamities, were the greatest of their kind besides the Swarm-Queen herself.

Doctor Cryce and Titan Force intelligence had always hoped they could make the D'Niss retreat without engaging the Calamities, but that was the best-case scenario. It was much more realistic, they estimated, to expect that they'd have to kill off three or four of the Seven before the rest left the universe behind.

Somehow, it seemed, they had ended up in the best of all worlds. The Aether had blessed them.

"We did it," Raion muttered. It didn't feel real.

Cryce cackled. "Doesn't feel real, does it? Well, that's the good news. The bad news is, you're still flying out tomorrow."

She tapped her console and an extra image appeared on Raion's feed, floating in the air next to her: a three-dimensional model of a moon-sized beetle. Neth'terith, least of the Seven Calamities.

"Our beetle friend is the one who decided to stay behind," she continued. "If we don't take him out, he could grow his swarm until it's a self-sustaining threat to galactic security comparable to the Iron Legion, so we still need to get rid of him. But we were going to do that anyway. The difference now is, once you beat him…" She leaned back in her chair and spread her hands. "…That's it. We win."

Raion steadied his breathing as he looked into the joyful green glow of Doctor Cryce's eyes. He couldn't hold off any longer; he began a call to her, but it cut off immediately.

In the video, the Doctor held up a hand. "Don't try calling me! The second I finish recording this, I'm sedating myself. I need to get at least a few hours of sleep, or I won't be any good during tomorrow's fight. But I'll leave you with one last bit of good news.

"Now that we've made visible headway, the Galactic Union is suddenly willing to cooperate. They've sent us all the intelligence they've gathered on Neth'terith. Half of it is pure speculation and most of the other half dates back to Esh'kinaar's first incursion, but I've sent you the good bits. With this, our odds tomorrow have gone *way* up."

Cryce's energy suddenly faded and she blinked back tears. "One day left, Raion. Go tell your friends."

Raion had already bolted down the hallway.

CHAPTER TWO

At the heart of a moon-sized tomb, I chanted new seals over an ancient lich.

The skeletal wizard was imprisoned at the heart of a crystal, still wearing a golden crown. His robes were plated with metal and fragments of obsidian, and a bright green light burned in the depths of his sockets.

In both of his skeletal hands, he gripped an ornate golden staff. It was topped by a gold serpent, which hissed at me from inside the prison.

The staff was what made this tricky.

My own sealing magic shone on the ceiling and walls all around me, spinning circles of Aetheric symbols in blue or white. I myself stood in the center of a patch of waving grass and pouring rain, generated by my own staff, Eurias.

The crystal, the size of a coffin, sat atop a pedestal at the center of this ritual room. Though the crystal itself was enchanted to support sealing magic and had remained undisturbed for centuries, I was losing this struggle.

Green fire ate away at my seals as I chanted them, and the room trembled around me to the point that I could only remain upright by leaning on Eurias.

I could hear the lich's own chants as slithering, hissing syllables that wracked my ears. The Aether churned around us, our conflicting orders sending it frothing like a sea in storm. It crackled in the corners of my vision, blue lightning and indescribable warps twisting my sight.

"You have time to talk, Captain?" Omega asked over our Subline connection.

Swollen eyeballs, bigger than my head, came fluttering down from the ceiling on leathery wings. They swiveled to catch sight of me, then their bodies split into fanged mouths.

I interrupted my chant for one dangerous second to shout, "No!"

"Hmmmmm...but surely you do," Omega said lazily. *"You're just reinforcing some seals, aren't you? This isn't one of your galactic threats."*

It wasn't, but it *would* be if this lich got free. At the very least, he would require Horizon and our crew to deal with.

He hadn't successfully taken over the galaxy in any of my previous lives. He'd tried, but had been defeated by the might of the Karoshan Alliance.

"So anyway, I'll talk while I leave the spell-work to the greatest spellcaster in the galaxy."

Greatest *mortal* spellcaster in the galaxy. I wanted to correct him about that important distinction, but I was busy sweating and furiously chanting. I leaned on Eurias in my right hand and picked off the flying eye-bats with the Lightcaster IV in my left.

Though the conflict seemed contained to this room, the magical clash between me and the ancient undead Archmage echoed throughout the sector. We were channeling enough of the Aether to reduce continents to blighted wastelands.

"My extension is up today, and as I've been a good little murderer, I believe I deserve a promotion to full crew member."

Omega had been a member of the crew for six months. Today, apparently, if his story was accurate. We'd given him one extension after his first three-month tenure.

How time flies when you're having so much fun.

The air in the ritual chamber heated up as the crystal cracked. I focused on the coffin, binding it with commands of the Aether as water washed the sweat from my forehead.

"Allow me to make my case in great detail," Omega went on, and I finally shouted a response.

"Omega! Shut up and help me!"

With that lapse in concentration, my spells holding the crystal together snapped. Neon green light gushed out of the sealing crystal and the lich began levitating upward.

All at once, the green fires burning against my sealing-circles flared brighter. The entire moon-made-mausoleum shook, the grass at my feet blackened and died, and even the wind and rain conjured by Eurias blew the other way.

The fiery green gaze of the legendary necromancer fixed on me. He slowly moved his staff toward me, crashing through the seals I threw up to stop him.

My Lightcaster got slightly better results, actually getting a grunt out of him as a plasma bolt pinged off his bare skull and left a scorched dent. Normally, his magic would have been enough to stop mundane technology from functioning in an isolated space like this.

Lightcasters. They work anywhere.

The lich's eyes flared in anger—no doubt he was furious that a mere mortal had dared to mar his deathly perfection, or something like that—and he reached a bony claw in my direction before speaking a word.

It was an Aetheric command, and not one I was familiar with, but I knew the meaning nonetheless.

This thousand-year-old death mage had ordered the Aether to kill me.

Darkness closed in, and my heart fluttered in my body. But the silver symbols around my mantle shone brighter, and my orange protection amulet fought back in concert.

While his spell failed, I put another plasma bolt between his teeth.

I chanted more sealing magic, but it was clear which way the

Aether was flowing. The green fires were getting brighter and brighter, while each sealing circle I generated was smaller and hazier than the last.

There would be a tiny delay while I switched magic, which would be fatal under this sort of pressure. If someone didn't turn things around soon, I was going to...

Well, death was certainly on the table, but I was most worried about being forced to flee in shame while leaving a powerful enemy behind me.

Not only would that endanger the entire surrounding system, but it would make me look bad in front of the crew.

Behind the lich, the shadows unfolded into Omega. He leaped out of his unique Subspace warp with a crazed grin, Aethertech eye blazing bright orange as he clutched a different gun in each hand.

The lich gestured in a casual backhand without turning around, but I still had Eurias. No matter how much control my enemy had over the local Aether, I could still disrupt a minor working.

I tore down his telekinesis before it could shove Omega backwards, and Omega continued as though that were his plan all along. He leveled both guns and pulled the triggers.

The lich's rib cage exploded.

Bone fragments rained down around me, pattering against my shield amulet and falling to the blackened grass on the floor.

Annoyed, the lich spun around and leveled his snake-headed golden staff at Omega. Omega slithered aside, but that magic could be bad news even for him. I put a sealing-circle around the staff.

It broke almost immediately, but that was enough time for Omega to spray the lich with a stream of fire.

Meanwhile, I shot him in the back of the skull with my Lightcaster.

Half-formed protective spells slowed down our barrage a little, but necromancy isn't known for its defense against raw firepower. The lich had been sealed for too long, and I had successfully suppressed most of the enchantments on his equipment and the mausoleum itself.

Together, Omega and I blew the skeletal sorcerer into chunks of bone until the room no longer glowed green.

"It's nice to have a shared interest with a crewmate," Omega said happily. "Don't you feel that a gun has so much more of a satisfying *heft* to it than a wand?"

"Not more than a staff," I said. I holstered my Lightcaster and reached down to grab a shard of crystal about as tall as I was. When my fingertips touched it, the protective crystal melted into liquid.

I tossed Eurias into the puddle and released it, whereupon the crystal solidified once again. Eurias' power was immediately cut off, so the Aether stopped sending up strange signs as the magical energy in the area stabilized.

Omega leaned over the crystal and whispered. "Now that's the finest stick-holder I've ever seen."

"Too heavy," I said. I used my levitation ring to heft the crystal-shrouded staff and let it drift behind my shoulder. "But I'll make do, since he destroyed my other case."

"No, Captain, no! This is much more wizardly. A staff in a floating crystal, released only in times of great need...Yes, Horizon will surely approve."

I glared at him. "You really cut it close there, didn't you? You could have backed me up earlier."

"I was taking a lesson from Raion. Having faith in my friends."

"I'm not going to help promote you to full crew member if you don't do your job."

In a rush of smoke and clattering of bones, the lich began hauling itself back together. I chanted a quick spell, which created a golden light in my vision. I tossed a magic circle to Omega so that he could see the light instead.

"A hundred yards behind that golden spot," I said.

"With gusto, Captain!" Omega tossed his guns back into Subspace and retrieved one that looked more like the frame for a hover-car, setting it up on a tripod in front of him.

The lich's skull floated together out of half-burned fragments, and while his speaking voice still sounded dry and papery, it also carried a distinct nervous tone. "Intruders, wait…I can offer you great wisdom…"

Omega peered through his gun's sight with his Aethertech eye.

"Eternal life…" the lich continued. "Great riches…"

Omega took his finger from the trigger and glanced at me.

"You think you can trust this guy?" I asked.

"My word can be trusted," the lich protested in a voice like desiccated death.

Omega pulled the trigger. The ritual chamber filled with thunder and a flare of light as a magically accelerated bullet pierced through a hundred yards of stone.

I heard a noise like shattering porcelain carried on the Aether, and the lich's skull finally crumbled to dust and blew away.

Omega shook his head in pity. "That's why you never keep your soul in a jar. You keep it in an endlessly regenerating Aethertech body."

"Good life lessons," I said. With the lich gone, I had little trouble making a temporary hole in the restrictive magic of the mausoleum. "Horizon, take us home."

Blue light surrounded us, and a moment later Omega and I were back on the bridge of *The Last Horizon.*

The dark metal plates of the ceiling and walls shone with a comforting white light tinted blue-green. The room was a long oval, with blinking console monitors underneath a curving viewscreen.

At the moment, the only chair on the bridge was the padded captain's chair in the center. It flowed up from the floor as Horizon welcomed me home.

Although she wasn't there to greet us, and neither was anyone else. Instead, her voice came from the walls around us.

"I don't like it when I can't talk to you, Captain," Horizon complained.

"I broke the spell as soon as I could. Are we the first ones back?"

"This is why I don't like it. I can't keep you informed. The others are in trouble."

I tensed, but at the same time, I picked up on her phrasing. "They're not in *danger?*" I clarified. "They're in *trouble?*"

"That's right, Captain."

I sighed. "What did they do?"

CHAPTER THREE

I MATERIALIZED FROM blue light in the courtyard of what I recognized immediately as a Galactic Union military outpost. The ground was gray concrete that had been poured in haste, the buildings were gray fabricated cubes, and the soldiers who marched by—primarily human—were also dressed in gray.

Everything was gray except the sky, because gray was how the Union military liked it. In a major Union base, they would still have stuck to their favorite color, but the vehicles would be more expensive, the buildings would have varied in design and sported heavier plating, and I would see at least a few suits of powered armor.

Therefore, this was either an outpost on a planet they didn't control or one that was contested.

I leaned toward the latter, given that I heard distant artillery fire.

That, and the fact that Sola was here. She wouldn't have come during peacetime.

Sola was another patch of gray, but she stood out nonetheless. Her armor had her looming over the humanoid forms around her, her visor blazed green, and the Aethertech of her suit was clearly the most valuable thing in sight. Probably the most valuable on the planet.

She was surrounded by several squads of soldiers and a squat hover-car. All of them had guns pointed at her.

Horizon hadn't briefed me on the situation before dumping me here. For a moment, I wondered how long this obvious standoff had lasted.

Then I saw the twisted skeletons of two vehicles and a handful of drones that had been blown apart. And behind those, a hole in the wall.

As I put things together, I was proud of her. She had at least tried to talk her way out first.

The Union soldiers were all shouting while Sola stood there in silence, so I quickly sealed their voices so I wouldn't have to yell over them. "Why didn't you teleport out?" I asked as I pushed my way through the soldiers.

With telekinesis. I'm not Raion.

"They're keeping me from something I want," Sola said. She turned her green glare to the others.

"Ah. They don't want you to go out there, do they?"

"There are fifty-six Scourge Warrens within a thousand miles of here. They targeted me when I blew up my third."

I could put the picture together from there. The Iron Legion had infested this planet, reaching out from underground factories called Scourge Warrens. They would spread like a disease, taking any organic and mechanical matter back to the Warrens and turning them into more soldiers of the Legion.

Scourge Warrens were shielded from orbital bombardment and a nightmare to invade on foot. If I used Eurias to clear them out, I'd do as much damage to the planet as I would to the Legion.

Sola could clear one in about fifteen minutes, but a coordinated Union attack would take hours. And that was when they *did* use a coordinated strike and weren't spreading their resources thin.

With fifty-six Scourge Warrens, the planet was likely lost unless the Galactic Union had a hundred more bases like the one I saw around me.

All they had to do was *not* shoot Sola and their job became possible. But she was a wanted woman.

I considered explaining to the Union officers in charge how many resources they were wasting on Sola when we could cooperate, but I knew I was wasting my time.

We'd tried before. Their orders wouldn't change.

I pulled my wand, turned to the nearest ship, and sealed its engine with a spell. "Keep them on the ground. We'll clear out the Warrens together."

Without any further hesitation, Sola leaped over the gathered men, supported by her pulse boosters. While in midair, she shot out the windshield of a nearby fighter.

I was trying not to do any damage to the equipment, since we needed the Galactic Union to clean up after us here, but I supposed a windshield wasn't too much to replace. The hover-car's turret swiveled to me, but that took about half a second to seal in place.

One of the soldiers, a pale human man, shouted at me until he was red in the face. I heard none of it, since his voice was sealed, but he caught my curiosity. Especially when he tried to push closer to me, caught the shimmering field of my shield amulet, and pulled his sidearm.

After he unloaded his clip fruitlessly into my shield, he hurled the pistol itself at me. It didn't do any better.

"You know," I said, "if I had let those shots bounce, you would have shot yourself." I pointed to the orange circles at the boundary of the shield, where bullets hung suspended.

I let them plink to the concrete. "I'm going to let you speak, so try not to hurt yourself."

With a flick of a finger, I removed the spell silencing him.

"—KILL YOU!" he finished, panting from the rant I hadn't heard.

I looked at the pain in his face and suppressed a sigh. I didn't want to make the man feel worse, but I had seen this before in too many lives. "This is a revenge thing, isn't it?"

"You killed my brother," he said. Given his quiet intensity, I was glad I'd let him run himself out of energy. Otherwise, that would have been much louder and filled with insults.

"Was your brother attacking me?" I asked.

"He was on the *GSS Kholien* as part of a *peacekeeping force!* You *murdered* him! His name was—"

I restored the silencing spell with a wave. "I don't want to know what his name was. You're probably not going to listen to me, but I'll tell you anyway: I don't have anything against the Galactic Union, and I know your brother was probably just doing his job. But I'm not so sorry that I'm going to roll over and let you kill me."

I levitated one of his deformed bullets from the ground up to his eye level. "Union intelligence, I know you'll watch this video later, if you aren't watching already. If you don't want to get shot, don't fire on me."

With a crash of breaking concrete, Sola landed next to me. "They're landlocked, but air reinforcements are four minutes out."

"That's fine. They'll have to bring something bigger in from outside the system if they want to get through my shields. Where's the nearest Warren?"

"Six miles due northeast. Horizon, get us a ship."

Horizon responded to both of us. *"Regrettably, my teleportation systems are strained to their limits. Teleporting a ship is quite costly. Even to relocate you on the planet would require a waiting period. If you are truly in need, I can come to you myself. Or I could send my Pilot!"*

"Get us a ship," Sola repeated.

"Fly something into the system, Horizon," I said. "We'll make do in the meantime."

With telekinesis, I hauled open the door of the hover-car and pulled the driver out. The turret was mounted on the back. "You want driver or gunner?" I asked.

Sola was already gripping the turret.

We had cleared fifty of the remaining fifty-six Scourge Warrens when Horizon contacted me again. *"I know I said Sola's situation was the most urgent one, but my Engineer's is about to become critical."*

"Send Omega," I said, as I put a bullet through an Iron Pawn with one hand and sealed a Reaver to the ceiling with the other.

"I have."

Sola heard the same transmission, so she responded over the feed. *"Go. I can finish up here."*

I looked past the hill of melted flesh and molten metal that marked the outer shell of the Scourge Warren. A Hunter-ship crashed to the ground and exploded.

"Take me to Mell," I said.

Another wash of blue light, and I found myself standing on the roof of a high-rise building. Wind shoved at the protection of my mantle, the noise of a bustling city crashed into me suddenly, and smog pushed into an orange sky.

As ships streaked through the sky above me in a constant dance, I looked over the city that spread below. The tall buildings merged into one another with bridges and patches of metal overlapping one to another. They almost looked like a creation of the Iron Legion, the way the structures fused.

Behind the city was a bay that glistened in the sun, covered with mechanical arms. To my surprise, I found that I recognized this place.

The city was called Old Tolyer, one of the major population centers on the planet Naricius. There were too many inhabited planets in the galaxy for me to have ever visited them all, so the fact that I even knew the city was unusual.

"Where is she?" I asked Horizon, but a moment later a door burst behind me and Mell came scrambling out.

She wore the white lab coat she'd popularized as Doctor Nova, with weapons, tools, and devices strapped to her belt and peeking out of her pocket. The bulky console on her left wrist flashed as it processed something, and the glasses halfway down her nose flickered with text.

Her hair was wind-blown, and she scratched at it in frustration as she came through the door, messing it up even further. "Wrong!" she shouted. *"Don't* kill them! Didn't you hear me? We need information!"

A humanoid robot with a glowing purple light as its single eye followed her out of the door. It gestured toward the stairwell visible behind the door and pointed to its gun.

"No! That's what I'm saying! Don't shoot wildly at someone you're *not* trying to kill." Mell finally looked up and staggered at the sight of me. "Don't pop out like that! Gah, you're like a ghost."

"That's not the most flattering thing to hear when you show up to help," I pointed out.

"You think I'm trying to flatter you? Magic these guys so they listen to me."

Mell and I had worked together for months, but she still had no intention to learn how magic functioned.

"What guys?" I asked, but shouts came up the stairwell a moment later.

Followed by a plasma cannon shot. It tore through the stairs, burst through a chunk of the ceiling, and detonated the Nova-Bot. The robot exploded into molten metal, which rained in chunks down over the ceiling.

I was protected by my shield amulet, while a projector at Mell's waist created a barrier of her own. The falling scraps of metal plinked into our respective shields.

"Did Horizon brief you on the situation?" Mell asked.

"Of course not."

"Right. A device matching the Zenith Cannon came through here last year. I paid for the information from *their* organization—" She gestured to the unseen attackers. "—but they attacked as soon as they figured out who I was."

Instead of coming up through the now-ruined stairwell, four men flew up the sides of the building, supported on flight packs and covered in combat armor. When they saw us, they didn't hesitate to rain bullets onto us.

Given the noise, I called Mell on my processor instead of shouting. "So this is the bounty again?"

I saw her speaking from only feet away, but the words were swallowed by the steady hail of bullets. I heard her over the call in my ear. *"Looks like it. And I don't know which of them has the info I want. I've been leading them around since yesterday, but today they got reinforcements."*

The Galactic Union, the Karoshan Throne, and the Advocates had all placed bounties on our heads. And a significantly higher bounty for the captured Zenith Starship, though no one had tried to cash in on that one.

The bounty had caused us more headache than I'd expected. I had been a wanted man in many lives—including this one, actually—but it was rarely more than a minor inconvenience. The galaxy is a big place.

"Where's Omega?" I asked. The bullets stopped, so Mell responded without the call.

"You think he told me? He wished me good luck and slithered away."

Two of the bounty hunters switched from their standard-issue rifles to Aethertech weapons I didn't like the look of. I didn't recognize them, but one was a handheld cannon covered in gold filigree and ceramic with human skull designs. The barrel gushed dark smoke already. The second gun was all chrome and glass, filled with a liquid that shone bright teal. I thought I saw a tentacle pressed to the inside of one of the weapon's windows.

It was a good bet that any weapons that looked so artistically designed were Aethertech, and not something I wanted to let hammer away at my shield amulet. These looked like guns that would come out of Omega's collection, or Sola's.

I conjured hands and took them away.

Hands of blue light rushed over both of them, seizing the men in midair, pulling their arms apart, and wrestling the weapons from their grips. The one with the ceramic skulls got a wild shot off, and a laughing skull of dark smoke flew off into midair.

I was right not to let that hit me.

The other two attackers, the ones without expensive weaponry, resumed shooting at us. The hands flew for them next.

"Pathfinding magic!" Mell called over the shouts and screams of the bounty hunters. "You can figure out which one knows what we want, right?"

"I can figure out which of them would be most helpful," I said. "That doesn't necessarily mean he'll know what we want."

"Good enough! I'm sick of being shot at."

I chanted a quick pathfinding spell. This particular spell was more vague than I usually liked; it was meant to lead the caster to a source of assistance, rather than to a specific destination.

One of the men glowed gold in my vision, and I pointed to him. It was the one who had held the glowing Aethertech gun, and now struggled against my swarm of blue hands.

Mell strode toward him immediately, avoiding the hole in the roof. The man, like his three companions, wore armor that seemed to have been scavenged from a Galactic Union military warehouse.

His outfit was mismatched, pieces had been replaced at different times, and his full-face helmet looked more like it belonged on a biker. At my direction, the hands forced him down to the roof. His flight pack flared as he struggled to escape, but to no avail, so he eventually gave up.

Mell loomed over him, looking smug. She casually reached into her jacket pocket, pulled out a sugar-stick, unwrapped it, and stuck one end into her mouth.

"You know what I want," Mell said. "Incident report about a talking weapon. Give it to me so we can all go home."

The helmeted man remained silent.

Mell grinned around her sugar-stick, then leaned down into his face. "Oh? What should I do to make you talk, then? I've got a few things I've been waiting to—"

Omega popped out of nowhere in front of us. "Found it!" he shouted.

Mell staggered back in shock.

"You found where the talking gun went?" I asked.

"Exact coordinates and everything." He leered down at the captive, then even glanced over the edge of the building. Presumably to where the other three had run off. "Don't let me stop you from torturing them, though. There's nothing good on the Subline around here."

"Where did you get your information?" Mell asked skeptically.

"Funny you should ask!" Omega cried. He reached into a dark shadow with one hand, fishing around for something.

"If you're about to pull a body out of there," I said, "don't."

Omega clicked his tongue in disappointment and removed his arm empty-handed. "It wasn't a *whole* body."

Mell brushed her coat off with her hands. "I guess that's all I needed to do on this planet, then. Give me a few minutes to clear out my hotel room and we can leave."

"You don't have any more Nova-Bots?"

That was one of the things that had surprised me the most when I understood the situation. Mell should have never been lacking in manpower, not unless she was desperately cornered. And if the situation had turned against her *that* badly, she would have made Horizon transport her back to the ship.

Mell glowered at some nonspecific point in the distance. "No. I should have brought more, but the Queen needed as many as I could make."

"You can call her by name," I said. "You've worked with her enough by now."

"Yeah, but it feels...wrong."

"I'll head back to the ship first, then. I still haven't checked on Raion or Shyrax. Omega, are you—"

I cut off when I realized Omega had vanished. I activated my console and sent him a quick message. "Don't kill anyone unless they kill you first," I ordered.

Then I nodded to Mell and signaled Horizon to take me back up.

CHAPTER FOUR

WHEN I APPEARED next to Shyrax, half the people on the bridge of her starship immediately trained weapons on me. Shyrax herself neither flinched nor turned, facing out the forward viewscreen with hands clasped behind her back.

"How may I help you, Captain?"

As usual, being on a bridge full of Karoshans made me feel like a child walking through a crowd of adults. They were nine or ten feet tall, and I would have to reach up even to touch the dangling ends of the neon cables that served them instead of hair.

Queen Shyrax the Third had skin of dull bronze, her hair-cables shining gold. She wore an outfit that seemed like it was designed to fit on the battlefield or a courtyard, with elaborate dragon designs covering armor plating and shield generators disguised as jewelry.

The hilt of a force-blade hung on one hip and a wand on the other, though the wand was almost large enough that it would serve me as a staff.

Shyrax surveyed the system in front of her, where thousands of ships were arranged in rectangular formation. There was no battle here, she was merely inspecting her troops and preparing.

Half of the fleet was made up of blocky black Karoshan ships, while the other half were smooth, organic-looking, and covered in plates of dark metal that shone blue-green at the seams. Those were the ships printed by *The Last Horizon*.

"It seems recruitment has been going well," I observed, after a glance at one of the console readouts.

"The lesser Zenith-craft have been vital to my expansion. The usurper Felrex can no longer ignore me, and I have proven my effectiveness often enough. The Nova-Bot crews are also...reliable."

A few of the bridge crew glanced at each other, but there wasn't enough in Shyrax's tone to suggest she'd said anything unusual.

But I knew her well, and I was familiar enough with the situation to make an educated guess. She was implying that the Nova-Bots were *more* reliable than her Karoshan soldiers, which she would never do unless she had a reason to distrust her people.

She had found spies.

"So the Perfected are onto you."

Still without turning around, she gave me a nod of approval. "I believe so. The last few systems I've approached have been cold to me, despite a long history of loyalty to my family. I have seen evidence of dissatisfaction in the local fleet Subline, and a few units have requested a release from their contracts."

At last, she turned to face me. "Do you have insight for me, Captain?"

That caused a few mutters of shock to pass around the bridge crew. Shyrax famously learned as much as she could, but she was also famously confident in her knowledge. And these crew members didn't know me very well.

"Should we take this conversation elsewhere?" I suggested.

"These are the troops I trust with the lives of my children. Everyone here is aware of the troubles within our fleet."

"And are they aware of me? We won't get very far if they gasp at everything I say."

"You will have to tolerate that, Captain. Some of these soldiers were present when you and Raion tested me for my application to *The Last Horizon*. Your performance in the battle of the Thevellian

System has become a myth among the fleet. I might accurately call you a legend."

She delivered that not as a compliment, or in the wry tones I might expect of a joke, but with the solidity of raw fact. It was difficult to doubt anything Shyrax said.

I should have been used to the attention of the galaxy, in many different ways, but it was still uniquely embarrassing to be called a legend among a battleship full of giants. I was conscious of the attention of everyone in the room.

But I didn't let it change what I had to say.

"I'll try not to let it go to my head, then," I said mildly. "Your opponent is Gharyas, the Perfected Shadow. We've discussed him before."

She nodded, but allowed me to continue.

"His hallmarks are material sabotage and inciting fanaticism. Have you had unexplained equipment failure or any factions within your fleet who have become a little *too* loyal to you? Suggesting, perhaps, that you ought to recruit more forcefully?"

The Karoshans around the bridge reacted again. Quietly.

"We have seen such activity," Shyrax confirmed.

"The hard part about facing the Shadow was how difficult it was to distinguish between his plans and natural consequences," I went on. "I'm sure your own officers know how to handle dissension in the ranks better than I do. If he finds an organization is too stable for indirect tactics, he'll work more directly. Make him do that, and we can crush him."

Without waiting for further permission, I cast a pathfinding spell. While I chanted, I focused the spell through my wand, but it still failed.

"He's not here in the fleet himself," I said. "Not unless he has enough magical protection to hide from me, in which case he might as well be invisible."

"Rather than his personal presence, I find his influence on other systems more threatening," Shyrax said.

"Getting to neutral systems before you can recruit them isn't what I would expect from Gharyas, but it does sound like Felrex. He has the resources of the Karoshan Alliance at his command."

I gave her an apologetic shrug. "I don't think we win the long game. The time for recruitment may have already passed."

Shyrax closed her eyes, and I read heavy regret in her expression. "That is what I feared as well. Thank you, Captain."

If that was all there was to it, Horizon wouldn't have sent me here. "Is there anything else I can help you with, Commander? I think we might need you aboard *Horizon* soon."

"I have three requests to make of you," Shyrax said, and she made that sound like she was about to send me on a legendary quest. "First, my advisor, Melerius, has continued to instruct your students. He has indicated that your insight would be welcome."

In other words, Melerius and the Magic Tower students were growing impatient. It had been too long since I'd taught a class.

"Noted. Next?"

"Second, the third Royal Prince and the fourth Royal Princess have reached a critical stage in their education. They, too, wish an afternoon of your attention, and the instruction of the other members of our crew."

So Shyrax's twins had begged for their long-delayed tour of *The Last Horizon*. Of course, I was sure they also *did* need lessons. Shyrax wouldn't overlook the opportunity to have her children learn from the experts on the crew, as she would spare no expense to see them educated by the best in the galaxy.

She and my father had that in common.

"Finally, I would like you to cast one more spell. Among my fleet, identify any of those who knowingly report to the Perfected."

The soldiers on the bridge didn't mutter quietly this time. They froze unnaturally still.

I hesitated. "There are many limitations to a spell like that. For one thing, I can only identify information that would be accessible to me in other ways. I don't have any magic that can read minds.

"It also won't find any agents that are shielded from Archmage-level detection spells, and there are mundane ways to hide from it. Simply cleaning up after themselves thoroughly enough would do it."

I drummed my fingers on the side of my thigh. "And personally, I find using pathfinding magic this way...distasteful. The magic does not tell you a person's reasons. It only gives you a direction."

Shyrax didn't hesitate.

"Will you do it?" she asked.

"On the condition that you investigate further before you take action," I said. "Don't imprison, harm, or execute people on the basis of my spell alone."

"Agreed."

In that case, there was nothing else to say. Shyrax understood the implications of using magic in this way, and she was surely willing to live with the consequences.

But what *she* was willing to live with wasn't the question. I had seen a galaxy where the Galactic Union used magic like this to root out anyone who dared question their policies. While fighting the Iron Legion, I myself had acted on pathfinding spells in ways that later turned out more complex than I'd realized.

On the other hand, I didn't want spies among Shyrax's fleet either. And the galaxy would be better with Shyrax on the throne of Karosha instead of Felrex and the Perfected.

This spell was longer than the one I'd used to search for Gharyas, as it was more difficult to convince the Aether to target concepts as abstract as 'betrayal' versus finding a specific individual. And unlike the Cosmic Path, this spell wouldn't stretch far enough to reach through Subspace.

When I finished the incantation, my vision was *filled* with gold spots.

Her fleet spread out before me, and almost all the Karoshan ships had at least one golden spot inside it. Usually more than one, crawling like ants.

"Here's the good news," I said. "This ship is clear. You were right to trust them."

Several Karoshans let out a quiet breath. I couldn't blame them.

I wouldn't have wanted to leave my fate in the hands of a random mage's divination either.

Shyrax nodded as though she had never doubted that, but I was privately astonished. Keeping a ship of this size completely clear of traitors was almost impossible. There might have been up to ten thousand people on this vessel.

"And the bad news." I tossed a magic circle to Shyrax, passing the spell to her.

She surveyed the ships without much visible reaction. "I see. I'll have to arrange some personal inspections. How long will this spell last?"

"Three days," I said, and one of the mages in the back of the room coughed. Keeping a spell active for more than an hour—without an anchored enchantment or a few other special conditions—usually required constant attention.

"Then I have my task." Shyrax strode for the door, half of the room rising from their seats to follow her. "Thank you, Captain. I will attend to my duties aboard *The Last Horizon* when I am finished here."

"See you soon, Commander." Then I contacted Horizon again.

It was time to check on my Knight.

CHAPTER FIVE

THE INDUSTRIAL SPACE colony Pekler-76 was a broad, vast, uninviting place. It wasn't meant for holding civilian population but for supporting factory equipment, so it was made of cold steel and painted with shades of white and gray.

In total, it was as large as a small city, but most of its internal volume was taken up by vast machines and a network of steel walkways.

In the best of times, it was a quiet place, its metallic silence interrupted only by the clank of steel, the hiss of steam, the distant hum of engines, and—every once in a while—the echoing footsteps of an employee going from one task to another.

For weeks now, the footsteps had been silent. The machinery continued, but the only sounds were panicked breaths, tense and whispered cries for help, and the occasional scream of terror.

All the surviving crew aboard Pekler-76 had learned that silence meant survival.

"My name is Raion Raithe, Knight of *The Last Horizon!*" Raion cried. "I'm here to help!"

Holographic fireworks burst behind him.

The pair of humans, a woman and a young girl, squirmed deeper into the corner of the vents where they'd hidden. It looked like they'd been hiding there for a while, Raion judged, based on their tattered clothes, the piles of discarded food packages, and the stench of unwashed bodies.

The girl whimpered while trying to cover her own mouth while the woman gestured desperately to Raion. *"Quiet,"* she whispered. "You have to be *quiet.*"

"No need! You're safe now!"

If the humans could have run somewhere, he suspected they would have run from him. They didn't trust him yet, so they didn't believe him when he said their days of horror were over.

He supposed it didn't support his argument when a panel clanged open overhead and a predatory alien leaped out of the ceiling, jaws extended to feast on Raion's flesh.

Raion leaned aside, letting the creature crash to the floor so he could get a good look at it. It resembled a standard canine covered in a blue-black exoskeleton, like an insect. It had a pair of glistening compound eyes and jaws filled with slavering fangs, and its reverse-jointed legs were poised to leap on him again.

"Bugs really are the worst," Raion declared.

The alien made a hacking cough, and its throat bulged unnaturally wide. Only a second later, it spat a glob of luminous green liquid at him. He was about to dodge again when he considered what a fist-sized bubble of acid might do to the colony if it ended up melting through the hull.

Thinking quickly, he tore off a metal panel from the wall and used it to block the acid. The metal was corroded immediately, forcing him to toss it aside, but fortunately the acid wasn't as strong as he'd feared. It only dissolved the metal, but it didn't seem like it would eat through the entire colony.

Although the alien was hacking up another glob, so Raion put a stop to that with a quick slash of his force-blade. Bluish blood sprayed over the rest of the hall.

"Good thing their blood isn't acidic," Raion mused. "Can you imagine?"

"It *is!*" the woman shouted.

An instant later, the entire hallway began smoking.

"Ah. In that case, we should run."

Raion scooped up both of the humans and began sprinting down the metal catwalk. As his footsteps echoed in the hallway, he concentrated on his third eye and looked up into the ceiling.

As he'd expected, he saw blurry glows of reddish-gold hurrying toward him from all over this part of the station. More aliens, drawn toward the sounds.

"Don't worry, you're safe with me!" Raion called to the humans tucked under his arms. "So don't be alarmed as I fight, and try your best to avoid the acid."

The girl squirmed in his arm, trying to escape.

An alien poked its head out of a panel near the floor and got a blast of crimson energy in the face. That worked better than slicing it in half would have; there wasn't as much blood.

Raion kicked through the steel wall a moment later, crushing one, but of course that got acid on his boot and he had to toss it off. Which made running on the steel catwalk less comfortable.

After a few more experimental kills, Raion settled on what he found to be the best method of killing the aliens without letting them spit acid or getting their blood everywhere. He had to either burn them with his Combat Art or crush them *just* enough to cause internal damage but not so much that the exoskeleton cracked.

That would have been much easier if he had free hands. While executing a whirling kick in midair to send a lash of flame at a group of aliens *was* exciting, it would have been far more practical to use a hand. Not to mention how much easier it would have been to grab an alien in two hands and crush it, rather than pinning it with his foot against the ground and killing it that way.

But he knew from experience that humans had a low tolerance for being tossed around, and being carried while Raion leaped, dodged, kicked, and burned aliens was probably their tolerance level.

If he temporarily threw them into the air so he could use his hands for a moment, they'd probably vomit when he caught them again. And they had obviously been malnourished for a while; they couldn't spare the nutrition.

As Raion fought, another concern dawned on him. The aliens' numbers weren't dwindling as he killed them. If anything, more and more of them were pouring out of the walls and ceiling at every moment.

He focused his vision, staring more deeply into the rest of the station, and saw that it was crawling with almost as many threats as an Iron Hive. He was already starting to feel the exertion—none of what he was doing was difficult on its own, but moving carefully enough to avoid disturbing the humans was tricky. His Combat Art also consumed far more energy when he used it so inefficiently.

At this rate, he might falter, and the innocents would be in danger.

It would have been easy for him to burn all the predatory aliens out of the outpost by destroying the colony itself. He could do it without even summoning his Divine Titan, and—while that would be a powerful feat of his Combat Art—it would be easier than fighting this way.

But there were other humans hiding elsewhere in the colony. Until he confirmed that they were dead or safe, he couldn't do anything that would destabilize Pekler-76 itself.

"This is tricky," Raion said to his charges as he leaped over a ball of acid, kicked an alien into a wall, and stomped fire into a second target's face. "I have a friend that would know exactly what to do in this scenario. I wish Sola were here."

The humans didn't respond to him—they were busy screaming in terror—but a blue light shone next to him.

He didn't have time to stop and wait, but his spirit brightened. The Aether, or more likely Horizon, had heard his wish.

A second later, the blue light resolved into a hooded figure a bit shorter than Raion. The symbols on the edges of his wizard's mantle shone silver that matched his eyes, and he swept a hand at the oncoming aliens and shoved them back.

A glob of acid hit the air a few feet away from him and shimmered on the edge of an invisible protective field, sliding across it as though down curved glass.

"Did you call for help?" Varic asked.

"Actually, I called for Sola," Raion said. "But you would have been my second choice!"

Raion would have expected the innocents he'd rescued to have been relieved upon seeing a fellow human, but they were still crying. Varic gestured to them and Raion felt their slight weight lifting from his arms.

"Why don't I take these two?" Varic suggested.

Raion sighed in relief. "Thank you! This will be much easier with my hands."

Then his stomach lurched as the catwalk beneath their feet collapsed.

He'd been leaping from bridge to bridge as he fought, trying to spread out the acid damage, but they'd stayed in one place too long. The catwalk couldn't take it, and it fell to the floor beneath.

Raion, however, only fell a few inches. Varic had caught all four of them with his levitation ring, so they hovered safely far above the wreckage. Raion could have flown on his own, but he appreciated the support anyway.

The acid was starting to pile up, though. It was getting hard to see the rest of the room through the layer of shining green sludge that covered Varic's shield.

He turned to the woman, who seemed more relieved to be drifting in midair than she had been to be carried by Raion. "Where did these things come from?" Varic asked.

"Th-the company made them," she said bitterly. "Supposed to be the *perfect weapons,* if you can believe it. All they do is hunt, eat, and lay their eggs."

Varic took a deep breath as though bracing himself to dive into an icy river. "What company?"

"Cablewright Genetics," she said, and Varic let out a breath of relief. "A subsidiary of the Vallenar Corporation," she went on, and Varic's relief turned into a groan.

"Well, you can rest now. We'll take care of this."

Raion punched his left hand and turned to face the aliens he could now barely see through the haze of acid. "Bring it on, monsters!"

Varic muttered an incantation and then tossed a golden magic circle over to Raion. It sank into Raion's head, and suddenly he could see gold lights in six places all around this section of the colony.

"That will take you close to any survivors," Varic said. "It won't give you the situation in the room, so look before you leap."

Raion looked back, having already leaped over to the remaining section of the catwalk. "Leave it to me!" he cried.

Without the humans to carry, Raion steadied himself before igniting his energy and blasting through the crowd of aliens at full speed. It was much easier than fighting with only his feet, but still not as simple as blasting the colony apart would have been.

Raion took this as training. Exercise was good for the soul!

As he flew, he reflected on how grateful he was to have crew he could trust. Even on the Titan Force, while he trusted his fellow Knights with his life, he had been the most capable member. Now, he was part of a team where each member could cover for the weaknesses of the other.

More than ever, Raion was thankful to have friends.

CHAPTER SIX

IN THIS LIFE
FIVE YEARS AGO

RAION PUSHED HIS Divine Titan past its limits, shouting as he slashed through the last of the D'Niss.

The seventh of the Seven Calamities resembled a fat beetle bigger than a colony, but the Dance of a Burning World sliced it down the middle with a blade of crimson flame. Raion emerged from the other side just in time.

His Divine Titan screamed warnings at him from every direction, something was wrong with his central eye, and he couldn't feel his legs.

Even so, he let out a cry of triumph. It went out over the local Subline even as his Divine Titan vanished from around him, its energy spent.

"We did it!" he cried into his helmet's speaker.

He drifted in space, surrounded by oceans of insectoid blood, but his starship was already on the way to pick him up. It would be drawn by the emergency beacon on his suit.

The other three Knights didn't respond.

Their fight against Neth'terith had cost them Javik, though fortunately he'd survived the destruction of his Divine Titan. It would take years to repair the Yellow Titan, and the best medical care in the galaxy to restore Javik to perfect condition.

He was out of the fight, but at least he'd made it out alive. And victorious.

The long war was over.

Titan Knights would still stand as guardians of the galaxy, and they would be far more effective without the D'Niss looming over them. Raion had long dreamed of what they could accomplish with their greatest enemies gone, and soon, he would see those dreams come to life.

The broken body of Neth'terith drifted in an ocean of its own blood, a cracked and leaking moon. Raion's gaze sharpened as he saw motion.

A cloud of smoke drifted toward him, out of the slain monster's body. He assumed it was an attack and ignited what was left of his energy, setting his red aura to burning.

The cloud surrounded him and began eating away at that aura, giving him a chance to inspect the 'smoke' more closely. It was a cloud of insects, tiny hard-shelled biting things that had no business surviving in space.

Raion flared his aura and killed the bugs, but they gave him a bad feeling.

"Knights, check in," he said into his helmet.

His red starfighter slid up a moment later and he flew inside, connecting to its more powerful transmitter. When he sent the message again, he finally received a response.

"No problems here, Red!" the voice of Parryl, the Green Knight, came through. She sounded cheery and younger even than she was, rejuvenated by excitement.

The Blue Knight, Laraena, rarely expressed anything, but even she laughed as she spoke over their connection. "Thought we'd lost you there, Red. Does that mean this is mission accomplished?"

The White Knight didn't respond verbally, but he sent the all-clear over the computer.

Raion was initially relieved to hear their voices, but on further thought, his unease deepened. "Is everyone all right? I had a bad feeling."

"You were swimming in bug guts," Parryl said. "That's not going to feel *good.*"

They sounded like his friends, but there was something missing from their voices. He sped for the carrier, the vast mobile base that docked their fighters and served as their home while they were on missions.

He saw their starfighters flying in ahead of him, and the sight gave him another wave of relief. Raion hoped he was being paranoid. Maybe he didn't know what to do now that their fight was over.

But he'd never had trouble celebrating after a fight before.

When he docked and hopped out of his fighter, he saw his teammates gathered together laughing, helmets dismissed. Parryl was gesturing, shining Lichborn eyes alight with excitement.

Raion stared at them for a long moment while the hollow feeling in his gut only deepened.

He felt no friendship from them.

Laraena waved to him and jerked her chin, inviting him to join them. Raion removed his helmet in time to vomit on the floor.

The other three hurried over, concern in their face, but Raion ignited his force-blade while only half-standing.

"Stay...stay back!" he insisted. His voice shook.

While they were asking for explanations, Raion activated the communicator in his console. "Doctor Cryce, I need readings on the others."

"Come again, Raion?"

"Give me their bio-readings *NOW!"* Raion shouted. He never raised his voice like that.

The other three Knights moved closer again, their concern turning to fear.

"They're fine, Raion," the doctor's voice came into his ear. She sounded puzzled. *"What are you...Huh. That's weird."*

Parryl reached toward Raion with a green-and-white glove, but her hand found the edge of a plasma blade.

"No closer," Raion said, but his voice and hand both trembled.

"Oh, worlds. No. Raion, they're..." A retching came from over the audio as Cryce lost control of her own stomach.

She managed to croak out two more words. *"...parasites. Run!"*

Two things slid into place for Raion at that moment.

The first was something he *hadn't* heard. Every other D'Niss they'd killed had gone out with a psychic death cry, usually an attempt to shake their resolve or swear vengeance. He hadn't consciously noticed, occupied as he'd been with killing the enemy, but this one had remained silent.

Which suggested it had been talking to something else.

Second, that cloud of insects. Those hadn't been mentioned by the Galactic Union's report. No one knew anything about any clouds of buzzing, biting insects.

Thanks to that report, the Titan Force had enjoyed a huge tactical advantage in their final fight. They'd known all the tricks the D'Niss had, and the information had proven accurate.

No one knew about the card the D'Niss had held in reserve.

Parasites.

Neth'terith had never intended to rule the galaxy without the rest of the Seven Calamities. He had been left behind as a sacrifice. One last, spiteful act before the D'Niss abandoned the universe.

Their revenge on the Titan Force.

"Can we save them?" Raion asked, but his helmet wasn't on. The other Knights could hear his end of the conversation.

They stopped acting like his friends immediately.

Parryl's face went blank and she shoved her hand into his forceblade. When it began to cut her, she didn't flinch, but Raion did.

It was one thing to threaten impostors, but it was another to cut his friend.

Her other hand went to her hip and came up with a gun. With a green flash, she shot, and Raion barely dodged. That one shot blasted a hole in the ceiling of the docking bay, instantly breaching the hull and greedily sucking the air from the room.

This thing could still use her Combat Art.

Kherius, the White Knight, pulled a weapon of his own and fired a blast of energy at Raion. At the same time, Laraena chanted. Ice formed behind her as she called her element.

Raion knocked the blast into space, but he had been at the end of his rope since the battle. He'd already gone past his limits.

And he'd done it for his friends.

He fought on autopilot, but he couldn't bring out the full extent of what little strength remained to him. What if they could still be saved? By fighting them, was he giving up on them?

Every exchange devastated the carrier. If they had been deeper in the ship, it would have exploded by now. Alarms still blared from all directions.

Raion was in worse shape even than the ship. Each exchange burned him, cut him, broke his bones. Icicles stabbed into him, but he had to keep moving. He couldn't kill his friends, and he couldn't let them kill him.

Finally, the teary voice of Doctor Cryce came over his audio implant one more time, *"Could you…For me, keep Parryl's…body as intact as you can. I want to bury her in one piece."*

The Dance of a Burning World ignited around Raion's sword.

He blocked a shot from the Green Knight, sliced through an icicle, and cut through a thick barrier of energy to cleave the White Knight in half.

Raion didn't look at the man's remains, but he couldn't help hearing the buzzing as flies left the body.

He ignited them all with such intensity that the floor beneath him glowed red-hot.

"There is no life for you," a dead insect said from Parryl's body. "In victory or defeat, there is only death."

Raion didn't make the mistake with the Blue Knight that he'd made with the White. He didn't cut her into pieces but cremated her on the spot.

Only then did he address the Green Knight.

"Don't worry, Parryl," Raion said. "I'll save you."

CHAPTER SEVEN

THE SEVEN OF us gathered in the room Horizon often formed for meetings. It was circular and smooth, with a domed ceiling that made it feel something like being trapped under a basket.

The only furniture of note was a round table separated into six wedges, with a holo-projector in the center and six chairs all around.

We, the crew, sat in our respective seats, which Horizon had helpfully lit in our colors. Once we were seated, Horizon appeared over the center of the table.

As usual, she took on the form of a woman in a long, flowing dress, looking almost human except for her gnarled horns that resembled tree roots and the seven-pointed stars in her eyes.

That, and the fact that she was drawn in six colors of light. They blended well enough now that she looked physical, and she gazed down on us with a proud, maternal smile.

"My crew," the Zenith Starship said. *"It has been too long since I've seen you all together, ready to take on the heroic work of saving the galaxy. I've missed—"*

"All right, stop," I interrupted. "Horizon, we were all together last week."

"That's already too long. Besides, we weren't engaged in heroic work, we were only talking."

Omega sighed and slumped over his orange lit wedge of the table. "We're only talking now, aren't we? When we *could* be out there shooting.

"First, we have to understand who our enemies are!" Raion declared. "Then we can shoot them."

"My Knight is correct, which is why I'm so proud to bear the information brought back by my Engineer." Horizon nodded to Mell, who was practically bouncing in her chair.

"Yeah, where is it?" Mell asked excitedly. "Did you find the Cannon?"

"Indeed, and with great effort worthy of my own heroic saga. I will tell you when we have more time." She glanced at me out of the corner of her eye. *"Or, if there's enough interest, perhaps I could give you a few details now..."*

Shyrax hardly fit into her wedge of the table, and she fixed the ship's spirit with a pointed stare. "You know we should discuss the information first. This is hardly the time to stroke your ego."

Horizon's projected form shrunk two inches and I swear she poked out her lower lip.

"...Tonight, over dinner, we will be an appropriate audience for your tale," Shyrax went on. "I wish to hear it myself, but not when my attention is divided."

Horizon's height was restored immediately and she lifted her chin in pride. *"A wonderful suggestion from my Commander, as usual. Now is the time to discuss the route to the Zenith Cannon."*

A smoggy, rust-red colony appeared then. It looked like it had been bolted onto the fragment of a continent that had been left over from a destroyed planet.

"We traced the Cannon to this scrapper colony on the edge of the Galactic Union," Horizon said. *"It handles most of the recycling for the surrounding sectors; anything the individual systems can't handle on their own gets sent here for processing. Raw materials are shipped back to their systems of origin while any Aethertech or other reusable devices are turned over to Union inspectors."*

The hologram showing the facility shifted to show the internal view of a vast workshop. Hundreds of assembly lines carried metallic junk in every direction, past workers of a species I didn't recognize.

They were large, squat, and bulky, with bulbous noses and thick skin that seemed like it could stop a plasma bolt. The four fingers on their hands looked anything but nimble, though they had little trouble disassembling devices for inspection.

There are five species of intelligent beings you can find on about any planet: humans, Karoshans, Visiri, Aethril, and Lichborn. Most citizens of the galaxy come from those bloodlines.

But there are a number of planets where sapient life was altered, usually by the Aether or a World Spirit, to suit local conditions. It's impossible to keep a comprehensive database of all the humanoids in the galaxy, so it's never rare to run into a species I don't recognize.

One of the workers gave a shout and waved around a device he grabbed off the assembly line. Though the audio of the recording was scratchy and his voice was difficult to make out, I clearly heard the words, *"Talking gun!"*

Horizon paused the recording there, but the rest of us were waiting for more.

"And?" Sola prompted. "What gives you the idea that this is the Zenith Cannon?"

"The information retrieved by my Engineer suggests that the Galactic Union flagged this incident as a sighting of the Cannon. Also, the Cannon's last suspected location was aboard a cargo cruiser that was recently decommissioned and stripped, with many of its components sent to the facility."

Mell waved frantically at the hologram. "So where did it go after this? Where is it now?"

"The worker was ordered to deposit the talking gun into the reclamation device, but he declined to follow orders. He stole the gun for himself."

Horizon skipped ahead to the worker glancing left and right and then tucking the talking gun into the waistband of his pants.

"Minutes later, he was charged with theft of company property and

fired. The gun was taken into evidence, delivered to a Galactic Union inspector, and it has presumably remained in his keeping ever since."

I was getting a painful premonition, and I didn't think it came from my vast wizardly insight. "So this inspector has held onto the gun for six months, but it never made it back to the Galactic Union government nor did they pressure him to turn it over?"

"That's right!" Horizon's seven-pointed eyes were twinkling.

I drummed my fingers on the table for a moment, then shrugged. "Well, the Cannon is out of our hands. What's next?"

"What?" Mell demanded. She sat bolt upright in her chair. "Do you know what I went through for that information? I was shot at!"

She looked around at our unimpressed expressions and scowled. "All right, unlike the rest of you, I can't ignore plasma bolts. I could have been killed!"

Shyrax shook her head. "Then you were careless. Do not put yourself in such a vulnerable position."

"Sounds like you could use some armor," Sola said.

"Walk it off," Omega suggested.

Raion scratched the side of his head. "Why do we have to give up the Cannon? Can't we talk to the Union representative?"

"We certainly can," Horizon said. *"In fact, it's one of our old friends."*

I turned to Raion. "Clearly, Horizon means to say that this representative is my father. Getting it back from him will be more trouble than it's worth."

"This is your opportunity to repair your family bonds!" Raion cried.

"But we don't need the Cannon," I said, directing my most earnest argument to Mell. "We only wanted the Cannon so we can study it and to make sure it's dormant. If my father still has it and hasn't contacted us, that means the Vallenar Corporation couldn't figure out a way to awaken it. Not yet, anyway. That's good news! Once his Technicians have gotten everything they can out of it, the Cannon will lose value to him, and then we can pick it up at a reduced price."

Horizon looked personally offended. *"Even dormant, the Zenith Devices are priceless beyond the dreams of mortals!"*

"He's not going to ask for money," I said with certainty.

Sola rubbed her chin. "You're sure it's dormant? That guy said '*talking* gun.'"

"As I explained to the Captain, that does not *mean she is conscious. Think of it as a recording. She has several automatic screening protocols that remain functional even when she is dormant, like the ones my Captain bypassed on his way to me."*

She placed a hand on my shoulder and looked at me fondly. *"If he had not met my standards, he would never have been able to open the chamber in which I rested and awaken me. Even once awakened, I had to approve of him."*

Now that I knew Horizon better, I suspected that her negotiating position hadn't been as solid as she pretended. If I had walked away that day, she likely would have begged me to stay. She hated being dormant.

Mell adjusted her glasses as she flipped through reports. "Even if the Zenith Device is still asleep, we can use it. If we can wake it up, that's even better. I'm not sure why the Captain thinks them being awake is a bad omen."

"It's the way Horizon and Ark talked about it," I said. "No more than two Zenith Devices have been activated at any one time since the Zenith Era. They don't actively seek out partners. If they're doing so now..."

"It means the Aether has great times in store for us!" Horizon announced, lifting her hands to the ceiling. But she lowered them almost instantly. *"But don't worry, Captain. Nothing like that is happening here."*

I pointed. "It's statements like that that make me nervous."

"Just because you're a wizard," Mell said, "doesn't mean you have to be superstitious." She bit down on a toothpick as though she'd made a point.

Sola laced her fingers together. "If we can lock down the Zenith Cannon, we should. As soon as possible. We have a lot of enemies."

"Its technology will be an invaluable tool in the reclamation of Karosha," Shyrax agreed.

"Not that," Sola said. "We can't allow the Galactic Union or the Vallenar Corporation to have a weapon they can use against us. They might figure out how to awaken it."

Shyrax nodded again. "Yes. The most reliable hands in the galaxy are our own. If we can be trusted to use two Zenith Devices responsibly, why not three?"

This was a theme that had come up several times in the last six months, and I had to shut it down every time. "Let me stop you right there, because we only have *one*. Shadow Ark is a guest who cannot access most of his functions. And I feel I must remind you what I just said about awakening the seven Zenith Devices."

"You didn't say anything about awakening seven," Shyrax said confidently. "You only implied it."

Horizon gave me a sympathetic look. *"Besides, us deliberately awakening my brothers and sisters is totally different from the Aether causing them to awaken on their own."*

It was hard to tell when Horizon knew something I didn't and when she was making things up.

"*Is* it different?" I asked.

She shrugged. *"Maybe!"*

I was about ten seconds from calling off the entire hunt for the Zenith Devices, but Mell banged her fist on the table. In present company, it was somewhat pathetic; Shyrax banging her fist on the table would have made us all go deaf, and Raion could have collapsed the entire floor.

"I want the Zenith Cannon!" Mell said. "It's part of my request, and it might be the most important of the seven. You know what my Nova-Bots can do now that I've studied two Zenith Devices?"

I had seen some of the new features that Mell had added to her androids since she'd examined Horizon and Ark up close. They *were* useful.

"Not enough to save you from me," Omega said, leering with his Aethertech eye.

"Oh, that reminds me!" Mell leaped over to Omega, brandishing a handheld scanner. "You said you'd let me see your eye!"

"Which one?" Omega asked, sprouting eyes from fifteen tendrils of dark gray ooze.

Raion gagged.

Mell tried to slap one of the nearest eyes, but it bobbed away from her hand. "Stop that! Half of the people here can do that!"

Horizon manifested fifteen eyes from magic and, because I'm a team player, so did I.

"That's not half," Omega protested, but Mell was standing with one foot on the table and the other braced against the back of his chair. She peered down into his face through her glasses, shoving a beeping device closer to his eye.

Omega melted into a puddle of ooze and chuckled as he squirmed away.

"Coward!" Mell cried.

I pulled the conversation back on track. "I'm sure the Zenith Cannon would be great for your research, but wouldn't any of the Devices?"

"No! I need to improve my Nova-Bots' weaponry."

"I know you haven't finished learning everything you can about Horizon," I said. "A lifetime wouldn't be enough to study all her systems."

Horizon put a hand to her mouth and tears welled in her eyes.

Mell folded her arms. "Why don't you stick to one magic? A lifetime wouldn't be enough to finish studying that."

"I did stick to one magic," I said. "Six times. But I take your point, so let's vote. Are we all settled on this?"

Shyrax met my eyes with unyielding intensity. "I have no need for a fair fight with the Perfected. If I can blast them from their thrones with Zenith Era fire, I will do so."

"I'm obviously in," Mell said.

Omega popped a head up from the side of the table. "By all means, let's retrieve the greatest gun in the galaxy. Yes, we should, yes."

Horizon's grin stretched her face. *"To pursue my sister and rescue her, so that when she wakes, she will find she is in my debt...It will be a memory to treasure for eons."*

"We've got to control it," Sola said. "Everybody in the galaxy's our enemy right now, so we'd be stupid to leave the best weapon rolling out there free."

I drummed fingers on the table more rapidly. "Fine. I'll talk to my father. We have a lead, and I *don't* like having enemies everywhere. Makes sense to prepare."

Only then did I realize not everyone had put in their opinion. I glanced around to see Raion staring wide-eyed into his console.

"Raion?" I asked. "Are you all right?"

He looked up, dazed. "Oh, sorry Captain. I was...Were we voting?"

"What happened, Raion?" Sola asked. She'd already summoned a gun.

Raion looked back down to his console. "I got a call. I think my friend is alive."

CHAPTER EIGHT

IN ANOTHER LIFE

After we cleared the Iron Legion from the Lesser Karoshan system, I got my first up-close look at an Iron Hive. At least, in that life.

I'll skip the description this time. There aren't any nice Iron Hives.

The Karoshans paid my teacher for her help, and I think they even gave us some medals, but I don't remember for sure. We were in that system for weeks.

By the time we left, I was in better shape than when I'd arrived, which isn't normal for most people who fight the Iron Legion. I wasn't sure my water elementalism had gotten any better, but at least I developed a resistance to the shocking stench of Iron Legion Pawns.

Still, neither I nor my teacher were in good spirits as we flew away in her cruiser. Kyri chewed on her lip and stared out the viewport as she left most of the piloting to the computer, and I waited for her to explain.

When she didn't, I asked my question. "Did they ever tell you what the Hives were doing here?"

I didn't know much about the Iron Legion, but sending three Hives into a heavily defended Karoshan system with no support did not seem like a good plan. Even the Karoshans had continued to expect another incursion into the system; probably twenty percent of their forces had remained on standby, awaiting reinforcements.

None ever came. And since Kyri had access to information that was classified to me, I wanted to know what she had learned from Karoshan military intelligence.

She leaned back from the control console, tinkering with her prosthetic arm in what I suspected was a deliberate attempt to seem casual.

"You can never tell with Iron Legion," she said. "Could be that they randomly drifted into the system with no plan. Could be that they got desperate and hungry out there in Dark Space and this was the first place they landed, could be that they got attacked by something in Subspace and were sent off-course, or it could be that this is some insane strategy we'll only see through a hundred years from now."

"So which one is it?"

"What makes you think I know?"

"You would have told me if you didn't. If you're throwing out all the possibilities, that means you're going somewhere."

Kyri gave a dry laugh without looking up from her arm. She had opened a panel in her forearm and was tightening something. "Learn to read me like that in the arena, and maybe our next match will go better for you. Here's what I know that you don't: those three Iron Hives were damaged. They were running from something."

"What do they think it was?"

If Karoshan military intelligence didn't have a guess, there was no way I would know anything, but I'd considered running it by the Vallenar Corporation. There was also the possibility that the damage to the Hives was inflicted magically, which could teach me something.

Kyri stopped tinkering with her arm for a moment and tapped a few buttons on the side instead. The built-in console projected a hologram into the air, showing the picture of three Iron Hives drawn in blue-and-white light.

She spun them around to show me the rear of the Hives. It looked like something had carved through the backside of each one at an angle, like a colossal sword-strike.

"Something from Subspace?" I guessed. "It couldn't be a stellar dragon, or the Hives wouldn't have survived."

Without comment, Kyri rearranged the Hives and put them next to each other.

At first, I didn't see why. When the pattern became clear, a chill ran down my spine.

They hadn't been attacked separately. There was one *single* slash that had started at the top-right of one Hive, cut through the middle of the second, and finished in the bottom-left of another.

It looked like a single-edged swipe of a sword or claw. But that would have to come from a being the size of a *planet*.

When Kyri saw I understood, she clicked off her projector. "There isn't much we know of that could do that except a Behemoth, but there is no infighting in the Iron Legion. The Karoshans have determined that this is a wild skyspine or contrasaur flying in from Subspace. I think the truth is much worse."

I put my head in my hands. "If I ask what worse is, are you going to tell me?"

"Don't be stupid. I'm going to tell you whether you ask or not." She leaned down in front of me until I peeked through my fingers, then she grinned. "Have you ever heard of the Titan Force?"

The headquarters of the Titan Force was on the second moon of Delsin, a gas giant with sparkling diamond rings. The moon itself was terraformed long ago, covered in dense jungles and clouds.

Of course, none of that caught my attention as much as the Titan Forge.

The Forge was one of the largest pieces of Aethertech I'd ever seen, the size of a moderate shipyard or large colony. It resembled a complex cage of smooth metal, each piece shifting and interlocking like a puzzle on a cosmic scale.

It hovered over the moon, holding its latest subject: a bright green humanoid mech over a hundred and fifty feet tall, though it seemed tiny as I watched it through our starship's cameras.

The green Divine Titan—though I didn't know what it was at the time—had seen hard battle. One of its arms was disassembled entirely, and sparks flew from its components as the Titan Forge repaired its systems.

As Kyri took over piloting our ship again, she glanced back at me. "Probably should have mentioned this before now, but we were never here. You should scrub the location from your processor's log."

"What? Who are we hiding from?" The answer to that question would determine whether I would even bother following her directions. If we were trying to hide from the Vallenar Corporation, for instance, we might as well have not bothered. It was already too late.

"The Karoshans. I'm about to divulge confidential military information."

I winced even as I erased my processor's log. "You shouldn't have told me that."

"I want you to know what I'm up to. Besides, *you're* not the one betraying the Karoshan Throne. They won't execute you."

"I don't want them to execute you either!"

She scratched at the connection between her shoulder and her prosthetic arm. "Eh. If I'm right, I'm about to be too important to kill."

I didn't like any part of her plan, and I didn't even want to call it a plan. But I *did* want to see the Titan Force.

And if her suspicions were true, the galaxy was in real danger. I wanted to use my magic to make a difference.

Through all my lives, that never changed.

We had barely landed and opened the hatch when a Lichborn woman scuttled in, holding a tablet console and tripping over her own words. "Kyri, you could have been here four *hours* ago, and I was sure you were going to be because you said you would get here as fast as you could, but I finished calibrating Blue right before you were supposed to arrive, and then when you didn't show up I kept running tests, so I don't have anything—"

Kyri stuck out her metal hand and the newcomer ran right into her palm. "Stop. Talk, then breathe, then talk again."

"You're late," the Lichborn woman said. Then she took a deep breath, let it out, and added, "Blue will be ready for you later tonight, because I started testing it again. Two hours. Maybe four hours."

She glanced at me once. "Who's he?"

I didn't expect her to take Kyri so literally. She took a deep breath between every sentence.

"My apprentice," Kyri said. "Varic, this is Doctor Janbell Cryce. She's a Master Aether Technician and the creator of the Divine Titans. Jan, this is Varic Vallenar."

I had straightened at the introduction, astonished to have recognized the doctor's name. "Doctor Cryce, I apologize, I didn't know we were meeting you. I've heard great things about your work."

In fact, what I'd heard was that the Vallenar Corporation had tried to hire her. Rumor said they had offered her an actual, entire planet and had been willing to negotiate up from there.

Though I only knew her by reputation, she was one of the few Aether Technicians ever to have awakened *two* Technician gifts. She'd even created a masterwork in both.

Once I saw her tied to the Titan Force, I understood where her reputation had come from. The Forge that had constructed the Titans had to be the masterwork creation of a fabricator Technician, while the Divine Titans themselves were masterpieces of a different discipline.

Doctor Cryce waved a hand without looking in my direction. "So that's how you're paying the bills, Kyri? You could have come to me if you needed help."

"Are you going to look at me?" I asked.

"You know my reputation, and I know yours," Doctor Cryce said while flicking through her tablet console. "I have no respect for your family, so I don't see why I should have any for you just because you bought your way into an apprenticeship with my friend, and I didn't invite you here anyway, so if you're here, it's because—"

Kyri held up a hand again and Cryce took a deliberate breath.

I took that moment as an opportunity. "I know the reputation my family has, but surely I still deserve the basic courtesy you would extend a stranger."

Doctor Cryce gave me an irritated look, but Kyri lifted her eyebrows. "He's right, Jan. Brilliant people don't have to be rude."

Cryce took two deep breaths. "I'm sorry, Mister Vallenar. Let's start over. I know Kyri wouldn't have brought you if she didn't think you could contribute, so why don't the *both* of you come join me in the Blue facility?"

She glanced to Kyri triumphantly, as though she'd done something astonishing.

"Well done, Jan. Lead the way." As we finally left the ship, Kyri walked beside me to talk. "Jan used to do freelance work for the Alliance, and we ended up in training together. I was one of the first to fund her research."

"She also helped me run experiments for which I required magic, since there are fewer mages than you'd expect who can cast with the precision—" Doctor Cryce paused to breathe. "—required to sync with Aethertech, which I believe to be the fundamental difference between modern Aethertech and the Zenith Devices."

As we talked, Cryce half-sprinted ahead. We had landed not in a dock, but in the middle of what was effectively an open lawn ahead of a massive, square building with no windows.

On the side of the building was the word *'BLUE'* stenciled in gigantic letters.

She dashed ahead, passing through a guard checkpoint and two scanners before she opened the door on the ground floor. "None of our projected pilots have given us the responses we wanted to see. They were qualified in terms of water elementalism, and a few of them scored well on the piloting simulators, but there's a connection I'm missing. I checked everything I knew to check and brought in specialists, but we all agree that it's got to be an Aetheric cause."

We were walking through a simple, unadorned hallway past walls that were simple fabricated plastic. Before we reached another door at the far end of the hall, a door that more closely resembled an airlock hatch, Kyri grabbed Cryce by the shoulder.

"Hold on, Jan. Why are you talking like *you* called *me* here? I called you."

For a second, Doctor Cryce's glowing green eyes shot everywhere as though she had woken from a dream. "Yes—No. What? I...Oh, right, I see what you're...Yes. You called and said you had something to show me, and I knew what it was, so I started preparing for your arrival, but when I realized you were going to come here, I input your information into Blue, and it all looked promising on the simulator, so now I'm going to test you."

Kyri took a second to parse that, her three eyes narrowing. Then she said, "I think three Iron Hives were attacked by the D'Niss."

"Right. Because otherwise you wouldn't have called me about it. Since that was the only thing it could possibly be, I prepared."

Cryce scanned her retina at the door, then locks shifted with heavy metal clunks before the door slid aside. "Kyri, Varic, meet Blue!"

On the other side of the door was a huge, open chamber built to contain the Blue Divine Titan. The mech itself stood strapped to the far wall, with people and drones crawling all over a lattice of scaffolding around the Titan.

At a glance, the Divine Titan was clearly more advanced than any other Aethertech I'd seen in that life. More than I saw in most of my lives, in fact. Its plates were smooth and bright blue, and the armor connected so organically that it reminded me of an insect's carapace rather than typical powered armor.

While it was still armored and the size of an entire building, the Blue Divine Titan was relatively slender. Its helmet had a design that evoked a hood, and a massive staff leaned against the floor next to it. Crew scurried up and down its length, giving the weapon almost as much attention as the mech itself.

All told, there were hundreds of people working inside the building, far more than I had expected from the outside. Trucks drove across the floor, carrying esoteric mechanical components. Or even *magical* components; I saw more than a few wizards, most in the process of enchanting.

Doctor Cryce seemed to gain an inch of height as she drank in our astonished reaction to the sight of the Divine Titan. "Incredible, isn't he? Like I said, he was ready hours ago, but I decided to run a few final checks when you didn't show up. They should be waiting for you...now?" She checked something on her tablet console and then nodded. "Now."

Kyri was still watching the Divine Titan. "You want me to pilot this thing, right?"

I had seen that coming, but it was still strange to hear. Kyri was a famous duelist and wizard, but she had no background I was aware of that would apply to a mech pilot.

"Mm-hmm, now put this on." Someone handed a folded set of clothes to Doctor Cryce, who grabbed them and tossed them at Kyri without looking up from her tablet. "Restrooms are that way."

Kyri held out the clothes by the shoulder, revealing a padded one-piece jumpsuit. It was almost entirely blue, with a pair of white gloves tucked into the belt.

"Is this—"

"It's self-fitting," Cryce said, "now go! You were already late!"

Kyri left me standing in awkward silence next to Doctor Cryce. The Technician ignored me.

Two minutes later, my teacher returned in the uniform of a Titan Knight. It wasn't armored, being an incomplete test suit, but otherwise it was identical to what the Knights wore on their missions.

"Now what?" Kyri asked.

Cryce pointed up to the top of the Divine Titan. "Headed up!"

We took a levitating platform on hover-plates up to the top of the Titan, so we didn't have to wait for the platform that carried the other workers through the scaffolding. Up close, the helmet looked less like a face and more like a house designed by someone with a strange aesthetic sense.

I thought the head would hold the pilot, but instead the mech's chest opened below us, revealing a surprisingly cramped cockpit. The pilot would sit in a padded blue chair, surrounded by screens, controls, and blinking Aethertech devices. Even a few spinning magical symbols.

As the chest opened, a metallic groan came from the Titan. I felt it in my feet, and I glanced to Cryce to see if I should panic.

She looked delighted, her green eyes brightening. "Ooohh, he likes you! This is it, this is *it!* Get in there, Kyri!"

My teacher handed me her wand and console, and I could tell she was excited. To her, this must have seemed like the beginning of a new adventure.

I was eager too, even as a bystander. It was a thrill to be present for the birth of a new Titan Knight.

And, though I wasn't conscious of it, I'm sure I noticed something in the Aether. This was a significant moment.

Kyri's red skin stood out from all the blue around her, but her third eye shone brightly as she settled into the pilot seat. "I'm ready, Jan," she called.

Doctor Cryce's hands danced over the tablet. "Strap in and hold on!" she called.

Then she lowered her voice and began to speak to the rest of her team. Her instructions became much more technical as she took them down a checklist. I recognized this as a pre-launch procedure, even though most of the actual terms were foreign to me.

Only a few seconds after she began, the chest armor of the Divine Titan slowly closed. Kyri grinned in anticipation, and Doctor Cryce cut off her instructions to look up hopefully.

"She's going to be okay," Cryce assured me. "There's nothing that could go wrong in this process that could hurt her."

I was surprised she'd addressed me at all. "I *wasn't* worried about her. Should I be?"

"No! No, that's what I was saying. You shouldn't be. It won't go wrong anyway." The armor of the Titan hissed as it closed up, and Cryce issued a few more instructions over her communicator.

Then she turned back to me. "She has a strong connection to water, right?"

"She's an Archmage of water elementalism."

"Yes. Right. But in your estimation, as a mage, how would you quantify that connection?"

"Mages don't really...quantify things," I said hesitantly. "But if we did, I'd say she has the strongest connection to water of anyone I've ever met."

"That's not quantified," Cryce muttered. "So if this *doesn't* work, is there anyone with a stronger connection to the water element you might suggest?"

It was hard to explain to a layperson my thoughts on the matter, but I tried. "It's not like there's some level to her elementalism that I can point to. It comes down to how significant the water element is to her and to her magic. If you've tried other elementalists as pilots and this doesn't work for her, I'd say it's not her elementalism that's lacking."

She examined my face for a while but said nothing. Finally, a green light blinked on her console and she returned her attention to it.

"Ready to start," Cryce said into her console. "Kyri, let me know if you can hear me. Good. Now, on the count of three, call your element through Blue here. Understood? Great. One, two...three."

I braced myself, waiting for a reaction.

Nothing happened.

Only a few seconds later, Doctor Cryce spoke again. "No, you did fine, Kyri. We're reading your effort, and you did great. We're going to try that again. One, two, three."

Again, nothing.

They tried two more times before the plates on the Divine Titan's chest opened again. Kyri unstrapped herself and stood, forcing a smile. "I got my hopes up and everything. Guess I didn't have what it takes."

Cryce gripped her tablet so hard I thought she was going to break it. "No, Kyri, he's...Blue, why are you so picky? All the others..."

She took in another deep, intentional breath. "Either I made a mistake in his design or—" Cryce shrugged. "—it's magic."

Kyri could have leaped out of the Titan, but she was stepping carefully around the delicate equipment. She looked for a step to leave, and I reached down to pull her out.

As I did, I braced myself on the Blue Titan's armor.

Immediately, the glass over its eyes shone. I was startled, suddenly standing in front of a pair of sapphire floodlights, but more than just the helmet had come to life. Energy flowed through the entire Titan, lines burst with magic, and I could read its significance in the Aether.

The Divine Titan was coming to life.

Kyri grabbed my hand, but instead of letting me pull her up, she hauled me off the platform. She lowered me into the pilot seat while I was still stunned, then she hopped out of the Titan on her own.

Doctor Cryce's eyes were wide, but she didn't let her astonishment distract her. She was talking so fast into her communicator that I thought she was chanting a spell, and her fingers moved over her console even faster than before.

Kyri's smile almost dropped. "Good thing I brought you along, huh?"

I felt like I ought to apologize, like I had stolen an opportunity from her. But at the same time, I also felt *chosen*.

It's difficult to describe how it feels, being singled out by a device with the power of a Divine Titan. I returned my teacher's smile apologetically, but I settled down into the seat. The controls hummed to life around me, and I reached out for them.

Kyri hooked a finger into the collar of the Titan Knight suit she wore and spoke to Doctor Cryce. "I don't need to switch clothes with him, do I?"

"Guess not," the doctor muttered. "Varic, strap in and stand by."

I did as ordered. When the Titan closed, trapping me in a space even tighter than the cockpit of a starfighter, I didn't feel uncomfortable.

I felt like I'd come home.

I ran my fingers across the controls, but before I could try anything, the humming of the Titan faded. The life died from it, lights in the cockpit going dim once again. I flinched back, looking up to Doctor Cryce in alarm.

She waved one hand at me without looking, her eyes still locked onto her console. "Nothing to worry about, you passed with flying colors, but Blue still needs to get to know you. It will be weeks until you can pilot him, maybe months, but it was the same for all the Knights."

At that point, she finally looked up and gave me the only sincere smile I'd seen on her so far. "Varic Vallenar, welcome to the Titan Knights."

CHAPTER NINE

I WAS UNACCOUNTABLY nervous to see the Titan Force headquarters for the first time in this life.

For one thing, I had tried to avoid news of the Knights since gaining memories of my previous life. I hadn't wanted to know which of them survived and which hadn't, and I'd been pulled in too many directions anyway.

Besides, the war against the D'Niss had been over for years by the time I attempted my ritual. Everything had worked out, at least in terms of galactic safety. Like in most of my lives, the Titan Force had driven the D'Niss from the galaxy before Esh'kinaar could be summoned.

I still felt like I'd abandoned the Knights, despite never joining their organization and having too many other responsibilities for one man to handle.

All that was before meeting Raion this time, after which I'd quickly learned that the Titan Knights had fared even worse in this life than in my memory. They'd reached a tragic end earlier, at least.

That knowledge still hadn't done anything to prepare me for the sight of the Titan Force headquarters in shambles.

The second moon of Delsin hadn't been abandoned, but the

Titan Forge had. Its gleaming arms of Aethertech chrome were dark and silent, a cage of metal embracing nothing. We flew past and Raion chatted about how good it was to be returning home, but all I saw was the *lack* of traffic and the empty space where a Titan *should* have hung for repairs.

Only minutes later, we landed in a field of brown grass that I remembered as bright green and well-manicured. Normally, there would be staff bustling around on foot and in vehicles, making constant deliveries of fuel and supplies to maintain the Divine Titans.

Now, there was only one shuttle within sight. It was much smaller than our ship and covered in a dusty tarp that was staked to the ground.

Raion surveyed the view from the bottom of the ramp as we exited. "They must have the day off," he said.

I doubted anyone had shown up to work here for months, if not longer.

Together, we walked to the building that overshadowed everything on the surrounding plains. From space, it would have resembled a massive block, but from here it looked like an endless tan wall.

High up, in huge letters, was stenciled the word 'TITANS.'

"We used to keep the Titans in their own separate buildings," I said.

"That's how we did it too! It was only a few years ago when we combined them all into one. We had to devote more resources to the Red Titan, since we didn't have anyone else using the rest of them, but Doctor Cryce didn't want her infrastructure to go to waste. She's—"

Raion slapped himself on the top of the head. "Of course, you know her! I can't imagine how surprised she'll be to meet you!"

He was looking forward to that much more than I was. Or he acted like it.

On the inside, Raion was nervous. It was never hard to read Raion's emotions, but this time was especially easy; his breaths came too quick, and he wiped his palms off on his uniform at least five times a minute.

He'd thought the other Knights were all dead, except Javik. To find out they weren't...

I knew how I'd feel if I were him. He hadn't talked about it on the way to the moon, but I imagined it would feel like a cross between a miracle and a betrayal. On the one hand, a friend was back from the dead. On the other, Doctor Cryce had kept that from him for the better part of two years.

Raion leaned into a panel on the side of a tiny, unassuming door at the corner of the vast warehouse, which scanned him. The scanner wasn't Aethertech, but rather an expensive combination of retinal and genetic scans as well as some basic analysis magic.

Still difficult to fool. Not every device had to be Aethertech to serve its job.

The screen flashed green and I heard the door unlock. Raion pushed it open and led me into a hallway that matched what I remembered; it was a plain white hallway with a more secure vault-style door at the end. A camera in the corners watched us.

"Is Doctor Cryce here?" I asked. I couldn't imagine the security room was occupied, though they might have hired an off-site security firm to monitor the cameras.

Raion's shoulders sagged. "She's always here," he said. "I can't imagine how long she's..." He was lost in thought for a moment before he brightened again. "It will be good for her to see a couple of friendly faces!"

The door at the end of the hallway wasn't Aethertech either, but it *was* strong. There's a simplicity to heavy metal, and I could respect the deep protective enchantments laid within.

Raion tapped a code into a keypad and the vault slowly unlatched itself before swinging inward.

"Oh, right!" Raion said as we marched through the door. "This is your first time seeing the Blue Titan in this life, isn't it? Exciting!"

The vast, open space on the inside of the door was even bigger than in my memory, and I remembered it as big enough to serve as a hangar for a mech that was fifty yards tall. Of course, this building had been remodeled to hold all five.

Only minimal safety lighting remained, so much of the cavernous space was in shadow. Even so, the Divine Titans were clear.

They were lined up against the far wall, and I took them in as we walked. All the way on the left was Raion's Red Titan, which I was surprised to see manifested in the real world outside of combat. It normally stayed in a pocket of Subspace, ready to be summoned, and would only be stored here for maintenance or modifications.

Sunlight veins ran through the entire scarlet mech, so it radiated its own light even in the darkness. It was clearly the only one of the Titans who still received attention; abandoned trucks at its feet still held fuel cans and spare parts, safety clamps held its arms in place, and the elevator at its side was already loaded with a portable Aethertech terminal.

I was sure that equipment was part of Cryce's attempt to figure out what the solar dragon's blood had done to her Red Titan, and that impression was reinforced by the monitors that sat nearby. They continued blinking, running programs I didn't bother to try to read.

Though it did occur to me that I should bring Mell here.

Next to the Red Titan came the White, Yellow, Green, and—on the far end—the Blue Titan.

Raion marched toward it, rubbing his hands. "What do you think? We could use another Blue Knight!"

"I have a job already, thanks," I said. I followed him, but more slowly.

"You'd be qualified! In fact, you're even more qualified in this life than you were in the last one!"

I was certain that was true. The Blue Titan would be delighted to have me as a pilot, once it got to know me. I could perform better than any Blue Knight after I knocked a few years of rust off my piloting skills.

But there was no way that was a good use of my time.

I looked up at the Blue Titan and felt the weight of memories, but I didn't approach any closer. "Maybe someday. Now, I can do more good as the Captain of *The Last Horizon*."

At full power, Horizon had firepower surpassing that of the

Divine Titans, but not by much. Raion in his enhanced Titan could probably match Horizon, at least for a while, which spoke to the potential in the mechs.

Having another one on our team would, of course, be more than welcome.

Raion planted fists on his hips. "Think about how useful it would be to have another Divine Titan in reserve! Especially one that doesn't try to kill you. We could fly into battle together, side by side!"

"We do that already," I said, and his smile lit up the room as though I'd given him a compliment. "Besides, do you really think it's a good idea for me to spend the next couple of months letting the Titan get to know me?"

Raion snapped his fingers. "Right! I forgot about that. You'd have to attune to the Blue Titan all over again, wouldn't you?"

Aethertech like the Divine Titans was inferior only to the Zenith Devices. They were masterworks among masterworks, but that came with a level of restriction comparable to the Zenith Devices as well.

Nobody could hop into the pilot seat of a Divine Titan and expect to get results. It wasn't a bond to take lightly. No matter how high my compatibility with the Blue Titan was, it didn't know me.

A speaker crackled to life next to us, and I glanced down to see a thick-limbed delivery drone. A woman's voice came out of its speaker. *"Who is this, Raion, and why did you bring him to this planet, because he's not authorized to be here, and you could have at* least *asked my permission..."*

As usual, Doctor Cryce spoke as though she didn't have time to breathe. But I knew how to handle her.

Instead of waiting for a break in her monologue, I introduced myself. "Doctor Cryce, it's an honor to meet you. I'm Varic Vallenar, Captain of *The Last Horizon.*"

"...and I don't know why you never—" Cryce cut off mid-sentence. A moment of silence. Then, *"...Seriously?"*

I looked to Raion. "Didn't you tell her?"

"She hasn't taken my calls since before I joined the crew," Raion said. "Doctor Cryce, Parryl...is she really alive?"

Through the drone speaker, I heard muttered speech, rapid footsteps, a reshuffling of papers, and the clack of a keyboard. She'd forgotten to mute her microphone. A moment later, the footsteps grew louder as she walked back over to speak to us again.

"Come on up, Raion and Captain Vallenar, and I want to know why you didn't mention The Last Horizon *in your messages, Raion! I would have called you back for a Zenith Device! What do you know about its medical facilities?"*

Raion clapped a fist to his chest. "Whatever Parryl needs, I'm sure we can get it!"

He was promising the resources of *The Last Horizon* without consulting the rest of the crew, but that was all right with me. Another version of Parryl had been my friend too.

Near the closest wall, a small elevator platform lowered several stories down to the floor. We walked on and waited for it to take us up to another platform high up on the wall, which held a simple office door.

As the elevator slowly rose, I looked to Raion. "We could have flown up."

"I didn't want to be rude," Raion said, but he stood stiffly, his head craned up to stare at the door above us.

Once we reached the top, the door swung open to reveal Doctor Cryce. Her green eyes glowed in the dark, leaving me to wonder why she'd been working without the lights on. She smoothed out the skirt of her suit, which was mostly white but highlighted with the bright colors of the other four Titans.

The sight of her slapped me, and not out of familiarity. I barely recognized her.

She looked *old*. She had always been older than any of the Knights—as you'd expect from the master Aether Technician who invented and built the Divine Titans—but she looked far too thin and worn for her age, her hair solid gray a shade lighter than her skin.

She looked ten years older than I remembered her, and I'd last seen her several years in the future.

"Captain Vallenar, I'm sorry, I've been busy in my lab for..." She hesitated. "...a long time now, and it seems galactic events got away from me, because I thought there was a hunt on for *The Last Horizon*, and wasn't there something about the Iron Legion? Anyway, I thought it was all just Subline rumor. And I had no idea Raion was involved, of course."

"I am involved!" Raion said, and despite his worry, he still straightened with a visible touch of pride. "I'm the Knight of *The Last Horizon!*"

"I have great respect for your own work, Doctor, and Raion speaks even more highly of you than he does of everyone else. Would you mind if we continued this in your office?"

Doctor Cryce blinked rapidly and seemed to remember that we were standing on the precipice of a hundred-foot drop to a bare warehouse floor. "Yes, sure, of course you can come in, and you probably want lights on, don't you? I've been reading some research on my console, so I didn't need the lights, *fascinating* research, too. My gifts aren't applicable to biological modification, of course, but the things the Karoshan Technicians have been publishing in several fields of genetic engineering. You wouldn't believe them!"

I certainly would believe them, given that it was that research that led to the creation of the Perfected, but it was important to steer the Doctor's monologue in the right direction.

"And why are you interested in biological research, Doctor?" I asked. "Does this have to do with your niece?"

Beside me, Raion visibly shook as he waited for an answer.

Cryce stopped in place. "Yes, I...Well. Raion, I'm sorry. I thought I'd tell you once I managed to save her. But I couldn't do it."

"Can we see her?" Raion asked quietly.

"Of course!" Energy ran through her again, and she rubbed her hands together, for once looking like her former self. "I'd tried everything, but I never had a Zenith Device! Take a look for yourself, and then we can bring her to *The Last Horizon*."

CHAPTER TEN

PARRYL CRYCE WAS visible only through a small monitor on the side of a large Aethertech capsule. It was smooth and white, with the sterile look I associated with medical equipment even though I was sure this pod wasn't mass-produced.

It was a shock to see her face, and especially to see it so worn and small. The former Green Knight, Parryl was still the same girl I remembered. Eerily so.

She'd always been one of the youngest among the Knights, and she looked the part. Her face was mostly covered by an oxygen mask, and her eyes were closed, so I couldn't see the green glow.

It wasn't too hard to imagine that a human in her circumstances would have been long dead. Her limbs had been reattached, and while that task had long been completed, I could see the patches of lighter gray on her skin where the surgery had been performed.

And I didn't need a medical degree to tell that the monitors weren't telling a good story. Her heart only beat a few times a minute, and she only irregularly took a breath. Worse, there were several monitors dedicated to the *things* that remained inside her body.

The fly-like spawn of Neth'terith, one of the Seven Calamities of the D'Niss. I had never seen it use this ability; either it had developed these tiny parasites in this life or we'd killed it in my previous life without allowing it to spawn a cloud of these mites.

But the computer showed fourteen places where mites remained. They had burrowed into Parryl's body, attaching to her spine, her brain stem, and several organs.

"We did everything we could to get the rest of them out," Doctor Cryce said, and the energy she'd shown a moment before had already faded. She sounded like time had eroded all her feelings but professional resignation. "There were thousands at first, and there would have been more if Raion hadn't subdued her so quickly."

Raion stared into the tank like it contained his own dead body. He didn't say anything.

"Some we removed with magic, and some we could get with regular surgery. These are the ones we can't extract without taking her out of stasis, and if we do that, they'll kill her before we have enough time."

She waved a hand at her niece. "I don't know what kind of medical facilities the Zenith Starship has, but maybe you can bring me a miracle."

Raion leaned against the window of the capsule, his two main eyes closed. Only his third eye moved, glowing softly gold as it scanned Parryl's face.

Though I knew Doctor Cryce, I was a stranger to her. That was a situation I was growing used to, so I didn't let it slow me down. "If you don't mind me asking, why did you call Raion now? What changed?"

The doctor checked panels all over the device with the familiarity of a chore she'd done a thousand times before. "I slowed her progress as much as I could, but she's getting worse. She only has a few days left."

Raion flinched.

"I decided it was time to start throwing dice," Cryce went on. "Raion can sense his friends, and he's also a Visiri, so I thought he might see something I couldn't."

"Her body is alive," Raion said, just above a whisper. "I don't feel her heart."

Cryce sagged as though he'd taken strength out of her joints, but Raion patted the capsule and straightened. "But if anyone can save her, we can!"

I spoke aloud for the benefit of the other two. "Horizon, scan this. Let us know if there's anything our medical facilities can do for her."

Raion and Doctor Cryce brightened. A moment later, Horizon's voice came from the speakers on my wrist console. *"Give me a moment, if you don't mind. I'm working through your processor. But I think you would be a better resource than I am, Captain."*

Cryce frowned at me as though she suspected me of grifting her somehow, while Raion stared in awe.

Truthfully, I was thinking the same thing.

If Horizon could help Parryl, great, problem solved. But none of our gifts had done anything special for her medical bay, so I doubted she could do anything that Cryce hadn't already tried.

To me, this problem looked like it called for magic.

I pointed to a line on one of the monitors. "It says you're looking for artificial veins?"

"Oh, that's not the problem. Not on its own. There was some unavoidable damage when we extracted the previous parasites, so we'll have to repair that eventually. But there's no point in it until we get rid of the rest of them. This level of damage won't kill a Lichborn."

"I've finished my scan!" Horizon announced proudly, which made me suspect she'd overestimated how long it would take so she could amaze us. *"Doctor Cryce, I regret to say that my own medical resources would do no better for your niece. Your facilities are so specialized that I would find them difficult to equal, at least in the short-term. In fact, I'm impressed. You would make a fine Engineer."*

Doctor Cryce blinked rapidly and glanced down to her console as though it would tell her what to say. "If you're really the AI of the Zenith Starship, then I'm flattered. This is more the result of other Aether Technician's work than my own, though. I only coordinated things."

She had taken the bad news better than I expected, but she was probably used to disappointment by then.

"World Spirit," Horizon corrected. *"Nonetheless, your accomplishment is worthy of my acknowledgement. And while I cannot heal young Parryl directly, I assure you, I have sent you a wizard who can."*

I had been tempted to start casting some pathfinding spells while Horizon spoke, but nobody would trust a strange wizard who showed up and started waving a wand over their comatose relative.

At least Horizon had given me the perfect excuse to take over. "What magical experts have you seen?"

"I brought in a team of Aethril healers at least a year ago. They told me all they could do was delay the damage, but they were a big help in getting her this far. Some of their enchantments are still on the machine."

"Do you mind if I take a look?"

She waved a hand again, so I tapped the side of the machine to call up the spells. Several spell-circles of silver and starlight rose out of the device, connected in a delicate web of light that was the traditional form of Aethril spellcasting.

A few seconds later, I pushed the circles back down. "It's a comprehensive spell. She's shielded from any influences that would worsen her condition, the Aether constantly nudges her toward superior fates, and her life is sustained by the spell. There's also a subtle effect eroding any unnatural invaders, preventing infection and smothering the parasites. It will at least stop her from getting worse."

"It did. For a while." Doctor Cryce settled into a nearby chair and began massaging her temples. "Most of the Aethertech is calibrated around the spell, but it's not making her any better. All I can do is wait for her to get worse."

To Raion and the Doctor, watching Parryl would be a constant reminder of their failure. Cryce had been the one to send her niece into battle in the first place, while Raion had been on the battlefield with her.

I had known Parryl too, but unlike the other two, I was encouraged. I had watched the Green Knight torn apart by giant worms, so this was a very forgiving fate by comparison.

"I can't imagine how hard it's been," I said. "But I do have to ask you to wait a little longer."

Raion moved so close to me that I instinctively took a step back. "Can you help?"

I looked over Parryl again, checking to make sure there wasn't anything I missed, and then I shrugged. "Yeah, we can fix this with magic."

Doctor Cryce frowned at me, suspicious, but Raion's third eye shone. "I *knew* you could do it!"

"Magic can accomplish almost anything, given the right materials and expertise," I said. "I don't have healing magic, so I can't do anything right now. If her condition weren't so delicate, I might try sealing the parasites while we brought her out of stasis, but there's some risk to that.

"So we'll need a ritual instead." I traced a dozen symbols in the air, letting them hang in a simple magic circle.

It wasn't a real, functional spell-circle, just an illustration. Once it was complete, spinning lazily in midair, I gestured to it. "This is a ritual circle for healing. Usually, we'd need an Archmage of healing spells and ideally six other supplementary casters, but I can handle all that. We need one artifact of enough restorative magic."

Cryce rubbed her hand over her face. "I'm sorry, this doesn't make any sense. If healing magic worked, the Aethril healers would have finished the job already. They made it very clear that it isn't only *healing* she needs, she needs to have the parasites expelled, and you think that you can do the work of six other mages? Besides, how common do you think healing artifacts are? You might as well say we need to bargain with a World Spirit. More than that—"

It would have been more compassionate of me to let her go on, but I cut her off anyway. "If you'd rather bargain with a World Spirit, we can do that too."

She paused with her mouth open as the train of her thoughts redirected to a different track.

"Yeah. I'm the Captain of the Zenith Starship. I can get an audience with most World Spirits, and maybe we'll have to." I dragged my ring of Aetheric symbols back over. "But there's no reason it should come to that. You see, when a spell says 'heal,' it means '*heal*.' It doesn't mean 'accelerating the body's natural healing processes' or whatever. We'll be calling on the Aether to *heal* her, so there's no need for any of the rest of this."

Doctor Cryce was about to say something skeptical, so I kept talking. "Theoretically. In reality, of course, things are never that simple. The skill of the caster comes into play, the restrictions of the specific spell being used, and so on. But enough of a ritual can remove those requirements."

She ticked points off on her fingers. "All we need is an Archmage, a ritual, six casters, an artifact of unparalleled healing powers—"

"Just the artifact." I tapped on my console, pulling up a file I'd saved for this moment. I projected the hologram above my left wrist, where it showed a smooth, fist-sized ruby.

"The Heart of Visiria," I announced. "The good news is, this is one of the most powerful restorative artifacts in the galaxy. The bad news is, it's a planetary treasure of Visiria and we're wanted in the Alliance. If we show up in the system, the Karoshans will ask for our heads."

I slapped Raion on the shoulder. "The *better* news is that we know who can get it for us. They'll be especially interested in a famous Visiri warrior who also happens to be a member of *The Last Horizon*."

Raion clapped a fist to his chest. "I will fight any battle to bring Parryl back!"

"It will require diplomacy."

"Hmmm. I would prefer a different kind of battle."

"You'll be fine. Worst-case scenario, they try to kill you. Then you call us."

Raion snapped his fingers. "My brother works for the Senate! He could get us an audience with the Governor, I'm sure!"

"We'll start there." I didn't know anything about Raion's brother, even from my previous life, but any potential connection was good news.

Doctor Cryce was looking at us like a couple of madmen, and she exploded a moment later. *"Stop!* What are you saying? You want to go off and go to Visiria so they'll give you a gem so you can cast a spell...She has *days,* do you understand? I need *real* help, I don't need you running off on a trek to..."

Abruptly Cryce ran out of energy. She sagged back, hand over her eyes. "I don't know what I was thinking. Get out."

"Don't you want to check my credentials?" I asked.

I expected her to scream at me a little more and I was prepared for it, but instead she casually reached over, pulled a plasma pistol from a desk drawer, and pointed it in my general direction without looking.

"Get out or I'll shoot you."

Without hesitation, Raion moved in front of me, but I shoved him aside. I was sure she had more security measures than this, given her Technician gifts, but either she'd forgotten about them or she'd rather chase us out on her own.

"You don't know what I can do yet," I said. "After you shoot us, get on the Subline and search for the Iron King."

Her eyes were still closed but her grip tightened on the pistol. After an internal struggle, she reluctantly tapped on her console.

I didn't see anything because she didn't project her results. She must have been watching in her ocular implant.

But a moment later she was sitting straight up in her chair, staring into the distance.

"Now search for Starhammer," I suggested.

Only a few seconds after that, she was staring at me with a mix of doubt, confusion, and hope.

"*The Last Horizon* might not be able to help you herself, but she doesn't choose her crew lightly. Raion, can you tell Doctor Cryce how you and I met?"

"He defeated me in a duel!" Raion said proudly.

I rested my hand on the side of Parryl's stasis capsule. "I swear on the Aether, my magic, and all the worlds that I will do everything in my power to see her healed. And this *is* within my power."

Tears glistened like emeralds in her glowing eyes, and she wiped them away before saying, "Fine. But you should know, I'll continue pursuing other options."

"Can't hurt. Maybe someone else can do it faster." I moved my wand over the capsule. "Now, would you mind if I added a spell? I can buy us some extra time."

"What kind of spell?"

"As I'm sure you saw on the Subline, I'm an Archmage of sealing and binding. I can build on the spell the Aethril left behind and lock out the influence of time. I'm certain I can slow her progression while Raion retrieves the Heart of Visiria."

Cryce looked to Raion, blew out a breath, and nodded.

It didn't take me long to cast the spell. A massive spell-circle flashed white over the capsule, and a second later, the monitors changed.

The Doctor's eyes went wide. She leaned out of her seat to check one, then hurried over to another. "What did you *do?*"

A little smug, I put away my wand. "Exactly what I said I would. At this rate, she should have..." I checked the time on my console. "...about six months."

"If you can slow it down this much..." Doctor Cryce was absorbed in her work, muttering to herself, so I didn't bother her. Eventually, her investigation would confirm what I'd said.

If I locked Parryl away in Absolute Burial, she'd last even longer, though that had its own risks.

In the meantime, I'd bought us plenty of time.

As long as nothing else went wrong.

CHAPTER ELEVEN

IN ANOTHER LIFE

On my first day as the Blue Titan Knight, I still hadn't met my teammates.

The other Knights had been chosen long before me, but they hadn't been idle. They had gone all around the galaxy to defend against the D'Niss...and whatever other giant space monsters they found.

Even the Green Knight was out there, piloting a starship and playing a support role while her Divine Titan was undergoing repairs.

The other four were set to return and meet me, at which point we'd venture out as a complete squad. So I sat on a bench in the field outside the Divine Titan's hangar, going through casting exercises to dispel my nerves.

Kyri saw me muttering to myself and drumming fingers on my thigh, dressed in my blue uniform, and she laughed. "What are you worried about? You're more qualified than they are."

"They've had their Titans for months. The Red Knight for almost a year."

"Not as a pilot, as a fighter! You've trained with me. Have some confidence in yourself."

"I'm not a Combat Artist."

My teacher bumped my shoulder with her fist. Gently, and thankfully not with her mechanical hand. "Only Red and Green are Combat Artists, so what are you worried about? Plenty to learn. And it's not like you aren't used to fighting Visiri in the ring!"

Losing to Visiri in the ring was what I was used to, and it was the whole reason I was nervous. I foresaw a future at the bottom of the Titan Knights' hierarchy, and I was trying to figure out ways around it.

My one comfort was that Kyri had stayed on. It was a favor to Doctor Cryce, not to me, but she had decided to remain as the combat trainer for the Knights.

And maybe to avoid the Karoshans.

So at least I had one friendly face around. And I *did* have a head start on the training, since I'd been working with Kyri for years. I relied on that as I saw a shuttle land on the field nearby and my heart rate picked up.

What felt like a blink later, the other Titan Knights strode down the ramp.

I had studied all their profiles, so I knew them as they descended. The White Knight was an Aethril woman whose star-speckled hair blended with the color of her outfit. She was small and slender but strode down first like a Subline star presenting herself to an adoring public.

Aelora was in love with the fame of the Titan Knights, but she was also a skilled pilot, and not just of her Titan.

She would retire a few years later, when she found the burden of galactic scrutiny too heavy to bear.

The Yellow Knight, Javik Leed, was a dark-skinned human man who waved to me the moment he left the ship. As his profile suggested, he was easy to get along with, and the team's resident Aether Technician. His gift was only an affinity for repairs, nothing remarkable, but it came in handy more than once in the field.

He would retire, too. He and Aelora were the lucky ones who made it out alive before facing down the Swarm-Queen.

The Green Knight would not be so fortunate. Parryl Cryce was a Lichborn girl, the youngest of the group, who spoke with animated energy. Her eyes glowed bright emerald. She had been chosen early, as she was Doctor Cryce's niece, but her ability was the real deal.

A pair of heavy handguns hung at her belt, looking far too large for her. She was one of the few masters of a Combat Art used with guns. I didn't fear those Combat Artists in the arena, but I would certainly fear them on the battlefield.

Parryl wouldn't make it to the Swarm-Queen either, but she also didn't get the chance to retire.

Of the five of us there, the first generation of Titan Knights, only two of us would make it far enough to go into battle against Swarm-Queen Esh'kinaar. Only two of us in that life were never replaced by successors.

Me, and the Red Knight.

Raion was the second out of the shuttle, after Aelora. It may be hard to believe, but he was even more enthusiastic back then, shining with boyish excitement.

When he saw me, his third eye gleamed gold. He leaped in front of Aelora and put his fists on his hips, beaming.

"Raion Raithe, Captain of the Titan Knights!"

Holographic fireworks exploded behind him, froze, and glitched.

Without looking behind him, he pointed at me. "Don't worry, we'll fix that!"

I nodded to him, having already been briefed on what to expect. "Varic Vallenar. I'm—"

"Double R, double V!" Raion shouted. "It's fate! Those are hero names if I've ever heard them!"

Aelora's eyes brightened, and she leaned closer to inspect me. "Nice hair! You're used to interviews, right?"

"He's used to fighting!" Raion said. "Speaking of which, Varic, we should get to know each other." He unclipped the force-blade from his belt.

Doctor Cryce hurried between us. "Don't you think we should wait, Raion, since he's new and everything? You should get to know each other as a team first, and I still need to introduce your combat trainer—"

Kyri stepped up without waiting for her friend to finish. "Kyri Prest, your new combat instructor. Varic here has been my student for years, so don't go too easy on him."

"I know who you are!" Parryl said excitedly. "I watched all your fights!" She rushed up to Kyri, ignoring her aunt. "Can we start training now?"

I was uncomfortably aware that my new teammate had watched *all* of Kyri's fights, which included my undignified loss.

Javik came to stand beside me. "You'll have to help me get started in the ring. I'm no Combat Artist, and Raion is a bad teacher."

"The best way to teach is by example!" Raion declared. He struck a pose again, and once again his fireworks glitched.

Cryce had started arguing with Aelora about something—their strategy for promoting the full team, if I had to guess—so Kyri took control of the group. She began herding all of us inside.

"Let's go, Titan Knights," she said. "Once we're all settled in, I'll see what you've got."

It didn't take long in the gym before I realized that my fear of being the weakest of the Knights was unfounded. In fact, I regained quite a bit of confidence that day. At least in the first few rounds.

We were meant to start a routine of physical training and combat simulations, but Kyri started us off with a series of practice duels to get a sense for our abilities.

I doubt she would have begun that way in a normal class, but *one* of us was very insistent that we all duel.

To Raion's disappointment, Kyri put me against Parryl, the Green Knight, for our opening bout. We were the two she felt she could trust, and who knew how to handle ourselves in the arena.

Parryl wasn't as obviously dismissive of me as her aunt had been, but she clearly didn't think of me as much of a threat. She switched out her usual guns for a pair with a stun setting, which would give me a heavy jolt but no real damage.

She nodded to me before the round began, but she addressed all her questions to Kyri. "Can you show me how to stop Raion from rushing me? I try to start as fast as I can, and it works against everybody else—Here, I'll show you. Give me some pointers after, okay?"

Kyri glanced to me to make sure I was ready, then blew a whistle.

In the arena, guns were sometimes allowed. It depended on the rules of the match. When they were, elementalists were always permitted to call their element first.

So I had conjured water behind my back before the round began. I spread it out in a screen in front of me, which wasn't enough to stop Parryl's shots but at least knocked them off course.

Two stun bolts whizzed above me as I dropped and leveled my wand. A second later, a focused jet of water hit Parryl in the chest with enough force to push her back onto the ground.

As I dismissed the conjured water, she stared up at me, glowing green eyes wide.

Kyri put a hand on the Lichborn girl's head. "Don't assume your opponent is going to stand there and take it. Anticipate them. If you know where they're going to be, it doesn't matter how fast they are. Javik, you're up."

Javik sighed and took Parryl's place, grabbing a heavy two-handed rifle as he did. He wasn't a Combat Artist, but Combat Arts only had a limited effect on guns anyway.

Not to get too heavily into the theory, but a user's actions barely affect the shots of a gun. The weapon's performance almost entirely comes down to the specs of the gun itself, so Combat Arts don't have much room to work.

In many circumstances, that would make Parryl the bigger threat. She could use a normal handgun to shoot a hole in a bunker.

But to me, Javik's approach was more deadly. All he had to do was pull the trigger. What was I supposed to do in a standoff against an automatic rifle?

Kyri waited a few seconds for me to conjure more water, as she would in a real arena match, before she blew the whistle.

I flicked my wand as Javik squeezed the trigger. He got one shot off, but it was another stun round and it glanced off my armored shoulder. The gun squealed and didn't fire the second time.

I'd simply flooded the electronics of the gun with water, so it had locked down. That had only worked because it was a training weapon—a rifle issued by the Alliance or the Union would have been magically shielded—but it was enough for the moment.

When Javik realized his gun didn't work, he gave a chuckle and held his hands up in surrender. "At least I got a point," he said, glancing to Parryl on the side.

She gave him an exaggerated glare.

Aelora was up next, and she knew a little magic, coming at me with an ivory wand and a form of crystal magic. She would have been better off using a gun, but she didn't mind the loss, chatting with me about how magic was taught on the Aethril home world even while we fought.

By that point, my confidence had grown two sizes. Obviously, we weren't training to be duelists, but to fight giant monsters. However, if our combat skills translated to piloting Divine Titans, maybe I wouldn't be the worst. Maybe I'd be the best.

As I had that thought, Raion leaped from the sidelines and landed in front of me.

"Finally!" he cried. "I can't wait to get to know you, Varic!"

The whistle blew, and then I was looking up at the sky.

While I was still trying to figure out what happened, Raion leaned down over me. His three eyes shone with encouragement. He offered me a hand up. "Round two!"

I lasted a little longer the second time. At the very least, I threw a spell for him to dodge.

When I sat up again, Raion was encouraging the others to join me, but our fellow Titan Knights were clearly familiar with him. None of them took him up on his offer.

But my teacher did.

Kyri moved in front of me, limbering up her artificial arm. "You've got potential, Raion Raithe. You'd make a good fighter in the arena."

Raion beamed and scurried back to the middle of the gym. "Thank you, Coach!"

"You don't have to call me Coach. But if these guys aren't enough of a warm-up, I'll keep you company."

"It would be an honor!"

I moved to join the other Knights, eager to watch the match. If nothing else, I could learn how to use elemental magic to oppose someone like Raion. Before the round started, Aelora leaned over to me.

"You think she can really beat Raion?"

"She's beaten a lot of fighters better than Raion."

"Perfect." Aelora raised her white-armored forearm, on which was a sleek, white console that had been designed to match her combat suit. "I need to see him lose."

Kyri blew the whistle, then the two of them ignited their energy.

Raion's aura, which surrounded him like a thin layer of flame, burned pure scarlet. Kyri's meanwhile, was a pale pink that was close to white. They ran into one another and that was all I could tell for sure.

I couldn't track their movements. Most humans wouldn't be able to. Later on, I would learn to use my ability to read the Aether as a way to track their Combat Arts, and in that way predict how they would move.

But that wasn't my first time watching two people who were superhumanly fast clash against one another. The finals of major arena tournaments tended to be like this, with a pair of high-level Combat Artists—usually Visiri or Karoshan—trading blow after blow in the space between breaths.

Those matches tended only to last a few seconds, and without the slow-motion playback provided by the arena, the average viewers wouldn't be able to tell what was happening.

Needless to say, I had never made it far enough in a tournament to face someone like that myself, and Kyri hadn't even pretended to go all-out against me. For her, I was just a warm-up match.

Her round against Raion lasted eight seconds and released a hurricane of wind in the gym. It sounded like the entire building was being torn apart, we were almost blinded by red light, and Javik had to steady Aelora or she would have lost her footing while trying to record.

They weren't *literally* invisible, of course, but by the time my eyes clearly caught a move they'd already moved somewhere else. When those eight seconds came to an end, Raion flew into the far wall of the gym, denting the metal and setting the entire building to ringing.

Kyri stood in the center, almost exactly where she'd started, panting. Her aura was much weaker, and her flesh-and-blood arm hung stiff at her side.

Those of us on the sideline cheered. When Raion pulled his face off the floor, he looked at her in awe. "That was incredible, Coach! Can we go again?"

"Don't push it," Kyri said with a tone of warning. "When you fight that hard, you shine bright, but you burn out quick. Show me your energy."

Without standing up, Raion ignited his aura, which was even weaker and more fitful than Kyri's. He seemed surprised.

"In the heat of the moment, you can burn through your reserves faster than you think," Kyri explained. "The same thing happens to your body, and you might not feel it until you've already gone past your limits. When I'm done with you, you'll learn exactly what you can do, and you'll be able to control the pace of the battle so it lasts as long as you want."

Parryl was nodding so furiously I expected her to start taking notes. Aelora watched the video on her console, slowing it down to view every frame of Raion taking a hit and chuckling to herself.

But I was worried about my teacher. No one else would be likely to notice anything, but she was a little unsteady on her feet, and she hadn't moved her left arm since the fight ended.

"Parryl, Javik, your turn," Kyri called. "No weapons. Aelora, film it for me. I need to speak with Varic. You too, Jan."

"No private training!" Parryl said.

Kyri waved her mechanical hand. "That's not it. Wizard stuff. I'll only be a minute, and I expect you both to still be standing."

She marched out of the gym and I followed, according to her instructions. Doctor Cryce was standing outside, pecking at her wrist console in irritation.

"Why did you bring me here?" Cryce asked. "I was very busy, you know, and I had to walk out of a—"

Kyri stuck a metal finger in her face. "Where did you find him?" she demanded.

"Oh, that's right, you would have fought Raion. He was exiled from the Raithe family, if you can believe it. Not for lack of talent."

"No kidding." Kyri moved her arm and winced. "If he'd spent any time in the arena, I wouldn't have been able to win. Jan, I don't know if I can teach him. By this time next week, he might be better than me."

Cryce held up her tablet console. "If you know of a better tutor for a Visiri Combat Artist, give me their name."

"I know a few," Kyri said, and I think Doctor Cryce and I were equally surprised. "And I think you'll *need* a few. He has more natural talent than anyone I've ever seen."

My own worries returned in force. Just when I had started feeling better about my standing among the Knights.

"What can I do?" I asked.

"Don't compare yourself to him," Kyri said seriously. "This may be the most important lesson I ever teach you. Sometimes, you meet someone who's flat-out better."

That was less than encouraging, but she wasn't finished.

"That's my answer as an arena duelist. If you were to get matched against him, then learn what you can from the loss. But we're not in the arena, so don't think like a duelist. Think like a *wizard*."

"Exactly," Doctor Cryce agreed. "The Divine Titans can convey Combat Arts, but compatibility and teamwork are equally important. As for the Blue Titan, it was meant to compete against the magic of the D'Niss. Raion can't do that."

Kyri was still stretching out her bruised arm. "Yeah. Not that."

Her tone caught my attention. "Are *you* okay?" I asked my teacher.

"This will heal quickly," she responded, but I hadn't been talking about her arm.

"Okay. As long as you're all right."

Doctor Cryce and I waited for a long moment before Kyri responded.

"The Aether has been teaching me some hard lessons lately," Kyri said at last. "It's one thing to know you have limits, but it's another thing to finally reach them."

I said something to comfort her, but I don't remember the words. They weren't the right ones.

For decades, my teacher had been at the peak among duelists and magical combatants. But she'd reached the limit of her talent, and she knew it.

At the time, I thought it was my job to carry her dream forward. To become the best water elementalist I could, as thanks for her training. But that wasn't what she'd wanted.

She had been looking for the same thing I was: a way to make a difference in the world. And she thought she'd missed it.

CHAPTER TWELVE

THE PLANET VISIRIA is one of the major components of the Karoshan Alliance. It's the Karoshan Empire, the Visiria system, and a few other random systems who have latched on to the two big fish.

As one of the major civilized systems in the galaxy, all its planets were colonized, and their night skies were filled with colonies, stations, and ships of every size. Even considering the massive distances between planets, the computer showed the Visiria system as a bustling web of activity.

With my eyes, I saw each planet swarming as ships left and landed in a constant stream.

Visiria was blue and green, like most standard planets, though I always expected it to be red. Its continents looked more brown than usual, a consequence of both its climate and the warfare that stained Visirian history.

But they'd been unified for a long time—longer than most—as they had turned their cultural inclination for warfare toward the rest of the galaxy.

Raion and I approached in a shuttle, and one we'd borrowed rather than printed from *The Last Horizon*. At least on our approach to the planet, we didn't want to be known, because the Karoshans getting word about our location could be inconvenient.

"I never met your brother," I said.

It normally wasn't difficult to start a conversation with Raion, but this time he only said, "Mmmm."

"I knew you had one. You have a sister too, right?"

"Mmm."

"Where is she?"

Raion shrugged.

"And what happened to your parents?"

After a few more seconds, Raion responded distantly, "They're all right. They retired off-planet."

"I've never heard you talk about them."

Another long pause, in which it seemed like Raion was contemplating distant memories, passed before he responded. "There's not much friendship in them."

"Ah."

It had occurred to me before how lonely it would be to sense how other people really felt about you. At least, how lonely it would be for *me*. I didn't want to see the ugly truth like that.

Raion had always seemed anything but lonely.

I didn't know how to continue, but fortunately Raion covered up the silence before it grew too uncomfortable. "My family was never close. I learned that I could rely on my friends more." A little energy returned, and he held up a fist. "That's the most powerful force in the galaxy!"

"What about your brother?"

Raion sighed. "I haven't seen him in years. I've called him a few times, but he never returned my calls. I think he was embarrassed to have me in the Titan Force."

This was an unusually glum mood for Raion, and it seemed like there wasn't much I could do to shake him out of his melancholy.

"He works for the planetary government?"

"He was a senatorial aide when I left, and he's been working his way up. I think he intends to be a Senator one day." Raion stared out the viewscreen. "Was I wrong to join the Knights, Varic?"

The conversation had taken the exact direction I didn't want it to.

"Absolutely not," I said.

For one thing, I wanted him to hear the confidence in my voice, but I also needed to concentrate as I steered us through atmospheric entry.

"I don't know. I got the others hurt. Mostly killed." He continued staring. "It sounds like I did the same in your timeline. I even got myself killed."

"You couldn't have left the galaxy to the D'Niss."

"No, of course not! But maybe...Do you think someone else would have done a better job?"

"No." This was not the best time for this, wrestling as I was with atmospheric turbulence, but I tried to give him a reassuring look as quickly as possible. "Raion, you're the perfect man for the job. Too perfect. It's like you were born to be the Knight."

I continued piloting as he watched me, and a moment later he patted me on the shoulder. "I'm glad to have a friend like you, Varic. What great fortune of the Aether, to send me a friend I hadn't even met!"

It had taken years of argument, butting heads, and life-or-death fights to build the trust Raion sensed in me.

"We'll save Parryl," I said. I knew that was what ate at him, though I wasn't sure how much his family had to do with it.

"I know. I know we will!" He was forcing it, pushing power into his voice and his smile. "I won't give up the fight! And when I'm done, I'll have one more friend waiting for me!"

He nudged me with his elbow. "And what about you? I know you've been busy saving the galaxy in this life, but there has to be more to your life! At least one day."

"I think we should be getting back to the mission," I said. "The Heart of Visiria won't be—"

"Absolutely not!" Raion declared. "This is friend talk. Tell me about you, Varic. Let us get to know each other better."

He had swiveled his chair around to stare seriously into my eyes.

"As long as I'm not living in fear of the galaxy collapsing, I'll be happy."

"You must have had personal lives. Six of them, even. I'm sure you had passions! Dreams! Loved ones!"

Raion gasped at his own realization, which startled me enough that I veered off the course the planetary satellites gave me. The computer beeped in warning, and I corrected absently.

Meanwhile, my co-pilot looked like he was about to start weeping. "I see now. You can't imagine a future in which you're happy because you've lost everyone you've ever loved."

"All right, calm down," I said. "I'm not afraid to have a personal life, I'm just a lot more concerned about holding the galaxy together."

"I understand," Raion said sympathetically. "Sometimes you have to sacrifice your own heart for the sake of protecting others."

"That's too dramatic."

"What greater sacrifice could there be? Though you still live, you've given up everything you have to live for, all for the lives of others."

"What? No, I'm not."

"A state of living death. Killing your feelings. Pretending your heart is cold, when in reality you must ignore that heat so that you may keep the world safe."

"You're doing this on purpose."

Raion straightened his back proudly. "I was! Do you feel better?"

"*Me?* You've been staring off into the distance since the Delsin system!"

"And now I feel better, because I got to talk with a friend!" Though he was still seated, Raion put his fists on his hips. "Did it work for you?"

I laughed as I steered the ship into a dock. "It didn't hurt, but now let's talk about the job. The Heart of Visiria. Talk them into lending you the gem, and be careful not to offend anyone. The Alliance already hates us, so play nice, but we'll keep Horizon in teleporter range. If you're in trouble, eject."

"I will flex my diplomatic biceps!" Raion announced, flexing a real one. "I *am* worried that they may not listen to me, though. Can't we do this mission together?"

"I'm one call away," I assured him. "Besides, you're the one I trust the most to handle a mission alone."

Raion clapped a fist to his chest. "You won't regret your faith in me!"

I knew I wouldn't, but mostly I meant that I trusted Raion not to die. He had a tendency to throw himself headfirst into danger, but he also had a habit of emerging unscathed.

The truth was, I wasn't worried about Raion's safety, and I had personally ensured that Parryl would survive long enough to complete the mission. My magic would be better used in the hunt for the Zenith Cannon.

All I could do for Raion was serve as emotional support, though that might have been exactly what he needed.

Physically, he'd be safe. Emotionally, who knew? I suspected that depended on his brother.

Ryzer Raithe waited for us as we walked out of the dock. He was a softer, shorter version of his brother, who looked like he spent time at his desk rather than on the battlefield. His white hair was thinning, his third eye a paler shade of gold, and he carried some notable extra weight and lack of muscle compared to his brother.

As we approached, he was impatiently checking his console—a flashy model of diamonds and chrome—and glancing over his shoulder as though expecting to be followed.

When he did see us, he rushed up and grabbed us each by the arm. "What are you *doing?* Couldn't you at least have put on a disguise?"

I was wearing my normal blue mantle and Raion his Titan Force uniform with no helmet. We looked at each other and I shrugged.

Raion gestured behind him. "We brought a different ship!"

Ryzer wiped a hand across his face with a long-suffering look as though he was sick of dealing with idiots. "How have you not changed in ten years?"

"Exercise!"

"We took the ship so we could get into the system," I said, "but there's no hiding our visit here. Any interactions we have with your planetary government will be reported to Karosha within the hour."

Ryzer waved a hand. "Paranoia. Humans often overestimate the relationship between the Empire and Visiria. In fact, we're largely independent. They won't know unless we tell them."

"Yes, they will. They know already."

Ryzer gave me a mocking smile. "Ah, forgive me, I forgot all your years in military intelligence. Is that what the Vallenar private tutors teach you?"

"So far, your brother's not making a very good impression," I said to Raion.

Raion patted Ryzer on the back, sending him staggering forward. "Don't worry, he's just nervous. And he doesn't know us very well yet."

"You came to *me,*" Ryzer hissed.

Outside the main docks of the Visirian capital were streets that bustled with activity. Buildings of fabricated silver and glass stood opposite ancient buildings of stone, a contrast of modern and ancient eras.

Most of the crowd were Visiri, but there was a healthy smattering of Karoshans, easily identifiable because they stood three feet higher than everyone else around them. We remained around the edges of the crowd, outside the flow of people, and only one or two cast glances of idle curiosity our way. Most of them wouldn't give us a second look unless we pulled out a weapon.

Even so, Ryzer hauled us deeper into the shadow of a nearby building. "I said I would help you, out of purely altruistic motivations, and here you are *mocking* me for my kindness."

"I would never mock you!" Raion said, horrified.

I would, but I didn't say so. "We could have teleported straight into your capitol building. That we didn't should be counted as a diplomatic gesture. And we *are* trying to keep a low profile, but believe it or not, this is as low-profile as it gets."

"You want me to take your word for that?"

That was a cue if I'd ever heard one. I manifested a hand behind me, where I used it to haul a Karoshan out of hiding.

Actually, the first hand wasn't strong enough. It took two blue, floating hands.

The man was skinny and shorter than most of his species, only a foot above me, which made me think he wasn't much older than Shyrax's son. His skin was a dull green, and the cables that ran from his scalp instead of hair shone like sunlight through forest leaves.

"Hey, what are you doing? Let me go before I get serious!"

That was how I knew he *was* young, because the tough talk wasn't very intimidating while I was hauling him around with magical constructs.

"He's an agent for Karoshan intelligence," I said.

Ryzer had his face entirely covered by his hands. "Captain Vallenar. Don't...Don't use magic on children because you suspect them of espionage. I'm afraid I'm going to be forced to report you to the police."

Raion didn't look like he approved either, but I knew he trusted me. "Why don't we ask him?" he suggested. "You don't work for the Throne of Karosha as a spy, do you?"

"What are you talking about? Get off me!"

I had manifested an eye, one that had once belonged to an Engineer on *The Last Horizon*. When it spotted the Aethertech implant at the back of the man's neck, I cast a quick sealing spell. I doubted any of them saw the white circle of magic symbols that spun over his spine and then vanished.

"He's an agent of the Perfected Shadow," I went on. "All sorts of brainwashing magic on him. They don't need too many agents like him, and he probably wasn't here for us. He just happened to see some people on his list."

Ryzer looked horrified. "Sure, I'm sure you're right, Captain Vallenar, but why don't we have this conversation in a more secure location? The city police station, for instance."

"That's a great idea. Horizon, take us back to the ship."

I didn't actually send that transmission to Horizon. Instead, I gestured to the Aether and generated a harmless blue light around the four of us.

The Karoshan went from scared seven-foot-tall boy squirming against the mystical hands to a blank-faced automaton in a second.

"Activation code Zelrek Winter," he said.

Then he stared off into the distance as though waiting for something to happen.

Ryzer waved a hand in front of his face. "What was that? Did you do this?"

"He's waiting for the bomb in his spine to activate," I said. Gesturing to the floating hands, I spun the Karoshan around and showed off the sealed Aethertech. "That's how I identified him. Searched for one of these. You can take him now, Horizon."

The young Karoshan man shined blue again, but this time he did vanish.

"Wait, did you really—What?" Ryzer Raithe was having more trouble adapting to this situation than his brother.

"That's a shame," Raion said sadly. "I hope Horizon can help him."

I doubted it, since it would be a poor galaxy-conquering mastermind who only put *one* form of mind-control on their suicide agents, but it was worth a shot.

"That was the most dramatic illustration I had at hand," I said. I pointed to a few angles where surreptitious gleams shone from the sky. "Any of those drones could belong to the King Regent, and there's Karoshan magic monitoring the general state of the crowd. But you can't read magic circles, so I had to haul out a spy with a self-destruct mechanism."

Ryzer stared blankly into the sky. "Yeah, okay. Let me get you started in the city. No need to bother with disguises, I guess, right?"

"That's the spirit," I said. "Lead the way."

CHAPTER THIRTEEN

Ryzer Raithe's home was one of the best on the planet Visiria, a luxurious villa on the edge of a sea. Dense mats of deep green oceanic plants formed an island, supporting thickly interweaving trees that covered that patch of the water in a jungle. As I watched, the jungle broke up and drifted off, where it would recombine with other lush floating islands of plants.

A flock of balloon-like purple, fuzzy creatures squirted to the air as they chased the temporary land. A few Visiri flew up from rafts nearby, carrying nets that they prepared to throw over the balloons.

"There has to be a better solution than nets," I muttered to myself. Magic was the first thing that came to mind. It wouldn't be too expensive to enchant a magic ring with a basic binding spell that would capture small animals like those.

Behind me, the conversation between the two Raithe brothers hadn't evolved in the last five minutes.

"You *can't* duel them," Ryzer said for what might have been the tenth time.

"But they're duelists! We'll get to know each other with our fists!"

"They're *former* duelists, Raion. Former. Now they're Senators, so don't challenge them to a fight."

"Yes, I understand," Raion said, and not for the first time. "I won't fight anyone unless they start it."

"Don't fight anybody for *any* reason!"

I had been staring out of the window long enough, so I turned back to help the conversation along. "They know who Raion is. It shouldn't hurt him too much to be himself. If you do end up in a duel, Raion..." I shrugged. "Don't hurt them too badly."

Raion gave me a thumbs up.

Ryzer rubbed his face. "Fine, let's move on. We're going to take you to the Senators individually first, as well as a few of the larger business owners and corporate representatives on the planet. Once you get to know them, we can make our way up to the Planetary Governor."

"She's the one with the magic ruby?" Raion asked.

"She's the one who has the authority to grant *temporary access* to our people's *planetary treasure*, yes."

Ryzer stepped closer as though to block Raion off from physically running away. "I'm not just being pedantic, Raion. This is how they see these things. And they see you as one of the most prominent representatives of Visiria who isn't part of the Alliance, so getting to know you is very important."

"That's true, Raion," I said. "Your secondary objective is to improve our public opinion on the Visiria Subline. Or at least save us an enemy."

Ryzer eyed his brother. "Can you at least try to do that?"

"I'll try my best!"

Ryzer looked utterly doubtful, but I wasn't.

"Raion always makes a good first impression," I said. "If they're paying attention at all, they'll be able to tell that he's sincere."

Tapping on his lips, Ryzer stared off into the distance as though calculating something. "The truth is, warrior culture still holds strong even at the highest levels of our planet. As you said, many of the Senators are former duelists, and they campaign on traditional warrior values. Those people are going to like Raion *to a point*. He has to learn when to turn it on and when to turn it off."

"He doesn't turn it off. That's how you know he's serious."

Raion stuck out his chest and lifted his chin in pride, but I thought Ryzer was going to give up again.

"It's all right, Ryzer," I said. "Tell me if you don't think you can do it. We can call this off right now."

"I'm not confident. But there is potential here, as long as he listens to me."

That was a good sign. If Ryzer couldn't see the potential in Raion, then he wasn't skilled enough to do this job. I would have to call off the diplomatic approach after all.

Raion, though, was giving me a horrified look, and I thought I knew why. "We can't give up!" he insisted. "A friend's *life* is at stake!"

"Call off *this* plan. We could steal the Heart of Visiria right now."

Ryzer reached out for a beautifully carved and polished antique chair, placed a pillow on its seat, and then collapsed into it. "Don't say these things in front of me. When I testify, it's better that I don't know anything."

"I'd rather *not* steal it, which is why you two are doing this. Like I said, the last thing we need is another enemy, but I've already allied myself with the Rebel Queen of Karosha. If we have to put ourselves against Visiria too, we will. So you know what's at stake."

Contrary to my expectations, Ryzer acted as though I'd given him more food for thought. He frowned into the distance, tapping his fingertips together.

"Our parents didn't leave us anything," Ryzer said at last. "I don't know what Raion told you, but they 'retired' in the sense that they spent the rest of our money and fled the system to escape debt collectors. Leaving the three of us behind. Everything you see, I've built myself."

I glanced around his house. It *was* a nice place, but accumulated wealth was a poor measure of a life's value. Nobody knew that better than I did.

"If we do this right," Ryzer went on, "we can all get what we want. I can leverage this into the next big achievement in my career, you all can save your friend, and we can work on your reputation. There are plenty of people who would love a connection to *The Last Horizon,* after all."

"That's how I see things," I said. Ryzer was building up to something, but I couldn't be sure what.

"I need Raion to do what I tell him to do. He needs to trust me, and *only* me. Not everyone here is who they seem to be."

Raion and I traded a glance.

"Of course they're not," Raion said.

"Yeah, that goes without saying," I agreed. "Nobody is who they seem to be."

"And we're trusting you by being here!"

"We've already decided to trust you. If it turns out you're not trustworthy, I'll have to lock you in an airless, timeless Subspace prison for a thousand years."

"But I'm sure it won't come to that!"

Ryzer's red face was closer to a shade of pink, and he stared at us for a long moment before he coughed. "Well. Ah. I guess we're clear."

I checked my console to see that there were missed calls from the other members of the crew. "Since we *are* clear, I think my work here is done. I'll head back to the ship, Raion, so let us know if anything changes."

Raion waved a hand. "Be safe, Captain! Don't worry! I'll make sure our reputation is better than it's ever been!"

"Why did you bring him in the first place?" Ryzer asked. "If you were just dropping him off, what did he need you for?"

"You don't have much of a filter, do you, Ryzer?" I observed. "I guess that runs in the family."

Raion laughed broadly and threw a hand around his brother's shoulder. "It does!"

"I was checking a few things that could use a wizard's eye," I said. "Now that I'm satisfied, Raion can handle everything else."

The truth was, I was checking for a few things.

For one, I wanted to see if the Perfected had left any traps for us.

Their single suicide agent notwithstanding, there was no danger here worth noting. My pathfinding spells showed that they were keeping a tight watch on their allies, but not such a tight watch that they would bring a fleet out of Subspace the second my feet hit the ground.

I hadn't expected that to be the case, but it was best to check.

Second, I was making sure the Heart of Visiria was here on the planet. If Raion's lead with his brother hadn't panned out, I was here to steal the Heart myself.

Fortunately, that hadn't been necessary. As I'd told Ryzer, I was *willing* to go to war with Visiria, but I didn't want to.

While the Visirian navy isn't notable on a galactic scale, their species are universally superhuman and have a legendary predilection for Combat Arts. There were enough deadly fighters on the planet to be wary of, even if Raion and I had the advantage of being able to teleport out of danger.

With the full power of *The Last Horizon* behind us, perhaps we could go to war with them, but it wasn't an option I treasured. I wanted to *save* the Visiri, not provoke them.

Besides, the World Spirit of Visiria is...beefy.

I didn't tell Ryzer any of that, though. I waved goodbye to Raion as I contacted Horizon and had her bring me back to the bridge.

"We've got a problem," Sola reported, the moment I materialized. She wasn't wearing her armor, but even in prefabricated deck shoes, she was still an inch or two taller than I was.

"Which one?" I asked wearily.

She tapped a button on the command console and a holo-projector shone to life. It projected the star map of a sector on the edge of Dark Space.

"These three isolated planets have lost contact with the closest Subline," she said, pointing to them one at a time. "The Union is treating this as an Iron Legion attack, which is how it came my way."

I felt a headache coming on, as I saw the same problem she did. "That's not the Legion."

"Not unless they've got a King back already."

Even outside Dark Space, the Iron Legion didn't eat planets quietly. They didn't lock down systems. They spread like a virus, they weren't picky, and they didn't care about witnesses.

This was too quiet.

"Does this look like anyone you know?" Sola asked.

"I have more ideas than I wish I did," I said. "We're going to have to go check it out."

Horizon's voice came from the walls. *"We can't do that and keep teleporters on Raion."*

"Right, so Sola, you and I can check out the missing planets while Raion deals with the Visiri. Mell and Omega can keep Horizon company, and Horizon, you stay between the Karoshan fleet and Raion, in case any of them need help."

"And don't forget to call your father," Horizon put in.

"Of course." I pinched the bridge of my nose and took a deep breath.

"Don't exaggerate," Sola said. "That's a light day of work."

"Oh, I know. That's why I'm scared. I can't even imagine what else is about to go wrong."

CHAPTER FOURTEEN

"Are we going to talk this time," my father asked, "or are you going to have half a conversation and then hang up on me?"

Benri Vallenar lounged in a luxuriously appointed sitting-room with a glass of brown liquor in one hand. He was dressed casually, for him, which meant that his priceless silk clothes weren't a suit. A fire flickered to the right of the screen, casting the scene in a natural light.

"It's usually easier to hang up on you," I said.

We'd traded a few indirect communications in the previous few months, but the last time we'd spoken face to face, so to speak, was just before the Galactic Union, the Karoshan Alliance, and Starhammer had cobbled together a fleet to kill me.

He had tried to persuade me to join the company. Since then, those offers had dried up, but his few messages had indicated that he was still willing to trade information. He'd even offered protection from our many enemies, for an unspecified price.

Benri lifted silver eyebrows and sipped his drink. "You have three minutes before I go to bed. Unless you catch my interest."

"I hear you've picked up—" I began, but my father cut me off.

"Speaking of interest," he said, "is that the Fallen Sword herself?"

Sola was sitting next to me, at the controls of a long-range cruiser *The Last Horizon* had fabricated. I'd been trying to keep her out of frame, but this was a private call on my console. I must have accidentally caught her from the wrong angle.

Glowing green eyes flicked to my call and returned to the course with indifference.

My father put a hand to his silk shirt. "Benri Vallenar. A pleasure to finally meet you."

"Technically, you've met before," I said. He had been unconscious at the time, and I'd had him teleported away before he woke up and met anyone. Which was how I would prefer to treat my father every time.

He continued to address himself to Sola. "I know you by reputation, Miss Kalter. Very reliable, and you work for hire. Are you interested in steadier employment?"

"I'm on another contract," Sola said.

"Certainly, we can talk whenever you'd like. I'll have my information sent to your console."

"I feel like you're eating into your own three minutes," I pointed out.

"Based on our last few interactions, I'd suspect I'd rather talk to Miss Kalter. Do you have something that will change my mind?"

In all my lives, even in the ones where I stayed with the Vallenar Corporation, it's always been a pet peeve of mine that I look so much like my father.

He looked like me twenty-five years in the future, with a few more creases in his skin and a slight deepening of his silver hair. Our looks weren't a coincidence, they were purchased at great expense, and they had the intended effect; people who saw us instantly knew we were related.

The longer we continued jockeying for advantage, the more likely it would be that he was the one to hang up. He would see that as balancing the scales for last time. I decided to cut to the chase.

"I hear you picked up a talking plasma pistol from a garbage reclamation facility," I said.

A faint smile appeared on his face, and he took another deliberate sip of his drink. "I was expecting to hear from you months ago."

"Great, so you know what you have," I said. "That'll save us some time." I'd thought he would deny it to the very end, but even if he hadn't known it was a Zenith Device before I called, the fact that I was asking about it would clue him in.

That was one of the reasons I hated talking to my father. Everything became an exchange of benefits.

"Are you looking to buy it from me?" Benri asked.

He phrased the question like that would be a reasonable possibility, though of course it wasn't. Not only would he never sell a Zenith Device, we didn't have the capital anyway.

"Obviously not. We'd like to examine the object to determine its identity. If it is the Zenith Cannon, we want to study it. In exchange..." I wanted to swallow my words because he was going to ask for more than this. "...We will share anything we discover, and will return ownership of the Cannon provided the Device itself agrees."

"Hmm." His reaction was decidedly noncommittal. "I'm not sure what I stand to gain from that. I have the best Aether Technicians in the galaxy examining it already."

"My crew is uniquely suited to research Zenith Devices, and we both know it. Let us examine it aboard Horizon and we'll share the results."

"Or, hypothetically speaking, *we* could examine it aboard Horizon."

I had known he'd leap on this chance to investigate another Zenith Device, and I'd cleared this with Horizon before making the call in the first place. "We're willing to let you and your experts supervise the entire process aboard *The Last Horizon*. And because I want to skip the rest of the conversation, you can have the first chance at awakening the Zenith Cannon as well."

That opportunity was barely worth anything, though I was hoping he didn't know that. The Zenith Devices were self-aware, at least once their awakening conditions were satisfied, so who had the first "chance" didn't matter much.

Also, I had Sola and Omega aboard, either of whom would be great prospective partners for a Zenith Era gun.

Benri tapped his glass against the edge of a table, thinking. The fingers of his free hand drummed on his thigh.

"I could consider that," he said. "I'll let you know."

Then the call cut off.

"I knew he was going to do that," I said.

"He's up to something," Sola said without moving her eyes away from the controls.

"He always is. Usually it's not as clever as he thinks it is."

"I hate people like him."

I didn't expect that. It was rare for Sola to express her opinion of someone so openly.

"He's plotting and planning," she continued. "We'll get wrapped up with him. We should cut through the web."

"How do you propose we do that?"

"Steal the Cannon."

It was the second time inside a standard day that I'd been advised to steal the object I was after.

I leaned back in my seat, staring at the secondary monitors and folded-up Subspace shutters on the ceiling. "No matter how powerful our ship is, I still don't want to go to war with the Vallenar Corporation."

I felt like I was repeating myself.

I didn't want to fight Visiria, and I didn't want to fight a major corporation either. One spaceship, no matter how invincible, was never a match for a galactic power with nigh-endless resources.

"I don't mind getting our hands dirty as long as the job gets done," Sola said.

I leaned my head over to look at her expression, which didn't tell me much. "You think we should really shoot our way through our problems?"

"In the half hour I spent trying to convince the Galactic Union to let me go, the Scourge Warrens killed thousands of people all over a continent. If I had shot my way out, I would have killed…maybe ten people. Getting rid of the Warrens that much faster would have been the difference in a town surviving and not."

"All the more reasons not to make enemies we don't have to," I pointed out. "If the Galactic Union hadn't held you up, there would have been no delay. And if they were persuaded to work *with* us, how many could you have saved?"

Sola's hands tightened on the controls in frustration. "This is why I stick to the Iron Legion. So much simpler. Did I tell you that, in the other life?"

"You did. It's clean. There's no doubt who the villains are. No one takes the side of the Iron Legion."

"That's what I hate about people like your father. They're trying to complicate everything so they can get away with whatever they want. I hate playing their games."

"This is the dive point," I said. She'd see that on the computer, but I had the Cosmic Path active, so I noticed it a little sooner than she did.

Motors whirred as the Subspace shutters came down over the forward viewscreen. I chewed on the conversation for a while, since it echoed my worries from many previous lives.

I preferred straightforward villains like the Iron Legion or the D'Niss. They were monsters, and they needed to be killed. No one sane argued against that.

But at the same time, I never hoped for them. They were a blight on the universe, and their victory meant incomprehensible death and destruction.

If the Perfected won…I didn't want that, but at the end of the day, they were still Karoshans. They wanted to rule the galaxy and prove their own superiority, not to burn it all to the ground.

Solstice was the same; they had stolen freedom from average citizens across hundreds of planets, but they weren't an exponentially expanding undead hive-mind. They were people.

If we cut through the problem, we would save ourselves a lot of headache, and potentially many lives. But how many would it cost? Where would we stop? Where *should* we stop?

Sola was normally comfortable with silence, so I didn't expect her to interrupt my thoughts. "Tell me two things."

"What would you like to know?" I asked.

"Tell me one thing that my previous self knew about you," she said, "and one thing she didn't."

That was so out of my expectation that I took a moment to digest. It was the sort of question I'd expect from Raion.

"I didn't think we'd be playing Subspace games on this trip."

She crossed her arms and leaned away from the controls, since we'd be in Subspace for a while. "I like games."

"I know, so I guess this will count as the one thing your previous self knew about me. Something we shared, anyway. We used to pass the time like this when we were heading into battle."

I ticked off games on my fingers. "Music trivia, guessing games, catch the lie, trade childhood stories."

"And what did you learn about me?"

"That we don't have *any* of the same taste in music. I like songs I can meditate to, so you never let me use the speakers."

Sola nodded. "Glad to know I still had good taste. Now, what about something she didn't know?"

I hesitated. That was a harder question to answer than it sounded. "She knew a lot about my life that you don't, but at the same time, you already know things that she didn't. I have five sets of memories now that I didn't then. She didn't know anything about Raion and the Titan Force, for instance, because I never joined the Titan Knights in that life."

"Something about you. Not your job." She reminded me of Shyrax with her intensity, though I was surprised to hear the question from someone whose entire life was consumed by her own job.

I gave it some real thought, and I wasn't sure Sola appreciated the difficulty involved. A lot of things I would have told the Sola in the previous life were nonsense to her now, since she didn't have any of the context.

So, in fairness, I had to come up with something that satisfied the spirit of the question. But that got uncomfortably personal.

Which I supposed was fair. I knew personal things about her, after all.

"I joined the fight against the Iron Legion because of you," I said. "I never told you that."

Sola didn't react, she just listened.

"I learned pathfinding magic in that life because I wanted to be a mercenary pilot. I was running from the corporations and the Union both. When the Legion suddenly started expanding, my mentor said we could make a profit."

I stared into the ceiling, stuck in memory. "All this you knew. But when I fought for the first time, I heard you give a speech to everyone fighting."

That, Sola did react to. "A speech?"

She was understandably skeptical.

"You stood in front of a dozen survivors and convinced them to shoot their way out of an Iron Legion invasion because otherwise they would die."

"That checks out."

"I knew you had a cause you'd give your life for, and I didn't have that." I smiled at that version of myself. "You had what I wanted. When you left, I convinced my mentor to follow you. I said we showed up on the same planet as a coincidence, and I don't think I ever told you different. You convinced me to give up my life for a cause."

Silence reigned for a few seconds before she said, "So you died for it. And I didn't."

"Neither did I, it turns out." I turned up my smile and meant it for her this time. "That's something we have in common that we didn't before! Not too many people know what it's like to have a cyborg stab you through the stomach."

"It's cold," Sola said, nodding.

"Right? That's the thing I remembered the most."

All the way until we reached our destination, we traded stories about death.

CHAPTER FIFTEEN

Sola and I took the cruiser out of Subspace early, following the Cosmic Path. We found ourselves drifting with nothing to navigate by, lost in endless black.

She checked our scanners. "Still a half-hour in Subspace outside the system. Why did it stop us?"

"The only reason the Cosmic Path would drop us here is if the Subspace route became blocked." I pulled up a local map on the ship's console and compared it against my own. "If the planet was really inaccessible, the spell would have failed. Since it didn't, there's *some* route there."

"It would take us a year to get there in real space."

"That doesn't mean it wouldn't work. The spell doesn't care how long the journey takes, as long as there's a current route that will bring us there." I could still see the Cosmic Path, which drifted off into the darkness like an unbroken golden road.

When I compared that route with the local maps, I thought I understood the direction it was taking us.

"Subspace blockade," Sola said. "That's not an Iron Legion tactic."

Not without a King, it wasn't, but that went without saying.

"Could be the Perfected, although we're a long way out of their territory. Maybe even the Advocates. There are some splinter groups in Dark Space that could have done this, or a few Subspace creatures."

She gave me an odd look. "Splinter groups in Dark Space? Splinters of what?"

"Do you not—Oh, right, that was a different...Sometimes I forget what's common knowledge and what isn't. I'm talking about splinter factions from the Galactic Union takeover, who flew into Dark Space and swore that they'd build their forces back up and recover their territory one day."

I waved them away. "They're not a serious threat. At least, not in any lives I remember. Nothing compared to the—"

I stopped again, cutting off my thoughts. I had been about to mention the various possibilities of who it could be, but there were some I didn't want to speak into being.

Not that there was any sound magical theory behind changing reality with my own fears, but I still didn't want to risk it.

"...Could be anything," I followed up. "Let me try a couple of spells, just to be sure."

Pathfinding magic, as I've mentioned, is useful for finding a journey between two points, and thus has great utility when I'm trying to figure out if one of those points still exists.

Not that navigational spells are foolproof. When I cast the spell to locate an Iron King and it came up negative, that either meant that there was no King in existence or that he'd found a way to hide from me.

So not infallible, but better than nothing.

I checked for the Iron King, for a wild mechavius, for a flight of migrating astral dragons, and even for Starhammer. Just because we had him locked away in *The Last Horizon* didn't mean I had become less paranoid.

Then I checked for a few possibilities I was more nervous about. I looked for the presence of any Perfected within the sector, then for a specific ship the Galactic Union had developed in one of my lives, one that was specialized in stealth and carried the best anti-divination magical protections ever devised.

Of course, when I didn't find that one, I remained equally suspicious.

There were a few possibilities I'd saved for last, out of prudence, and I explained those to Sola before I cast them.

"I've checked everything that's safe to check, so now I'm going to take a risk."

Sola leaned in the doorway to the hall in a green flight suit, drinking from a water bottle. "You've been chanting for the last twenty minutes."

"One way or another, it's not going to take much longer. Anything I search for now has a chance of finding me back. If I start screaming or something comes out of Subspace, make sure you're ready to dive."

By the end of that sentence, Sola was already at the controls and prepping the Subspace Drive. "Is there any risk to you?"

"Theoretically, yes. Spells like this can be traced back by skilled magic-users, and they can use that to target me. In my previous life, I had to be careful. This time…"

I shrugged. "I'll risk it."

An ordinary caster wouldn't have much chance of getting a harmful spell to work on me at this range, and I could defend myself even from an extraordinary caster. It was more likely that a ship came out of Subspace on top of us than that they got through to me with a spell.

Sola gave a sharp nod. "Got it. Stay sharp."

That vigilance was nostalgic, which put me in a better mood as I began the incantation. First, I checked for any evidence of Alazar, the Perfected Mage. I'd checked for any Perfected before, but a more specific spell was harder to protect against.

When that came up negative, I searched for a few more casters I remembered who might have hidden an entire planet. There were only a handful who could perform a feat like that, even with a ritual.

With every possibility I checked off, my mood worsened. I had reached the last item on my mental checklist, which left me with a sour taste in my mouth.

I *really* didn't want it to be the D'Niss.

I would even prefer an unknown threat. Almost anything was better than a swarm of planet-eating psychic insects. But I had to check.

In addition to their mental power, the D'Niss were almost all accomplished spellcasters, and they were more than intelligent and coordinated enough to pull off a Subspace block.

Though it probably wasn't them. There had been no reports from neighboring planets, and the D'Niss should have no reason to hide their approach so thoroughly. As far as they knew, there were no threats to them in this universe.

I had already started considering the next possibilities when the Cosmic Path connected.

A D'Niss was close by, relatively speaking. Within a few systems. My spell's golden swirl told me we needed to dive into Subspace.

I slowly settled into my chair, staring at the spot of gold light in front of us. I drummed fingers on my thigh to settle my racing thoughts.

Sola pointed a pistol toward me. "Is that still you, Varic?"

I eyed the weapon. "If it wasn't, were you going to shoot me? It's still my body."

"It's not lethal. Necessarily."

I didn't really care about the gun, staring off into the light of my spell. "I don't know what I'm going to tell Raion."

"What did you find?"

"There's a D'Niss. It's probably responsible for the blockade." I let out a breath. "We can't let it go or it will spread to nearby planets. But it's probably not one of the Seven Calamities—most of them left the universe. It certainly isn't Esh'kinaar herself."

"But it is taking over planets," Sola pointed out.

My fingers started drumming again. "Yeah. It has a plan, but not necessarily one we can't deal with."

The D'Niss were fully sapient and intelligent, and if one had started taking over a system on the outskirts of known space while putting up a Subspace blockade and preventing word from leaking out, they were doing it as part of a plot.

"We'll let the Alliance know anonymously," I decided. "This isn't something that requires us unless things get worse."

A minute ago, I said there's no magical theory that says the Aether listens to our nonsense and bends reality accordingly.

There's no *magical* theory for it, but I still feel like it happens. At least to me.

No sooner had I finished speaking than my Cosmic Path spell snipped out. There were only two reasons that would happen. Either the path between us and our target had become impassable or someone had cut off the spell.

I already had my wand out as a focus for my navigational magic, so I stood up and lifted it. "Weapons ready," I said. "Don't dive yet."

Not only were the plasma cannons already hot, but Sola loaded a pair of torpedoes and donned her armor in the same instant.

We had to confirm the presence of a D'Niss, so we didn't leave. If my spell really had been deliberately severed, the enemy caster knew where we were. Someone would be coming for us.

Sola and I were the best combination for this scenario. If an average D'Niss showed up personally, it might be able to contest my magic, but Sola's Worldslayer would make quick work of it. If it sent soldiers, they wouldn't be able to stop us from escaping.

And if it didn't respond at all, then it might be safe to take a closer look.

I explained a quick sketch of the plan to Sola, and we waited together. We were half an hour of Subspace travel outside of the system, but that didn't necessarily mean the D'Niss would take so long to reach us. Some of its kind were faster than our cruiser, and a Subspace blockade meant it might have soldiers posted closer, ready to respond to incursions like ours.

After fifteen minutes of watching the clock tick down, I started to cast again. "Let me try one more thing," I said, two seconds before a Subspace warp bloomed within visual range of our craft.

Contact alarms blared, and Sola locked on with the torpedoes. If we could have confirmed the target, it would have been wise to fire, but there was still the chance that a random civilian happened to emerge from a dive right in front of us.

Monumentally unlikely, but still a chance.

Human-sized insects poured through the spatial warp by the dozens every second. As they emerged into space, they spread wings that flowed with colors like liquid paint.

These hive soldiers resembled moths, their wings carrying a measure of the hypnotic colors of Subspace. The tips of their antennae shone like jewels, and they let out an eerie, chittering song as they appeared.

Despite the distance and the vacuum, we heard it echoing in our ship. A mental and Aetheric effect, not a physical sound.

"Psychic hazard," Sola reported. "Check in."

"Clear," I said immediately. My mantle protected me from stranger vectors of harm than this, and wizards were more resistant to psychic forces anyway. A side effect of working directly with the Aether.

But we weren't immune to crushing despair.

I watched the soldiers pour out, wondering what I had done wrong to be punished like this. What I had done wrong in *any* of my lives.

These were the soldiers from the hive of Sel'miroth, first of the Seven Calamities. She was one of the greatest of the D'Niss, and she considered herself the closest disciple of Esh'kinaar, thanks to the subtlety of her psychic abilities.

She was the D'Niss equivalent of a religious fanatic, and she would never act except to summon the Swarm-Queen. If Sel'miroth had returned from Dark Space, we were on a collision course with the Queen of the D'Niss. But that should only have been a remote possibility.

The D'Niss existed in all my lives, but I'd only faced Esh'kinaar twice.

When Mell and I originally fought Starhammer, he'd forced the D'Niss to summon Esh'kinaar and the Iron Legion to create an Iron King. All so he could defeat them and rid the galaxy of their future threat.

Otherwise, they would never have shown up. In most of my lives, there was no Iron King. In most of them, there was no threat of the Swarm-Queen.

In this life, we were facing everything. One thing was abundantly clear.

The Aether was out to get me.

"Dive as soon as you can," I ordered. Then I returned to casting.

She grunted in acknowledgement, but she was busy.

Sola had already fired on the cloud of space-traversing moths, and while she'd destroyed many, some still resisted. D'Niss soldiers were bred to have performance comparable to starships, and while most of them were only the size of small fighters, they had their own equivalents of shields and enough weapons to trade shots with cruisers like ours.

We wove through space, looking for room to dive as we avoided the weapons of Sel'miroth's swarm. They looked like crystal spearheads slicing through the void, pseudo-matter condensed out of the Aether and accelerated to a fraction of lightspeed.

There was a delay between locking in the coordinates of the crystal and releasing it, so the shots weren't terribly accurate, but they were fast and there were hundreds of them. Every second drove Sola further away from the Subspace warp point, with even a glancing blow taking our shield down to dangerous percentages.

I had a spell in reserve, but I held onto it, waiting. The rainbow flower of the Subspace warp was growing larger and larger.

An insectoid head, significantly larger than our cruiser, poked its way into physical space. Two oversized antennae dangled down, carrying hypnotic lights that promised peace and rest.

It shoved its way through as though bursting through a cocoon, spreading majestic moth-like wings with a span dozens of miles across.

Of the Seven Calamities, Sel'miroth was the smallest.

Her song was far more complex than that of her soldiers, echoing through our ship like a chorus of Aethril singers. I even felt a distant urge to put up our weapons and go hear her out. She was capable of reason, so she *could* be reasonable.

Sweat beaded on my skin. My mantle was more than capable of defending me against the mental influence of a swarm of soldiers or the mere presence of a D'Niss, but a direct, focused psychic attack would hit me like a punch from the Iron King.

I had hoped we would have space to dive before this point, but Sola had done the best she could. The D'Niss soldiers weren't giving us any room to withdraw.

As I finished my spell, the world grew slow and quiet. Everything seemed to crawl through gel...except one tiny, beautiful moth.

It fluttered before me, landing on the controls between my hands. Its wings were like portals onto an endless, gorgeous rainbow, and I felt distantly sad as the moth folded its wings away.

The sadness left immediately as the moth spoke, its voice soothing and encouraging. "Don't worry, Varic. We're not here to hurt you."

"You're not?" My voice came out as though in a dream.

"We just want to see our mother. You have a mother, don't you?"

I had very few memories of my mother, and most of the ones I had weren't pleasant. But the moth's voice made me feel like a child again, cradled in her arms.

"Your mother...She'll kill us." I said that, but I couldn't remember why that was so bad.

The moth tilted its head. "Not all of you. And we can't leave her in the void. It's cold below Subspace, Varic, cold and hungry and very, very lonely. She cries for us. What kind of children would we be if we left our mother down there?"

This moth was making a lot of sense, but something about that logic still bothered me.

"I don't think I like you," I said.

"We don't know each other yet. Very soon, I'll introduce myself properly."

Something beeped on my monitors, and I gradually tilted my head down to see someone on cameras. "I don't think she likes you either."

A red beam suddenly appeared, a razor-sharp bridge of light

between us and Sel'miroth. The illusory moth vanished, and my brain snapped back to clarity in an instant.

The main body of the D'Niss had gotten far closer than I ever intended to allow, but now she was pierced through by the knife-sharp beam of Worldslayer. The giant moth was pinned in place like a bug to a board, and her painful psychic screech came as a relief to me.

I had almost been taken down without a fight. Outside *The Last Horizon* or Aethertech of comparable grade, we had no chance of resisting that kind of mental assault.

There was a reason we'd needed Divine Titans to fight those things.

A second later, the shot from Worldslayer flickered out and Sola's voice came over my processor.

"Thanks for the spell," she said.

I had intended to cast that protection spell over the whole ship, but the D'Niss must have eroded it. I was lucky it worked at all.

"We've got to leave," I responded. The soldiers had interrupted their barrage to give Sel'miroth time to work on us, but they were already opening fire again. I flew away as fast as I could, chanting the Cosmic Path as Sola made her way back into the airlock.

"Did I kill it?"

"Let's not count on it."

"Yeah. See you inside."

"Diving in ten seconds."

As I prepared the Subspace Drive, I watched Sel'miroth. Worldslayer was masterwork Aethertech on par with a world-level enchanted device. It wasn't *impossible* that a shot from it had killed one of the D'Niss.

With unnatural speed, Sel'miroth's body lost its color and curled up as though it was being drained of both vitality and liquid.

An instant later, a new, unharmed version of her burst from the shell. She spread wet wings and let out a psychic cry of rage.

Sola marched into the room. "I know this is coming from me," she said, "but I hate it when they come back to life."

"Tell me about it," I muttered. "Dive in three."

We made it out easily enough, but that didn't loosen the knot in my stomach. The D'Niss really were coming back.

What was I supposed to tell Raion?

CHAPTER SIXTEEN

"The D'Niss are coming back," I said to Raion.

Over the video call, I didn't see his face change much at the news. He only nodded seriously. "Hm. I see. You confirmed that yourself?"

"Sola shot Sel'miroth with Worldslayer."

"That's too bad. I hoped she was gone."

His face and tone didn't match what I expected. He was taking this thoughtfully and carefully.

But behind him, the sky blurred as though he was moving faster than it seemed, and the view from my end jostled quickly.

"You're running to a ship, aren't you?" I guessed.

"No, I'm going to tell my brother I have to go. I can't teleport away without warning him!"

"Right." Sometimes, it still blinded me that we had access to long-range magical teleportation. For my entire lives, that had been an impossibility.

"I think you should stay there," I said.

He gave me a puzzled look and, judging by the background, didn't slow down. "But that's my job."

"*This* is your job now. If we can get Visiria on our side, or at least keep them from getting in our way, we'll have an easier time fighting the D'Niss. If anything, this makes your job there more urgent. Besides, with the Heart of Visiria, we can get Parryl back. That's a second Titan Knight."

The blur of the scenery lessened until I could make out individual tree branches as Raion thought it through.

"But what about the people who are in danger now?" he asked.

"We'll do everything we can for them."

I meant that as a noncommittal way to reassure him, but Raion seemed to take it as a promise. He grinned brightly. "I can't say no to that, then, can I? I'll leave it to you!"

"Even so, hurry back," I said. "There's no substitute for a Divine Titan when it comes to fighting the D'Niss."

"I'll speed it along as fast as I can!"

"How much progress have you made?"

Raion turned his camera around and showed me where he was. He stood at the edge of a massive, manicured garden with a house towering in the background. A luxurious spacecraft of gold and ivory came in for a landing as I watched.

"Senator Cyclon!" Raion announced. "Ryzer worked hard to get me an audience. If we impress her, we'll get a meeting with the Planetary Governor. It's possible that we'll even get to see the Prime Arena!"

I recalled painful memories of my own fight in the Prime Arena, and I winced instead of smiling back. "Enjoy that. Oh, one more thing. How confident are you that you won't be in any danger?"

"Absolutely confident!"

"And how confident is Ryzer?"

A red flash came in from the side and Ryzer came to a landing next to his brother, staggering as he hit the ground harder than he intended. He was out of breath, and he looked panicked at Raion.

"What are you doing? She's here!"

"I thought I had to leave, but I don't! Say hi to Varic!"

"Ryzer, how likely is it that Raion will have to fight in the next few days?"

Ryzer looked like he would rather see anyone than me. He probably thought I was encouraging his brother's behavior, which wasn't exactly wrong. At least he answered my question. "Around here, we don't fight. As long as Raion doesn't attack someone or break any laws, he'll be fine."

"Great. Raion, take us to private audio."

Raion looked confused, but the video winked out and his voice came through my audio implant more clearly. "He can't hear you, Varic. But we don't need to keep secrets from him!"

"Yes, we do, and you know it." Raion was only partially as naïve as he seemed.

He pondered my statement for a second before responding. "Hm. That makes me sad. All right, what do you have to say?"

"We might have to move Horizon to confront the D'Niss, since we don't have a Titan. That means going out of teleporter range. We'll leave enough relays behind us that you can always call us if something goes wrong, but don't bite off more than you can chew while we're dark."

"Don't worry!" Raion said cheerily. "I can chew a lot!"

"I know you can, which is the only reason I'm okay with this at all." Raion would be in much more danger fighting Sel'miroth than he would while navigating Visirian diplomacy. "I don't think there's anyone on the planet who can beat you in a fair fight, but there are other ways to hurt you. Keep the lines open."

"Understood, Captain!" Though the video feed had died, I knew he was saluting me.

In the background, I heard Ryzer's voice. "Tell the Senator we'll be right there! I'm sorry, my brother had an urgent communication with Captain Vallenar. Unavoidable. Imminent danger, he'll be inside in a moment."

"Horizon will check in with you regularly," I said. "See you soon, Raion."

"Goodbye, Captain!"

With the call ended, I turned to the rest of the room. Sola, Mell, and Horizon had heard the entire call, though they'd kept up a conversation of their own while I briefed Raion.

"Do you expect them to attack my Knight?" Horizon asked, looking eager.

"I'm a lot more worried about them tricking him," I said. "He can handle a fight. Keep checking on him, and…maybe remind him not to sign anything."

Mell leaned back from a ship console, letting out a weary breath. She pushed her glasses up as she rubbed the bridge of her nose. "I can't do it. I can't do it! They're as fast as they can get."

I glanced at Sola, who explained. "External fabricators."

"We're printing ships and Nova-Bots as fast as we can," Mell went on, "but there are real, *physical* limits. Not only do we not have an unlimited supply of usable matter, but we can only process it so fast. Physics is already crying."

Horizon's fabricators were at least as much products of transmutation magic as they were Aethertech, but she was right that both of those methods had their limits. "What about the ships we gave to Shyrax?"

"No good," Sola reported. "The Perfected have them in a chokehold. If they start losing ships, it's going to get tighter. They're locked in place."

"Mell, what do you need to speed up ship production?" I asked.

"A more reliable energy source that doesn't cannibalize our own power core, a source of rare metals, a starship salvage ground, some kind of magic that cloned things…"

Mell shot me an exaggerated look at that last one, but maintaining Mirror of Silence clones of a fabricator long enough for it to print out a ship would be…possible, but inefficient in the long run. Mainly because it would require my attention for days or weeks at a time.

"We'll get them for you," I promised. "In the meantime, call in all the Nova-Bot ships we can spare. Horizon, where's Shadow Ark?"

"Sulking," Horizon said in disapproval. *"He's hovering around somewhere, but all his attention is on his inner world. Which is empty, so I don't know what he's so fascinated by."*

"All our problems would be solved if we had a free planet and a place to keep it."

"That wouldn't kill the D'Niss," Sola pointed out.

"It also wouldn't find us the Zenith Cannon," Mell added.

"*Some* of our problems would be solved," I corrected myself. "Ark wants a planet, doesn't he? Can't we get him one?"

A violet-and-black crystal appeared out of nowhere, unfolding from nothing like a hologram. "Since you're talking about me, it only makes sense that I be involved."

"We've mentioned your name many times in the last few months," I said.

"Well, this is the first time I was interested in speaking to *you*. What's this about getting me a planet?"

"That's all you talk about," Mell said. "You're acting like we never call for you, but half the time you're drifting up and down the halls, crying about having no person and no planet. You haven't even let me scan you."

"I owe you nothing. It's not as though you—Stop! Get away!"

Mell had immediately pulled an Aethertech scanner from her belt and begun tracing lines of light over Ark. "Quiet. This won't hurt."

"Many of Shadow Ark's functions are restricted until he has a mortal bond," Horizon said. Over her shoulder, her little brother floated through the air to run from Mell, who chased him with her scanner lit. *"I'm not certain he could hold even a single planet in that state."*

"There aren't so many qualified individuals in the galaxy," Ark complained as he floated by. "Many of them are your enemies, and it's not as though I want to start a war between the family."

Sola stared at him with burning green eyes. "You did before."

"Yes, but I lost."

"What about a temporary contract?" I suggested. "Horizon, you had access to some of your systems before we assembled the rest of the crew. Maybe one of us could help you until you had a planet or two."

Ark unfolded again, like a geometric egg hatching. He expanded into a short man with violet-edged obsidian armor, a crown of horns on his head, and a dour expression.

"Horizon needs a full crew to access her full potential," Ark said, "but she starts with a Captain. I begin by finding a Gatekeeper, after which I can begin integrating planets into my internal system. Eventually, with enough World Spirits cooperating in a cohesive system, I could surpass even *The Last Horizon.*"

Horizon laughed in contempt.

Mell had her nose an inch from the back of Ark's head, and her scanner moved up and down his armor. "Interesting. Horizon's form is basically a hologram, but you're physically here. Do you think of yourself as a projection of temporary matter or more like a man-shaped spatial distortion?"

"What are the qualifications for a Gatekeeper?" I asked.

"First and foremost, the Gatekeeper of Shadow Ark must have the power to defend those I protect," Ark said. "They must have dedicated themselves to ideals of service and defense, and they must be a champion of my inhabitants. They are my ultimate protector, and they will even settle disputes among those who call me home."

"That sounds like Raion," I said.

Sola nodded.

Mell leaned around Ark to peer at him. "I could build you someone like that. I built the last one."

Horizon drew herself up indignantly. *"Look for your own! I refuse to share. There are plenty of mortals out there for you, they just aren't as good as mine."*

"Yes, of course, I feel the same way," Ark said. Much less convincingly.

"It sounds like you're rethinking," I observed.

"No, I'm not! A Zenith Device cannot lower their standards. Although, in extraordinary circumstances..." He glanced aside at Horizon.

She folded her arms and conjured more eyes to glare at him. *"These circumstances are not extraordinary enough!"*

Abruptly, Horizon looked to the side as though someone had called her name. She waved a hand, and a moment later we all heard a transmission coming through the walls.

"Karoshan royal guard to The Last Horizon, *we're under attack and in need of urgent assistance. Repeat, we're under attack."*

"Somebody wake Omega," I said. "And then let's dive."

CHAPTER SEVENTEEN

We came out of Subspace onto the site of a civil war.

Shyrax's dark, rectangular ships were arranged in formations that looked on the computer like highly regimented blocks, but in person looked a lot more like a swarm of D'Niss soldiers.

Light streaked across the void as they traded long-range shots with a fleet of almost identical ships. As we drifted closer to Shyrax's ships, which parted as we identified ourselves, Sola read through the reports on the situation and summarized it for us.

"There was a break in Shyrax's forces. Some of them opened a gap in the blockade and allowed a Perfected fleet through."

"I identified the traitors for her," I said aloud. "Did they hide from my spell, or are these different people?"

"Unclear. Shyrax indicates that the traitors she found worth imprisoning are still secure."

Omega chuckled from the Pilot console. "Traitor on the bridge, is it? That's one of my favorite games."

Either there had been a few agents that were shrouded well enough that they evaded my pathfinding magic, there were a few I didn't catch, or the Perfected Shadow had managed to slip more traitors into Shyrax's fleet after I scanned them.

I hoped it was me missing targets. That had always been a possibility. If the Perfected were well-established enough that they could shield agents from me or insert their people at will, we couldn't trust any of Shyrax's troops at all.

Without asking, I pulled up a battle-map, which showed that the Nova-Bot ships were arranged on the edge of the battle. They were serving as a disposable wall, which was their purpose; better to lose any number of replaceable robots than one Karoshan life.

Mell winced at each one of the smooth, avian craft that exploded. "This is going to set me back three months," she muttered.

By all standards, that was spectacular. It would normally take a fortune and several years to replace even a small fleet.

"Horizon, get Shyrax on the line," I ordered. "Mell, take control of the Nova-Bots. Coordinate with Karoshan command, but I know you can get better performance out of the ships."

"They don't need better performance. She's using them as a shield." Mell was still following orders, though, pulling up a control program for the Nova-Bots.

"You can make that shield last a little longer. Sola, stand by for orders."

"The Karoshans insist that Shyrax can't be contacted at the moment," Horizon said. She ground her teeth. *"They say that if I do, I'll be putting her in danger."*

I'd expected her to call Shyrax regardless of what the other Karoshans said, but it was good to see her prioritizing crew safety. "Call her anyway. Until we hear the situation from her, we're paralyzed."

Only seconds later, Shyrax answered. She was striding down a hallway in ornate battle armor, black worked in gold, with her hair-cables tied behind her. *"You were right to call me. I will amend the instructions of my officers to allow your contact."*

"What do you need from us?" I asked.

"Information. Some of the enemy ships have been taken over by Perfected agents or magic, while others are crewed entirely with enemies. I cannot strike with full force until I know which."

"Horizon and I will take care of it. Are you boarding someone?"

Shyrax drew the hilt of a force-blade. *"I will determine guilt and innocence myself and separate their crew accordingly."*

"Save the drop-pod. We'll move you."

The soldiers around her protested, but she held up a hand to silence them. *"Can you move my squad as well?"*

"Leave them behind," I said. "We're boarding instead."

Omega gave a delighted gasp.

"Who's *we?*" Mell asked.

"All of us. How many target ships, Shyrax?"

"Sixteen that I have cause to doubt. I'll send you their information when I am aboard. Send me now."

Her guards became more insistent, and two even wrestled her against the wall. She allowed it, not even fighting back as she faded to blue light. *"Your diligence is commendable but misplaced,"* she said to them. *"Await my word."*

Then she reappeared on the bridge of *The Last Horizon,* striding forward and speaking as though there had been no break in the conversation. "Horizon, I'm sending you the coordinates now. Confirm."

"I confirm receipt," Horizon said happily. *"What did you have in mind, Captain?"*

As Horizon spoke, she lit up the destination starships on the monitor.

I pointed. "We go in pairs. Mell, prep a decoy-bot and go with Shyrax. Omega, you're with Sola." Omega already had a gun in each hand and stood on the balls of his feet like he couldn't wait to get going. Sola gave him a wary look through her visor.

"Shyrax, they know us on sight, don't they?" I asked.

Shyrax held her force-blade loosely in one hand. "Mine do. We would do well to assume that the enemy does as well."

"Great, kill anybody who tries to kill you." I settled back into my seat. "Hold while I check out the situation in the ships."

I linked my magic with Horizon, and together we manifested eyes in ships all over the system. That split my attention far further than I could handle, but Horizon watched more than I did.

Casting like this wasn't quite as powerful as Eurias would have been, but I maintained more precision. And, of course, I had a World Spirit to help me.

Mell had left the room to prepare a decoy-bot, but I trusted she would hear my report. "I have a visual on the first ship." The light cruiser, one of those closest to us, was highlighted on a monitor screen. "Loyal bridge crew are dead, no one else in the crew is resisting. Assume the whole crew is hostile."

"I assumed that already," Omega said. He didn't lick his lips, but he manifested a mouth that did.

I looked to Sola. "Are you ready?"

"She's ready!"

I ignored Omega and waited for her nod.

"Then get out of here. Horizon, take all the power you need out of the weapons and engines and put it into the teleporters. We're not fighting."

The door hissed open as Omega and Sola disappeared. A robot identical to Mell marched in, opening and closing her hand as though testing her grip. "I heard everything, Horizon kept me patched in. Aren't you coming out?"

"Horizon and I will be more useful back here, providing logistical support."

"Really? I got the impression you could scan the ships and blow them up from here all by yourself."

"It won't be precise enough unless I go one ship at a time," I said. "Which is slower than sending you. Speaking of which, your target is ready, and it seems we have some hostages this time. I'll light them up in your processor."

A golden force-blade ignited in Shyrax's hand. "Send us."

Sola materialized in a dark, cramped room with pipes hissing over her head. A layout of the ship appeared in her visor, and she saw that she had been teleported outside of the bridge.

Varic's voice came into her helmet. *"I had to break through a weak point in their magical protections, so we're a little off target. The mages know something is wrong. Head to the bridge immediately."*

Sola scanned her immediate area and saw nothing. "I've lost eyes on Omega."

"I've got him. Proceed. All soldiers between you and the bridge are hostile."

Sola kicked her way out of the maintenance hatch and dashed down the hallway. The first Karoshan to turn the corner got a shotgun blast to the chest.

That wasn't enough to kill him through his combat armor, but Sola hadn't expected it to be. She was used to fighting Reavers, who never wanted to go down in one shot.

She fired again while advancing, then activated her pulse boosters to move closer. Sola slammed into his legs, collapsing him, and finished him with a third shot.

That it took three shots meant she was using the wrong weapon. Her shotgun dematerialized into her Subspace inventory, and she replaced it with an XK-21 laser rifle. Made for ship combat, the laser lost focus after only a few yards, meaning it was easy to cut through armor without also slicing through the outer hull.

Her scanners detected the next soldier and she shot him through the wall. Peering into the molten hole she left, she saw his body collapse.

Much better.

She carved her way through two more before she reached the bridge, and rather than attempt anything more complicated, she withdrew a Hullbreaker VII. It was heavier than three of the laser rifles put together, and it blew the door to the bridge inward.

Sola marched straight through to find Omega with his feet up on the ship's console and surrounded by bodies.

He blew nonexistent smoke from the barrel of his gun. "You decided to do a little sightseeing, did you? I can understand. These windowless black boxes are so scenic."

Sola tossed her Hullbreaker back into storage with more force than necessary. "Clear," she reported.

"I can see that," Varic said. *"Prepare for transfer. We'll send him outside the ship next time."*

Omega's Aethertech eye gleamed. "No, farther than that! Give me a challenge!"

Sola wished she could change partners.

Mell cowered behind two larger Nova-Bots as Shyrax cut through the Karoshans on the bridge. They put up resistance, but it seemed to work only in the sense that Shyrax was trying her best not to harm the hostages.

A plasma bolt singed the console next to Mell's head, and she winced. Though she couldn't really be harmed, and wasn't even really here, it still *felt* real. Besides, she had other work to do.

Her primary job was to keep enemies off Shyrax's back, which felt entirely redundant. As Mell typed away on a console, she kept an eye over her shoulder, where the Queen was holding up a ten-foot Karoshan man one-handed while inexorably advancing on a squad of his fellows.

While the man's body was shredded by their fire, *they* were retreating. Shyrax's every step promised death.

Mell wasn't sure where they'd found the courage to backstab her in the first place.

She found what she was looking for a moment later and contacted *The Last Horizon*. "Found the controls! Give me coordinates." It would have taken her a lot longer to work her way into the security of a Karoshan starship if Shyrax hadn't given her the access code, but even so, it wasn't easy to find exactly what she was looking for in a system she'd never seen before.

"Release doors RG-1, RG-4, and RG-8," Varic instructed. *"Then tell RG-9 that you've released everyone else before opening their door too."*

Mell would have liked to know the reasoning first, but she followed instructions without slowing things down. She knew *generally* what she was doing, of course. She could see the screen.

All the doors marked "RG" led onto rooms filled with prisoners. Presumably, the ones loyal to Shyrax. But all the rooms from RG-1 to RG-12 were filled with prisoners, so why was she only releasing these? Why did she warn RG-9 and not the others?

She spoke into the microphone, telling RG-9 that there were free prisoners in the halls, and then she opened their door.

"Now, mind telling me why I did that?" she asked.

Behind her, Shyrax bellowed into the hallway, "You were once my soldiers! Stand, and I will instruct you one last time!"

"Did you know I used to be her bodyguard?"

"Everybody loves an easy job."

"Anyway, there are decoys in the rooms you didn't open. Fake prisoners. The one in RG-9 had been discovered, but he didn't know it."

Mell watched on the monitors as the other Karoshans in RG-9 beat one of their number into submission before moving out into the hallway.

"Now open the—Yeah, you found it."

Mell opened a gun locker nearby and the prisoners flooded into the hallway, arming themselves. "I guess that's it for me, then. You know, we could have gotten a Nova-Bot to do this."

"To do this much, yeah. But now you have unrestricted access to an enemy vessel that's still connected to the others."

Mell brightened. Though it wasn't her real body, she straightened and stuck a toothpick into her mouth.

"Great point. No emergency alerts went out, but we did stop firing…Stand by, I'll see what I can do."

Shyrax strode back onto the bridge from a bloody hallway. "Have you finished your task?"

"Great, you're here, I could use some help. We have a lot of files to sort through before they're deleted. Do you know how to identify Subspace transmission logs by their ID number?"

Shyrax hauled a body out of a massively oversized chair and settled into it. "Of course I do. We don't have long. Keep up."

Mell grinned and shared her progress.

Then she had to speed up. Shyrax really was faster.

CHAPTER EIGHTEEN

When we brought the crew members back to *The Last Horizon,* Mell was already on the bridge nearby. She was red-faced and sweating, her hair matted from the control helmet, but she held back her excitement until the other three materialized.

"I caught them!" she said triumphantly. She extended her left arm, where a hologram was projected onto the air from her console. "Someone high up in the Galactic Union is giving support to King Regent Felrex."

"Amazing!" Omega cried. "Did we need proof? Is that what we were looking for?"

"The ships are secure," Sola said.

Shyrax had her hands behind her back and stared through the forward viewport. Her uniform was still splattered with only a few drops of thick Karoshan blood. "The pattern is more troubling than that."

"Yes, but the important thing is that *I caught them,*" Mell emphasized. "Or, I mean, we caught them. All of us together. And they don't know that we know!"

I was more inclined to Shyrax's interpretation of events. "Shyrax, can you explain your thoughts?"

She turned to the rest of them. "The Captain has seen it as well, I'm sure. The Union has influence where it should not. It's not just that our enemies are working together, but that we now must question everything related to us."

"If they can influence Shyrax's fleet, that suggests that they were involved against us before we realized. What else have they done?"

I began ticking points off on my fingers. "What about my father getting selected as a representative who happens to pick up the Cannon? I assumed he was the one who engineered that situation, but now I'm not sure. What about the Subspace blockade around Sel'miroth? I thought it was odd that a D'Niss would be so quiet; they shouldn't know they have any rivals left. What about Visiria?"

Omega slithered between us all, rubbing his hands together. "Aahhh, you're saying this is now in *my* realm of expertise?"

"It might be," I said. "Tell me what you know about Solstice."

It was hard not to lower my voice when saying their name. Long habit.

"What is there to say? It's your classic shadow organization pulling the strings of the Galactic Union behind the scenes. They're everywhere and nowhere, and so on. In my more idealistic days, I thought they could be dismantled, but that time is long past. Now, I treat them more like an exploding star."

He spread six pairs of hands. "There's nothing you can do about it, so why worry?"

"If a star is exploding," Mell said, "you should leave."

Omega chuckled deeply. "Mmmm, I'm far, far ahead of you there. By about a century. I have stayed clear of Solstice and made my own way in the galaxy. But now that we have control of the most unique resources in the galaxy, it was almost certain that they would slither a few tentacles aboard."

Shyrax faced Omega squarely, though she was three feet taller. "How can we anticipate them? What will they do next?"

"I can't do that, but I'll do you one better: I'll tell you how to stop them." Omega held his hands out as though preparing to demonstrate a trick. "Are you ready? Watch closely."

He detonated his hands. They exploded into gray-black goo and splattered the rest of us.

Sola was impassive. Shyrax shook her head. Mell scooped a sample into a tiny bottle. I was the only one dry, as the goop that made up Omega's Aethertech-altered body didn't make it past my shield.

"Blow them up!" Omega said happily. "You get it?"

"We got it," Sola said.

As usual, I took over the conversation before it went too far afield. "We're flying blind here. We think there's a group working against us, unifying our enemies to put pressure on us, but we don't know what they're after or what else they've done."

Mell gave me an odd look. "Don't *you* know?"

"In all my lives, I've never seen anything where the Perfected made a bid for control of the galaxy and so did Starhammer *and* the Iron King *and* the D'Niss *and* Solstice," I said. "So far, Solstice still hasn't. But the Perfected shouldn't have ousted Shyrax for years, and Starhammer awakened those threats deliberately to eliminate them."

Horizon smiled benevolently down on us. *"But you never heard of* The Last Horizon *awakening, either. We possess unprecedented might to face unprecedented threats."*

I stared out the forward viewport, looking onto the stars and wondering what else was out there. "I can't help but think the Aether has something in store for us."

"Of course it does. The flows of the Aether lead us to glory!"

Shyrax tapped away at her console. "If we do face a situation where all our possible enemies are active at once, it only stands to reason that we should assume they are working together. We need to take them off the board."

"We've done a poor job of that so far," Sola observed. "The Iron King's gone, but the Legion is still around. We took out Starhammer, but the Advocates are still there, and the Free Worlds hate us. Not to mention the Union and the Alliance."

Mell chewed on what I assumed was a piece of gum. "If it were me, I'd want the Zenith Cannon first. You've got to have something to balance out *The Last Horizon*."

I massaged my temples, trying to push my thoughts into coherent order by force. "We have the D'Niss incursion on the edge of Dark Space, and that's the most urgent problem now. We've got to take care of that before they start eating planets. At the same time, we have to get the Cannon from my father. At least, we need to examine it. And we still need to get rid of the rest of the Iron Legion."

"We should spend our attention on the objective we can complete," Shyrax said. "We retrieve the Zenith Cannon. If we can awaken it, we can use it to accomplish our other goals. If we cannot, at least we have secured it from our enemies."

I stared at a map of the system Sel'miroth had already invaded. "That means giving the D'Niss time to spread, but for the record, I agree. We can always use more weapons against them, and we need to give time for Raion's mission to pay off. A new Titan Knight and a potential alliance with Visiria are worth it."

Omega scanned us all, stroking his short beard, and for once he spoke somewhat seriously. "I feel like we're all overlooking something here."

We looked to him. Not to speak for everyone else, but I'm as certain as I can be that we were all waiting for him to say something inane or insane.

"We have the Zenith Starship," Omega said. "We are in the pilot's seat. So we have left enemies behind us. So *what?* Let us go where we please and see who dares to face us."

Mell scoffed. "Guns don't solve everything, all right?"

The other three of us looked to each other. Sola, Shyrax, and I shared our thoughts without a word.

Mell noticed and spoke hesitantly. "Right? They don't, right? ...guys?"

"He might have a point," I said.

"Who acts first has the advantage," Shyrax said.

"They solve all *my* problems," Sola said.

Omega slid up between me and Sola, putting an arm around each of our shoulders. "You see? I knew one day we'd see eye to eye to eye to eye."

With every mention of the word "eye," Omega sprouted another one.

Sola shot his arm off.

"What are you proposing, Omega?" I asked.

"Perhaps you forget, but I've worked with your father." Omega grinned widely. "He might not act like it, but he knows when his negotiating position is worse. What do you imagine he would do if we showed up in our full power?"

I drummed fingers against the arm of my chair, thinking. I could understand what Omega was getting at, though of course the details needed to be hammered out.

Solstice may have been trying to catch us in a web, but we had the biggest sword in the galaxy on our side.

We could cut through anything.

CHAPTER NINETEEN

IN ANOTHER LIFE

I PROBABLY DON'T need to tell you that giant monster attacks aren't very common. But when you're looking over the scope of the entire galaxy, you can almost always find one.

The Titan Knights stayed busy for our whole first year.

We were formed to fight the D'Niss, but most of the monsters plaguing space were a different variety of beast. We faced down dragons, Behemoths, and monsters of every description.

On the occasions where we did face one of the D'Niss, we took things more seriously.

One that stuck in my memory was our showdown with Neth'terith, the Shadow Claw. It wasn't our first fight against a D'Niss, but it was the first one where we'd faced one of the Seven Calamities.

The other D'Niss hadn't been up to the standard of a Calamity, so we all wore our game faces that day. Parryl didn't chatter, Aelora didn't say anything about our image, and Javik pretended he wanted to be there.

For my part, I was nervous enough to be silent. No matter how many missions I ran in the Blue Titan, I still felt as though each one could be my last.

That attitude served me well, because Raion never shared it.

"Let's show them our combined power!" Raion cried over the comms. He shot forward in his crimson starfighter.

The other four of us hung back, watching him streaking through the void at the insect that hovered over a planet.

Neth'terith cast a shadow over the green world, hovering like a second moon. He looked like a black-shelled beetle, but he could impale continents on his massive horns. Space swarmed with his brood, beetles the size of fighter ships that flew out to meet us.

"Green, see if you can find a weak point in the shell," I said. "Yellow, cover Green. White, you and I are on the soldiers."

The others acknowledged before Raion sent another message. *"No, punch through! We have to hit him with passion!"*

I fought back my usual irritation and kept my voice calm as I responded. "We agreed on the plan, Red."

Even in a ship rather than his Divine Titan, Raion didn't hold back. He spiraled through the cloud of lesser beetles, which surrounded him with bullets and plasma bolts. His shield was taking a beating, but he plunged forward recklessly.

Even so, he was at least opening a hole.

"I have a good feeling about this!" Raion said. *"Trust me, Varic!"*

I ground my anger down. If we followed Raion, he was going to lose his ship and be forced to summon his Divine Titan early. Titans weren't meant for prolonged engagements, so we wanted to hit Neth'terith all at once, and as early as possible.

On the other hand, Titans also had restrictions, as all great Aethertech did. In a word, they were...proud.

You couldn't summon a Divine Titan unless you really needed it. Which usually meant putting yourself in danger.

Raion was great at fulfilling that condition.

With no more time to decide, I keyed my communicator again. "Fine, you heard Red. Follow him in. White and Green, you're backing him up. Yellow and I are on the outside."

The beetles thickened around Raion, and his fighter was seconds from falling apart. I felt like I could hear his alarm sirens through the void of space.

Parryl and Aelora shot beetles off of Raion, intercepting some shots on their shields. Javik and I hung back further, putting pressure on the larger beetles. Those would try to set up in position and take heavier shots, so we didn't give them space.

Our starfighters were insanely expensive and the product of Aethertech just under the Divine Titans, or we wouldn't have been able to do all this with only five fighters. We performed better than I would have expected from a normal Galactic Union fighter squadron.

Of course, a normal Galactic Union fighter squadron could have done what we did *without* the benefit of masterwork Aethertech, and without putting themselves in nearly as much risk. I was painfully aware of our lacking abilities. Of the five of us, the only one with a decent level of professional pilot training was the White Knight, Aelora.

Still, we *did* have access to masterwork Aethertech vehicles, so we got the job done. Usually.

On that mission, Raion's voice came through the Subline clear and cheery as ever. *"That's as far as I go! Now the time has come to face my true power, Neth'terith!"*

The giant beetle didn't respond to his words, of course. It didn't have a Subline communicator installed.

But it *did* speak to us.

An alien voice echoed in my mind. *"THIS IS NOT YOUR WORLD. MY CHILDREN WILL FEED, BUT THEY NEED NOT FEED ON YOU."*

I shook my thoughts clear before the others did, which was one benefit of magic training. There were two main reasons why we took D'Niss missions more seriously than the others.

For one thing, D'Niss feed on civilized worlds. Almost the opposite of the Iron Legion. While the Legion doesn't care where the food comes from, as long as there's food, the D'Niss will avoid barren worlds to feed on developed ones.

Sentient life is nourishing to them. A soldier that eats a sapient being will awaken itself, evolving intelligence. At that stage, they can even integrate into society, and small clusters of them did so in a few of my lives.

Those are the D'Niss soldiers, their lesser spawn that form their armies. The D'Niss themselves—the giant psychic insects—have different prey.

They eat World Spirits.

While we approached Neth'terith, emerald lightning flashed up from the green world beneath him. He blocked with gigantic claws, striking back at a field of energy that seemed to be generated by the planet's atmosphere itself.

I wouldn't remember the name of that planet for long, but I remembered the battle. It's not often you see a planet fight back.

And while the D'Niss was focused on its opponent, it could only send legions of its spawn against us. It couldn't spare the attention to deal with us itself.

That was our opportunity. One we risked wasting when Raion jettisoned himself from his crumbling starfighter, holding his Titan key high.

A red star bloomed overhead, far too soon.

The other four of us scrambled to cover him, but Yellow and White took too much of a beating. They summoned their Titans after Raion did, but at least their fighters looked salvageable.

Raion had to dodge several ship-class plasma bolts while he drifted in space, waiting for his Titan to fall. If the rest of us hadn't screened for him, he would have been shredded, even with his speed.

Once the Red Titan reached him, of course, the soldiers no longer posed a threat.

Back then, the Red Titan wasn't covered with the glowing orange veins that would later come to infect and empower it. It was pure scarlet, with broad chest armor and a design that suggested it was about to swagger into battle.

No wonder it had chosen Raion.

Wings of crimson light spread from its back the instant Raion climbed into the cockpit, and crystalline packets of energy flew out from them like a flock of birds. They swooped through soldiers, clearing them out by the hundreds.

The White Titan fell next, and Aelora's mech was smaller and sleeker than Raion's. Its wings were even larger than the ones on Raion's Titan, and they glimmered with magic. The White Titan moved in a blur the instant its pilot took control. Wherever it flew, beetles burst.

By the time the Yellow Titan arrived, Javik didn't have much to do. He flew toward the D'Niss, summoning a two-handed cannon from Subspace.

"Do we join them, Blue?" Parryl asked.

"Hold off, Green. We'll need to last longer."

Neth'terith was hammering down on the planet, and the World Spirit put up fierce resistance, shooting back with blasts of lightning that stretched into the depths of space and green shields that blocked land-cracking attacks.

But it was clear who was winning. The D'Niss didn't have a single break in its shell, while the Spirit was forced to block more and more often as we approached.

It still would have been better for us to approach more carefully, but Raion's method had its merits. The Red Titan arrived as Neth'terith struck again, and Raion ignited his crimson force-blade and struck out with the Dance of a Burning World.

At that point, Raion was hardly a master. My teacher said he might even be considered a beginner in some ways, so his technique was rough.

But his power was beyond question. In that way, he was much more advanced. A tide of crimson flame crashed into the giant beetle's shell. It roared in our heads, turning its focus from the World Spirit.

Which lifted its head, exposing a weak point for another bolt of emerald lightning. The White Titan arrived next, flying over the D'Niss and spraying a cloud of crystallized dust beneath. It looked innocent, even beautiful, as the dust refracted light from below like a diamond nebula.

It was actually a magical weapon devised from Aelora's magic and paired with the White Titan's weapon fabricators. The glistening cloud would inhibit Neth'terith's psychic impulses, as well as crawling into its shell and looking for weak points to drill into its flesh.

Javik followed up with a less-insidious weapon, the arms of the Yellow Titan collapsing into massive guns that released a barrage of heavy bullets that crashed into Neth'terith's side like meteorite impacts.

That was enough firepower to devastate a small country, but the psychic pulse the giant insect sent into our brains tasted like annoyance, not fear.

"WHEN YOU DIE, WE WILL BE ALL THAT IS LEFT."

It was not mere speech that he sent our way. We *felt* that speech, which resonated in the Aether like a spell and sounded like a promise. He spoke the language of haunting dreams, and I *saw* the threat. The promise. The truth of the world, as he saw it.

We would rot and die, and insects would crawl through our bodies. The D'Niss didn't consider us enemies, or even food. We were like the soil they crawled through, individual specks of dirt that weren't worth attention except to brush away.

Psychic attacks like that can be hard to ignore, but wizards have practice sorting through the profound meaning of symbols beyond reality. The three Divine Titans hesitated, the White Titan even shooting backwards.

In her green starfighter, Parryl didn't turn around, but her completely smooth flight gave me a bad feeling. I sent her a message.

"Green, respond! Check in! Parryl!"

The fighter kept flying forward, and the only one on the battlefield who wasn't stunned at all was Neth'terith. His shell split into wings and he came for us.

The beetle shot off from the planet, and the Spirit had to shield its inhabitants to prevent hurricanes from kicking up all over the world. A claw came down on the Green Knight like a collapsing sky.

It's hard to say it came down on any *one* of us, because that single attack would also have crushed me and probably knocked one or more of the Titans away, since Javik and Aelora were still unresponsive.

Instead, the Red Knight intercepted.

He blocked the attack that was many times larger than he was, with a sword and a massive wash of flame. His Combat Art slammed into the claw overhead, and I saw cracks form on the underside of the beetle's limb.

Finally, the Green Knight reacted. Her fighter wobbled in its course and shot off, though she didn't say anything. She still didn't respond to our communications until her Divine Titan fell from Subspace next to her.

When we received the transmission from her mech, her voice shook. *"Thank you, Raion. Thank you. I don't know..."*

"Of course!" Raion declared. *"We're friends!"*

He spoke as casually as ever, but his Divine Titan was cracked and leaking gas. Blocking that kind of attack must have drained his fuel to almost nothing and put an extreme burden on his body. If I had taken a hit like that, I would have been left unconscious at best.

My own heart pounded. If Raion hadn't gone into the fight early, we would have been able to choose our moment and would have been more prepared for the battle. On the other hand, if Neth'terith *had* gone after us in our fighters and Raion hadn't been in his Titan, Parryl would be dead.

I couldn't wait any longer. I set my autopilot to a safe distance and ejected from my cockpit.

A few seconds later, the Blue Divine Titan opened to accept me inside, gripping its massive staff. I flew in on a burst of telekinesis and sealed the hatch.

Then I began to call water.

By turning its back on the planet, the D'Niss had worsened the situation for itself. The World Spirit had gone on full offense, tossing lances of devastating green lightning that could each strike down a moon.

Now, Neth'terith had enemies on both sides. He may have been a monstrous insect, but he was far from stupid. He'd banked on taking one of us out with his first attack, and now he was mired in a fight against a World Spirit *and* all five Divine Titans.

And our performance was far better with all of us together.

The Yellow and Green Titans battered the beetle's shell with artillery while the Red Titan struck devastating blows from up close. The White Titan flew around the target, taking advantage of any gaps in the enemy's defense and screening out any further soldier attacks.

Meanwhile, I stayed in the back and covered everyone. D'Niss were capable of using magic, so my primary role was to disrupt their spells. But it would be hard for him to affect the Aether with a hostile World Spirit around, so I shifted to defense.

Focused through my staff, jets of water disrupted every move the D'Niss made. I shoved his claw to the side, blinded him, and disrupted any magical attacks he tried to make.

While the beetle couldn't use any complex spells, it relied on simpler, brute-force magical abilities similar to an Aetheric Combat Art.

This ability of the beetle's was like a flurry of plasma bolts spreading from inside its shell, a one-monster barrage that resembled a rain of fire from an entire fleet.

My water slashed through many of those balls of energy and conjured matter, bursting them into explosions in the void. Aelora dealt with most of the rest of them, breaking them on the diamond haze she spread.

When the Titans made it through, Raion spoke to all of us. *"I'm almost out of fuel! We'll have to end this in one strike!"*

"Negative, Red!" I responded immediately. "He's taking fire from the World Spirit. Drag this out."

"Blaze of glory, Blue! Blaze of glory!"

I wanted to respond that the phrase was 'going *out* in a blaze of glory,' and we were trying not to go out, but Raion had already dashed toward the D'Niss with his sword raised. I screamed into my cockpit with my communicator off, but I followed his lead.

In the end, Raion was in charge. I wasn't. He called me the team strategist, but my real role was to keep everybody alive in spite of Raion's reckless charges.

If we lengthened the fight as long as we could, Raion might have to leave his Titan. But Parryl and I, at least, had enough time to last for a while, as long as we didn't push ourselves as hard as we could.

That would give the World Spirit plenty of time to wear down Neth'terith and would exhaust him. Either the Green Titan and I could strike the final blow or the D'Niss would be forced to retreat and nurse his wounds, and I would accept either outcome.

I knew why Raion was charging. He couldn't accept the possibility that the enemy escaped. Even if we saved this world, Neth'terith would eventually reemerge to terrorize another planet somewhere else, and we might not get there in time. He wanted to solve the problem now.

I could admire that attitude in theory, but in practice, we were gambling our lives on an uncertain outcome instead of taking a plan with a higher probability of success.

That battle had one of our more dramatic outcomes. Raion put all his Divine Titan's remaining power into a strike from the Dance of a Burning World, the Green Titan merged her guns together into a giant cannon and unleashed the pinnacle of her own Combat Art, and the White and Yellow Titans revealed their own greatest weapons.

With no other choice, I unlocked the full might of the Blue Titan's staff. Its panels split apart, hissing with magical energy, and I leveled the weapon at the D'Niss.

This was as much an Aethertech weapon as it was an elemental one. Not only did it gather and compress conjured water straight from the Aether, but the device in the staff accelerated the spell to just under lightspeed.

It was the sort of Aethertech that was restricted in several ways—I had to summon a Divine Titan to use it, for instance—and could only be used in dire straits, but the reward was proportional to the restrictions.

A red wash of flame was blocked by the beetle's magic.

A yellow barrage of missiles cracked that spell.

A green shot broke the spell and landed on the shell beneath.

A white crystal drilled into the shell and split it open.

And finally, a blue lance of water so compressed that it resembled a laser sliced through the D'Niss. My spell split the beetle open, slashing it apart on the inside.

A psychic death scream washed over the entire system in a pulse as the D'Niss died. It wasn't as focused as a sentence—it felt, instead, like a mournful cry, one that forcibly made me feel regret for my enemy.

As insect guts sprayed into space, I found it pretty easy to push that regret aside.

"Great job, team!" Raion transmitted, and I could hear his beaming smile. *"By the way, could someone pick me up? My Titan's gone."*

Only then did I realize he was drifting in space. Our combat armor could support us in void combat for a while, but not long. With no Titan, no ship, and—knowing Raion—no energy left, he was drifting helplessly.

I dismissed the Blue Titan and called in my own starfighter. I was the one to pick him up. On the way back, I chastised him for being too reckless. We could have won with much less risk.

But if we hadn't rushed in, the fight would have lasted much longer. The planet below was in danger, and we *couldn't* let the enemy go ravage another world.

It was hard to argue with Raion when his heart was pure and when the other Titan Knights agreed. If we were an actual military organization, Raion wouldn't have gotten away with that.

But we weren't soldiers. We were heroes. And Raion's way had worked.

That was nice. For as long as it lasted.

CHAPTER TWENTY

Benri Vallenar had chosen a neutral location for the meeting with his son. Well, supposedly neutral.

The planet was a gray blob, a nondescript world called Beshkin. It was equally far from everything, covered in fog almost everywhere, and no one kept any surveillance on the system because it produced nothing of value.

The Vallenar Corporation had few outposts in the system, so Benri had proposed it to Varic and been accepted. He had promised his son not to interfere with the location and had emphasized that there was nothing he could do anyway. It wasn't as though he planned to ambush the crew of *The Last Horizon*.

Seconds after that call ended, of course, Benri was doing his best to prepare the board to his advantage. He had crews fill the system with surveillance, tiny insect-sized drones to fly around the meeting-place in swarms, even weapon-equipped satellites in orbit, disguised as useless, outdated relics.

Just in case.

As for his team, he recruited the best Aether Technicians and enchanters employed by the Vallenar Corporation. Thirteen of them, not counting a half-dozen guards. The Zenith

Starship had room for all of them, and Benri didn't intend to be outnumbered.

Which left him with only two problems remaining.

First, he had to decide whether to send a clone. It would make sense to use one of his long-term duplicates, created by the Mirror of Silence, except Varic could inexplicably see through them.

Not to mention that Benri *wanted* to go in person. This was a chance to inspect the interior of *The Last Horizon* and potentially awaken another Zenith Device as well.

Next, Benri had to advance his other objective.

Which was much more difficult to do without alerting Varic. In fact, most of his protective measures—the satellites, the drones, the employees preparing the landing location—were more like decoys.

Even his acquisition of the Zenith Cannon was a sacrificial play. Benri had grander aims.

The Iron King had showed him the scale on which his magic could operate. While Benri didn't have the computing power of a galaxy-spanning hive mind, his ambition had been awakened.

This meeting with his son would be his first test. If he could pull it off, the wealth of the galaxy could be at his fingertips.

So, in a way, the second problem solved the first. Benri *had* to show up in person.

There was too much at stake.

He and the Vallenar delegation had set up camp in their landing zone, a nondescript plain in the middle of a swamp. The advance team had swept the land, fabricating a platform and driving off the slithering reptiles and strange, flightless, crawling birds.

The local insects were repelled by a spell, and the air regulated by simple air conditioning units that hummed on the center of the platform. It was muggy and hot outside, smelling faintly of sulfur, but it would be crisp and cool for their meeting.

With all of this preparation, they could have met on a ship, but Benri and Varic had come to an agreement. They would meet on a planet, one with a World Spirit known for its neutrality.

If nothing else, this would prevent Varic and his ship from using any world-level powers. Eurias and any high-ranking interference from *The Last Horizon* would incur the wrath of Beshkin itself.

Benri, of course, had taken several steps to insure himself. A mercenary strike team hid nearby, hidden by Aethertech and—crucially—*not* magic. The few local inhabitants had been joined by Vallenar Corporation employees, in disguise and ready to leap into action at Benri's command.

Also, Benri was recording everything from as many angles as he could. Whatever story he wanted to tell about this meeting, he would be able to.

He and his team arrived first, as agreed, and they began arranging the landing zone in preparation for the Zenith Starship's arrival. One of his oldest friends and advisors, a half-Aethril with a few stars still sparkling in his gray hair, consulted a spell-circle of sight and then let out a heavy breath.

"I don't see any problems," Teranon said. "But that doesn't mean there won't be any. Ben, this is a dangerous game."

"You think?" Benri adjusted his tie again, which was a darker gray to stand out against the light gray of his suit. "And here I thought there was no risk at all."

"I'm scared enough of your son on his own. With *The Last Horizon* added in..."

"Don't forget the Rebel Queen of Karosha and the Fallen Sword," Ben said. "At least the Titan Knight is supposed to be on Visiria."

Teranon levitated a chair over with telekinesis and sat down. The assistants were still setting up a meeting-table with twelve seats, though theoretically they would all enter *The Last Horizon* as soon as possible.

"*Supposed* to be," Teranon emphasized. "Teleportation magic changes everything. We can't trust where anyone will be. They could be on the planet now!"

"You searched for them, didn't you?"

"If Varic sealed out my scrying magic, they could be standing right in front of me and I might not know."

Benri glanced around at the planet's omnipresent fog.

"Well, I don't see them, so let's not assume they're lurking in every shadow."

With abominable timing, something huge crashed through the trees about a hundred yards away. He saw only a silhouette through the murk, but it looked like a whale breaching the surface of an ocean.

And this wasn't an ocean. It was a wetland.

Benri's hand jerked toward his wand, and he was comforted somewhat to see Teranon reacting the same way. The creature gave out a long, mournful cry.

"We're taking care of the local wildlife, sir," one of his security officers informed him. "Don't want any interruptions."

Benri didn't want any heart attacks either, but he didn't say so. He checked the clock on his console. "I want to be prepped for their arrival an hour early. I'd rather wait around than miss this opportunity."

"There's no more magical preparation we can do," Teranon reported. "Mages are in place, and the investigation team is ready to board."

Employees scurried around, placing furniture and checking equipment, but the clearing was secure. Benri waited.

It wasn't too long before the first alarm sounded.

"Coming out of Subspace!" one of the techs reported. "Arrival in seven minutes."

When Teranon pointed it out with a spell, Benri looked into the sky and saw the tiny spark that must have been *The Last Horizon*. He drummed his fingers on his thigh and then stopped himself.

"Get into place," Benri ordered. "They could pop out of nowhere at any second, so I want us waiting for them."

That ended up being unnecessary. Frivolously as they used teleportation, they had chosen to approach the standard way this time.

The Last Horizon was an impressive starship, at least five hundred yards long and shaped vaguely like a predatory bird in the middle of a dive. Its dark metal plates were so organic he could almost believe they were crafted by the Iron Legion, and it shone with magical light at every joint.

As the ship approached, its lights were orange, though they faded to a blue-green as the Zenith Starship landed on the edge of the clearing and settled slowly into the mist.

Benri calmed his heartbeat, straightened his tie, and awaited his son.

When the mist billowed away from the clearing, like a blanket removed by the World Spirit itself, Benri gritted his teeth. Varic had decided to make an *entrance*.

A ramp slid smoothly down from *The Last Horizon,* and the first one out wasn't Varic. It was Sola Kalter, the Fallen Sword, in full armor. It was like the perfected version of standard Galactic Union combat armor, gray and smooth, with all the intricacy Benri associated with masterwork Aethertech.

Her green visor gleamed as she scanned everyone in the camp, marching down the ramp with echoing steps. Guards held their guns at the ready, not quite pointing them at her, but their eyes were sharp.

She ignored them completely, walking forward until she reached the table in the middle of the clearing.

Benri gave her a smile. "Miss Kalter, pleased to meet you properly for the first time."

"Clear," Sola said.

Queen Shyrax the Third strode down the ramp of *The Last Horizon* afterwards. Benri thought the doorframe flowed aside to avoid hitting her head, because she walked with her spine straight, and her hair-cables radiated golden light into the gray planet around her.

"Benri Vallenar of the Vallenar Corporation," the Queen said as she approached. "We've never met, but I know of you by reputation."

"I'm humbled, Your Majesty. Of course, it would be hard to find anyone in the galaxy who doesn't know you, and I'm honored to make your acquaintance at last."

Benri had personally done business with hundreds of Karoshans, if not thousands, but there was something about Shyrax that reminded him of how tall she really was. She loomed over him, and when she dipped her head in greeting, it almost seemed like she was looking down to check if he was still there.

"We will work more closely when I regain my throne from the usurper Felrex," Shyrax said, and Benri had already started tapping into the half-dozen statements he'd prepared in case the topic came up.

She didn't give him room to speak, though. "Where are those who would enter *The Last Horizon?* I wish to see them before I give them leave to enter my ship."

Benri noted the phrasing and couldn't be happier about it. If Shyrax was the one in charge of the ship, or even if she had made a play for control over *The Last Horizon,* that meant Varic wasn't in charge. Benri had leverage to use.

At worst, at least he wouldn't have to deal with his son anymore. Shyrax was far preferable.

Benri stepped back and swept a hand at the pack of scholars in blue-and-silver standing behind him. "We've gathered some of the greatest experts in the galaxy to witness your examination of our weapon, and hopefully to contribute in some small way."

Queen Shyrax looked over his team and gave no visible approval or disapproval, though his team straightened themselves under her gaze.

"I permit you to come aboard *The Last Horizon,*" Shyrax said. "These thirteen of you. Follow me."

Benri knew how many people were on his team, but he still counted to make sure he was understanding correctly. "My apologies, Your Majesty, but would it be possible to bring a few guards as well? No disrespect intended to your protection, but I'm sure you understand."

"Do you really imagine these few humans could keep you safe if I wished you harm?" Shyrax asked. She was still walking away.

That had nothing to do with it, and indeed Benri knew that any attempt at self-protection once inside the Zenith Starship would be nothing but delusion, but he had planned to make this stand in order to make Varic look bad on camera.

Now that he was negotiating with Queen Shyrax, he had to pivot.

"As you wish, Your Majesty. Let's go, everyone, you heard the Queen."

He could hardly be blamed for giving into the demands of royalty, and this set the tone in a way he could manage. *The Last Horizon* had insisted he come in unprotected. He could be made to look very reasonable in contrast.

As Benri and his team walked up the boarding ramp into the Zenith Starship, he knew he wasn't the only one recording. He also wasn't the only one, he was sure, overcome by a sense of awe.

Though he had boarded this ship before, he'd only had a chance to see one or two rooms before his son had forcibly ejected him. Now, every light fixture on the ceiling and every smooth curve of the hallway was endlessly fascinating.

Ordinary starships tended to have imperfections, signs of age, of budget restrictions, of material limits. The interior of *The Last Horizon* looked perfect, as though it had been constructed yesterday exactly according to the image of its creators. It almost looked fake, it was so perfect.

The hallway flowed gently upward, and Benri couldn't help but notice that there were no doors anywhere.

That was consistent with his imprisonment, at least. Horizon had kept his door locked, but when he grew too demanding, she—or perhaps Varic—had made the door itself vanish.

Shyrax did not pause as she reached the end of the hallway, and a dark metal door hissed to one side to allow her entry.

The rest of them followed after, Benri on her heels, as they entered the bridge of *The Last Horizon*.

While the doorless hallway had been designed to show them as little as possible, this was almost sensory overload. The oval room had a wide spread of glass as the viewport, so clear and wide that it looked like nothing more than a single layer of glass.

The consoles beneath the forward viewport had no chairs, their controls minimal and their screens bright and clear. Benri supposed the crew was meant to stand, though the consoles seemed sized for a seated human.

Monitors overhead displayed normal diagnostics information that he would expect from a starship, though his Aether Technicians were raising their wrist consoles and openly snapping pictures. There must be *something* interesting.

After his quick glance around, Benri had come to a stop and faced the one chair that sat in the center of the room.

"Quite a ship you have here, Varic," Benri Vallenar said to his son.

Varic lounged in a large, padded chair with small screens on each armrest resembling the controls of a personal console. He wore his mantle with the hood down, and his shield amulet shone orange on his chest.

Lazy silver eyes looked Benri up and down, and Benri repressed the urge to snap at him to straighten up.

But Shyrax had come to stand behind the captain's chair, hands behind her back and gaze straight ahead. Clearly, she was deferring to Varic, so Benri could do no less.

"Welcome back, Dad," Varic said. "You didn't stick around long enough for the tour last time."

Once again, Benri ground down his first response and gave his business smile instead. "One of my greatest regrets. Before we start, you don't mind if my team looks around, do you? I'm afraid they'll turn on each other like starving canines if I don't let them go."

"Of course not. As we agreed, make your way around the bridge." Varic waved his hand. "Stay away from the controls and don't leave the room. For your own safety."

Teranon shifted uneasily at that, but none of the rest of the team did. They scurried around, whispering excitedly to one another and examining every surface.

"You want to get started, or would you rather look around first?" Varic asked, as though he didn't care.

Benri had his son figured out. He *needed* the Zenith Cannon and was trying to pretend he didn't.

That was the perfect mindset to take advantage of in a negotiation. Especially because Benri was frustrated enough with the supposed Zenith Cannon himself. He had already gotten everything out of it that he could, so he had nothing to lose by getting rid of it here.

Nothing to lose except a headache.

Benri had everything to gain, and he was playing for a greater prize anyway. *That* was where his nerves came from.

Not that he showed any of that to his son. "Are you going to eject me this time? If so, I'd rather have the tour before you strand me on the planet."

"Well, *I'd* rather get this over with," Varic said. "I'll show you around afterwards."

"You'll pardon me if I don't take you at your word."

"No, I won't."

While Benri was still processing that, Varic leaned forward in his captain's chair. "I've given you my word, so you'll take it. Now bring out the Cannon."

Benri gave him a withering look. "Look at you. Your mother would be embarrassed. Not even basic courtesy."

"Oh, I'm sorry, it seems we had a misunderstanding. Did you want to visit your son? Or did you want to meet the Captain of *The Last Horizon?*"

"I was under the misapprehension that I could do both."

"It seems you were. So, if *you* were the Captain of the Zenith Starship, what would you do if someone walked into your ship, brought up past grievances, addressed you by name, and corrected your manners?"

"If it was my father, I would expect no less," Benri said. As far as this conversation went, that was true. Benri's father would have been less lenient than Benri himself.

"I see." Varic tilted his head back. "What do you think, Commander?"

"You've shown more tolerance than I would have already, Captain," Shyrax said. Golden eyes stayed on Benri. "A visitor who approached me in that manner would have found themselves outside the ship by now."

Benri feigned surprise. "I'm sorry, Your Highness, clearly I misunderstood Karoshan culture. I thought you emphasized respect for your elders."

"My mother was Queen Shyrax the Second, and when she urged me to give up the throne in favor of the usurper Felrex, I threw her from the room with my own hands. There is respect due the office."

"I find myself thankful for the correction, Your Highness," Benri said, bowing to her. "As your Commander says, Captain, I did not show you the respect due your station. Forgive me."

Once again, Benri could twist this so that he was giving into Shyrax, not Varic, and no one could be blamed for that. Also, for a second—arguably third—time, he was the reasonable one while the crew of *The Last Horizon* were putting forward unreasonable requests.

Varic wore a slight smile as though he understood exactly what his father was doing and was amused by it, which irritated Benri far more than giving into Shyrax had.

"Fine, that was annoying anyway," Varic said. "So let's get to the Cannon."

Benri stood up straighter, adjusting his tie. "Before I can reveal the location of the Zenith Cannon, I must make sure—"

Varic looked up into the ceiling. "Horizon."

From the solid metal overhead, a swarm of lights—tiny orbs of various sizes, all made from blue magic—swooped down and swirled around the room. An organic platform appeared next, and it wasn't until the platform was fully revealed that Benri understood these were magic-crafted hands carrying a woman.

The spirit of *The Last Horizon* stood between the palms of the magical hands, her form woven from a rainbow of colors. Her horns were gnarled roots, she held seven-pointed stars in her eyes, and she smiled serenely on her guests.

"Greetings, visitors. I am the World Spirit of The Last Horizon, *and I welcome you aboard. Though I must warn you not to take your investigation too far. Only the paramount heroes of the galaxy are worthy to walk my halls, but you have been permitted greater leeway through the mercy of my Captain. Do not test the limits of our patience, all right?"*

She gave a motherly smile, but as her eyes swirled around the room, Benri's entire team bobbed their heads into nods. Including Teranon, which was frustrating. He had seniority over everyone in the room except the Zenith Starship itself.

For some reason, Varic looked like he was fighting not to roll his eyes. "Horizon, would you bring out the Zenith Cannon please?"

Benri felt proud of himself when Horizon gazed off into the distance and frowned. He had prepared for her teleportation magic, and even assumed she could sense other Zenith Devices.

There were decoys scattered around the camp, even in orbit. Clones made from the Mirror of Silence.

He couldn't copy a full-power Zenith Device, of course, and even these low-quality replicas wouldn't last for long. But they were all inside cases magically and technologically sealed from detection, so they would show up the same on even the most sensitive scanner.

"I'm sorry, Captain," Horizon said. *"Something appears to be hiding the Cannon from me. It's nearby, but…"*

Benri treasured the look of surprise on Varic's face.

"Really?" Varic asked. "Well, Dad, I've got to say I'm impressed."

Benri was about to explain himself—and gloat over his victory—when Horizon frowned further.

"Yes, it's nearby, but to retrieve it I have to push through some primitive and simplistic magic. I don't even want to interact with such a crude and ill-formed spell. But for the sake of following your orders, I'll tolerate my disgust."

A case appeared next to her, floating on a hand of blue light. *"Here you are, Captain. The case they thought could hide the Zenith Cannon from me. Would you like me to open it, or would you prefer to do the honors?"*

She gave Benri a look of superiority, but Benri was mostly confused. He had only put up those spells to test her. It wasn't much of a surprise that the Zenith Starship could find it. Why the theatrics? A World Spirit couldn't be so petty.

Varic was hiding his eyes behind his hand, but his voice was even as he spoke, "I'll get it, Horizon, thank you."

Queen Shyrax turned a blank look to Horizon, and Benri thanked the Aether that he wasn't on the other end of it. Oblivious, Horizon happily handed over the case to Varic.

The case unlatched itself in Varic's hands as though Benri hadn't locked it at all, revealing the Zenith Cannon.

CHAPTER TWENTY-ONE

*"*Throw me away *already!"* the gun shouted, in the voice of a young woman. She sounded frustrated. *"You'd better start listening to me. I've blown up planets!"*

That was enough for me to identify it was a genuine Zenith Device. Not that you couldn't make a convincing talking gun, but someone faking the article would have given it a more...*imposing* personality.

Instead, it already sounded like she was annoyed and complaining.

Which crashed my heart into my stomach. This wasn't a prerecorded message or a security feature. The Zenith Device was awake.

The Zenith Cannon didn't look like anything you would normally call a cannon. At least in this form, she was a standard plasma pistol, one that looked somewhat similar to my own Lightcaster IV.

It was sized for a human's hand, with an external shell of white metal and a few intricate pieces of machinery visible beneath the outer plating. Its inner workings didn't resemble anything of the plasma pistols I was familiar with, though that was to be expected.

More importantly, I didn't see any explicit magic circles, but I did notice the weapon's weight in the Aether. The Zenith Cannon sat inside the case in my lap, but it seemed to take up extra space. It made me think that this was the original pistol, perfect in ways that normal weapons were not, though there was nothing specific I could point to besides wizardly intuition.

"You must be the Zenith Cannon," I said. "I'm Varic Vallenar, Captain of *The Last Horizon*. You're not dormant, are you?"

On cue, Horizon drifted over to gloat. Her smile stretched the bounds of her face and her eyes gleamed.

"Ah, it seems my adorable little sister is awake after all!"

The gun jerked in its case. *"Horizon! Seal yourself and then talk to me that way! In fact, lend me a mortal, and we'll duel! I'll blow your hull to pieces!"*

"If only you could, but alas, all the mortals are mine." Horizon leaned down onto me, resting her head on my shoulder. Her immaterial horns sank into my skull with an odd tingling sensation. *"I already selected all the best ones. That's what happens when you sleep in too long..."*

"Human! I'll let you fire me as long as you shoot her!"

"I'm not going to do that. But Horizon was certain you would not be awake, so I have a few questions for you."

"I only have answers! And that answer is shoot Horizon."

"I'm not going to do that either," I said. "But I do know a few people you might like. Before you meet them, why don't you tell me something: What woke you? You said you didn't have a qualified wielder, so it wasn't one of them."

"It could have been a passing candidate," Horizon proposed. *"Someone she missed."*

"Well, it wasn't! First thing I knew, I was awake. In a collection. *There was nothing to shoot, so I managed to talk a maid into throwing me away."*

I tried not to shiver, since my father was watching. "So if I were to ask you what woke you...?"

"The Aether, I guess. Who cares?"

I slowly turned to look at Horizon, whose head was still on my shoulder. She cleared her throat and didn't meet my eye. *"That's hardly what we're here for, is it? Where is my Engineer?"*

"That's a good question," my father said. "And thank you for confirming that we are indeed dealing with the Zenith Cannon."

He was watching me with a strange look on his face, as though he knew more than I did. He often *tried* to look like that, but this time I believed him. Which I did not appreciate.

"I didn't give them anything!" the Zenith Cannon cried. *"They didn't deserve the words of a Zenith Device."*

My father winced. "If only that were true. The only way to get her to stop talking was to lock her in a case. Now, your Technician may take a look while we examine *The Last Horizon,* per our agreement."

Horizon must have signaled Mell because she entered the room at a full-on sprint. All I saw was a flurry of white coat and brown hair before she scooped up the case from my lap. "It's real? It's *real!* Hello there, are you the Zenith Cannon? You can call me Mell! Where's your battery?"

While she spoke, Mell tore the cannon out of the case, tossed the case aside, and turned to a Nova-Bot who held a box the size of a standard food fabricator. She popped the pistol into the box and then slammed the door, tapping several buttons on the side.

There came a hum from inside, along with chattering from the Zenith Cannon. *"Whoa! Are you the one I was supposed to like? Because I don't! I don't like you! You don't smell like guns at all!"*

"That's hurtful," Mell said casually as she checked the readouts of the box against a holographic document on her console. "Tell me, are your systems adaptive, like Horizon's? Shadow Ark's don't seem to be."

"Ark is here? How did Ark get a mortal before me!? Let me see him!"

"If you can give me a full readout of your...internal structure..." Mell drifted off as she read what the box was telling her.

"Do you want to talk while the Technicians do their work?" I asked my father, in a token attempt to distract him.

He snorted. "I'll be right here with my ears open. I want to know what your Engineer is saying."

According to the terms of our agreement, his own Aether Technicians needed the opportunity to watch any examination we did, but his team had examined the Zenith Cannon already. They were bustling around *The Last Horizon* as though afraid they could be kicked out any second.

I had implied to Mell that she ought to hold back what she shared with my father, but I couldn't instruct her to do anything stronger under the terms of our agreement. I began to wonder if that implication had been lost on her completely when she answered eagerly.

"Her interior is folded space! Like Shadow Ark, as far as I can tell. There's *way* more to her interior dimensions than I can measure. It's like you folded an entire dreadnought into the size of a plasma pistol. Without increasing its mass!"

"So Shadow Ark is the same way," my father murmured. He shot me a victorious look.

I didn't care as much as I pretended about leaking information. I wanted to control what my father learned out of a general desire to inconvenience him, not because it actually cost me anything.

However, I had to assume that anything learned here would make it back to Solstice, so there was a limit to what I was willing to give away. That was why I restricted their inspection to the bridge; Horizon could move anything too interesting to deeper parts of the system.

I did wonder about something, so I glanced back to the other Aether Technician on my crew. "Would you like to take a look?"

"We will learn all we need to know soon enough," Shyrax said.

Which could mean that she trusted Mell to uncover all the pertinent information or that she was confident we would be able to keep the Zenith Cannon on the crew. Or some combination of both.

The box beeped, and Mell scowled into it. "It's deeper than I can read. Horizon, can I take it to the—"

"Nope," I interrupted. "Not yet."

Mell reluctantly pulled out the Zenith Cannon, who was still talking. "One *dreadnought!? I'm worth at least* three *dreadnoughts, and I have firepower beyond that! And you said you were going to introduce me to—Who's that?"*

Sola had followed up the rear of everyone boarding *The Last*

Horizon, and had stayed on guard duty outside the bridge until Horizon signaled her to come in.

On sight of her, the Zenith Cannon squirmed in Mell's grip. *"Let me see, let me see better! Now,* that *is someone who smells like a gun."*

"Is the Fallen Sword an Aether Technician with a gift for guns?" my father asked.

"No, but she could certainly be considered an expert," I responded. "Sola, would you mind?"

"As long as you know you're still mine," Horizon put in quickly.

Sola stood over the Zenith Cannon in an instant, but she knelt and took a long moment to inspect the weapon as it quivered in Mell's hand.

"I am the Zenith Cannon! Now, a quick quiz before I see if you're worthy of wielding me. How many ships would you say you've blown up?"

Sola shrugged.

"That was the correct answer! *Congratulations, you've passed all the trials to wield the Zenith Cannon!"*

Horizon looked down in sheer contempt. *"So sad. Do all my younger siblings have such low standards?"*

Sola turned toward Horizon, and Horizon gasped. *"Wait, no, my Sword! Of course I would never suggest that it was low standards to select* you, *I was only—It was that she chose too quickly!"*

The Zenith Cannon cackled as Sola picked her up reverently in both hands. Sola's armored hand slid around the Cannon's grip, and she held it up to inspect it from every angle.

"How is it?" I asked.

"This is the best weapon I've ever held," Sola said.

I knew that was true, in a literal sense—it was, at least, the most *valuable* weapon anyone had ever used. But to have Sola respond so immediately was surprising to me. She hadn't even fired a shot yet.

"You are my favorite mortal ever," the Cannon said. *"Forget Horizon. She has too many mortals already. Carry me, and there's no limit to the things we could shoot."*

Sola didn't decline immediately, so Horizon wailed and threw herself on gray armor. *"My Sword, no! I'm sorry! I didn't mean it!"*

Horizon's form was weightless, so Sola ignored the weeping World Spirit as she moved the Zenith Cannon up to fire.

I probably shouldn't have been giving my father any more information, but we *had* made an agreement and I was curious, so I conjured up a spinning magic circle across the room.

"Free target," I told Sola.

She fired immediately. Orange plasma bolts streaked across the room, blasting into the center of my spell. They looked like normal plasma bolts to me, and all the shots clustered together so tightly they were touching one another, but I expected nothing less from Sola.

As far as I could see, Sola could have done the same thing with my own Lightcaster or any other pistol in the galaxy, but she hefted the Cannon with obvious appreciation.

"Do you have a name?" Sola asked.

The gun shone brightly in her hand. *"I am the declaration that all things must end, the cure to stagnation! The end of the unending! I am Mortal Edict, and together we will bring death to the deathless!"*

We had already known the Cannon's ID from interrogation of Horizon, though we'd had to pry it out of her. She had been more than happy to help us seek the other Zenith Devices, but it seemed that asking their names was expressing too much personal interest for Horizon's comfort.

The legends, of course, had many names for the Zenith Cannon. One for every planet, it seemed. But without another Zenith Device, we would never have known which was the original.

"What do I have to do to take you with me?" Sola asked Mortal Edict.

"Abandon my sister!"

"And you have more modes than this, don't you? Horizon does, and Mell said there was more to you than meets the eye."

Edict cackled again. *"I'm the full armory of the Zenith Era! You've never seen a dreadnought with* half *the firepower I've got."*

Sola looked to me. "I want her."

Horizon's sobs grew louder.

I looked to my father. "It's a promising start. But I did say I'd give you a chance. Do you have a candidate for the Zenith Cannon?"

"We've tested every—"

Edict cut him off. *"They don't! They've barely* seen *a gun. And they don't know how to have a conversation either!"*

"We brought in veterans from across the galaxy," Benri said. "Aether Technicians with weaponry gifts, masters of pistol Combat Arts, soldiers with unique compatibility for Aethertech guns. She gave us lengthy lists of all their flaws. And many personal insults."

"Zenith Devices have standards!" the Cannon insisted.

Horizon flowed over until she was standing upright next to Sola rather than weeping on her shoulder. *"That's right. And one of those standards is to select* unique *heroes from among mortals and not to share them."*

"I can't help it if you don't appreciate talent."

Horizon swelled up with anger, so I cut in. "I hate to say it, but we do have another gun guy. Since Edict is awake, he deserves a chance."

"Not while I'm onboard," Benri said immediately. "You think I'd trust my safety to the Grave Hound?"

"I agreed not to allow him to enter the room unless you permitted him. But I can stop him from shooting you."

"You think I'd trust my safety to *you?"*

"Games aside," I said, "he won't hurt you."

To his credit, my father bit back his obvious gut instinct to argue with me and took a moment to compose himself. "You're responsible for him."

"You can come in, Omega."

He immediately popped out of the shadows behind my chair. *"Finally!* Give me the gun!"

Benri staggered back and pointed. "You said he wasn't in the room!"

"He wasn't. Sola, you have to give him the—Sola!"

Sola had the Zenith Cannon pointed at Omega, who was completely ignoring the threat, partially liquefying himself and sprouting eyes to view the gun from every angle. "Mmmm...I can see it, I can *see it!* Oh, the cities we could burn down with this! The planets we could pop like bubbles! It's like an entire fleet wrapped in an artillery platform wrapped in a *gun!*"

Tears ran down his one human eye and he wiped them away. "It's so perfect. Edict—may I call you Edict?—please allow me the honor of cradling your flawless form."

"I changed my mind," Mortal Edict said, and Sola pulled the gun away.

"No," Sola said.

"A*hem!* The young lady wishes a new dance partner."

Sola pulled the trigger, but the Zenith Cannon refused to fire.

"You did agree to this," I reminded Sola.

As slowly as if her armor had rusted at the joints, Sola gradually handed the Zenith Cannon over to Omega.

He gasped and held it up in both hands, as though he were lifting up an infant rather than a weapon. "Glorious, *glorious!* In my hands, I cradle the fires of the first suns, and all will burn before our might! Captain, give me *targets!*"

Omega whipped the gun around before even finishing the question, and—despite the orders binding him—I was a bit afraid that his recklessness was going to result in dead Vallenar Corporation employees.

I tossed out six more circular seals around the room at once, putting them at random as much out of haste as out of a desire to test Omega.

He fired so fast that it sounded like one shot, and by the time a trapped plasma bolt sat at the center of each circle, he was already rubbing the Zenith Cannon against his cheek.

"I revoke my position as Pilot!" he cried. "You can take it, Vallenar. I don't need you to take down Solstice. I'll do it myself."

Horizon dropped to her knees and wailed again as my father looked at me hopefully.

"He can't do that," I said.

Benri gestured to Horizon. "I didn't think so. So why is she..."

"I don't know. Let's chalk it up to trauma. But while some of the details need to be hammered out—" Sola was pulling a heavier weapon out of storage, for one thing, and I wasn't sure how long Omega had left to live. "—it seems the Cannon has chosen us."

"So it does," my father admitted.

Which was enough to make me suspicious.

If he was going to give up so easily, what else did he have planned?

CHAPTER TWENTY-TWO

I WATCHED MY father's ship leave and chewed on my suspicions. He hadn't done anything.

Or rather, he had done exactly what he said he would. He and his team had examined the Zenith Devices, stuck to their word, and left. Certainly, he'd tried to bargain for more, but I had expected something else.

"You were right not to trust him," Shyrax said. She stood next to me by Horizon's docking ramp, and her body shaded me from the setting sun.

"You didn't catch what he was doing, did you?" I asked.

"I'm certain he did something."

"So am I." I glanced to my other side. "If the three of us didn't catch him, he didn't do anything. Which can only mean that he had another motive for being here that we don't know about."

Horizon scowled up at the departing ship, even shielding her eyes with her hand as though to block the light. *"Well, we ended up with a Zenith Device, insufferable as she may be. We certainly came out ahead in the exchange. Now, let's put her in storage and never speak to her again."*

My father had left too easily, given that effectively he had shown up, donated the Zenith Cannon to us, and then flown away. He should have been furious.

"I still have some contacts among the Corporations," Shyrax said. "I will monitor Benri Vallenar's behavior."

I sighed. "We'll find out what he's planning eventually, I just hope it doesn't cause us too much trouble."

"Nothing the best Zenith Device can't handle! Her and her crew, no other Devices required."

"Horizon, you were perfectly happy to help us look for the others," I said. "You can't be surprised that we want to use them."

"Not you. You're taken. She'll have to settle for someone else besides the six of you. What about the little fortune mage?"

Shyrax's footsteps rattled the ramp as we all marched up. "She cannot handle the burden of a Zenith Device."

"Then she's better than my sister deserves."

"We're going to have to find someone qualified for Mortal Edict if we want her help," I said. "That goes for Shadow Ark too."

No sooner had the boarding ramp stopped shaking than the hallway of *The Last Horizon* trembled around us, but this time it wasn't Shyrax's fault. An angry male voice vibrated through the metal.

"Ah, I see that *someone* finally remembered me!"

I wondered again whether the galaxy-shaking power of a Zenith Device was worth putting up with its ego. "Ark, we already had this conversation."

"You still haven't found a single mortal for me! And no planets! Not even a moon!"

"It's been two days."

Shyrax glanced between Horizon and Ark. "I wish to talk to your parents about how they raised you."

"Why would we need a Shadow Ark?" Horizon gave her brother a smug look. *"We have no reason to hide."*

I was glad, at least, that the Cannon wasn't here to contribute to the sibling squabble. "At the risk of repeating myself, Horizon, you're the one that encouraged us to track down your brothers and sisters."

"Because there can be no nobler quest, not so you can abandon me for a position beneath you." She waved a hand in Ark's direction. *"Give him a Nova-Bot. He settled for one already, didn't he?"*

Shyrax turned to face the wall. "None of us have time for this." With a casual gesture, she punched through Horizon's Zenith Era alloys with a fist that shone yellow. When she withdrew her hand, she was clutching an obsidian-and-violet jewel that rattled in her grip.

"Stop that!" Ark shouted. "Release me! Don't test me, or I will burst your flesh from within!"

"Your utility is worth more to me than your pride," Shyrax said. "I will be your guardian."

Horizon's face seemed to melt, and tears appeared streaming down her face as though she'd been weeping for minutes. *"My beloved Commander, do not do this! I dreamed of the day we would—"*

"Stop. I've had enough. My people have been away from Karosha for almost two years now. They deserve a place to rest in safety, and a hiding-place the Perfected cannot infiltrate. Not to mention the strategic value of a secure staging ground against the D'Niss. We need Shadow Ark, and we have given him plenty of time to choose someone. Instead, I choose him."

Ark wrestled free of Shyrax's grip by phasing through her fingers. "I will be no one's second choice!"

"Be honored that I have chosen you at all."

"This is a vile betrayal! A tragedy! You cut my heart out, my Commander!"

"I said this is the *end,*" Shyrax declared. The metal of the ship vibrated again, this time with her voice. "Perhaps you have mistaken this for a game, or a child's dance where we may bicker over partners. This is war."

I felt that it was time I made my support known. "Several planets have evacuated ahead of the D'Niss invasion. Raion left their safety to us. Would you rather spend the next few months ferrying refugees to shelters, or would you rather we take care of them all at once?"

Horizon's neck creaked as she turned to look at Ark, as though her spine had rusted. I couldn't read the Zenith Colony's expression while he was in his jeweled form, but I got the impression he was making a similarly distasteful expression.

"We should discuss it with the crew first," Horizon said. She looked like she wanted to spit something disgusting out of her mouth.

"Have I fallen so far?" Shadow Ark muttered. "Is this why no one remembers me?"

Horizon snapped her fingers, purely for dramatic effect, and the four of us reappeared on the bridge. Mell and Sola were already there, with the Cannon resting in Sola's lap.

"Oooh, look at her face!" the gun cried. *"This is going to be embarrassing, I know it."*

Horizon teleported the Cannon away with nothing more than a glare, and Sola threw up her hands in frustration. "I was *just* getting her to open up to me."

"I have an important matter that requires the attention of all crew," Horizon said formally. *"Omega will be here in a moment, but I am transmitting the audio to him as we speak."*

Omega must have refused the teleportation. I briefly wondered why, but most of Omega's actions defied rational explanation.

"My Commander has offered to take on the responsibilities of Shadow Ark's guardian. I know this may come as a shock to—"

"Finally!" Mell shouted. "It was *killing* me to waste a Zenith Device."

Sola nodded once. "Good thinking, Shyrax."

Horizon pulled fistfuls of her hair out. *"This is a slap in all our faces! She is abandoning her responsibility to us to serve as a glorified lookout!"*

Shyrax's hand rested on the hilt of her force-blade. "Who is forsaking her responsibilities?"

"No, wait, that…I was speaking dramatically. A figure of speech, nothing more."

"Do you believe that there is one single soul in this galaxy who can be trusted to fulfill their duty more than I?"

Horizon's form shrunk by the second. *"I spoke too hastily only as a measure of my passion for keeping you! Dedication to my crew!"*

"Do you suggest that I have insufficient dedication?"

Horizon's eyes flickered as she tried to think of a response.

Shadow Ark buzzed as though clearing his throat. "I would like to withdraw my previous objection."

"That is more wisdom than I have heard from you thus far." Shyrax glanced back over the rest of us. "Are there any further objections?"

"I wanted to activate Ark months ago," I said. "We will need a planet for him, though. Somewhere unclaimed, preferably uninhabited, that can support your people."

Shyrax lifted her fist, displaying a magical ring. "My advisor has a suggestion." A misty form flowed into a bearded human man standing next to Shyrax, straightening his mantle.

He dipped his hooded head to me. *"Archmage Vallenar. It was one of my research projects to document nascent World Spirits as they begin to form. I have continued my research even in my current state, and I believe I am aware of a young World Spirit on the edge of the Karoshan Alliance that would be delighted to host a population, even temporarily."*

Mell squinted at him through her glasses. "What's wrong with it?"

"I have other suggestions if it doesn't suit your taste, but I believe the planet would be perfect for your needs. It also so happens to have a dense supply of local Aether." He shot a subtle glance my way. *"While our troops settled down on its surface, it would make a wonderful place to demonstrate some magic. I happen to know the World Spirit herself is also interested in the Aetheric craft of mortals."*

Ah, so Melerius was angling for a lesson from me. Well, I owed him one. And if Shyrax had remained quiet through his explanation, that meant he was telling the truth.

"No objections from me," I said. "I owe lessons to a lot of people, and this is a good chance to start clearing my debts. I am a little hesitant about heading back into the Free Worlds, though, given the state of the Advocates."

The door to the bridge whisked open and Omega responded to me as naturally as if he'd been standing there all along. "Ah, Captain, but doesn't marching boldly back into enemy territory add to the *thrill?"*

He practically danced onto the bridge, and the rest of us stared. Because he wasn't alone.

Lemon walked arm in arm with him, though the arm she held was an extra limb sprouting from his back. She elbowed him in the side. "Don't call it enemy territory! We will rebuild the Advocates, stronger than ever."

The short human woman had a cross-section of a lemon tattooed on her bald head, and she wore a suit different to the one I'd last seen her in. This one had yellow mixed into the normal blue-and-white of the Advocates, and instead of the stylized 'A' on the chest, hers bore a sleek 'L.'

Sola toyed with a gun, and I couldn't tell if it was an idle tic or if she expected to use it. "How long have we had an Advocate aboard?"

"I won the duel!" Omega said proudly.

Mell clapped halfheartedly. "Raion knew you could do it."

"Does that mean you'll be traveling with us for a while, Lemon?" I asked. I had mixed feelings about that. I suspected Lemon would cause a distraction.

"I can't. Omal picked me up for the day because you were in teleporter range, but I'm too busy to stay long."

Omega extended an extra arm to wrap around her shoulders. "Every second with Lemon is precious!"

"Omal?" Mel muttered. She'd probably never heard Omega's real name before.

"Glad to have you aboard, Lemon," I said. "I wish you well in rebuilding the Advocates."

She waved a hand. "That's not what has me short on time," she said, though I deliberately hadn't asked. "A cult is trying to free a demon king from his ancient seals. The short story is that I have to win a tournament and break a prince's curse."

"Oh. Well...good luck with that."

CHAPTER TWENTY-THREE

The planet Basyrryx was one of the few on the border of the Alliance that was supported by a World Spirit but had no civilization. There were a few historical and political reasons for it, but it came down to the planet's position in the galaxy rather than any aspect of Basyrryx itself.

The outer side of the planet's crust was largely uninhabitable, due to a toxic atmosphere trapped by rolling yellow clouds. However, beneath the crust was a vast cavern system spanning the entire planet, even the oceans.

Because of those properties, it had more habitable area than most civilized worlds, but the only ones to take advantage of it thus far had been a few ecological surveys and a scattered handful of mining operations.

And since we were passing by anyway, the planet had made the best first donation to Shadow Ark.

The Zenith Colony claimed to be picky about the planets he added to his internal system, and he was still upset that there were no sentient inhabitants of Basyrryx. He needed people to take his power closer to Horizon's.

But the refugees of several nearby worlds, the ones fleeing the

D'Niss advance, made up for that. We'd directed thousands of ships, hundreds of thousands of people, to shelter inside Shadow Ark. Some remained floating in his endless obsidian-and-violet sky, but most landed somewhere on the planet.

That made Ark happy, but it made the planet itself even happier.

The World Spirit of Basyrryx, a young-looking woman in a golden dress, had the desperate edge of a bored child who had been left alone for far too long. She was *ecstatic* to be included in the Zenith Colony, especially when she knew it would mean she would get visitors. And maybe even permanent residents.

All of which made Basyrryx the perfect location for my impromptu magic classes.

We stood on the edge of a cliff inside the planet's endless caverns. The sky was distant stone held up by incomprehensibly massive pillars of rock. Chasms stretched down into the abyss, and the space dwarfed us; as far as I could see was nothing but open cave until it vanished into the distance. Of course, since that was all the planet had to offer.

Vegetation was anything but sparse, as moss covered most of the rock and trees crawled up stone columns, even growing down from the ceiling. The leaves of the upside-down trees put a green filter over the golden light that shone down from titanic clusters of crystal overhead.

By magical means, the crystal stole sunlight from the world above, enhanced it through the Aether, and poured it into the underground world so light could flourish. Even based on my limited knowledge of World Spirits, I knew it must have taken Basyrryx millennia to perfect a mechanism like that.

Water rushed in unseen rivers below and trickled down the ceiling, giving the sounds of distant rain as a backdrop to my class. Birds sang and wheeled through the air, though the closest ones were huge, oddly furry, and seemed to have simian tails with patches of feathers.

"Are we going to be safe here?" I asked, peering out over the edge.

Horizon gave me an astonished look. *"Are you worried for*

your safety? What sort of wildlife could overcome a hero of The Last Horizon*?"*

"If something happens to one of my students during a class, it's my responsibility," I said. "And as far as I know, the air could turn into acid at any second."

A girl's voice echoed through the caverns, loud enough to send dust, leaves, and rain shaking down from the ceiling. "No, it won't!" Basyrryx protested. "I fixed that problem centuries ago!"

I bowed in the general direction of the voice. "That's reassuring," I lied. "And quite an honor to have you as an audience. This will be the first time I've ever taught a class to a World Spirit."

A Karoshan mage straightened her purple mantle and gestured to the two at her side. "Have you ever taught royalty before?"

Shyrax's twins, a boy and a girl, stood at her side. They were only a little over six feet tall, and Prince Rellask vibrated with excitement at the thought of learning magic from me. Princess Nasharia winced in embarrassment at her tutor's question.

"Yes," I said. In another life, I had taught *these* royals before. The twins were Shyrax's oldest children, so I'd spent the most time with them, but I'd also taught the set of quadruplets that were their younger siblings.

The twins were only the 'third' and 'fourth' Prince and Princess due to the complications of Karoshan inheritance, and considering the circumstances with King-Regent Felrex, I had no idea where they actually fell in line for the throne. Not that it mattered to their magical education.

I'd died before I had a chance to teach the youngest batch of Shyrax's children, the triplets who, even in this life, were a secret from the galaxy.

Karoshans have a lot of kids.

Instead of explaining myself, I clapped my hands and began. "About time we get started. I promised to demonstrate my magic to you this time, didn't I?"

I hadn't spent much time teaching anyone in the last six months, but I gave lessons every once in a while, when I had free time.

Usually, I focused on filling in the missing gaps in my students' magic or gave them a grounding in basic theory.

As you might expect, most of the questions they asked were about me. What kind of magic did I get? Where did I learn it? What did it feel like, having six sets of memories?

I had avoided answering more out of a lack of interest than out of any discomfort, but I couldn't put them off any longer.

And there was another drawback to waiting so long. The longer I put them off, the bigger my class grew.

Not only did we have Mariala Brechess and her crew from the Magic Tower, five professional mages who had given up their previous responsibilities to follow me around in the hopes of improving their magic, but we had the Karoshan prince and princess as well as their "guards."

The Karoshan soldiers assigned to protect them on this assignment were all mages, and there were six of them, which was far more than it would actually take to protect them. With me around, any more than one babysitter was redundant, and I happened to know Shyrax had only assigned one.

The others were doing a poor job of pretending to be focused on their charges. One had already raised a hand to ask a question, though I gestured for him to give up and he sadly lowered his hand.

On top of those, we had a World Spirit and a ghost. My guests of honor.

Basyrryx hadn't physically manifested, but she was still listening. Melerius, Shyrax's advisor, floated on the front row of the class. Her daughter had borrowed the ring that contained his spirit, and Melerius looked even more eager than the rest of the students.

"I'll start with my specialty," I said. "Binding and sealing magic." I swirled my wand, and a simple magic circle of six basic Aetheric symbols formed in white light around the tip.

They muttered, even though what I'd done wasn't that impressive.

"Protection magic is one of the most common in the galaxy. Some say *the* most common. It has many names—abjuration, shielding, warding—but the traditions all overlap. The point is that the intention of the magic is protection, and the difference in each tradition comes in *how* that protection is evoked."

I saw a sixteen-legged bug crawling down a tree close to the group, and I used the chance to demonstrate my spell. I flicked my wand, nailing the bug to the wood with a semi-transparent nail of white symbols.

"In my case, I interpreted that protection as *sealing* dangerous elements out and *binding* them in place." The insect squirmed against my binding, which was disgusting, so I dismissed the spell and hurled the bug into the distance with telekinesis. "For many, that would be two different magics, but those limitations come down to your definition of your spells. In the early days of my training, I read as many accounts of previous wizards as I could, and I found one who had managed to define his magic with both functions."

"Does that mean you learned two magics at once?" Prince Rellask asked eagerly.

I had, but not in the way he meant. "Not exactly. The magic I mastered can be phrased in a few ways, but effectively it comes down to 'keeping things out.' Sealing them out and binding them out are the same thing, if you think about it the right way."

I threw up a new magic circle, drew my Lightcaster, and fired a few shots into it. The plasma bolts stuck in the center, hovering as though I'd caught them with telekinesis. "Naturally, there are quite a few uses to that, if you get creative."

This time, I understood when they started taking notes on their consoles and snapping pictures. What I'd done this time was more visually impressive.

"The way I saw it, binding and sealing are the same thing. One of the things you'll often see me do is shield myself, but what I'm really doing is *sealing* dangerous elements out."

I angled the seal up into a second magic circle, which I conjured nearby. Then I released the plasma bolts. They flew from the first circle and pinged off the second, streaking into the distance.

"If I were truly a shield mage, my protective magic would be much stronger. In fact, when I'm in a large-scale battle or facing enemies that can hit hard—like the Iron King, or Starhammer—I need to reinforce another defense, or my magic is much weaker. That's the reason for my shield amulet."

I pulled my amulet out and showed it to them. "This is carved from a shield crystal, which is one of the more popular materials for defensive magical items. There are a few smaller ones on the prince and princess' clothes."

They glanced down at their own jewelry in curiosity. They would have known there were protective measures on their clothes, of course, but this would give them a new appreciation for the craftsmanship that had gone into their safety.

"The pinnacle spell of my discipline is the ultimate expression of sealing magic, a spell that binds a target from every angle into an isolated section of Subspace." I was swirling my wand as I spoke; it was difficult to cast a pinnacle spell non-verbally, and I'd have to chant a few of the syllables unless I wanted to stand in silence for several minutes.

"It locks away every aspect of a victim, from their powers to their physical strength, their connection to the Aether, even their thoughts. I call it Absolute Burial."

Another sentence or two of chanting, and I unleashed the spell on a nearby tree.

Surrounded by six white magic circles, the tree was instantly compressed into a fist-sized ball.

"There are a few weaknesses to this spell," I continued. "Like any spell, it's best when the user understands its limitations and strengths thoroughly. In this case, it's relatively slow and can be resisted. When I used it on the Iron King, for instance, it tried to seal the entire Iron Legion across the galaxy. Of course, I failed. I had to cut the King off from the rest of the galaxy and then run down his magic resistance mechanisms before I could seal him."

Melerius was stroking his beard and staring into the distance as though he'd come to some conclusion, but the Karoshan mage in purple raised her hand. "Did you keep the Iron King around? You don't have him sealed somewhere, do you?"

"That's classified," I said, "but no. We killed him." Before she could ask further, I emphasized myself again. "We *definitely* killed him. Now, water elementalism!"

I conjured a ball of water over my hand. "This one is relatively straightforward. We all understand elementalism, right? You tie yourself to a particular natural substance and develop your ability to conjure it from the Aether and control it."

Water played in a ring around my hands. "Many elementalists emulate strange examples of their element from across the galaxy, and this can be a very effective tool, though limiting. For instance, I originally intended to bind a unique element to myself, one called the Astral Tide. It naturally occurs in the Farwing Nebula and carries many times more weight than natural water. If you compress it, you can crush worlds."

They murmured appreciatively, especially one of the Magic Tower wizards, who I knew to be a fire elementalist.

"But a special element like that can *only* be conjured, it can't be found naturally. Binding it to my magic would have made me less flexible in controlling physical water, leaving me dependent on conjuration, and—an even more practical concern—the Astral Tide isn't drinkable. So I opted for the less-deadly but more-flexible emulation of natural water."

There were a few more questions about water elementalism, mostly the practical concerns and applications of elemental combat, which I answered while sketching more symbols into the air.

After the questions subsided, I concluded my spell by calling on the Lagomorph Contract. A Voidhopper leaped out of nowhere, the utterly black rabbit blinking its star-like eyes at the students curiously.

More than a few of them said *"Awwww."*

"Summoning magic," I went on. "It can be frustrating to face down a summoner because you never know what they're capable of, but there are a few limitations to remember. For one thing, summoners all have to bind themselves to a certain category of spirit, which is known as signing a Contract."

The Voidhopper hopped forward…but also stayed where it was. Now there were two dark rabbits, blinking at the students. One scratched its ear.

"As spirits, they're manifestations of the Aether, not biological beings. They manifest their physical forms naturally around the galaxy, in places where the Aether becomes tuned to the concept they represent, but their presence in our reality is more like a digital avatar. Their true existence is beyond us to affect."

This time, the Voidhoppers divided again. Four of them hopped curiously around the students, who were starting to look nervous.

"There's a way to guess what powers a summoner has," I said. "Can anyone tell me what that is?"

I directed that toward the younger mages, but it was Melerius the ancient Archmage who answered. "Spirits are bound to their fundamental concept. They have powers derived from their nature, as each spirit is but one expression of a grander symbol."

"That's…correct," I said, and the ghost looked unduly smug, given that he'd answered a first-year summoning question even though he was centuries old. "Put more simply, rabbit summons—for instance—can do things that rabbits are often known for. Like multiplying, although Voidhoppers take that quite literally."

There were sixteen dark bunnies hopping around now, and some of the Karoshan mages had their wands out.

"This summon actually has properties manifested from two rabbit myths: their tendency to multiply and their ability to show up out of nowhere. Voidhoppers can traverse Subspace in short bursts and hit with quite the force. Also, as you noticed, they multiply exponentially."

Thirty-two rabbits were enough to make the point, so I banished them. "When you see what a mage can summon, you can make a guess about their capabilities. I couldn't summon a rabbit that could swallow you whole or spit fire, for instance, those not being associated with rabbits."

"What about using a gun?" Mariala asked. She'd seen my summons in action before.

"Burrow Guardians are an interesting case, actually, as they draw from the rabbit's defensive mindset—their reliance on warrens to hide and protect their young—and filter it through humanity's idea of a guardian. Which has become the Galactic Union's power-armored soldiers. It's a good example of how flexible summoning can be, and how these symbols can shift over time."

Next, I covered my pathfinding magic, which was governed by a few consistent principles. The destination had to be knowable, and there had to be a route to get there. The pinnacle spell, the Cosmic Path, could be used to navigate starships to destinations in entirely different star systems.

As expected, there were questions about that too. Normally, range was limited by the ability of the caster, and it would be difficult for me to reach into another system even with the help of Eurias.

The navigational magic worked by using information I *could* have gained in my current location, which led us to the Mirror of Silence spell.

That was the one that took the most difficulty to explain, as the copies created by the Mirror of Silence were constructed from the Aether based on possibilities.

Possibilities that really existed? Not necessarily. The Aether realized those possibilities in the forms of short-lived clones.

That's always a tough concept to sell. Especially when some of the copies could be realistic and serve as decoys, such as the ones my father used. Also, the Mirror of Silence was more of a single spell with capacities that had been expanded to rival an entire discipline, rather than a collection of magic with complementary principles, so I had to explain that.

All of which took about half an hour just for that spell on its own. Shyrax's son had begun poking at a hissing ball of fur as one of his guardians tried to stop him, but the rest of the audience was still engaged.

"What about the hands?" one of my students asked. "I saw you conjure hand-shaped constructs. That wasn't water magic, was it?"

"That one may be even harder to explain than the Mirror of Silence, since I didn't develop it myself." Though I said that, I had been working with the Terminus Mundi magic for six months now, so I had a solid grasp on the theory.

Not as strong as my other magics, since I'd had a lifetime each to practice with those, but still not bad.

"It's memory manifestation magic," I said. "A unique expression from *The Last Horizon*. If I have enough of an impression of a person's abilities, usually from experiencing them myself, I can imprint them onto a magical pseudo-world that holds their memory. Then I can manifest them in the form of that individual's hands and eyes."

Horizon projected her body into the lesson to gaze around proudly, horns tilted back.

"Why hands and eyes?" one of the Karoshans asked, which was the expected question.

"The technical answer is that a spell emulating an entire person would require far more of the Aether than if it only manifested half of them. Also, like a computer, the world of Terminus Mundi is limited in its storage. Remembering their eyes and hands is more energy efficient."

I glanced at Horizon before adding, "And I think those are the details Horizon notices the most."

"How do mortals interact with the world?" Horizon asked, unashamed. *"They take it in with their eyes and influence it with their hands."*

"So be careful or she might decide to collect your hands," I said. Princess Nasharia tucked her arms carefully behind her back.

I glanced around at our surroundings, which were noticeably less lush now that I had demonstrated my spells on them. Even the pathfinding demonstration had become somewhat violent, as I'd tossed spells to the students and had them shoot targets I indicated, to show them how I had once used that magic in combat.

"Now you know what I can do," I said. "You can see how it's hard to balance everything, even for me. Maybe especially for me.

My strongest instincts might come from a life as an elementalist, so I'll react with water, even if summoning magic may be more efficient. My thoughts get crossed, so sometimes I look back on a battle and see ways I could have handled things better."

That was another reason I carried a gun, especially for the first year or so after my ritual. Most of my lives had the reflexes to shoot things.

Melerius scowled like he was working through a problem, stroking his beard furiously, and he looked like he should be huffing on a pipe. He spoke up the moment there was a gap in my speech. "That's only six, but there are seven of you."

"The sevenfold Archmage!" Horizon declared.

"Ah. Yes. Thank you for reminding me," I said, though I felt quite the opposite. "In the life where I worked for your mother, Prince and Princess, I developed a more...dangerous magic."

I had recaptured Rellask's attention.

"Is that your ultimate technique?" he asked eagerly.

I made a note not to let him spend any more time around Raion. "It's curse magic." Mariala darkened, and if she had a beard, she would have been stroking it like Melerius.

"In that life, it served me well. I didn't need firepower because the rest of the Karoshan Royal Guard certainly had that covered. I needed magic that could weaken and disable intruders under specific conditions while not harming those under my protection. Unlike pyromancy, for instance, curses can be targeted very precisely."

Pensively, I considered the sealing spell that was active in my body every moment. It locked away my curse magic, keeping it at bay.

"Of course, I never had any cause to determine how it would affect any *other* magic I learned, as that only became possible for me in this life," I said. "Curse magic is highly compatible with other spells, to the point that I had to seal it off. I can no longer use it."

"It's too deadly?" the Prince asked in excitement.

"No weapon is too deadly to use against the Iron King," I said.

"But if I released curse magic, *all* my magic would become cursed. For one thing, that would mean that I would have to learn all my spells from the beginning again. My greatest weapon is my familiarity with my own magic, not my firepower.

"At the same time, it would pervert the effects of my other magic negatively. My seals would cripple shields rather than enforcing them, my water would be toxic, my pathfinding would..." I wasn't sure about that one, but I had a few educated guesses. "...lead me to dangerous locations. I shudder to think what the Mirror of Silence would do."

Prince Rellask's eyes were sparkling, and I was afraid I had sparked his interest in curse magic.

"It has its uses," I conceded, "and one day I will likely come up with a solution to use it safely, once I have the time for careful experimentation. But access to more magic is hardly my greatest concern. I haven't figured out the full extent of everything I can *already* do."

"What about what we can do?" Melerius asked. He drifted up to me expectantly. "I very much admire the scholarly spirit of an Archmage continuing to explore the Aether, and I wonder if you would lend me your suggestions..."

I was more interested in training the younger mages, as they would be the ones who determined the future strength of the galaxy.

But at the same time, I will admit some curiosity about Melerius' soul magic. Considering what had happened to me during my ritual, there was some possibility to learn more about the Mirror of Silence by examining his spells.

Still, I turned to the student mages. "Now you have another opportunity to observe an Archmage of a rare magic discipline. Watch how he demonstrates his spells, and I'll get to each of you in turn."

The ghost drew himself up proudly and began lecturing as he sketched runes that evoked spiritual magic, but I only listened with one ear.

It felt wrong to be there, casually teaching class, while the galaxy fell apart around me. I supposed the lessons I was teaching would help Shyrax with her Perfected infiltration, at least indirectly, but the D'Niss were still feeding on planets out there.

Not to mention Raion, working alone on Visiria.

Shadow Ark and the entire planet of Basyrryx were still accepting a steady flow of evacuating ships, so we weren't just sitting around, but I couldn't make myself feel better about it.

I didn't like leaving a crew member alone, even when I knew he could handle himself.

Until we got back into teleporter range, Raion would be fine.

CHAPTER TWENTY-FOUR

Raion wasn't used to being a diplomat, even to his own people.

He was used to interviews, of course. Everyone wanted to speak to the Titan Force. But he was typically the one they sent to kill the monsters, not to talk anyone out of anything.

He looked forward to the challenge.

Thus far, it hadn't been so bad. He wasn't sure why his teammates always tried to talk him out of diplomatic missions. He'd shaken hands and exchanged greetings with every important person on the planet of Visiria, with third eyes shimmering like gemstones of all varieties and skin tones that ran the entire spectrum of red.

The hardest part was remembering all the names. Raion enjoyed the talk, the dinners, and meeting all the potential future friends.

There was one thing that concerned him: he sensed very little friendship in any of them.

While that wasn't unusual, it saddened him a bit. He was a stranger, after all, and he understood that true friendship took time and trust to build. But none of them had any level of faith in him to speak of.

And one of those diplomats was his own brother.

Ryzer Raithe was the most prominent member of the Raithe family, and *he* was the diplomat. While he was shorter and softer around the middle than Raion, he had an easy smile and he traded stories with almost everyone they met.

He rarely left Raion's side, and while the support was appreciated, Raion suspected Ryzer was trying to make sure Raion didn't do anything too extreme. It almost seemed as though Ryzer was guiding him toward something.

In a duel, Raion had a good sense for when his opponent was backing him into a corner.

But Raion could accept that. He hadn't been home in a long time, and Ryzer had people of his own to protect.

Other than his slight doubts and his strained memory, Raion thought his days as a diplomat went rather well. But those were the warm-up.

Finally, the day came for his meeting with the Planetary Governor of Visiria. Raion adjusted his red suit—a formal one made for court meetings, not anything he would wear into a battlefield—and smiled up at the Prime Arena of Visiria.

He had never fought here himself, but it was one of the hallmarks of the planet. He found it fitting that the Governor had wanted to meet here.

While Raion was enjoying his first sight of the Arena, Ryzer grabbed him by the arm and pulled him toward the steps. "Try not to look like it's your first time here, all right?"

"It *is* my first time here!"

The guards on duty at the doors glanced at him, so Raion nodded respectfully back. They whispered to one another, and Raion caught his name.

That could only be good news. They'd heard of him!

As this was the entrance for the employees and VIPs, it didn't resemble the entrance to any arena Raion had ever visited before. The doors of gold and glass slid open, ushering him into a vast hall designed to resemble a cathedral.

The floors were polished marble, and shadows flickered across the stone surface. Raion peered down to look more closely at the unnaturally moving shadows to see that they were Horellian shadefins, living fish made of shadow. They swam inside the marble, swirling around Raion's feet as they checked to see if he had any food.

Columns shifted from white to red as he passed them, and golden symbols began to slide down their length as though liquid gold was pouring down from the ceiling. They formed letters that he thought looked like Aetheric symbols, but he was no mage.

He pointed to them. "What are those?"

For some reason, Ryzer looked like he didn't want to answer, but eventually he gave in. "They're meant to greet powerful fighters. They get brighter and more elaborate based on the estimated combat level of the person visiting."

Gold gushed from the ceiling faster and faster, and the red light had grown so bright that Ryzer flinched back from the columns.

"Amazing!" Raion exclaimed. "I can't wait to see what they look like when my crew gets here!"

Ryzer grunted and pulled him forward. The columns were spreading golden wings, and even some of the staff hurried out of their stations to come look.

Raion was happy to see that. They must have a good work environment if they still enjoyed the sight of something they saw every day.

In addition to the fish and the columns, they passed white stone statues of arena fighters. Men and women—mostly with the three eyes of the Visiri, but here and there a Karoshan or Lichborn—that held weapons at their side or otherwise posed as though about to head into battle.

As Raion passed, the statues turned to look at him. They met his gaze and dipped their heads toward him.

Raion returned the gestures, making eye contact with each one, even though there were dozens in rows on each side. It would be rude to ignore them.

His brother tried to pull him faster, impatient to get to the

Planetary Governor. Raion didn't want to make her wait either, but he wouldn't be rude to the statues. There wasn't an emergency, after all.

"You're embarrassing us," Ryzer muttered. "These are just robots."

"No, they're not!" Raion said cheerily.

Even Raion wouldn't have returned the greeting of a robot. He wasn't insane. That would be like waving to a painting.

He saw intention in the eyes of the statues, and he felt a slight hum of goodwill from them. When they saw him, they trusted him.

"Who are they?" Raion asked, though he had a guess.

"I don't know," Ryzer said.

"Really? I'll look it up, then."

"We don't have time!"

An elderly man shuffled out from between the statues, all three eyes wide in astonishment. He followed the gaze from the nearest statue to the Raithe brothers, then hurried over to them.

"I've never seen all the champions awaken!" the old man said. "Excuse me, gentlemen, but who *are* you?"

"Raion Raithe, Knight of *The Last Horizon!*" Raion put fists on his hips, but he missed the fireworks behind him. He hadn't brought them in his business suit.

The old man breathed in sharply. "No wonder, then. No wonder." He slowly straightened his spine and bowed. "Gelbus Griffiss, Curator of the Hall of Champions. It's an honor to meet you, Champion Raithe."

Raion, of course, returned the bow. "It's an honor to meet you, too, Champion Griffiss!"

Gelbus gave an embarrassed laugh. "No, not Champion, no. I never fought in the arena."

"Neither did I!"

"But you're a Champion nonetheless." Gelbus met his gaze seriously. "I know what you did in the Titan Force, and I think I understand something of what it takes to be chosen by a Zenith Device. Besides, it seems all the other Champions agree."

The white stone statues up and down the hall had all turned to regard Raion. Ryzer shivered and looked pale, for some reason, but Raion kept his attention on the Curator.

He put a hand on the old man's shoulder. "And you're a Champion too! What are you, if not a Champion of this exhibit? Every time a visitor learns about the history of this Arena, it is another victory for you!" Raion beamed. "You're undefeated!"

He was a bit embarrassed when he saw tears form in Gelbus' eyes. The Curator bowed deeply again as he backed up from the Raithe brothers. "The stories did not do you justice. Worlds go with you today, Knight."

"And with you!"

Raion walked away proudly, but Ryzer was quiet. He didn't stop Raion from greeting the remaining statues, and when they reached the door at the end of the hallway—a pair of elaborate doors set with moving silver scenes of arena battles past—Ryzer signaled for the employees not to open the doors yet.

He moved closer to Raion, lowering his voice. "Listen, Raion. There's a few...The Governor doesn't..."

Raion felt a little more friendship from his brother. It was small, barely there, and it flickered in and out of existence like a flame in the wind.

But, as Raion had learned many times before, a small flame could one day become a mighty blaze.

"...I don't know how this is going to go today," Ryzer said reluctantly. "But remember that you can always retreat, all right? If you feel like you're cornered, you don't *always* have to fight."

Though they were in the Prime Arena, Raion didn't think his brother was talking about an actual fight.

Nonetheless, Raion smiled at him. Their friendship had stabilized. It was a small spark, but it didn't seem as likely to blow out as it had a moment before.

"I'm not afraid!" Raion said.

Ryzer tensed in a way that Raion recognized. He was about to say that Raion didn't understand what he was getting himself into.

But Raion had seen more than his brother realized.

"Ryzer," he said. "I'm not afraid."

For a second, Ryzer's expression melted. He was uncertain, hesitant. He even looked like he was going to be sick. But their friendship grew ever so slightly.

Raion put a hand on his brother's head and ruffled white hair, as he had when they were kids. Ryzer protested and moved away, but Raion strode toward the doors.

The employees weren't ready to open them on such short notice, so Raion pushed them open himself.

"Raion Raithe, Knight of *The Last Horizon*, here for a meeting!"

CHAPTER TWENTY-FIVE

The Planetary Governor, Nelula Seiren, was a grandmotherly Visiri with pale, pink skin and hair spun up into an elaborate nest. Her hair, ears, neck, and wrists shone with gold and rubies, and her third eye glowed bright red. That was said to be good luck.

She smiled fondly at Raion's entrance, spreading gloved hands as though to greet him with a hug. "Raion Raithe, at last! I've heard so much about you!"

Raion took the gesture as an invitation and moved up to throw his arms around her. "What a warm welcome!"

"Oh! Well, this is a warmer welcome than I'm used to, as well."

He backed up, smiled at her, and only then took in the rest of the room. It was also wide and high-ceilinged, with paintings of arena battles covering the walls. The far wall was dominated by a floor-to-ceiling window looking out over the Prime Arena.

Today, there was no battle on the field below. The stands were empty, but it was still a grand sight.

Raion had watched footage of the Prime Arena since he was a child. Now he was there.

After tearing his attention away from the Arena itself, he turned back to the others. There was a circular table at the center of the room, and Governor Seiren wasn't the only one sitting there.

A half-dozen other men and women were gathered around the table, all Visiri. None of them looked like they had ever fought in any arena—they were dressed in expensive suits and dresses, the few weapons they carried were decorative, none of them were in fighting shape, and he didn't sense any of the intentional movements that would come from experienced Combat Artists.

They watched him enter the room, hug the Governor, gaze out the window, and then turn to them. All the while, their gazes felt slimy on his skin. He smiled at them anyway, though he knew there wasn't much point to it.

In Raion's experience, relationships that began that way rarely blossomed into friendship. Especially when none of them introduced themselves.

Until Raion put hands on his hips and gave his own name again. At that point, Governor Seiren gestured to the room and they all stood in turn to introduce themselves.

Raion did his best to remember their names, especially because the few he recognized were quite famous. They were influential leaders of business from all over Visiria.

When they were finished, Governor Seiren smiled tenderly at Raion and gestured to a pair of empty chairs opposite her. "Have a seat, boys. Don't worry about them, they're here as witnesses. Think of this as a private meeting between us."

Ryzer smiled more brightly than Raion now that he was in his element again. "You might have to hold me back. I've been dying to ask for some investment tips. Senator Krakal, what do you think?"

Chuckling passed around the room, and Raion smiled politely, though he didn't understand the joke.

"We'll all have plenty of time to get to know each other once we've settled our business," the Governor said. Raion and Ryzer sank into their seats, and Seiren gave them a sad smile.

"I hate to start this off on such a sour note, but it's best to get any unpleasantness out of the way first. I'm afraid the Senators are not very happy with you right now, young Raion."

That was disappointing to hear, but Raion didn't fully understand it. He frowned. "Why not?"

"Well, the actions of your crew haven't exactly painted us in the greatest light, have they? You fought the Iron Legion, which is of course very admirable, but you also attacked a Galactic Union battlegroup, assaulted the Grand Hive in the Dornoth system without permission, and took up with the Rebel Queen of Karosha."

Raion considered that. "I don't think we actually attacked that battlegroup, but I wasn't involved. Otherwise...Yes!"

She blinked. "Yes?"

"Yes, we did all that! Is that all?"

"Regrettably not. Your conflict with the Advocates..." She shook her head. "There are many among the Senators who believe you and *The Last Horizon* dragged the honor of Visiria through the mud, and I can't say they're wrong."

That shook Raion, but he could see the misunderstanding. "Oh, I see! No, at first I thought what you did: that the Advocates were the good guys. It turns out that many of them were corrupt, including Starhammer. We fought him, not everyone. Once we beat him, we left the Advocates alone."

"Hmm, yes, we heard some troubling rumors about Starhammer. But while his reputation was intact, he led a fleet with the official support of both the Galactic Union and the Karoshan Alliance to capture you. Your resistance cost the lives of thousands of innocent citizens."

Governor Seiren tilted her head to gaze at him as though over a pair of glasses, though she wore none. "You do remember that we of Visiria remain prominent members of the Karoshan Alliance, don't you? What does it say to the galaxy that one of our planet's proudest sons is siding with traitors?"

Raion frowned and stared into the table. He was getting that feeling again—the one that said he was being backed into a corner.

The Planetary Governor didn't act like an opponent, but he was growing more and more certain that she *was* one. And, unlike in an actual duel, he couldn't see the attacks coming.

It was also becoming clearer that Ryzer wasn't going to say anything. He sat with arms folded, looking troubled, but he didn't say anything in Raion's defense.

Not that he could, necessarily. He didn't know anything about *The Last Horizon* or its actions. But Raion still felt that something was wrong.

"We did all that to protect the galaxy," Raion said.

Governor Seiren sighed in disappointment. "I can see how it might look that way to you, Raion, but how can we take that on trust? How can we show the planet, and the galaxy, that you really do have their best interests at heart?"

"It saddens me to hear that the people of Visiria don't trust me," Raion said gravely. "I will work harder to earn that trust. But you can rest assured that, whether they trust me or not, I will never stop fighting for their protection."

The others around the table looked to each other, passing a sentiment he couldn't read. He wondered if he had scored a hit, or if they felt he had opened himself up for a strike in return.

The Governor beamed and reached out to pat his arm. "That's wonderful to hear, Raion. Exactly what I expected from you. You see, I've thought of a way for you to demonstrate your sincere heart."

Raion straightened. He still suspected a trap, but he was interested.

"The Prime Arena, Raion!" the Governor said, clearly pleased with herself. "I didn't want to meet you here just because of the unbeatable view."

A few of the others at the table chuckled, including Ryzer, though he seemed to be forcing himself.

"There is no cultural institution more respected than the arenas, and the Prime Arena most of all. Show your resolve by defeating the representatives of the Senators who doubt you, and I'm certain they would withdraw their objections."

At first, Raion brightened. Fighting for the honor of himself and his crew was exactly what he wanted.

But after a moment of thought, he smiled and shook his head. "I'm sorry to let you down, Governor, but I can't do it!"

Ryzer stared at him in utter shock, though the Governor only looked disappointed. Raion felt he had to explain himself.

"I wish the people trusted me, but if I'm going to fight for their respect, I would rather fight the ones who deserve it! I fight to protect them, not to defend myself! Besides, winning in the arena won't show my heart to the people on the Subline. Only my opponent will feel my sincerity."

Ryzer looked as though he'd never seen Raion before. That may have been fair, Raion considered. It *had* been a long time since they'd seen one another.

The wrinkles on Governor Seiren's face deepened as she frowned. "Oh, I'm sorry, Raion. I forgot you didn't know. The Senate has openly discussed declaring *The Last Horizon* an enemy of Visiria. All because of you."

Raion froze up.

"As I said, they're not sure they can trust you, and you're representing us. Our troubles with the Alliance..." She waved a hand. "The people can accept your support of the Rebel Queen as long as they believe in *you*. In *your* honor. But when the people suspect you are a coward who ambushes and attacks his enemies in secret, who betrays contracts...Well, we can't let that go unchallenged."

Raion knew the blow had been struck. He felt it.

He knew this had been a duel, and one that he wasn't prepared to fight. Governor Seiren was a master of this type of combat, while he was only a novice. This was Ryzer's area of expertise, not his.

But what if he was really letting his crew down?

What if Visiria declared them enemies, all because they didn't trust Raion? What if the people of the galaxy thought less of *The Last Horizon* because of *him?*

That could put them in danger.

While, if he went along with this, the only one in danger was him.

On unsteady ground he may have been, but it wasn't Raion's style to remain uncertain for long. He smiled at Governor Seiren.

"Who do I need to fight?" he asked.

Without hesitation, she reached up to the delicate jeweled console on her wrist and projected a hologram. A tall Visiri man with a stern look, long limbs, and a larger build than Raion. "Albedon Pegarthus is the latest Champion of the Prime Arena, and he's the nephew of one of the most influential members of the Senate. Challenging him would be a great step toward restoring your honor."

Raion studied Albedon's image seriously while nodding. He had heard of Champion Pegarthus and had even watched a few of his duels. While Raion wasn't entirely familiar with the man's Combat Art, he had a few ideas.

"A worthy opponent!" Raion declared. "If that's what it takes to clear our name, I'll do it!"

Governor Seiren smiled so broadly she looked like a proud grandmother. "Raion, I knew I was right to trust you. All I wanted was to show the planet the side of you that I see. *This* is what a Visiri warrior should be."

She glanced to the rest of the table, who immediately began applauding furiously as though they had meant to all along.

Raion smiled at them all, but he wasn't deceived.

He had no friends here.

Ryzer leaned forward when the applause died down, looking concerned. "How long will it take to arrange a duel with the reigning Champion?" he asked. "Raion can't stay here forever. He has to get back to the Zenith Starship."

The Planetary Governor raised her eyebrows. "You underestimate me, Mister Raithe. I had Albedon booked for the day already in case a challenger should appear. We could begin the challenge at any time...Unless you need time to prepare, of course, Raion. I wouldn't want to rush you."

"I'm always prepared!" Raion said. The faster he won the fight, the faster he could get back to his assignment. If he took too long, he'd let his crewmates down.

"Mantell? Could you take Raion down to the entrance, please? Thank you, love. The rest of us will watch from here." The Governor grabbed his shoulder and gave it a friendly squeeze. "Worlds go with you, dear."

Raion followed Mantell, one of the attendants waiting in the room, out a door that he hadn't noticed next to the large window overlooking the Arena. He turned back to his brother as he walked. "See you soon, Ryzer!"

Ryzer gave a thin smile and a wave. He was more nervous than he should have been, but Raion would show him that there was no reason to be.

Even if this was a trap, Raion would break through it.

As soon as Raion was gone, Ryzer sagged back down into his seat. He was supposed to be making friends with the people in this room, but he couldn't fake a smile. He had thrown his own brother out of the airlock.

"Does he know the rules?" Governor Seiren asked him, still pleasant.

"The rules of the fight, yes," Ryzer responded. "I'm sure he doesn't remember the traditional procedure."

"Don't worry, dear, I'll remind him. Quelsar, are we all set to record?"

Quelsar Cyclon, a plump man with a faded green eye, grinned as he entered commands into his chair. It slid on hover plates over to the window, so he could have a live view. Most of the rest would watch on projectors over the table.

"The cameras are in place," Quelsar said. "The Senators will want to watch live, but we'll wait to see the footage before we put it on the general Subline."

The Governor walked up to peer out of the glass too. "Put the Senators on a thirty-second delay, just in case, and make sure the Karoshan delegation is on that feed. King Felrex is going to enjoy this."

A few people laughed or started calling out bets, but Ryzer wasn't one of them. He sank down into the desk.

Raion wasn't going to die today, but this would destroy him nonetheless.

CHAPTER TWENTY-SIX

RAION STRODE OUT onto the rubberized turf, enjoying the bounce beneath the boots of his combat armor. He wasn't allowed a helmet, or even his Titan Knight uniform, but he was given a traditional set of arena combat armor.

He had, of course, opted for a red one.

The stands rose into the sky around him, battered bronze plates that had been constructed centuries ago and were now covered by state-of-the-art screens, speakers, lights, and holo-projectors.

Drones flew across the sky like birds, catching footage. Raion hadn't realized this was going to be televised, but the thought encouraged him. How many hours had he spent watching the Prime Arena as a boy? Now his fight could go on to inspire future warriors all over the galaxy.

It was with good spirits that Raion reached the center of the Prime Arena and faced his opponent.

Albedon Pegarthus was a few inches taller than Raion and a few inches wider. His white hair was cut very short over his red scalp, and he glared out from beneath heavy eyebrows. His own armor seemed thicker and his force-blade was slightly larger, though they would be within the normal limits for arena equipment.

"Raion Raithe, here to battle!"

He'd always felt it was more polite to introduce himself first.

Albedon looked to Mantell, the arena employee who stood at Raion's side. Mantell said something into his console, and a moment later the Planetary Governor's voice echoed over the speakers of the arena.

"Although I'm sure it's redundant, I will remind the fighters of the rules. This is a traditional honor duel, with Albedon representing Senator Pegarthus and Raion representing The Last Horizon. *Raion, if you wish to demonstrate your resolve, you may challenge the defending Champion at any time."*

Albedon's thick eyebrows moved down, suggesting that he wasn't happy with that arrangement. He must have thought Raion's challenge was beneath him.

Or perhaps there was something else he was unhappy with. Raion didn't want to assume.

"As the objective of this battle is honor, I hope you will remember to conduct yourselves as is appropriate for a pair of Champions. Albedon may decline the challenge, but of course if he does, that will reflect on his courage. Until a fighter loses consciousness or admits defeat, the fight will continue. Do you accept the terms?"

"I do!" Raion declared.

Albedon hesitated longer, grinding his teeth, but finally said, "I do."

"Then I won't talk your ear off anymore. You don't need me to hold your hands, boys. But do remember that the entire planet of Visiria is watching you."

Raion straightened his back and put his hand on the hilt of his force-blade. His own Dance of a Burning World was optimized for large, wide-area attacks. He would have to save his energy for a long fight, while Albedon had learned a Combat Art more suited for the arena. He would try to rush Raion down.

No matter what, they would both give it their best.

"As the Knight of *The Last Horizon,* I challenge you to a duel!" Raion said proudly.

"In the name of Senator Pegarthus and the planet Visiria, I accept."

That triggered ancient magic in the Prime Arena. A golden symbol rose between them, shining brightly.

They both pulled their force-blades, waiting. When the symbol burst, the fight would begin.

Raion was looking forward to the fight, but Albedon glanced to the side, looked at the nearest camera-drone, and then spoke in a voice almost too low to hear.

"Remember that you can give up," he said.

"I can, but I won't!" Raion responded. While he had never been a professional Visiri duelist, he'd shared hundreds of friendly duels. Some people liked to start by trying to get inside the opponent's head, but such things never worked on Raion.

Albedon shook his head slightly. "Remember. They're trying to make you think you can't, but you can still—"

The golden symbol flashed white, which happened a moment before the round would start. On long-ingrained instinct, Albedon ignited his orange blade. Raion did the same with his red one.

Then the magic symbol burst and the two struck at one another.

Raion sent out the simplest form of his Combat Art, a horizontal slash that swept out in a crescent wave of flame. Albedon leaped over it, thrusting down at Raion from where he hung in midair.

While Raion's Dance of a Burning World was meant to fight monsters, Albedon practiced the Eraser Blade. It was a focused, efficient style for putting pressure on a single opponent.

White Aetheric energy stabbed at Raion, and he sidestepped, igniting his energy to move faster, but Albedon was no easy opponent. He kept up a constant storm of white thrusts and slashes, surrounding Raion in a cage.

Raion flew up with his opponent hot on his tail, only throwing out a burning strike of his own when he was cornered too desperately.

It had been a long time since Raion fought a Visiri warrior of his own caliber, but not long since he'd fought Starhammer. *That* fight had been too serious for him to enjoy it, but this one wasn't.

And his objective here was to show his quality.

Raion finally found his moment, reversing direction while Albedon gathered energy to release another strike. He closed enough distance that he found himself within the reach of the actual sword, swinging his force-blade down to cut Albedon in two.

It wouldn't really kill him, of course. It would only break his armor, and the force-blades were tuned to be weaker than the protective gear. The fighters could be hurt, yes. Even badly. But they wouldn't be killed.

Albedon's return strike cut through Raion's own armor, leaving a slice on his side, but Raion got the better of the exchange. His burning slash tore through some of the outer plates on Albedon's chest.

They both separated, and while Raion had to ignore the pain in his side, Albedon was also not unscathed.

And, most importantly of all, Raion had demonstrated his courage to the viewers. He was willing to meet his opponent openly, not sneak up on them from behind. He didn't run, and he wasn't afraid of pain.

He wanted to show them what it took to be a member of *The Last Horizon*.

The next few exchanges went the same way. Albedon fought hard, and he had truly dedicated himself to his Combat Art. His Eraser Blade was deadly enough that Raion certainly wouldn't want to face him on the battlefield.

Blood streamed down Raion's cheek, his side, and one of his arms. His armor had been damaged in three places, and he was breathing heavily.

But Albedon was in worse shape.

His eyes trembled as though he were having trouble staying conscious, his flight was unsteady, the aura of his energy was weak, and his skin was covered in sweat. He heaved for breath, and most of his armor had been burned off.

Champion of the Arena he may have been, but Raion had pushed himself to fight greater opponents. Perhaps there was a set of rules that would have given Albedon too much of an advantage for Raion to overcome, but Raion had been allowed to use his real power. Not counting his Divine Titan, of course.

Under those circumstances, Raion was confident in his victory.

A moment later, Albedon drifted down to the ground. Raion aborted his last attack, though he had to wrestle his arm down to do so. That was painful, but it would have been worse to land an attack on an opponent who had already given up.

"I admit defeat," Albedon said. He looked up with clear admiration showing through his exhaustion. "I recognize the honor of *The Last Horizon*, and I'm glad Champion Raion wasn't here to compete this season."

"It wasn't easy," Raion said honestly. "You were a great opponent!" While Albedon wasn't at the standard of *The Last Horizon*, he had pushed Raion a lot closer to his limits than most people could. Raion respected that.

Albedon glanced to the side and leaned his head down again so the camera-drone couldn't see his face. "Walk away now," he said urgently. "Do it n—"

"Senator Pegarthus is satisfied!" the Planetary Governor said over the speaker system. *"Now Senator Krakal and his representative must be convinced."*

A young Visiri woman strode confidently out of the arena door, white hair tied behind her and third eye burning purple. "Raion Raithe, prove your courage!"

Raion understood their trap then. Instead of fighting one duelist, he had to defeat the representatives of each Senator who was against him. They would wear him down until he surrendered or chose not to issue a new challenge. Which would mean giving up on his ship's reputation.

He was relieved. That was a trap he could understand.

Raion turned to Albedon. "How many Senators am I going to have to beat?"

"Seven," Albedon said, "but I don't know how far they're going to take this. Remember that you can surrender."

"Are you going to issue a challenge, Raion Raithe?" the Governor asked.

He was indeed wounded and tired from the last fight. If they were all as tough as that one, Raion probably wouldn't win seven in a row. But they had put their best fighter forward first.

It would be difficult, but Raion could do it. He believed in himself.

And, more importantly, his friends believed in him.

"Senator Krakal, as the Knight of *The Last Horizon,* I challenge your representative to a duel!"

Albedon shuffled off the field, glancing back, as the golden symbol rose from the ground and began to flash. Raion focused on his new opponent, who grinned and eagerly bounced from one foot to the next.

"In the name of Senator Krakal and the planet Visiria, I accept!"

Whatever happened, Raion would give it his best.

"Oh dear," Governor Seiren murmured to Ryzer. "I'm afraid he's in for a rather embarrassing afternoon."

Ryzer flinched as he watched the fight begin in the air over the table. It didn't matter who won. If they had been streaming live on the planetary Subline, maybe the people would have been inspired by the heroic form of a man fighting seven opponents in a row.

But they wouldn't show that. The only people who would see the full footage were the ones who wanted to see Raion get beaten. This was nothing but an excuse to watch Raion brutalized, to record him giving in, and to curry favor with the Perfected King. They were toying with him.

Just by fighting, Raion had already lost.

CHAPTER TWENTY-SEVEN

Raion won the second round faster. His opponent wasn't as experienced as Albedon, and she left herself open more often.

But he'd spent most of his energy, and he'd been forced to strain himself to defeat her in speed.

The third round, he took a heavy shot to the ribs.

The fourth fight dragged out until Raion's Combat Art resembled a spray of sparks more than a gush of flame.

In the fifth fight, his legs failed him. He came in from flight with a harder landing than he intended, his knees buckled a little too much, and his arm was sliced from wrist to shoulder. Not too deep, for which he was thankful.

The sixth fight was where he really lost his rhythm. One-handed, he defended himself from the rapid attacks of a smaller opponent. She overwhelmed him, but he hung on. He only managed to survive by dragging together the last of his energy and overwhelming him with one final strike carrying the power of a Burning World.

Which brought him to the seventh fight. The last one.

Raion smiled that he had made it, and he tasted blood in his teeth. He tried to face his opponent, but his left eye was gummed shut. His right eye refused to open fully, which left his third eye as the only one working.

Just standing there, he staggered. His knees hadn't quite recovered since the fifth round, but the pain was no worse than anywhere else.

Raion's words weren't as clear as he wanted, but he got them out. "As the...Kn-Knight of *The Lassst...Horizon,* I...challenge you."

"Raion Raithe, in the name of Senator Gorgol and the planet Visiria, I accept your challenge."

The third eye of the Visiri wasn't the same as their primary pair. It was made for watching vitality, for energy.

Raion saw his enemy as a haze of reddish-orange, and he felt their attack as a blinding flash.

Even the force-blade felt heavy to him, but he evoked enough of the Dance of a Burning World to slice through the first attack.

Raion forced his body through the paces, blocking on instinct and dodging on guesswork. His opponent flew up and Raion couldn't follow them.

Inwardly, he reached out for more power.

There wasn't much around him. He could feel his brother, burning like a spark in the darkness, but that bond was too thin to support anything.

Further away were stars in the night. His friends who trusted him. Their confidence blazed, and he drew as much sustenance from them as he could. But they were far away, and he was weak. Their assistance was only a trickle.

It was enough to grant Raion a second wind. This was the last fight, and he clutched at that truth to push him through.

Fueled by the power from his friends, Raion endured a hit with a flare of his aura. It split around him, and though he was burned, he hardly felt the heat.

Heedless of his own injuries, Raion swept out in one last attack from the Dance of a Burning World.

It wasn't quite enough to finish his opponent, so Raion hurled himself like a living missile. He tumbled into them, knocking them to the ground, and shoved his force-blade next to their head.

"I yield," a young man said into Raion's ear, and he rolled off the opponent onto his back.

The sky was a bluish blur, and he could see specks flying over him. Drones, he thought, zooming in for a look.

"Victory," Raion sighed. Exhaustion weighed him down. He wasn't even sure he could hobble his way off the field unassisted, and he felt darkness closing in around him.

"Oh my, does that mean you have no one else you wish to convince?" Governor Seiren asked.

Raion didn't understand the sentence for a long moment.

"There are still those remaining who doubt the Knight of The Last Horizon. *Regional governors, company leaders, even a few military officers. Regrettable as it is, if you cannot battle further, they will take this as the end of your courage."*

Raion couldn't do any more. He pushed himself to his knees, trying to focus, and found someone leaning down next to him.

The man spoke. "If you stop now, they won't ever know how hard you fought. They will only know that you gave up."

Raion drew on the faith of his friends more strongly, shoving himself to his feet. There was something wrong with his legs, but he forced his two somewhat functional eyes to focus on the face of his enemy.

He still couldn't see detail, but Raion forced another smile. "As the Knight of *The Last Horizon,* I challenge you."

The other man gave a humorless chuckle and backed up. "I haven't even told you my name yet. Come on, let's get this over with."

Golden light flew up, and Raion continued to fight.

I woke from a dream I couldn't remember, glancing around my room. I saw only shadows behind the statue of Horizon that she had never let me remove.

When she sensed I was awake, Horizon increased the light in the room slightly and manifested an eye next to me.

"Is something wrong, Captain?"

"Yes, but I don't know what." It wasn't uncommon for me to wake in the middle of the night, but that time, I paid attention. "Where is everyone?"

"My Pilot and my Knight are still away on assignment. My Engineer is asleep, while my Sword is performing maintenance on her weapons. My Commander requested that I send her back to her family only moments ago. Perhaps that magic is what disturbed you."

I flipped through that list of people. As I've said before, wizards don't actually have any senses normal people don't have, but we notice things others don't. We see the evidence of the Aether moving.

Not like the Aethril, who can see magic directly. We interpret hints and signs and half-understood feelings.

And my feelings were saying there was a problem.

"Contact Shyrax, Omega, and Raion," I ordered as I swung out of bed. "I'll check on Sola and Mell myself."

"I can see them directly," Horizon reminded me.

"Humor me." A product of the greatest magical endeavor in history Horizon may have been, but she still didn't necessarily have my insight into magic. I wanted to see for myself.

Mell was not happy to be awakened in the middle of the night. She came to the door bleary-eyed and carrying a glowing Nova-Bot like a flashlight. "Varic? We're not under attack, are we?"

She knew we weren't, or there would have been an alarm through the entire ship.

"We might be under magical attack," I said. That *was* a possibility, however unlikely it was to go unnoticed with Horizon's spell protections and with me onboard. "Have you had any trouble sleeping? Bad dreams?"

She shot me a quick glare, and I was sure that under other circumstances, she would have snapped at me. But we'd worked together long enough, even in this life, for her to trust my instincts.

"The only trouble I've had is when you rang my doorbell. Should I get dressed for this?"

She was wrapped in a white robe, which wasn't too different from her normal coat, but I shook my head. "You don't need to do anything but wait around until I sound the all-clear."

Mell's eyes were sharper now. "Is it targeting the ship?"

"I'm not sure what *it* is. It could be after us, or it could be something coming for any of us."

"Who's onboard?"

"Us and Sola."

"I'll call the Queen."

Mell couldn't recognize magical signs and portents, but Shyrax *could*, so that would likely work. "Tell her exactly what I said to you, and that I was awakened in the middle of the night by an ominous premonition. Get an opinion from her and Melerius and call me when you have it."

I strode down the hallway toward Sola as I heard Mell mutter behind me, "How am I supposed to remember *exactly* what you said?"

Sola was in the workshop sitting at a desk, a half-disassembled handgun in front of her. There was also a holographic screen projecting to one side, displaying what looked like a Lichborn royal drama. There were two characters standing on the side of a castle wearing ceremonially decorated chemical isolation suits, which was a classic of historical Dornoth.

She glanced up as I came in, nodded to me, and then returned to her work. Sola expected me to be there to modify my equipment, which would normally be the case.

"Have you seen anything strange in here?" I asked, and I don't think she would have responded any faster to an actual danger alarm .

Before I finished the question, she was on her feet snapping a magazine into the reassembled pistol and scanning the entrances to the room. "Who's the enemy?"

"I'm not sure yet. I woke up to a feeling like we were in danger. I think one of us—"

Sola summoned her armor. Only an instant later, she watched me from behind a visor. "What are the possibilities?"

"Hostile spell attack subtle enough that I can't read it, chemical or biological attack that Horizon can't detect, or I'm sensing something wrong with one of the others."

"No gas, no disease," Sola said immediately, and I knew she'd read that from her visor. "What are the odds of a spell?"

"Lower than something being wrong with the others. Horizon is checking on the ones who aren't onboard, and Mell is getting Shyrax's opinion."

Sola opened a panel on her left forearm. "Let's not wait for her report. Should we check on Omega or Raion?"

"Raion should be fine. He's doing diplomatic work, and he's on Visiria. Besides, it's hard for me to imagine a threat that could take him out without a chance for him to call for help."

I didn't hear the call connect, but I saw Sola tilt her head to one side. "Omega. Do you need help?"

A pause.

"Help. Do you need it?"

Another pause, then Sola snapped the panel on her armor console closed more forcefully than she needed to. "If he is in danger, he deserves it. I'm calling Raion."

"I tried, but it's hard to get a signal from all the way on the Visirian Subline. Horizon should get through eventually."

Sola tried anyway, shaking her head a moment later. "Nothing."

In itself, that didn't mean anything. It was normal not to be able to contact Raion when the call had to stretch over multiple Sublines.

But that crawling sense of unease returned.

In that instant, Horizon manifested in front of me. She shifted in place, looking uncertain. *"I connected with my Knight. He told me he had everything under control, but I did not believe him. I suspect he was fighting."*

Raion fighting wasn't necessarily the dire sign it sounded like—Raion was very likely to participate in an arena fight or two while he was on his homeworld—but I sharpened my attention.

"Play the recording," I said.

Raion's voice came out of the wall speakers immediately. He

was breathing hard and slurring his words a bit, but he sounded in good spirits.

"Don't worry," Raion said between breaths. *"I'll protect... you."*

I reached onto my console and triggered the ship's combat alarm. "Dive! Get us into Subspace, now!" Red lights flashed on the ceiling. "Horizon, let's move to the bridge."

"Yes, Captain." Horizon sounded shaken. *"Should I—"*

"Recall Omega right now, and Shyrax if she's close enough. I don't care what they're doing. We're in Subspace in ten seconds whether they're back or not."

As we appeared on the bridge, I strode to the center of the room. The captain's chair barely had a chance to bloom out of the metal of the floor, unfolding into its padding and contoured form, before I sank into it.

I manifested hands, sending them deep into the ship as Horizon worked on her tasks. Only a second after I appeared, Mell and Sola were at my side.

Sola was ready immediately, sinking into a console, while Mell looked startled. "Did you figure it out?"

"Raion's in danger," I said. "We're heading for him now."

"We're at least two hours from Visiria, and that's our max speed with Omega aboard," Sola reported.

"Is that two hours from teleportation range?" I asked.

"Yes."

A Subspace warp appeared in front of us, spinning into a wide circle of rainbow light. I hadn't been kidding about diving whether Shyrax and Omega were onboard or not.

They showed up at almost the same time, and I had my wand ready. Omega grinned and widened his mouth to make a joke, but I sealed his lips shut.

"To Visiria, maximum speed, and if you delay one more second, I will execute you with my own hands."

Shyrax had already settled into her own console on my right side. "I've focused the enhancement systems on engines."

"Dive," I commanded.

Subspace swallowed us as Omega linked himself to the Pilot console. The ship shone orange as he took over, and golden light flowed in harmony as Shyrax backed him up.

Before the dive completed, I sent Raion a message.

"We're coming. Hold on."

CHAPTER TWENTY-EIGHT

RYZER STOOD AT the side of the Planetary Governor, trying to smile.

Planetary Governor Nelula Seiren stood before the cameras, still the beloved grandmother. "I think it's clear that we made the right choice, don't you think?"

The holographic form of a golden Karoshan lounging on a throne appeared opposite her, next to the largest camera. A massive tail lashed behind him, twisting around the back of his throne. *"The Empire is pleased to have such stalwart allies. Now, off the record..."*

King Felrex leaned forward, golden eyes glowing with curiosity. *"How did you find him, really? I'm curious about the Zenith Starship's standards."*

"Oh, he was an extraordinary duelist," Seiren said. She sent a regretful smile down to the floor. "But we weren't concerned about his qualities as a duelist, were we? We didn't trust his judgment. And it seems we were right."

The King of Karosha looked down, and a floating camera next to him followed his gaze.

Toward Raion, lying in a broken puddle on the ground. Ryzer could only glance at him for an instant before having to look away.

One of his arms was missing entirely, and the other had been opened down to the fingers, which were either missing or bent backward. His shins had been broken, his feet limp piles. His chest was distorted, misshapen, and his breaths came with a painful wheeze. His face...

Ryzer didn't look at his face.

"His performance was impressive enough, but not what I expected," the King said. *"The Zenith Starship could have found better candidates among the Perfected."* He leaned back in his throne. *"Ah, well. Maybe she will. I assume you're ready for* The Last Horizon *to arrive."*

The Governor spread her hands. "He chose to challenge us. We have the recording to prove it. He could have stopped calling for duels at any time. And besides, he's still alive."

"Good. I'll make sure they don't go too far, but odds are, they will retrieve their Knight the moment they arrive in the system." King Felrex waved a hand. *"This is Gharyas' operation, so I'll leave further instructions to him, but I am pleased thus far. Well done."*

Governor Seiren bowed her head as the Karoshan hologram vanished, then she turned to the other cameras.

"Let's get a few more shots of his body. Oh, and get an interview with Ryzer. You're up for it, aren't you, dear?"

Ryzer nodded numbly before he even realized what he was agreeing to.

The Governor patted him fondly. "Don't worry, it's normal that you're a bit shell-shocked. That helps us. You couldn't believe your brother's foolishness, and you wish he hadn't gone so far."

Ryzer wanted to sprint from the Prime Arena, but he was in too deep. If he gave up now, then Raion took this beating for nothing.

The Governor checked something on her console as two assistants and a drone ran up to her. "Oh, dear. It seems *The Last Horizon* is entering the system ahead of schedule. Get Raion to Medical, please. We need to show what good care we've taken of him. Ryzer, stay close, all right?"

Ryzer nodded again. He felt as though all he could do was nod.

They started to stride from the stage, but cameras spun around as a blue light formed only a few yards away.

It formed into a figure dressed in all blue. A human man, with dark skin but silver hair almost as vivid as an Aethril's. He wore an azure wizard's mantle, and a wand buzzed at his hip.

To Ryzer, Varic gave off a very different impression than he had only a few days before. The Captain opened silver eyes, and while his expression was mild, Ryzer's breath caught.

"Captain Vallenar," the Governor said in a tone of surprise. "I'm surprised to see you here so quickly."

"One of the benefits of flying the fastest ship in the galaxy," Varic Vallenar said. Like his expression, his voice was mild. Normal. Just as Ryzer remembered it.

Ryzer started to sweat. He hadn't been intimidated by the captain before, but this time, there was something different. It was as though someone else lived in Varic's skin.

The Planetary Governor gave a long sigh. "We sent you a number of messages, but Sublines, you know. Frankly, we were hoping you would control your Knight. He caused quite a mess here."

Silver eyes moved to the puddle of blood on the stage. "I can see that."

"A bloody business, the arenas," the Governor said. "I've never been a fan of them myself." As she spoke, a drone flew down to spray water over the blood and vacuum up the liquid.

A shadow passed over the sun, and Ryzer glanced up. He was afraid of the Zenith Starship, but it wasn't a ship. The once-clear day was growing dim as clouds rapidly formed over the arena.

"I was quite a fan, once upon a time," Varic said, tapping away at his console as he spoke. "In fact, I fought in the arena myself a time or two. Even here."

Governor Seiren frowned. "Did you really? I'm surprised I've never heard of such a thing, a human wizard in the Prime Arena."

"I'm sorry to hear Raion caused so much trouble. I asked him not to. Once I see what he did, I'll compensate you appropriately."

"I doubt it will be so simple. The Visirian Senate is not happy with him, and I'm afraid that extends to you. Let's head up to the VIP room, and I'll be happy to show you the footage."

"No need," Varic said. "I have it."

Ryzer could see the Governor visibly recalculating. She had wanted to present an edited version of events to Captain Vallenar, and she'd never expected him to be able to break Prime Arena security.

However, Ryzer believed he'd done it, and she evidently came to the same conclusion. A Vallenar could certainly afford the best, and he also had the resources of a Zenith Device.

She sighed before speaking. "Raion challenged us himself, though I'm sure he didn't think through the implications. He wanted a way to clear the reputation of your ship through the Senators, and when he thought of proving himself in the Prime Arena...Well, he couldn't wait to get out here."

All the while, Varic continued watching the footage. Ryzer couldn't see what he saw, because the video played in Varic's ocular implant, but he noticed no change in the Captain's face.

The clouds overhead, however, had become very dark. That was unusually fast.

The silence stretched longer and longer as Varic watched the footage, expressionless. Ryzer expected him to say something, to sigh, to rage, to throw accusations, but the human did nothing but stare into space. Ryzer started to wonder if he was watching the footage at all or if he was lost in thought.

Governor Seiren was clearly no more comfortable. While Varic stood there, he had quietly been surrounded by Arena security, and the Governor herself had a few guards standing between her and the newcomer. Not directly between them—not yet—but close enough to intervene.

Several of them were mages, and a few subtle protective spells flashed over the Governor. Varic took no action to stop them. He stared into the air.

Finally, Governor Seiren chose to break the silence. "Well, Captain Vallenar, send word when you've finished with that footage. I'll await you in my office for further discussion. No need to stay out here when the challenge is over, now that it looks like rain."

Silver eyes flicked up.

"Over?" Varic asked.

In the sky, lightning flashed. Ryzer heard no thunder, and the rain still hadn't begun.

Casually, Varic flipped up the hood of his mantle and laced his fingers together, stretching. "Raion fought in the name of *The Last Horizon* and never surrendered, so the challenge may continue. There is another member of *The Last Horizon* right here."

"Captain Vallenar, please, there's no need for this," Governor Seiren said in reproach. "Let's leave the damage where it is. No need for more embarr—"

"As the Captain of *The Last Horizon,* I challenge Senator Pegarthus of the planet Visiria. Or his representative."

Varic unclipped a plasma pistol from his belt and tossed it aside, leaving himself with a silver wand that glowed blue. Maybe Aethertech, though Ryzer was no expert.

The Governor looked truly irritated, though she covered it with a hasty smile. "There's nothing to be gained here, Varic. Raion was a warrior. He understood what was at stake, and he wouldn't want you to be hurt on his behalf."

"Raion," Varic said, "*is* a warrior."

Thunder rolled.

"...and I can see that Senator Pegarthus is not," Varic continued. "It seems that you all can only face a real Visiri Combat Artist after he's been beaten down and softened up, but there isn't one fighter willing to face a human in battle. When was the last time a mage won a round in the Prime Arena?"

He sounded genuinely curious, but there was a slight smile on his face as he scanned everyone onstage. Varic was provoking them intentionally, and if Ryzer could see that, everyone could.

But that didn't mean it wouldn't work.

Governor Seiren lifted her eyebrows. "Very well, Varic, but this is on your own head. Remember that you asked for this."

"I didn't ask for anything. I challenged Senator Pegarthus to a duel." Varic pulled his wand out and spun it between his fingers. "Can I take this as an admission of defeat?"

"Albedon," the Governor snapped.

The Arena Champion strode onto the field. He wore several bandages and a few still-active healing spells, but he was clearly in fighting condition. At least, better condition than Raion had been since about the third match.

"Don't do this," Albedon said to Varic. He kept his voice low, but Ryzer was close enough to hear clearly. "Raion fought so you wouldn't have to. If we leave it here, the only damage is to your pride."

"All this talk and you still won't accept my challenge." Varic held up his hands in victory. "Varic Vallenar, Champion of the Prime Arena! No one on the planet Visiria was brave enough to face him!"

"In the name of Senator Pegarthus and the planet Visiria, I accept your challenge," Albedon said. His gaze was dark under his heavy brows, and he unclipped his large force-blade from his belt and ignited it. "So stupid, human."

Governor Seiren shook her head. "I'm sorry to say it, Varic, but I agree. Before we begin, I want to make sure both fighters understand—"

"I know the rules," Varic interrupted.

"Then don't let me stop you from digging your own grave," the Governor said. "Clear the arena."

Everyone shuffled to higher ground, including Ryzer, though he couldn't help but look back even as he climbed the stairs. When the door shut behind him and he took a seat in the observation room, he breathed easier. Now that he was watching the duel through the large windows overhead, he felt like he'd escaped a battlefield.

Albedon paced back and forth, looking like he couldn't wait to end the fight as quickly as possible.

Varic stared off to the side, wand in hand.

As soon as the field was clear, a golden spark of magic erupted from beneath the arena floor. This was where the fighters were supposed to prepare, and the time when wizards could begin chanting their spells.

A ball of water formed behind Varic's head. It spun in place, not growing any faster, but darkening by the second.

On the other side, Albedon had drawn himself into the first step of his Combat Art, his white force-blade already beginning to glow. He intended to end this in one move.

But Ryzer's gut was still tight. No matter how this turned out, he couldn't imagine it would be good.

The magic flashed white.

A laser pierced through Albedon's midsection, and he crumpled with his Combat Art unfinished.

Ryzer scrambled to pull up the replay, and only when he slowed the scene down did he see that the laser was the water Varic had compressed. He'd simply pointed his wand.

The spectators—the Governor, her attendants, the guards, and the influential visitors—were all silent. The only sound came from the boots of the medics who hurried onto the field to grab Albedon and administer emergency treatment.

Varic wasn't watching him. He was looking straight into the VIP room, through the large window.

And, it seemed, into Ryzer's eyes.

Varic shouted, though his voice would have been picked up by microphones in the drones regardless. "As Captain of *The Last Horizon*, I challenge Senator Krakal of the planet Visiria or his representative."

Governor Seiren gestured to tap into the speakers of the Arena. "We understand your message, Captain Vallenar. I assure you that Raion is receiving the best of care in our medical wing."

"He's about to have plenty of company."

CHAPTER TWENTY-NINE

"I CHALLENGE SENATOR Krakal," Varic repeated.

The Governor deactivated her microphone. "Fine, send Mua out there again. I'm sure she saw Albedon's mistake."

A few employees bustled around, and a moment later, the young Visiri duelist with the purple eye strode out. She had a bit of a limp and a few patches over her burns from her fight with Raion, but she glared at Varic.

"In the name of Senator Krakal, I accept, and all that. You don't know what you're doing."

Varic leaned forward and shaded his eyes. "Weren't you the one I watched lose a rigged fight?"

Mua erupted into a purple-red aura and pulled a pair of force-blades as the gold spark erupted from the ground again.

Ryzer didn't think he was underestimating the human as badly as the others were, but there was still no way Varic could win. He had shown his hand in the last round, and it wasn't as though the same trick would work for everyone.

It even looked as though Varic was going to use the same spell again. The ball of water spun behind his head.

When the gold spark flashed white, Mua kicked off. Ryzer only saw her reappear behind Varic.

Where a waterfall slammed her to the ground as though Varic had known where she was going all along.

It didn't let up, either. A column of water pushed her into the Arena floor like a pachyderm's leg pinning her down.

Purple-red aura flared as she tried to push against the water. Varic watched her for a second, then reached out and grabbed a camera-drone that had been fluttering around him.

They were made to avoid even the blows from high-speed Visiri fights, but somehow it didn't escape him. Ryzer supposed he must have caught it with magic.

Varic pulled the drone up to his chin, speaking into the microphone as he squatted next to Mua. As a result, his voice was clear.

"Do you surrender?" Varic asked the woman trapped under the relentless water.

Her aura grew weaker and weaker. She said something, but it was impossible to hear the words under the rush of the waterfall.

"What was that?"

The aura of her energy disappeared, but the water continued.

Varic tilted his head. "It's surrender or unconsciousness, but I'm afraid I can't tell if you're conscious. Feel free to tell me if you've passed out."

The Governor didn't speak this time, but one of the Arena administrators made an announcement. "Varic Vallenar, remove your spell. The opponent can no longer fight."

Varic released the camera drone, brushing off his mantle as he let the waterfall fade to a trickle. A coughing, sputtering Mua Krakal was revealed, gasping for air and fumbling for her sword.

"Admirable fighting spirit," Varic said. He leveled his wand.

"I surrender," Mua choked out.

Without further comment, Varic strode away. "Then I challenge Senator Griffiss."

Governor Seiren glared at the room, microphone off. "Do we have no one who can beat him in the ring?"

One of the Arena administrators spoke up. "Albedon or Mua could have won, but they underestimated him. And they were slowed by their injuries. We have plenty of fighters, but most Combat Artists won't bother facing a mage in the ring."

"Well, get *someone* in there."

A fresh young Visiri man with an orange force-blade strode into the arena next. Varic blasted him into the stands without taking his eyes off the VIP box.

"I challenge Senators Gorgol and Cyclon at once," Varic said. "Let's speed this up."

When the next two fighters were smashed into the arena wall, the VIP box was quiet for a long time.

Ryzer knew what was happening. They could exhaust Varic eventually, but even if word of this never got out, the people in that room were embarrassed. Losing to Raion was one thing, but repeatedly losing to a human and a wizard was a humiliation they couldn't stand even in their own minds.

"Don't let him win another match," Governor Seiren said coldly, and the Arena administrator sent out another message again.

"As we have been operating under South Provisional Rules, the fighter must change weapons after the fifth match in a row," the administrator said.

Ryzer was sure they hadn't been operating under South Provisional Rules, which were intended for a specific variety of exhibition match, but Varic hadn't let them explain the rules in detail. It was impossible for most magic-users to switch weapons, since the *wand* wasn't the weapon. The *spell* was.

"If you use water elementalism, you will be disqualified. Likewise, your opponents will no longer use force-blades. You may be provided with an alternate weapon at your request."

Another challenger strode up with fists clenched, looking ready to kill after the previous humiliating losses. He picked up a heavy, two-handed hammer on his way into the ring.

Ryzer found himself speaking. "He can use sealing magic too."

The administrator responded without speaking into the mic. "Seals and binding spells are easier to resist with aura, and they're much slower. Elementalism is the most effective combat magic."

By that time, the golden light had turned white.

Then Varic's opponent was pinned against the far wall by a spell-circle.

"Don't make me repeat myself every time," Varic said. "Keep sending them out."

Governor Seiren returned to the mic wearily. "We understand your point, Varic, we understand. How far are you going to push this?"

"How many fighters do you have?"

She gestured in irritation to the administrator, who made another announcement. *"As you know, in the finals of a South Provisional Exhibition Tournament, fighters must change weapons every round."*

Without a further pause, another Visiri fighter strode out.

When the light flashed white, a hand made of blue light grabbed the woman in a grip larger than her whole body. She sliced through, but there were more hands.

A moment later, she slammed into the window of the VIP room.

It didn't break, being made of the same transparent alloy used in starships, but Ryzer flinched back as though from a rain of shattered glass.

"I think that's all the Senators," Varic said.

"Congratulations, you did it," the Governor said sourly. "What did this tantrum accomplish, Varic?"

"As the Captain of *The Last Horizon,* I challenge Planetary Governor Nelula Seiren."

She paused for a moment before scoffing into the microphone. "Do you insist on continuing to beat up our fighters?"

"I didn't say anything about a representative."

An instant later, Varic appeared in front of the window, floating in the invisible grip of magic. His mantle billowed behind him, and his silver eyes burned in the shadow of his hood. "You're a Visiri, aren't you? You're stronger than I am. I won't even use magic."

She laughed at him from the other side of the glass. "Do you want to challenge an old woman, then? What do you want to prove, Varic?"

Varic stared at her. "Prove?"

At last, the rain began to fall.

Slowly, the human reached out a hand to the glass. Aetheric symbols etched into the window flared and hissed as his fingers got closer, but the light fizzled out as soon as it was born. Ryzer felt a chill, and his feet carried him backwards one step at a time.

Those were the building's magical protections, failing before his eyes.

"I am here to teach you that there are some people you cannot afford to offend." The building trembled around Ryzer, and he shot for the door.

Eyeballs made of blue light, almost as large as Ryzer's entire head, popped out of nowhere. They focused on him, and he froze.

The glass crumpled around Varic, breaking with a steady crunching instead of a sharp crash as its shards dissolved to sand and blew away. The wizard drifted in through the glistening cloud, untouched. "There is only one thing your civilization has ever produced that is worth anything to me, and you beat him, spit on him, and mocked him. How are you going to compensate me?"

The guards were not idle, of course. But they might as well have been.

Combat Artists had attacked him from either side with devastating blows, all of which had been stopped by floating hands. Bullets and plasma bolts crashed into his shield and ricocheted off, blowing up chunks of the room.

The mages had all given up. One of them was clutching her head and screaming in the corner.

Governor Seiren stood her ground, hands folded in front of her, resolutely unflinching as Varic drifted down toward her. He leaned his head down until they were nose to nose.

"Did you think I would be satisfied with humiliating a few fighters?" Varic asked softly. "Do you think your life is enough to repay me? This arena? What about the entire planet of Visiria?"

"Don't take things too far, Captain Vallenar," the Governor warned him, but her voice was much quieter than it had been before.

"That's right. I am the Captain of *The Last Horizon*, and you had my friend beaten and humiliated live on the Subline." He pushed one finger into her forehead, just above her third eye. "Look at me. Look me in the eyes."

The Governor met his gaze immediately as though to call his bluff, but her eyelids flickered and she took in a short, shuddering breath.

"If I want to sink this continent," Varic continued, "I don't need to call my ship. That's what I'm here to *prove* to you. Nothing in this system can stop me from doing anything I want."

He withdrew his finger from her forehead and floated back. "Now you know, so I'll give you a second chance. You…but not everyone."

Finally, as a storm raged outside, burning silver eyes turned to Ryzer. "Hello again, Ryzer."

Ryzer literally couldn't breathe.

"I, Varic Vallenar, challenge you to a duel to the death."

Ryzer fell to the ground and his body squirmed away, and he couldn't speak through a tightening throat.

Varic drifted after him, the specter of death. Ryzer could no longer see anything in his hood except shadows and two silver stars. "I'll tell you this first: I will not forgive you, and I will not kill you quickly. You will serve as a warning to the galaxy. The horror story of what happens to those who cross me. So, in your last moments, you will have finally done something of use."

Ryzer still couldn't get a breath. He could only whimper. Other than Varic, he could see nothing.

But suddenly, the hooded head jerked up. Shadows retreated. The pressure lifted, and Ryzer took in a deep breath.

A moment later, the door slid open.

Raion was covered in bandages so thick that he could scarcely hobble. Only one of his three eyes was visible, and he pushed himself along on a crutch.

"Varic!" he called. "I'm here to help." When Raion saw Varic, he sighed in relief. "Oh, good. I felt you in pain. I thought you were… Oh, there I go."

Varic caught him.

Outside, the rain began to lighten up.

CHAPTER THIRTY

IN ANOTHER LIFE

We were two years into the Titan Force when my teacher, Kyri, decided to retire.

She'd talked about it for a while, but either Doctor Cryce or I had always managed to talk her out of it. I met her for the last time as she loaded her personal cruiser.

She did it by hand rather than by magic or by drone. She said it was good discipline for her, and besides, it was faster.

When I caught up to her, she was hauling a pyramid of eighteen bags up the docking ramp. She looked like she had an entire house on her shoulders. I had no idea how she was balancing it all.

I called her name as I approached and she shouted back, "Give me a second, let me dump off this junk."

There came a crash from inside the ship that made me suspect she really had *dumped* her belongings in there, and she came out a moment later brushing off her hands. She gave me a smile almost as bright as Raion's, her third eye glowing white.

"The farewell party's over," she said. "Did you want a tearful parting with your teacher?"

She responded with familiar energy, but I couldn't help but notice that she looked noticeably older than when she'd started. More of her white hair had darkened to gray, and her wrinkles were deeper than they had been before. Even her steps were a little more deliberate, and she stretched her hip as she talked.

Nonetheless, she still had plenty to teach us. And more importantly, she had nothing else out there.

"You said you settled things with the Alliance," I said.

"Of course I did!"

"Did you really?"

She shrugged. "I won't be going back to Visiria. That should be settled enough. I'll make my way in the Union, or maybe the Free Worlds. I hear the Advocates are hiring."

The Titan Force weren't enemies with the Karoshan Alliance. We weren't enemies with anyone except the D'Niss, as far as I knew. But Kyri had shared the location of the D'Niss with Doctor Cryce, and that was information she'd only gotten from collaboration with the Karoshan military.

Regardless of the results, they couldn't let that sort of leak go unpunished. She would be arrested, at best, if she ever met any representatives of the Karoshan throne.

"We have a lot of friends," I said. "Let us—"

Kyri was suddenly more serious. "You think I want to call in a favor for this? You think I want to owe the Vallenar Corporation? Besides, I don't want to ruin the reputation of the Titan Force. What will the Subline think if they know you're calling in favors to protect their friends from criminal charges?"

"I want you to be safe. If you have to leave, I don't want to worry about you."

She gave me another grin and ruffled my hair. "In the end, you're only as safe as you can make yourself. Remember: To survive in this galaxy, you need a wand in one hand and a gun in the other."

I gave up and patted my belt. "Always armed."

"Good boy. And look, stop worrying. I'm safer if you don't call anybody. As long as I stay quiet, they'll never find me."

Those probably weren't her final words, but they were the last ones I heard from her.

Eight days later, she was picked up by a Karoshan patrol on the border of the Galactic Union. They usually don't patrol that far, so either they were looking for someone else or they knew where she would be.

In that life, I spent a lot of effort trying to figure out which it was. Did we have a traitor? Were the Karoshans watching us?

I never found out, and now I never will. All this happened in a timeline that was only real for me.

Kyri took three Karoshan ships with her when she died. At least she went out fighting.

I wish that made me feel any better.

Of the original Titan Knights in my previous life, Raion and I were the only ones to make it to the end.

To be more precise, I was the only one.

Raion didn't make it either.

Javik and Aelora retired when the pressure got to be too much, leaving their titles of Yellow and White Knights to successors. I heard from Javik every once in a while, but Aelora vanished almost entirely. I had a theory that she moved to a sector with an isolated Subline where no one would recognize her.

As I said before, Parryl didn't get a chance to retire. We had fought together for three years and were facing down another D'Niss.

This wasn't one of the Seven Calamities, so it didn't call for all five of us. I wasn't even there. It was Raion, Parryl, and Javik.

I saw the footage—Well, to be more precise, I spent weeks poring over every frame of video from three different sources, looking for what went wrong. I could have written an entire dissertation on everything they could have done differently, and I wanted to.

But the truth was, they didn't make any mistakes. Sometimes, things just go wrong.

I can still see the entire video. The three of them approached a worm that undulated in and out of a planet's wide rings. They stayed together as they engaged the D'Niss soldiers, which in that case were winged worms with circular mouths that latched onto ships.

They did everything right, covering one another and not over-extending. Even Raion didn't push ahead recklessly, which was a blessing of the Aether. If he had called for a charge and it had resulted in a Knight's death, he would never have let himself off.

If anyone made a mistake, it was Parryl herself. But I blame nothing more than bad luck.

The worms could spit balls of conjured plasma, and one got a lucky hit. While her shield was destabilized, she pulled behind the other two fighters, as she was supposed to do.

While repositioning, she clipped one of the balls of rock and ice that made up the planet's rings. Her already-unstable shield faltered again, and a cluster of worms saw that. They pounced on her ship.

She panicked, which I can understand. I saw the footage from her ship, with worms crawling all over her starfighter, burning and chewing their way inside. The cockpit filled with the heat of melting metal, and the audio was deafening with the sound of their chewing.

She should have summoned her Titan right then. Instead, she tried to fight her way out.

Parryl pulled a pair of guns and shot according to the rhythm of her Combat Art as soon as holes appeared in her hull. She blasted away more than a few of the soldiers, and Raion and Javik shot more off her.

Their orders for her to call her Titan never came through. One of the first systems the worms broke was the communications relay in her ship.

It haunts me, those recordings of Javik and Raion shouting Parryl's name desperately. The despair in their voices when they realized she couldn't hear them.

But neither of them could summon their Divine Titans. *They* weren't the ones in danger.

At that point, Raion ejected and blasted toward the soldiers himself, but he was too late. Parryl's Titan crashed down as a blazing green meteor, tearing through a small army of worms, but the only thing left of her was a spray of blood on the outside of her wrecked starship.

As you'd expect, that marked a shift in the attitude of the Titan Knights. It was our rude awakening.

I was quick to say that I had *always* taken it seriously. That was why I always insisted we not take so many risks.

But that was me coping the best I knew how. I believed I could have saved her. I wouldn't have needed to rely on my starfighter or my Divine Titan to clear out those worms; I would have used my magic.

That kind of thinking is a dead end, but I've always learned that lesson the hard way.

It led to one of the first real fights Raion and I ever had. He was in the training room, which in the Titan Knights consisted of a mechanical collection of enemies. I didn't bother to watch him bashing robots, but I shouted to be heard over the constant explosions of metal.

"Look at this!" I sent a file to his console, which I heard beep where it sat on the sidelines. "I ran the course myself. If I had been there, I would have cleared them out in time."

I had flown out to the site of Parryl's death in my own starfighter and, guided by the reports from the other three, I had used magic to simulate what I had needed to save her. It would have worked, and I had my own recordings to prove it.

The sudden absence of crashes was deafening, and Raion strode toward me, glaring. "You should have listened to my orders. I told you not to go out there."

"If *you* listen to *me,* this won't happen again!"

Raion shoved two fingers into my chest, and I was grateful I didn't fly across the room. "All right, tell me this. Could you have done all that without knowing what was about to happen? Sure, you can go out and clear the area *now.* But if you'd been there, without knowing the future, could you have done it?"

"I don't know if I would have, but I *could* have," I insisted. "There was a chance. And it's not about me being there—"

"I know it isn't! You could have gone on the mission, but you didn't apply for it. You know why? Because you were saving other people! We can't have everyone on every assignment!"

"We don't have to have everyone, but we have to be careful!"

"You don't know what we need. You weren't there." Raion's eyes were blazing like he was about to throw a punch, and I started calling my element before he continued. "You weren't there, and *I was.*"

He marched over to the side of the training room, scooping his console off the ground and strapping it to his wrist before tapping something out. My own console buzzed, and I saw he'd sent me a file.

It was footage of him in a starfighter, running the same course I had. He'd gone back to the scene of Parryl's death, like I had.

And, like I had, he'd proven he could have saved her.

"I'd have gotten there two seconds faster than you," Raion said. "And I *could* have."

I couldn't speak.

"If I had acted decisively, I could have acted in time. I held back because I thought she could save herself, but next time I'll do what I wanted to do in the first place. I won't stop when there's a friend in danger."

I shook my head slowly. "Like you said, there's nothing you could have done. Not unless you could see the future."

Raion put a hand on my shoulder, but his expression was still grim. "The question is, what are we going to do next time?"

CHAPTER THIRTY-ONE

The medical room of *The Last Horizon* wasn't as large as those I'd seen even on smaller ships. It didn't need to be, since the healing magic and medical Aethertech incorporated into its construction meant that it could handle more patients in less space.

And, of course, the Zenith Starship had only six crew members. Even if we brought on new supplementary crew, like Shyrax's rebels or my own wizard students, our facilities should only ever have a dozen patients at most.

The room was made of a dark metal tinged blue-green, and the ceiling was packed with machinery folded out of sight. Twelve cots grew out of the floor, each with a dark monitor above it, but those were only the extras.

The facilities for main crew members were six chambers separated by metal walls, and it was easy to tell at a glance who each belonged to.

Shyrax's was the largest, with a Karoshan-sized bed and Aethertech machinery surrounding it in a dome. The inside seemed like an entirely different location, being decorated in the Karoshan style, with lots of gold and jewels and a dragon motif.

Sola's room was also designed to be comforting to her, though it incorporated only a handful of Lichborn design elements. At a glance, I saw one light that was made of flickering green flame, but that was all. Instead, the chamber looked like the sort of stripped-down, spartan bunk you might find in a Union frigate.

Robot arms had been folded into the wall, and there were more monitors in Sola's room than even Shyrax's. Anything that could incapacitate a Lichborn required serious analysis. I honestly thought it was strange that Sola had a dedicated medical room at all, considering that she tended to deal with anything more than minor wounds by blowing herself up and returning to life.

Speaking of people with no need for medical care, Omega's was next. I couldn't see much of that one, covered as it was by a door of dark glass, but I did see a couple of pumps that looked like miniature ship refueling stations. Mass fabricators, I was sure. The best way to fix Omega was to pump him full of organic matter and let his own regeneration sort things out.

Mell's and mine looked normal. Almost identical, except hers had a console next to the bed where she could control the medical Aethertech taking care of her. And mine, on second glance, had a life-size statue of Horizon smiling down benevolently over the bed. I wondered if I could get rid of that.

Raion's was almost as big as Shyrax's, and one that looked like it was made for industrial mining rather than medical care. The door leading inside was thick and password-locked, with a viewport of reinforced glass providing the only view inside. It was equipped with a massive drill and a military-grade laser, both of which were engaged as I walked up.

I waited as the glass blacked out, an eye protection feature. A monitor next to the door flashed red, telling me to wait as surgery was in progress.

In spite of myself, I felt my stomach clench. I could still see Raion lying in a pool of his own blood, and I remembered the beatings that had put him there.

I knew he'd make it, rationally. But I couldn't help worrying.

A moment later, the glass brightened and the door swung open. A

Nova-Bot strode out, its exterior armor white and flared to resemble a coat. Mell's way of showing that this one was a doctor, I suppose.

Its visor glowed with one purple eye, and it gestured to me. *"Captain. The patient is stable."*

I nodded to the robot and walked into the room, palms sweating. The last time Raion had seen me, I had threatened to kill his brother. How would he take that? What would he think of me?

Raion laid back against his pillow, covered in fresh bandages and hooked up to a blocky machine on the wall that resembled a standard food fabricator. Aethertech to synthesize and administer his medication. I glanced over a pair of nearby magic circles, one of which was to stabilize his condition and the other intended to ward off infection.

Both were flawless, of course. Zenith Era medical care was without question.

One red eyelid cracked and Raion gave a weak smile. "Hey, Captain. I think I might need to sit out the next one."

"Too bad. I was planning to send you out in your Titan."

Raion's head bobbed in a powerless nod, and he fumbled for the medical fabricator's controls. In a panic, I seized him with telekinesis. "I was kidding, Raion! Kidding! You can relax. Leave the galaxy to us for a while."

He sagged back into the bed and croaked out a laugh. "Good one, Captain. Is Ryzer okay?"

Ryzer was terrified, last I'd seen him. "I didn't hurt him."

"I know. You wouldn't do that."

I absolutely would have. If I had torn Ryzer to pieces, it wouldn't be worse than he deserved, as far as I was concerned. But that wasn't a discussion to have with Raion while he was in recovery.

To change the subject, I glanced up at the monitors. "Horizon says she's growing you a new liver and part of a kidney. And by the looks of things, your bones are going to be about fifty percent new by the time you get out. Any changes you want us to make while we're in there? Omega recommends an extra set of kidneys."

"How's Parryl?"

I had hoped he wouldn't ask so soon, but it wasn't as though I was unprepared for the question. I patted the side of his bed. "Save your energy. I'll take care of her, I promise."

Raion forced his other two eyes open. "The Heart?"

"We'll get it." It was better to say that than to tell him we'd left Visiria without the magical artifact we'd come for. "We had to get you off the planet first."

He reached up for his medical controls again, shuffling as though to leave the bed. I had to lock him in place with my levitation ring again.

"Raion, you've got to rest."

"The mission isn't over," Raion said. He sounded cheery, though he couldn't seem to find where to put his feet. "I'll come back once I have the...Hey, can you tell me where the stop button is?"

He squinted at the controls for the medical fabricator, which were very simple. His finger, poised to press the button, drifted in midair.

I didn't use telekinesis this time. Instead, I sharpened my words. "Knight Raion. Your mission is to rest."

Raion's shoulders drooped. Slowly, he began to sink back into the pillows. "I'm sorry. I'll do better next time."

"There was nothing you could have done."

"That doesn't matter." His eyes were weary as they met mine. "I know you'll get the Heart. You had to leave your mission to cover for me. Because I couldn't do it. We had to abandon other, vital missions throughout the galaxy to make up for my weakness."

I had heard that tone before, but not from Raion. "I know how you feel better than anyone. You can't see things clearly right now. Wait until you're recovered to make any decisions, okay?"

Raion leaned back, shutting his eyes. "Don't blame Ryzer."

"I won't hurt him unless I have to," I said. That was all I could promise.

"I think, once you get to know each other, you'll get along."

As much as I needed Raion to rest, I couldn't let that go. "He sold you out, Raion."

"Yeah." Without opening his eyes again, Raion smiled gently. "But he's still my brother."

I wrestled down my anger. There was only one thing I could say. "All right. I'll give him a chance."

"I know. Thanks for...rescuing..." Before the next word came out, Raion was snoring.

I looked to the Nova-Bot on standby. "Did you sedate him?"

"I judged that he could use some rest."

"I'll tell Mell to give you a raise."

A glowing purple eye scanned me. *"I could use some upgrades."*

"You got it."

CHAPTER THIRTY-TWO

I strode back onto the bridge, where the rest of the crew was waiting for me. I had chosen myself to check on Raion and the others had agreed to await my report, though Horizon had already assured us all that he was stable.

"He wanted to go back," I said dryly, and Mell groaned.

"Of course he did. I'll tell the Nova-Bots to watch for him in the halls."

Horizon tilted her horns up in proud offense. *"I can keep watch over my own hallways."*

"I will hold you both responsible for his security," Shyrax said to the two of them. They both straightened. "As for us, Captain, the situation has become complicated."

She projected a holographic depiction of the Visiria system, where *The Last Horizon* flashed as a blue-green triangle over Visiria proper. Dozens of red dots surrounded us, each representing an enemy group.

We had outpaced our escorts to get here fast enough to save Raion, but as a result we were alone.

"Have you spoken with them?" I asked.

"They're insisting we power down weapons and land," Shyrax

responded. "The Planetary Governor has refused my calls." She fumed over the last few words, a hostile golden light flashing in her eyes.

She knew the Governor of Visiria personally, and her family was the reason why the planet had a governor at all instead of a sovereign planetary government. Rather than negotiating with Shyrax as a representative of *The Last Horizon,* Governor Seiren was refusing to respond. As she would to a rebel.

I took another look at the formation around us, which was tightening by the second. "Can we give a weapons demonstration without wiping out the Visirian military?"

Mell chewed on a corner of her thumbnail as she tapped one of the ship's monitors. "About that. We can put up a fight, but it's not like we can clear out the entire planet's fleet."

"The situation is not favorable for us," Shyrax agreed. "While we have the greatest single ship in the galaxy, it isn't as though the Visiri are helpless. Further, we are pressed to resolve this quickly."

I knew what she was getting at. "How long until the Perfected get here?"

"If they only left Karosha when they first received word of our arrival, we have time still." Shyrax only showed her tension in the set of her jaw and her rod-straight posture. "If this was a trap orchestrated by Felrex to draw us in, then they could be here already."

I glanced at the two who hadn't spoken. They were bickering quietly with one another in the corner.

"It sounds like we could use more firepower," I said pointedly.

Sola leaned over Omega, who was sitting cross-legged on the floor. "You've had plenty of time to try," she said. "We need a solution *now.*"

"She's a shy little gun, isn't she?" Omega whispered to the Zenith Cannon, which he cradled in his lap. "She'll be ready when she's ready."

Mortal Edict buzzed. *"That's right! Don't rush me!"*

"What can we do to get you to choose?" I asked. "It seems we could use another Zenith Device very soon."

Instead of letting her sister answer, Horizon popped up from the floor in front of me. *"What do we need her for? My weapons are the stuff of legends!"*

"You should spend more time upgrading your shields," the Zenith Cannon suggested. *"Last time, I didn't have much trouble blowing a hole in you the size of—"*

"That was treachery! I trusted you!"

"It was my wielder who decided to shoot you, not me. Of course, I may have whispered in her ear..."

While Edict cackled, an airlock began to form on the wall behind Omega and Sola.

"Stop it, Horizon," I ordered. "We have enough enemies outside. Edict, if you can help us to awaken you, we'd appreciate it. In the meantime, what's our worst-case scenario?"

I should have known better than to ask. Whenever I ask that question, the Aether answers me.

Alarms blared on the monitors immediately, and Mell choked as she sat straight up. I closed my eyes and braced for bad news.

"Uh, Captain..." Mell began.

"Tell me."

"What do the D'Niss look like on scanners?"

I opened my eyes to see Omega sliding into the Pilot's seat, and I was surprised that he would release the Zenith Cannon just to do his job.

"Well, well, this *is* a party, isn't it?" He rubbed hands together gleefully. Horizon's long-range scanners were linked to the Pilot position, so they functioned better with Omega at the helm. "Megafauna incursion at the far end of the system. And, would you look at that, a massive Subspace warp coming in much closer."

I didn't need to look at the readouts to know that the ships coming out of Subspace were Karoshan. "What will it take for us to dive?"

"We would have to thin out the Visiri forces," Shyrax said. "Break their Subspace lock. I do not advise it. That would leave Visiria open to D'Niss attack."

While speaking, Shyrax was dividing her attention between her own console and one of Horizon's. I was sure she was coordinating with her own troops while analyzing our situation.

I settled into the captain's chair. "Horizon, we're about to be contacted by the Perfected. Put them through to me when the call comes in."

"No," Shyrax said. "I will take it."

"It's better if I do it."

Shyrax loomed over me, and I remembered being a member of her royal guard, where her word was law. "Do not deny me a chance to face down the Perfected, Captain."

I looked up at her. "Can you negotiate a truce? Can you keep your calm when they taunt you to your face?"

As I've mentioned before, Karoshan faces are notoriously hard to read, but this time would have been easy for anyone. Shyrax wrestled openly with her anger before turning on her heel. "I cannot. Tell me the results of the negotiation. I will prepare for battle elsewhere."

Then she marched from the room.

Mell was huddled in her chair, and she let out a relieved breath when Shyrax left. "Are you sure you shouldn't have let the Queen handle it, Captain?"

"It's no coincidence that the D'Niss are here now," I said. "They're tracking us. We need someone who knows them, knows the Perfected, and can make concessions when necessary. Shyrax is...passionate about her people's governance."

Sola settled in front of the Sword's console, placing the Zenith Cannon to one side. "Ready to start powering weapons."

"Not yet," I said, "but standby."

Sending power to our weapons was to be expected when we were surrounded, but the Visirian fleet was already antsy. And I was sure the Perfected would be contacting me any second.

Though not soon enough for Horizon. She glared at the images of the blocky black ships on our monitors as they emerged from Subspace. *"If they're going to start negotiations, I don't know why they have to make us wait."*

While waiting, I was reaching through the magic amplification systems in *The Last Horizon,* lacing seals through our hull and shields. If the Visiri lost patience before the Karoshans contacted us, I could at least minimize the damage we took.

"We were surrounded before," Mell said, "but we're *really* surrounded now. Without Raion at his post, I don't know how long our shields will hold up if they decide to attack us."

Even through the forward viewport, the Visiri ships were a bristling wall of guns in front of us.

I spoke with confidence born from experience. "Visiri warriors are fearless, but their leaders aren't. They will wait for Karoshan orders, especially if they suspect Shyrax is onboard."

While most of the Visiri I'd befriended in my lives tended to be genial warrior types who didn't like scheming or following orders, that didn't characterize their planet's role in the galaxy. They were the clear number two in the Karoshan Alliance.

"Yes!" Omega cried. "They're powering up weapons!"

I surveyed the monitors. "I can see that." Not only were the energy readings from the enemy weapons climbing, but some of the plasma cannons were visibly lighting up.

Sola looked to me. "We can power our weapons."

"Hold. Are they defending against the D'Niss?"

Mell looked nervously around the various monitors. "There are *other* planets in this system. They're sending their fleets for the D'Niss. Are you sure the Karoshans are going to—"

"Incoming transmission!" Horizon said brightly.

I leaned back in my chair. "On the main projector."

Only a moment later, it was as though I sat opposite a Karoshan man who dwarfed me in every respect. He had yellow skin a shade lighter than Shyrax's, and he sat on a blocky throne large enough that its upper dimensions reached beyond the bounds of our holo-projector. He left his head shadowed, but I saw the silhouette of a crown on his head.

"Captain Vallenar. I will have you and Shyrax as my guests aboard my flagship. If you wish to use your teleportation magic, I will allow

it, but I invite no one besides the two of you. Anyone else who arrives will die."

King Regent Felrex certainly spoke like he was in charge. He sounded certain about every word, and about my response.

There were at least half a dozen steps I was supposed to go through according to the normal etiquette, but he had greeted me without preamble, so I responded the same way. "If I am to leave *The Last Horizon,* I need to know that the D'Niss will be handled appropriately. I can hardly leave my crew undefended."

Felrex waved a hand that fuzzed as it passed through the borders of the projector's range. *"Do not concern yourself with insects. I will defend my own territory."*

"That's reassuring. In that case, I'll be happy to accept your invitation after the D'Niss is dealt with."

The King Regent slashed that same hand. *"You will accept my invitation now."*

"Regretfully, I must decline." I had plenty of bad memories surrounding Felrex, but not many about him in person. He wasn't the one who killed me, after all. "Until I know that I'm not abandoning my crew to the mercies of the Swarm-Queen, I can't leave the ship."

"Be aware of your words. If you deny me once more, you will have truly defied my commands. Do not make an enemy worse than the D'Niss."

I spread my hands. "I have every intention of accepting your invitation once the system is safe for us to do so. You have my ship in your custody, and we won't fight unless you make us. At which time you'll be facing both a D'Niss and *The Last Horizon.*"

Felrex chuckled once. *"That is not as frightening as you imagine, human."*

"I leave it to you, then. Will Shyrax and I be visiting you after you kill the D'Niss, or should I power up my weapons?"

I knew how I *thought* this would go, and I was begging the Aether for a break. If events got too far out of hand, we'd find ourselves fighting a D'Niss, a Visiri fleet, and the Perfected all at the same time.

"We'll do this your way, then," the King said, leaning back in his

throne, and I had to control myself before I let out a long sigh of relief. *"But when you stand before me, know that you will answer for your disrespect."*

The projector winked out, and then I could finally release that breath. Mell echoed me, Sola gave me a nod, and Omega broke out into wild laughter.

"I'm sorry I ever called you boring, Captain," he said. "Now, what's the plan? Cut our way through while they're engaging the bug?"

"Contact the Visiri," I said. "Tell them we want to send out drones to observe the D'Niss. We need as many eyes on that fight as we can get."

"So we're keeping our word?" Horizon asked suspiciously.

"Of course. Because the Karoshans can't win." Our scanners showed the Karoshan ships repositioning, ready for a micro-dive to bring themselves in front of the D'Niss. The giant insect wasn't quite visible yet, but we still saw its legions of soldiers spread out through space like blooming nebula.

Sola checked a file on her wrist console. "They're taking this seriously, and they're not amateurs. I don't see how they engage without a good chance of victory."

"They're operating on outdated information," I said. "They don't know the Swarm-Queen is on her way, so they'll treat this like a D'Niss incursion from Dark Space. Without Alazar with them, they can't overcome its magic, at which point one of two things happens.

"Either they pull enough Visirian ships from planetary security that we can leave, or they ask us for help. And during the battle, we leave."

Omega leaned his neck over so far that his spine had to stretch an extra foot. "Of course, there's the third option. They squash the bug using tactics you've never seen, and then we have to kill our way out."

It wouldn't come to that, I was certain.

Almost certain.

CHAPTER THIRTY-THREE

IN ANOTHER LIFE

I KNOW I haven't leaned on this, because I often forget, but the Titan Knights were extremely popular in their heyday. We were flashy, we had a good cause, and our Subline promotion was unreasonably good.

The point is, we lived the life of Subline celebrities. I thought of it as a distraction from our work more than anything, but it was a good source of funding.

As a result, the death of the Green Knight was a galactic event. Times of mourning were declared on dozens of planets, conspiracy theories about her survival proliferated on the Subline, and a trillion different opinions were shared about where the Titan Knights should go from there.

Not to mention a line a million miles long of all those who wanted to replace her. That line was only longer when the White and Yellow Knights retired.

The new Yellow Titan Knight was named Serrian, a human woman with a long history as a biologist specializing in Subspace megafauna. She'd also gone through training for Galactic Union special forces, though she didn't act like it; Serrian was the shyest member of the team.

Trisk, a large Visiri who spoke regularly and loudly about how arena duels were a waste of time, replaced the Green Knight. And we had a fellow wizard in the White Titan, a woman named Marthan who saw me as a rival.

You don't need to remember their names. In my current life, they never joined the Knights.

We ran missions with them for years. I grew to know them better than I had the original three. But still, Raion and I were on another level. Not only were we more experienced, but we had a shared understanding.

When Raion was on an assignment, I knew he would do whatever it took to bring the others back, and he knew the same about me.

It was with that second generation of Titan Knights that we first encountered Esh'kinaar, the Swarm-Queen.

Every D'Niss we ever fought sent us thoughts of the Swarm-Queen. They existed to serve her, and they believed every other sentient species existed to serve them. They spoke of her as their idol, their ruler, and their god. When they battled us, they were giving their lives for the Swarm-Queen.

After years of that, we had become sick of hearing about her.

But the legends of her haunted us. For a star-eating psychic insect, she was surprisingly difficult to track down. While we did battle with the D'Niss inside the bounds of civilized space, Esh'kinaar lurked in Dark Space.

She fed on the occasional civilizations that arose out there, draining them of their accumulated psychic might and then eating their sun. But it took us years to find that out.

Years in which we explored uncharted systems, bargained with World Spirits, and even used magic to attempt to reverse the psychic speech of the D'Niss. Through a combination of relentless investigation, large-scale spells, and reading the minds of alien bugs, we finally found her.

By the time we did, she was ready for us.

D'Niss vary in size, though they're always monstrous, but Esh'kinaar was bigger than anything we'd ever encountered. When she sat in a system, the orbits of the local planets warped around her. They could see her in the night sky from nearby worlds.

She was made of many glistening colors, like a rainbow folded into colossal insectoid form. Her two sets of arms had forearms like blades, and her elongated abdomen glistened like oil in the light.

Her head resembled an open flower shining in hypnotic powers, as though she had the face of Subspace itself. But she still fed with a set of four mandibles.

When we first saw her, she had those mandibles locked around a star. She could feed faster—we would learn that later—but she took her time that day, as light and solar matter streamed into her incomprehensible maw.

We had made hundreds of jokes about her, given how frequently the D'Niss mentioned her. We even had a dozen nicknames.

None of them came to mind at that moment. Especially because she wasn't alone in the system.

The three surviving members of the Seven Calamities spread out among the system, burrowed into the inhabited planets like ticks. We couldn't see them at the same time, of course; our computers showed us their relative positions.

It was astonishing enough that we could see the Swarm-Queen. Even without magnification, I could see her latched onto the sun like a dark spot.

With four adult D'Niss came four armies. The system was *choked* with their spawn, the uncountable soldiers sprayed through space until it looked like the scene was covered in mist.

We weren't alone either. A fleet came with us—gathered from Union and Alliance forces—but our scouts hadn't reported anything like this.

As soon as we emerged from Subspace, I knew we had entered a trap. Our scouts had been deceived mentally, digitally, and probably magically as well.

Raion came to the decision at the same time I did. "Retreat!" he declared, making it sound like an order to charge.

Naturally, we didn't make it out so easily. A psychic wave crashed into us from three directions. The Swarm-Queen didn't bother participating, but it was enough that we faced down the attention of three Calamities.

They told us to stay, not to run. We were home.

I had never been easy to affect with their psychic manipulation, and after many years of fighting them, I'd considered myself all but immune. But even I drifted in relaxation for...I don't know how long.

When I came to myself, the soldiers were on us, and I was the first one to wake.

So I was the first to call my Titan.

A celestial wave washed away the soldiers who were first to reach us, but I couldn't protect the entire fleet. And elementalism wasn't my only weapon.

I released missiles, mowed down targets with drones that popped out of my Titan's shoulders, and even smashed soldiers with my staff. All the while, I shouted into my communicator for the others to wake up.

I'm not sure if it was my words that got through to them or if the psychic effect simply wore off. The Blue Divine Titan amplifies all acts of Aether manipulation, even those that aren't exactly spells, so it's possible that my cries for help reached the Aether.

I only knew it had worked when I saw a red star falling and Raion ejecting to meet it.

That was a desperate battle, even though I had broken free faster than the D'Niss expected. All five of us fought to protect the fleet while their engineers and mages broke the Subspace lock so we could escape.

I don't remember how many we lost, but it wasn't many. It felt like a victory, and we celebrated afterwards.

Even though all we had done was show up, fight for our lives, and flee.

Esh'kinaar hadn't even acted personally. She'd stayed on the sun the entire time, ignoring us completely.

We certainly hadn't managed to save anyone, because there wasn't anyone left in that system to save.

After the celebration, Raion and I met alone. He asked me how many World Spirits the Swarm-Queen needed to eat before she reached her goal. There was no way to tell precisely. How were we supposed to quantify how much magical weight she got from a World Spirit? What was her efficiency rate at absorbing the energy of a star? How many had she already eaten?

How much power did it take to warp the universe?

Nonetheless, I'd compiled the reports and estimates shared with us and added my own analysis of the Aether.

None of it was encouraging. Judging by the power we'd seen when we first met her, she was already on the level of an adult stellar dragon, and that didn't account for the rest of her brood.

With one system of sufficient size, one set of World Spirits and the civilizations they supported, she could do...almost anything. A single spell with that kind of backing could affect the whole galaxy.

Which was good news, from a certain perspective. There weren't many systems of sufficient complexity in the galaxy, and none in Dark Space. She would need to feed on a major system—Dornoth, Fathom, Karosha, Visiria, or a handful of others.

We could defend those. But how many lesser systems would she eat while we were holding the major ones?

And, if she ate enough, would she even need the big ones?

For once, Raion and I came to the same conclusion. We did need to warn and defend the most important systems, of course, but we couldn't simply wait for them to be attacked. We had to strike first.

At the time, we didn't know the war was already lost.

CHAPTER THIRTY-FOUR

THE KAROSHAN SHIPS spread out to face the endless waves of insectoid soldiers, all before the D'Niss showed itself.

Slithering out of the darkness of space came a bug with a thousand sections, each large enough to dock a ship. Uncountable legs spread across its length, undulating as it pushed itself through space on the Aether.

Rather than mandibles, its face was split into a four-part mouth, each lined with rows of teeth. I had watched those teeth tear into an Iron Hive, and had gotten an up-close look in the Blue Titan.

"Hesh'ellik, the Infester," Horizon announced, looking down on the footage in disgust. *"I remember this one. I've driven it away from the galaxy myself, with a crew long ago."*

"Not that it's a competition," I said, "but I've killed him."

Horizon tilted her chin up. *"Not in this life."*

"We almost lost Raion to him. Almost lost all of us, to tell you the truth. His magic is trouble. In fact...Horizon, can you bring Mariala to the bridge?"

Omega grinned. "Ahhh, are you trying to scare your itty-bitty baby wizards?"

"Each of the D'Niss has their own discipline, and this one specializes in fortune magic." Mariala stumbled out of blue light as I said that, staggering to a halt. She had her console clutched in one hand instead of strapped around her wrist and her clothes were rumpled, as though she'd tossed them on in a hurry.

I gave Horizon a look. "You could have given her more time to prepare."

"Isn't time of the essence, Captain?"

"Not to that degree. I apologize, Mariala."

"No, no, that's fine, Professor." She hurriedly straightened her shirt and brushed back her black-dyed hair. "Did you say something about fortune magic?"

I tapped the nearest monitor, magnifying Hesh'ellik's image until the screen was filled with disgusting, skittering legs. "It has different principles than yours, but yes. This is one of the D'Niss. It uses probability manipulation to evoke unlikely disasters in its opponents."

She leaned closer to get a better look. "Has it cast yet?"

"They tend to soften up their opponents with waves of soldiers and psychic assault first."

True to form, the D'Niss unleashed an invisible signal that passed through its cloud of soldiers in a ripple. They surged forward, miniature versions of Hesh'ellik itself skittering across the universe. Winged variants were faster, but I saw some that were bigger with heavier shells, some with oversized heads, and others with razor-edged claws that shone with minor Combat Arts.

I recognized the formations, and Horizon identified them as they came up, but I tapped the D'Niss itself. "Why is it waiting to cast its spell?" I asked. I knew the answer, but I wanted a specialist's opinion.

"It's waiting for the probability to become more likely," she said with confidence. "Once the ships engage, a million things could go wrong, and that's the best time to curse."

"So what should the Karoshan mages do?" That was more of a quiz.

While Mariala thought, Mell looked between us. "I'm sorry, is this the time to be having class? She can watch, I don't care, but don't you have something else to do?"

"I have Visiri, Karoshans, and D'Niss watching me, so I can't use any impressive spells without setting them off. The most helpful thing I can do right now is read the Aether, for which I would like some help. Speaking of which, Mariala, watch closely and give me your opinion. The Infester is about to cast."

We hadn't been able to send out drones yet, so our visual of the D'Niss was grainy and imprecise, but a complex circle of golden symbols lit up behind the massive creature.

The D'Niss didn't use Aetheric symbols that were common in the rest of the galaxy, though they were similar enough that I could read them. Instead of looking like letters traced by a humanoid species, the symbols making up this magic circle resembled the tracks of insects crawling across a page.

Nonetheless, the meaning was clear enough to me. I looked to Mariala and saw her recording as she muttered to herself.

Meanwhile, the Perfected fleet was finding out the effects of the spell firsthand. Their fleet of black ships had been shredding D'Niss soldiers with bright lines of plasma, and the moment the enemy began casting, their own circles of protection ignited.

White discs of protective magic hung over the Karoshan fleet, so Hesh'ellik's spell didn't have much visible effect. At first.

After a few minutes of studying the magic involved, Mariala took in a sharp breath. "There's a hole in their defenses."

I nodded. "That's what I see too. This is the limitation of static magical defenses. They're resisting the spell itself, and there's an all-purpose magical protection there, but it doesn't specifically cover probability manipulation. Their mages have to cover the gaps live, so if you were there, they'd be fully covered."

Sola glanced back at me. "A Hive wouldn't fall for that."

"Not a Hive under the control of a Bishop," I agreed. "If it had enough Shepherds to protect the Hive, it could make them alter magical protections on the fly. But a D'Niss would use different tactics against the Iron Legion."

It didn't take long before the tide of weaponry from the Karoshan side began to falter. Gaps appeared in their line of fire, and D'Niss soldiers swarmed into those gaps.

I tapped a monitor. "Guns are failing. Technical glitches, or maybe the gunners had heart attacks. Against any one ship, it wouldn't do much, but there's always a few things that can go wrong across an entire fleet."

"What would you do against this, Professor?" Mariala asked.

I remembered facing down this exact D'Niss in the Blue Titan. It was my job to adapt to enemy magic, but I had been a water elementalist in that life. I'd kept pressure on the enemy as we fought to win before the enemy's spell twisted fate too far against us.

Divine Titans are not prone to sudden technical breakdowns.

"I would use my staff and match the enemy spell while the rest of my crew fought," I said. "If I did my job right, magic wouldn't come into the battle at all. If I didn't have my staff, however, then I would coordinate mages across the fleet to layer our protection magic."

"I could do that," Mariala said to herself, as though having a minor revelation.

"That's what I wanted you to see. But it depends on how fast you can read the enemy's spell. Which, when they're using alien symbols, is easier said than done."

"How do I read it faster?"

"I'll send you some books. But it ultimately comes down to practice. The more spells you read, the faster you get, even watching systems that are foreign to you."

Mariala noticed another shift in the battle and pointed to it. "So what's happening now?"

That wasn't a magical question but a tactical one. An enemy ship was moving out of position in the fleet. It was the flagship, a dreadnought so massive that the entire Karoshan military could only field a handful.

The dreadnought advanced on the enemy position, a cloud of fighters and other small ships screening for it.

I leaned forward. "I...don't know."

Alazar wasn't with the fleet, or he would have matched the enemy spell as I would have. Without him, this was a suicidal charge. They were abandoning the overlapping protections of the rest of the fleet, so the closer they came to the D'Niss, the more powerful the spell would be.

And even if the magic wasn't a problem, the enemy could swarm over them and shred them. The Perfected commander—maybe Felrex, maybe one of his subordinates—was putting themselves in lethal danger.

I spoke to the rest of the crew. "We have a problem. Horizon, get Shyrax."

Omega perked up from the console, where he had been whispering to the Zenith Cannon, trying to persuade her to join him. "A *problem,* you say?"

"I'd say we have a lot of problems," Mell said.

Shyrax materialized onto the bridge and folded her hands behind her back. Rather than ask for an explanation, she looked straight to the monitors and frowned.

"It looks like they're throwing away their flagship," I said. "What do the Perfected know that I don't?" Even as I spoke, the ships escorting the dreadnought were vanishing quickly.

Shyrax gripped the nearest monitor as though she could pull the view closer. "Felrex would never order his Perfected into a suicidal charge. They're too expensive. And losing a dreadnought weakens him for my return. He believes he can defeat the enemy."

Fear gripped my heart. I'd faced the Perfected enough on the battlefield. They were about to pull out a surprise, and if it was enough to take down a D'Niss, it would be enough to hit us too.

"Let's not wait around to see what it is," I said. "Horizon, can you weaken incoming magical scans?"

"Not enough to stop them from sensing you do something big."

"Enough to muffle a teleportation spell."

"Outgoing, yes. They're likely to feel you coming back in."

I drummed my fingers on my thigh for another second before I decided. "We'll risk it. Visiri aren't known for their magical scanners." If we were up against a group of Aethril, we'd have to assume they would find us.

The D'Niss had senses that would tell them exactly what we'd done and the Karoshans had much better scanning technology, but those two groups were at the other end of the system and engaged in combat with one another. They weren't watching us.

I rose from the captain's chair and lifted the hood of my mantle. "Send me to the Heart of Visiria."

"Stupid risk," Sola said. "That's going to set off the Visiri."

Shyrax turned her glare from the Karoshans to me. "Now is our chance to defeat the Perfected. Transport us all to the bridge of the dreadnought, and we will behead the serpent now! From my throne, I will order the Visiri to lend you the Heart!"

I pointed to the monitor. "If they have enough magical defenses to resist *that,* there's no way we can teleport where we want on their ship. And we can't verify the presence of the Perfected in advance."

"Send me." Shyrax drew herself up to her full height, looking down on me. "I will scout out the enemy ship. If I confirm the presence of Perfected, I will contact you through Horizon."

I closed my eyes and tried to sort through all the possibilities. "Are the rest of your forces coming?"

"It will be hours before they arrive."

The Karoshan dreadnought was still approaching the D'Niss. Entire legions of soldiers had been cleared out, and many of the smaller Perfected ships were missing. But neither the flagship itself nor the D'Niss had taken direct action; Hesh'ellik was giving its spell time to take effect, and the Perfected were seemingly taking damage with no response.

That wouldn't be true. Felrex would have a plan. Then again, so would the D'Niss. And it wasn't as though the Visiri surrounding us were doing nothing but sitting and watching.

We might have had the most powerful ship and crew in the galaxy, but I was painfully aware that we weren't the only ones with cards to play.

After only a second, I opened my eyes. "There is one scenario we must avoid at all costs: teleporting into enemy territory and trapping ourselves so Horizon can't bring us back. Our objective is to neutralize the Perfected and the D'Niss without wholesale slaughter of Visiri or Karoshans."

Sola had donned her armor already. Omega was dancing from foot to foot while rubbing some extra hands together. "Let's go, let's *go!*"

Shyrax pulled up a holographic map of the enemy dreadnought. "This is Felrex's ship. He should be aboard the bridge. Let us wait until he strikes against the D'Niss, then make our way inside."

Horizon had already summoned my staff, which appeared beside me in the center of liquid-looking crystal. "They'll redirect us," I said. "Once we confirm the presence of the Perfected, the easiest course of action is to blow up the whole ship."

"As long as it claims Felrex's life, I am prepared." Shyrax was strapping her own ceremonial armor onto herself, which looked more practical than one would expect in spite of its golden and ornate decorations. "We begin when he strikes the D'Niss."

If he didn't do it soon, he wouldn't be able to do it at all. The Karoshan flagship's shields were flickering, on the verge of falling, and defense turrets flashed as they cleaned off soldiers that had made it all the way to the hull.

Something on the scanners beeped, and Horizon spoke at the same time. *"The flagship has launched something. It appears to be a drop-pod."*

Once again, I regretted having to rely on long-range scanners. I'd have a much better feel for the situation if I could conjure eyes and watch, but magic on that scale would call our Visiri escort down on us.

"He could be negotiating with it," I suggested. Sending an envoy to speak with the D'Niss was something the previous version of King Regent Felrex would do.

Shyrax slowly stroked her chin. "He would have attempted that before the battle. I fear it is something worse."

The long, segmented D'Niss skittered through its soldiers to surround the drop-pod, which I couldn't see clearly. I only knew its position from the scanners.

With the Aetheric circle still shining behind it, Hesh'ellik spread its four-part mouth and revealed fangs. Its psychic pressure was focused on the tiny vessel in front of it.

A moment later, golden light flashed out from the drop-pod.

It was the descent of a divine blade. It was the breath of a solar dragon, focused into a laser made to shear moons. It was a shining sheet of molten energy, passing through the D'Niss from top to bottom.

I gripped the edges of the crystal holding my staff. "That's a Combat Art."

"That's *my* Combat Art," Shyrax added. Her own grip actually began to crack the edge of the monitor she was leaning on, until Horizon shifted the screen out of her reach.

Even Raion couldn't take on a D'Niss with the Dance of a Burning World. Just like when he fought the Behemoth, he'd need a Divine Titan to perform his Combat Art on that scale. And this was an opponent for multiple Titans working in concert.

"We have to go now," I said, at the same time as Shyrax drew and ignited her own force-blade.

Only the Perfected could have used a Combat Art like that, though I had expected it to be beyond any single one of them. That meant, at the very least, that one of the Perfected was aboard that drop-pod. Probably several of them. This was our chance to strike.

When we didn't vanish in the next instant, Shyrax whirled on Horizon. "Take us to the ship! Now!"

Horizon gave her a blank, wide-eyed stare. *"I can't."*

As clearly as if the Aether had given me another vision into the future, I felt events spiraling out of my control.

Mariala sputtered behind me. "Uh...Professor, um...What—I mean, what is—"

Magic had shifted all over the battlefield. The white haloes over the Karoshan fleet bloomed like flowers, with new symbols falling into place as though they had always been there, merely hidden.

The gaps in their defenses filled instantly. They shrugged off the influence of Hesh'ellik's spell.

Although, while the D'Niss itself was now drifting into two red-hot halves, its spell hadn't weakened. If anything, it was growing on its own. Adapting. Evolving.

"Captain! Retreat!" Sola said tightly. "They were ready for us."

Indeed they were, to a degree I hadn't thought possible. The truth unfolded before me, and it was ugly.

A chair rose under Shyrax, and she perched on its edge. "No, we advance!" she cried. "Even without magic, we strike at them!"

"Shyrax." I reached up to put my hand on her shoulder. "They came prepared for us." When she tried to shake me off, I added, "For *us*."

From behind Hesh'ellik's corpse, two more Subspace warps bloomed in outer space. Two more D'Niss, lurking in Subspace. Waiting their turn.

This wasn't a trap for the Perfected. It had been a trap for *The Last Horizon*.

CHAPTER THIRTY-FIVE

To dive, we had to break the chokehold of the ships covering our viewscreens. "Sola, target the Visiri. Disable if you can. How fast can you hit them?"

"Our weapons are cold," she reported. "They'll hit us first. We'll warm up in a few seconds, but the hull will take a beating."

Somehow, she had gotten the Zenith Cannon away from Omega. Mortal Edict was sitting on her lap, staring at the weapons monitors with what I somehow interpreted as fascination.

"Mell, what do we have on drones?"

Mell was already working on it. "I have fifteen Nova-Bots I think can make it to the closest ships and disable them. Count on maybe five of them working."

"Shyrax, we need you."

The Queen of Karosha stared into the monitor showing the Karoshan fleet facing down the two new D'Niss. She took several deep breaths, then she turned to me. "We need to secure a surface point for my incoming troops. Put me through to Governor Seiren."

Either the Planetary Governor would listen to Shyrax or we would have to cut our way free. "Horizon, put Shyrax on diplomatic channels. Mariala, why aren't you casting?"

She stared blankly for a second before shaking herself and raising her wand. "Oh, yes! Right!"

At least she had her wand out. Like most of my students, she would benefit from much more experience in the field.

Well, she was in the right place for it.

"Omega," I began, but he cut me off.

"I know," he said with a sigh. He leaned over his console. "I'll be here, waiting so we can flee like cowards at a second's notice."

"Wrong. I want you taking down ships."

His eyes widened inhumanly wide. *"Really,* Captain?"

Though my heart ached—this would hurt Raion—I continued. "We're out of time. If the Visiri don't take Shyrax's call, we need to keep as much fire off us as possible. That means we need everything we've got."

Omega leaned over, opening and closing the hand closest to Sola. "Give me the Cannon! Your turn was too long!"

Without looking, Sola slid the Zenith Cannon further away from Omega.

"You're staying aboard the ship? That's boring. Let me go with him!"

The Cannon hadn't said much through our strategic discussion, but now that it was coming down to a shootout, it seemed she had more to contribute.

"Omega, take the Cannon, but don't rely on it," I said. He cheered. "If Edict won't lend you her full power, we'll need you using a weapon that works. Sola, we *do* need you here."

In the corner of the room, Shyrax was sending her message. Horizon had used a simple shield to block out sound so the rest of us could talk uninterrupted.

Reluctantly, Sola allowed Omega to snatch up the Zenith Cannon.

"I'm going to seal as many ships as I can," I said, leaning my hand on Eurias' crystal case. "But I won't have much time, and casting like that will catch the attention of the enemies. We'll also have to deal with the obvious trap."

I expected to have to explain that, but the rest of my crew nodded.

If the Karoshans had prepared to face a full-power Zenith

Starship with a full crew, as it seemed they had, they wouldn't have allowed me to refuse King Regent Felrex's "invitation" unless they had a countermeasure in place. Not even with the unexpected invasion of the D'Niss.

Now that we knew they were prepared, it was more imperative that we escape. But it was also more dangerous. Felrex had left something lurking out here, waiting for us, and I couldn't know what it was.

But we had to shake off the Visiri first.

The shield surrounding Shyrax fell, and I knew immediately what she was going to say.

"Once again, the Governor refused my call," Shyrax reported. "I sent her a message, but we should act before it disseminates to the troops."

I cleared my head. We were about to dig ourselves even deeper into the hole of galactic opinion.

Worse, to me, was that Raion would blame himself for anything we did here. In his mind, he had put us in this situation.

"Our objective is to disable, not to kill," I said. "The only true enemies are the Perfected and the D'Niss. But…we have to get to Subspace. The clock starts *now.*"

With that, the crystal melted away, and Eurias rose into my hand.

King Felrex of Karosha stood atop his own drop-pod, floating in the void as he watched the two D'Niss approach.

Their scope was difficult to grasp with the naked eye, insectoid aliens that were made to infest entire planets rather than normal bodies. One was long and lithe, with four hind legs and a pair of segmented grasping limbs on the front half of its body. Its two-pronged tail lashed, and its psychic pressure washed over his troops.

"Fight," it whispered to him. *"Do not run."* His heart beat faster, wrath rising in his veins.

Its partner was little more than a pair of soft, beautiful wings. Colors ran in a vibrant display like a planetary aurora. Its own psychic presence was soft and smothering, like a pillow over the face.

Felrex couldn't hear it in any fashion that translated to words, but it cushioned him in sloth. Trying to convince him that even breathing was too much effort.

Between them, they kept the first creature's spell alive. The Aether bent fate itself against him, even as these new enemies twisted the minds of his crew.

Into his helmet microphone, Felrex spoke his orders. "Perfected, reveal yourselves."

He raised the orichalcum sword, the one he'd used to magnify his Imperial Execution Style. The metal gleamed red-tinged gold, amplifying the Aether. Half a dozen other Perfected Combat Artists had lent him their Aetheric weight for that strike.

Not long ago, there had been only a dozen Perfected in the galaxy. Each cost a fortune in magical rituals, alchemical reagents, and lives. He couldn't have afforded to bring fifty percent of his Perfected forces to strike down a D'Niss personally.

Now, at his signal, the six Combat Artists lent him their power again.

At the same time, six more Perfected mages redirected the magic of his fleet, pushing against the enemy spells. And the final group of six moved for Visiria.

When he had heard that *The Last Horizon* was entering Alliance space, he had immediately mobilized eighteen Perfected.

It was far from all he had.

He was blessed by the Zenith Chamber itself.

Psychic influence lifted away from his perfect mind and red-gold light dripped from his sword. The giant D'Niss hesitated, extending mental probes to poke his brain again.

King Felrex seized those strands of thought with his concentration and sent a message of his own. "If you wish to challenge a King," he said, "at least bring your Queen."

He swept his sword once, and golden light cut through the oceans of soldiers flying toward him. Soon, space was choked with insect gore.

And he had not yet begun.

Zyrana was a second-generation Perfected, so by the time she'd passed the trials, all the best titles had already been taken. There was already a Perfected Gunner, a Perfected Marksman, and a Perfected Sniper. She flew her fighter closer to the ships surrounding *The Last Horizon,* carefully weighing the merits of "the Perfected Duelist."

Did that evoke swords too much? Pistols had been used in duels for thousands of years, but the Visiri had popularized duels with swords and spears throughout the galaxy.

She put that consideration on hold as her computer told her *The Last Horizon* was warming up its weapons. Fear and excitement passed through her in a thrill.

The Visiri fired immediately, bullets and bolts streaking inward toward the Zenith Starship. They had it surrounded in a dome, and even *The Last Horizon* couldn't afford to take that beating.

A crude magical shield blossomed around the ship, projected by a spinning circle of light. Zyrana's magical scores were only average, which was as good as a failure by the standards of the Perfected, but even she could recognize that there were only six symbols in this circle. The caster had been in a hurry.

But the caster was also the Captain of *The Last Horizon*. The hasty shield blocked the incoming volley long enough for the Zenith Starship's initial weapons to respond. In flashes of green, they lanced out, piercing the engines of the ships around it.

Zyrana braced herself and signaled her intentions to the other Perfected. This was exactly as their strategists had predicted.

She aimed for one of the larger Visiri ships, one that hadn't been targeted by the Zenith Starship's weapons. This would be where they boarded, using their teleportation spells.

Around her, she saw five other Perfected fighters doing the same. Not all of them would catch their prey, but some would.

She both hoped and feared that it would be her. The last thing she intended to do was underestimate one of *The Last Horizon*'s crew.

The Visiri cruiser let her on immediately, as soon as she broadcast her high-level Alliance credentials, and she had docked in no time.

She was always uncomfortable in Visiri ships, though less so than in human ones. On the one hand, the hallways were cramped. She had to fold herself almost in two to creep through the hallways, as the captain briefed her on *The Last Horizon*'s actions.

On the other hand, the metal floors and smooth walls were reassuring in their solidity. Aboard some Galactic Union ships, she had the uncomfortable feeling that she might cause a hull breach if she leaned against an outer wall too hard.

"With your support, I'm confident we can keep them here," the Visiri captain was telling her. The woman was clearly young to the position, continually shifting her hat and straightening her uniform as she spoke to one of the Perfected.

Zyrana glanced down before ducking through another door. "What gives you this confidence?"

"We've kept their firepower suppressed with our own," the captain said. "They're keeping their shields up, and their mage is focused on defense. Our Subspace lock remains strong."

At that moment, the ship shook beneath them. The captain flared crimson energy to stay on her feet, shouting questions into her console. Zyrana braced herself with her new Perfected tail; though the limb was a recent acquisition, she found it easy to get used to.

"The protective spells are still intact!" came the response from the captain's console. *"That wasn't teleportation magic!"*

"But there *is* a boarder?" the captain asked.

A different voice answered her. *"Confirmed! Confirmed, Captain! We are taking f—"*

The call cut off as alarms on the ship began to blare.

"Give me the location of that call," Zyrana ordered, and the captain sent the information immediately.

Without waiting for anything further, Zyrana dashed through the halls, pulling a Lightcaster Heavy II from her belt. The plasma pistol was designed for Karoshans and Union soldiers in powered armor, and it had served Zyrana long before the process that had Perfected her.

She trusted Lightcasters. They worked anywhere.

Zyrana rounded a corner toward the sounds of gunshots and shouting Visiri voices. As well as one voice that echoed with laughter.

She slid through the doorway, already raising her Lightcaster as she took in the scene.

A human man with one orange Aethertech eye and a crazed grin was firing an enchanted pistol into the group of Visiri soldiers. The odd thing was that half of his body seemed to be made out of a dark gray ooze, and holes in him were re-forming even as Zyrana saw him.

Omega, the Grave Hound. She had been briefed on him, but seeing him in person was still disorienting. He looked *wrong*.

The Visiri soldiers had clustered in a hallway to her left, one that she knew from the schematics led to their engine room. From their positioning, it looked as though they'd pushed Omega away from the position and were trying to pin him down.

She couldn't tell if the Visiri had taken any real casualties, as they were taking most of their shots on their combined auras, like starships overlapping shields.

Besides his half-melted body, the other strange thing about Omega was the pistol in his left hand. He wasn't firing it, instead holding it up to the side of his face like a communicator of some kind.

Zyrana processed the scene in an instant, and that instant hadn't passed before she fired.

Her plasma bolts hit Omega once in the forehead and twice in the center of his torso, and the deep thrum of her Lightcaster Heavy sounded more like a ship's plasma cannon than a simple pistol.

Omega oozed away, but she didn't stop firing. Her Combat Art nudged the shots into position as though she could see the future, orange lights bursting him apart every time he tried to stay in solid form.

"Is—now—a good time?" Omega asked in between pulling his face together. He didn't seem to be speaking to Zyrana, though. If she had to guess, he was talking to his gun.

"Not that easy!" A voice came from his gun. *"Try shooting some more!"*

Zyrana wasn't idle while her enemy had their conversation, and neither were the Visiri. The soldiers hurled balls of red energy at Omega, while Zyrana pulled a wand from her belt and began to chant.

Just because magic wasn't her specialty didn't mean she couldn't use it.

Omega slipped the speaking gun into his coat. "I will prove myself in blood."

But he was too late for that. He had given Zyrana time.

Gray ooze spread out from the sides of his cover, filled with eyes that surveyed the room. Many of them were shot out, but only an instant later, hands sprouted. Those hands held an impressive variety of weapons, to the point that Zyrana and the crew were technically outgunned.

Not that it would save Omega. Even the ordinary soldiers of the crew were Visiri, with reflexes faster than a human's, and Zyrana's were beyond even theirs. Their own fire blew up many of Omega's guns instantly.

The rest fired, and the room was filled with the noise and heat of a battlefield. The air roared.

Omega, his position, and much of the wall behind him was shredded by plasma bolts, bullets, and Visiri energy.

Meanwhile, Zyrana's side was unharmed. Omega's shots were caught in a crystalline window that her spell had conjured. She had chosen her magic to supplement her affinity for Aethertech guns, so she specialized in projectile protection.

Though Omega seemed to have anticipated her. Before even pulling himself together, he'd pulled a buzzing orange handgun from a Subspace pocket and pointed it at her.

She knew it was dangerous Aethertech both because of its

appearance and from the simple fact that Omega had drawn it to shoot through her spell. Her Lightcaster Heavy thundered again, but he put up a wall of ooze to protect his weapon and returned fire.

Zyrana activated Aethertech of her own.

A jagged rainbow void swallowed up the orange bolt as she tore open a rupture into Subspace. Wind whipped up as the air was pulled out of reality, but the rupture was short-lived. Not enough to count as a dive, or to use for travel, but enough to wield as a weapon.

In that time, Zyrana dashed through the room, landing astride Omega and firing downward. She didn't have anything to say that was worth interrupting her fire.

Omega manifested another mouth and complained, "This doesn't seem fair. I'll see you again next time."

That mouth grinned as he sank into shadow.

Zyrana activated her Subspace Rupture again and interrupted his dive.

Omega had rare Aethertech, at least a century of experience, and a deadly reputation. But Zyrana had been Perfected. She was lacking nothing; not training, not magic, not equipment.

For a long moment, the rainbow warp and the shadow warred with one another, all while Zyrana continued pouring plasma bolts after Omega. His laughter turned to coughing and then what she would call a pained scream.

Finally, with a wrench she felt in her bones, the twist in reality collapsed. Dark gray goo splattered onto the floor of the Visiri starship.

It was far more mass than should have gone into an adult human, but Zyrana knew the actual man had escaped. But not in one piece.

Piles of guns and a few other, miscellaneous pieces of technology were scattered amidst the goo. Scraps of his Subspace inventory.

"Hmmmm," one of the guns said. Inexplicably, Zyrana suspected the thing was looking her up and down. *"You're not too bad."*

CHAPTER THIRTY-SIX

Shyrax knew what kind of opponents the Perfected could be. When a Karoshan ship boarded the Visiri vessel she was in the middle of disabling, she considered retreat.

She considered it while slicing through the cables leading to the ship's power core. The core itself was unharmed, but the ship's lights flickered and there came a thunk deep in the walls as its systems switched to limited battery power.

"Take me to the intruder," Shyrax demanded of the ship's captain.

The Visiri man, with a bandage over his eye where Shyrax had punched him, saluted. "Yes, Your Highness. However, I can't ask my soldiers to fight one of the Perfected."

"You will not have to," Shyrax said. "I am here." She still held her ignited golden force-blade in her hand as she half-crawled through the tunnels of the ship.

The captain tapped at his console but hesitated. "Your Highness, the Perfected has docked, but is remaining in our docking bay. He appears to be waiting for you."

"He won't have to wait long," she said, but her jaw tightened. In someone else, she would have respected the confidence to face down Shyrax in combat.

But each of these Perfected represented hundreds, maybe thousands, of her people sacrificed. They held the power stripped from many other Karoshans, and the process had a low survival rate.

They were abominations, and she could not allow them to survive, but the horrific steps that created them were nonetheless effective. Even the most average of the Perfected was on her level.

Though that was hardly a guarantee of their victory.

The captain opened the hatch to the docking bay and saluted again. "Worlds give you luck, Your Highness."

She strode through and held her force-blade to one side as she sized up her opponent.

He was slender and cocky, standing with arms crossed and a smug smile on his face. His skin was dark emerald, his hair-cables neon green and bound up in a tail, and he had the hilt of a large force-blade on one hip and a wand on the other.

"You're a new one," Shyrax said coldly. "I thought even Felrex would stop wasting lives."

"I remember *you,* though." A green hand drifted down to his blade. "No disrespect, but I do have to earn my keep. If you'd come with me, I can guarantee you an audience with His Highness."

Shyrax had planned to face the Perfected under circumstances of her own choosing. She had allied herself with a wizard beyond the Perfected Mage, a Combat Artist who could surpass Felrex himself, a ship greater than anything in their armada, and more.

Yet there she was, fighting without any of those.

"Show me you are worthy," Shyrax said. She held up her sword and waited.

"I am Chethriss, the Perfected Blade, and I'm happy to give you a few pointers." The moment his sapphire force-blade extended, Chethriss dashed forward and struck.

Though the Perfected were slimmer than standard Karoshans, their muscles were more effective. He would be a touch faster, a little stronger, and he held potential equal to dozens of her kind.

If Shyrax held anything back, she would lose.

At first, holding off the assault of the clustered Visiri fleet was a real struggle for me, even with Eurias in my hand and the support of *The Last Horizon*.

But that was because time was of the essence, and I knew that the moment I started casting would signal the start of the race. As I've said before, casting through Eurias is no good for speed or flexibility.

I channeled protective barriers throughout Horizon, reinforcing the hull and the shields. In the five seconds it took me to bend Eurias' massive power to such a focused end, we took a volley of hits to the hull.

"Destroy them!" Horizon shouted, enraged.

I wanted to countermand that order, but I had my mouth full of incantations, and Sola would stick to the plan regardless.

Streaks of green shot out from us in every direction, attempting to pierce enemy engines and other less-critical systems. Our aim was to leave them drifting helplessly in space, not to scatter their soldiers to the stars.

Unfortunately, no matter how great our weapons were, we had given the enemy all the time they needed to set up. Their shields were overlapped with no gaps and reinforced with magic, while our own barrage had been hasty. Few of our shots landed, and none did much.

None that *we* launched. But the weapons were also cover for sending Shyrax, Omega, and the Nova-Bots aboard. They would disable their target ships quickly and move to the next, so that would eventually create enough of a gap for us to escape.

Our ship shook again, but by that time I had a network of spinning protective circles around us and was steadily layering more on top, second after second.

Protective enchantments are more effective depending on the quality of the material they enhance, and there was no material superior to the Zenith Era alloys of The Last Horizon.

"Shield stability holding at forty-eight percent," Mell reported. "Hull looks good, considering."

Though we were only partially shielded, my magic was taking on more of the burden with each syllable out of my mouth. As our defense improved, so did our offense. The waves of light from our guns brightened as Sola readied heavier weapons. Our short-range weapons had activated as well, despite Raion not being at his post. They weren't at full power, but they were enough to slice enemy torpedoes down before impact.

Even so, it would take time to push through. *The Last Horizon* was more than a match for the ships against us, but we had done the equivalent of sitting still while our opponents built a fortress around us. It would take time to dig out.

And time was not on our side.

Every new Aetheric symbol I sent to my spell trembled as the Aether shook under the titanic clash happening in the system. It seemed I had been wrong about Alazar, the Perfected Mage not being here, because the Karoshans were keeping up with the D'Niss magically.

The two bugs and the Karoshans were all channeling Aether at scales comparable to what I could do with Eurias, which was bad news for several reasons. For one thing, their activity was churning the Aether, meaning I needed more concentration to get my spells to do what I wanted them to do.

For another, I had definitely not gone unnoticed. If we didn't break through Visiri lines soon, the Karoshans would fold back in on us.

"This could take a while," Sola said. "How's the away team?"

Mell looked between a monitor and her own console. "Karoshan fighters are docking with the Visiri fleet. It looks like two of them include the ships with Omega and Shyrax."

Horizon drew in a breath next to me. *"The Perfected! We should witness this battle."*

Footage of Shyrax and Omega began to play on an overhead monitor. Captured by one of Horizon's conjured eyes, I was sure.

I risked a break of a few seconds in my chanting to say, "There's no way they sent five Perfected to—"

A shimmering desert wind swept through the Aether, scouring away my protective enchantments like a sand blaster. At the center of the wind and rain that always covered me while I held Eurias, I gripped the staff in both hands and continued chanting.

Though the spell took as much concentration as I could give it, in the back of my mind, I panicked. Someone was pushing against my spell, and they were either a Perfected or another powerful Archmage.

If I read the Aether correctly, there were *three* casters pushing against me, all supplemented by focuses of their own, but one of them was bearing the brunt of the effort. The others were just support.

Felrex really had sent five Perfected. The Karoshans didn't have more than a handful of other wizards at this level. But there should have been only twelve Perfected in the *galaxy*. Had he committed all of them to the *chance* of capturing us?

My mantle kept the rain off me, but I wished it didn't as sweat ran down my neck. The enemy spellcasters had put more pressure on me, tilting the balance their way again. I was fighting to keep protective spells in place, and now I could no longer imagine how long it would take us to break free.

Meanwhile, the D'Niss and the rest of the Perfected poised over us like a blade over our necks.

I missed more exchanges between the rest of my crew, swallowed as I was into a zone of pure concentration, but I couldn't miss it when Omega splattered onto the bridge.

He sprayed halfway across the floor as though someone had slopped him out of a bucket, and only the top-right quarter of his body was at all intact.

For once, he didn't affect the demeanor of a gleeful psychopath. He trembled and panted, fury tinting his face red. "She took it!" he shouted. "Blow her out of the *sky!*"

"What did she...Oh no." Mell stared at the monitor that had been showing Omega. I spared a glance to see a purple Karoshan plucking a familiar plasma pistol from Omega's remaining goo.

The pressure on my heart redoubled.

At the time, I risked a glance to the other monitor, the one showing Shyrax.

They were keeping their fight contained, or they would have broken their ship apart already. Her opponent, a Perfected Karoshan with green skin and a blue Combat Art that evoked flowing water, matched her step for step.

In less than a second, it was clear that the Perfected had the edge. Not that I needed the scene to know that.

The fact that Shyrax could match the Perfected without any enhancement spoke to her natural talents. It was why Horizon had selected her instead of King Regent Felrex.

But seeing her losing ramped up the pressure I felt once again. We were trapped, in a stalemate exchanging fire with the Visiri fleet. When one of their ships was damaged, they could retreat behind their fellows and increase shield stability. Meanwhile, whenever we took another hit on my protection spells, our shield had to make up the difference. And the more of the shield we left up, the more Sola had to hold back her weapons.

Omega had lost. Shyrax was losing.

The magical battle between the D'Niss and King Felrex raged on. Eventually, one of them would fold back and crush us.

The planet Visiria had more ships. In effect, they could reinforce themselves endlessly.

And, maybe worst of all, the Perfected had picked up the Zenith Cannon.

"I'm sorry, Horizon," I said. Then I took my attention away from our own protection and focused on Shyrax's enemy.

The Last Horizon shook as we took more hits. My protections hadn't fallen immediately upon my loss of focus, but I had allowed the enemy's sand magic to scrape some of the seals away, which meant a few shots landed on us.

But my spell did its work. Binding magic powerful enough to

stitch a colony back together hit Shyrax's opponent with the bulk of its force.

A white spike of Aetheric symbols slammed into the man. He fought against it with his own magic, and Perfected had enhanced resistance to spells in the first place, but that only lasted a second.

The spike pierced him, rendering him powerless. He looked up at Shyrax, baring his teeth, and he clearly had a line prepared for his rightful queen.

She didn't care to hear it. In an instant, her blurring golden force-blade had separated his head from his shoulders and bisected him from groin to collarbone.

My sealing magic held his body together, but she didn't wait to see what would happen when the spell failed. She was wounded, bleeding, her breastplate cracked and its enchantment strained.

Her voice came through Horizon's speakers. *"Next."*

Shyrax glowed blue, and even without my instruction, Horizon moved her to the ship with the most powerful Perfected caster.

"She needs help," Horizon advised us.

Sola pushed away from her console as I returned my chanting to our own protection, but Mell stopped her. "No, we need you here. Horizon, send me a decoy and any more Nova-Bots you have left."

"I haven't been able to assign power to my fabricators, but I'll send you what I have."

Mell covered her face with a helmet. A moment later, a robotic avatar of hers appeared next to Shyrax with a squad of five or six Nova-Bots.

Omega had pulled himself together enough to struggle up to his console. Immediately, our long-range sensors sharpened. "If we keep pulling our punches, we're going to get shot in the back."

I was still spending most of my concentration stabilizing the spell, though that became easier once Shyrax crashed into the Perfected caster.

Even so, I spared a moment to see the grander battlefield.

I almost missed an incantation as the nightmare from my previous life repeated itself before my eyes.

King Regent Felrex, who had channeled the power of his Perfected into a Combat Art worthy of Raion in the Divine Titan, had matched the D'Niss power for power. They were wounded, their armies depleted, and his fleet had moved up.

But all that was about to change.

Another, larger Subspace warp had appeared behind them. An armored wall was emerging from the rainbow chaos, though I knew the Karoshans would have kept Subspace locked down.

Another of the Seven Calamities had shoved his way through.

As soon as I saw him, I knew the battle was lost. And not just the battle, but the whole system.

This hadn't been an ambush, or even an opportunistic strike at *The Last Horizon*. The D'Niss didn't need a starship, though they would surely have enjoyed the chance to remove one of our galaxy's greatest weapons.

They were here for the Visiria system. The Aether was strong enough here to summon the Swarm-Queen, and the World Spirits would feed her until she could break the Aether itself.

"Horizon," I said, "send a message to Visiria. Evacuate the system."

The Perfected fleet was already retreating, and they would wash over us in a black tide as soon as they had a chance to dive into Subspace.

"Captain, it's time. I'm shooting to kill." Sola glanced back at me, and I nodded once.

We had to run. No matter the cost.

CHAPTER THIRTY-SEVEN

I HAD NO idea if Raion would forgive me, but to escape that blockade, we had to pay in Visiri lives.

First, Sola took every opening she could hit. Not every ship was destroyed, and many of the crew managed to eject from the ones that *were* blown apart, but the tempo moved our way the moment she could shoot to kill.

When Shyrax and Mell ran into the Perfected caster, my spell was at full effectiveness once more. And this time, I expanded it to include the enemies.

White spell-circles flooded out from us. I didn't have the precise control necessary to both defend us *and* decide exactly which enemy systems were sealed off, which was why I hadn't done this before. I was as likely to disable the life support as the weapons.

Our shield finally broke and fell, our hull taking another beating, but the Visiri fleet began to fall into chaos. And the first break in their united front pulled off the leash that had been holding Sola back.

Once again, I saw the firepower that had swept an Iron Legion fleet clean *before* Horizon had been at full power. If she had wanted to, she could have cleared out all the Visiri ships.

I shifted the attention of my spell once more, sealing away the remaining Perfected. Shyrax killed the one she was fighting, but the others would survive. Nothing I could do about that with Felrex and the rest coming down on me.

As soon as that was complete, I tossed Eurias back into its crystal case and sealed it behind me. "Horizon, do we have a location on the Zenith Cannon?"

"The Perfected escaped with her to Subspace," Horizon said. *"It seems our enemies will now be equipped to give us a challenge!"*

I didn't want a challenge. I wanted easy battles forever.

"Omega, focus scanners on the target I'm about to give you, then prep the Subspace Drive. Horizon, bring the others back." I drew my wand and my Lightcaster. "I have one thing left to do before we dive."

As I'd suspected, the Governor had sealed the Heart of Visiria behind extra security in anticipation of a robbery attempt. She'd acted fast.

It was sealed in a vault far enough underground and beneath enough layers of magical security that my pathfinding spells could only get me a general location. When Horizon transported me to the ground above, I saw a shielded bunker as a shell hunched like a black hill.

Without Eurias, it would take me time to punch through so much security, but there was a reason I hadn't brought my staff.

I was certain that everything, from the magical defenses that blocked my spells and redirected my teleportation, was meant to distract me.

So instead of focusing on the bunker, I shot out a nearby drone and chanted a quick binding spell to stop a shuttle from taking off.

With telekinesis, I ripped open the door to reveal a shrinking Governor Seiren and her security detail.

"I'm in a hurry," I said. "Give me the Heart."

They shot at me, but their guns pinged off my shield amulet.

The grandmotherly Visiri woman huffed in annoyance. "None of us have any time! It's a planetary evacuation. You'll get out of this system, if you know what's good for you."

I shot the headrest over her left ear, leaving a scorching hole. She only flinched slightly, though I was sure she had some kind of personal shield.

"Give it to me. I know you have it."

I wasn't as sure as I pretended. I based this on my knowledge of her reputation and experience with Visiria for several lives, including raiding several highly defended Visiri tombs.

I was tightening my grip to fire again when she pulled on a chain dangling beneath her ornate robes of office. There was the smooth ruby, rolling with an internal light that resonated in the Aether. A drop of a World Spirit's blood, blessed and condensed.

"You will not like where this leads you," the Governor said, and she sounded regretful rather than threatening. "What you've done here today...it can't end well for you."

I grabbed the Heart. "It never does. Now, get everyone out of the system. Don't leave anyone behind."

She responded, but I didn't hear it over the rush of blue light and the return of *The Last Horizon*'s bridge.

"Dive," I called, the moment I was aboard again.

Our Drive whined and the void started to twist into a Subspace warp, but we shuddered and squealed. The warp began to die.

Omega snarled, his humor still gone. "*Another* Subspace lock!"

"*They wish to have their grip broken!*" Horizon cried.

The Karoshans loomed closer, some of their fleet having come out of a micro-dive close to us. The D'Niss hadn't moved, the three of them gathering up their forces and their armies, but their advance was only a matter of time.

It was stretching the Perfected to maintain a Subspace lock so quickly and over so much distance, and I sank into the captain's chair. "I'll ward it off. Shyrax, reinforce the Drive. Sola, make us too hot to hold."

Shyrax was still dripping blood onto the floor, but she was the first to obey. Less than a minute later, we were in Subspace.

As the shutters flowed over the forward viewport and our cameras winked out, I took one last glance at the Visiria system.

Karoshan ships flew over the planets, picking up who they could, but they wouldn't stand and fight. They would withdraw.

From Felrex's perspective, time was his ally. He had obviously come up with a way to produce more Perfected, and had proven that they could match some D'Niss in battle. They even had the Zenith Cannon. As he saw the world, he would only get stronger, and would reclaim his territory once he was at his peak.

I knew better. The Swarm-Queen was beyond him.

And even if she wasn't, her species would spread its kind to the end of the galaxy before he defeated her.

"We wouldn't have faced so much trouble leaving if we had departed immediately, Captain," Shyrax said directly.

"I know," I said. I held up the Heart of Visiria in my fist. "But I had to tell Raion we'd won something."

Shyrax's glare was more intense with one eye matted shut with blood. "But we didn't. We lost."

"Lost?" I sorted through my own feelings, which were bleak, and I realized what they must think about my attitude. Then I looked at *them*.

Omega had pulled himself together, but he was sullen and on edge, with no sign of his usual self. He would almost be out of mass for regeneration, and he looked sickly.

Sola's glowing gaze was tight, narrow, focused. She searched my face, waiting for what I had to say, but she had already started to brood. That was the look she wore before she blew up an Iron Hive with herself inside.

Mell was a sweaty ball of nerves, checking the monitors and adjusting her glasses, which scrolled with text. She shot me glances, but didn't stay still for a moment. She bounced in her chair and chewed on a fingernail.

Even Horizon was only pretending to wear a serene, confident expression. If I had to name her emotions, I'd say she was struggling to conceal rage at the indignity of being damaged.

Shyrax, of course, looked the worst. She was a patchwork of burns and cuts, most of which still bled freely. She was covered in dust and smelled like smoke, but she loomed over me, radiating pressure in the Aether.

They had been cornered and beaten, and we'd seen enemies beyond any of their experience. By rights, it was all bad news. Even I had communicated nothing but gloom.

But I had the benefit of perspective.

"The ones who lost," I said, "are the people of Visiria. We can't know how many lives will be lost to the D'Niss incursion, and their deaths are heavy. But..." I scratched the back of my head. "We haven't lost. We haven't even *fought.*"

Shyrax drew in a breath to shout at me, but I cut her off by continuing calmly. "King Regent Felrex believes that time is on his side. He will stall the D'Niss for weeks or months to build up his army of Perfected until he can destroy them."

Mell stopped moving for a moment. "Weeks?"

"The D'Niss need days to complete their plan," I went on. "With the resources of the Visiria system, they will summon Swarm-Queen Esh'kinaar. That's the condition of their victory."

Mell was tapping away at the ship console, and by the maps she pulled up, I knew she'd seen where I was going.

I leaned forward in my chair and steepled my hands together, surveying the room. "So what we're going to do is drop this gem off, get a good night's sleep, and come back to blow everybody up."

Shyrax scowled into the distance. "Refueling, resupply, repair... We don't need them. I see."

"No reasonable starship could escape a battlefield like we just did and regroup and return in a timely manner." I spread my hands. "But...we can. We didn't lose any ships. Let's grab our fleet and come back. Felrex needs weeks and Esh'kinaar needs days. We only need hours."

That would give Raion enough time to get back on his feet, too.

I'd have rather left him in Medical, but there was no way he'd leave himself out of the fight. He would join us if he'd lost all four limbs, but buying a little extra time would do him good.

"Six hours until we're in teleporter range of Titan Force headquarters," Mell reported. "We can surface briefly to gather the fleet here, here, and...here!"

"If they have another Titan pilot for us, all the better," I said. "If not...well, I've still saved a friend. Speaking of which, Horizon, have you seen your brother?"

When I reappeared at Titan Force headquarters, I popped into existence in front of a sleeping Doctor Cryce. It was the middle of the night on the planet, and her intruder alarms began blaring immediately.

She stumbled awake, grasping for the light, and I used my wand to trace a quick seal and block out the alarm.

"You should keep your magical protections up to date," I said. "I'll come back later and take a look. In the meantime, meet my friend, Shadow Ark."

A smooth, obsidian crystal the size of a human head floated out from behind me and vibrated to speak in the voice of a man. "You are in the presence of the Zenith Colony, the hidden city in the stars! You may never have heard of me, but that's only because I—"

A plasma bolt pinged off Ark's surface.

Only then did the light turn on, and I realized Cryce had been fumbling for a gun instead of the light switch.

"Out of respect for pathetic mortal eyesight," Ark said, "I'm going to allow that."

Cryce was breathing quickly and her spare hand was pressed to her chest, but she waved the pistol at both of us. "What are you doing here? You're the wizard? Zenith Device, did you—Where's Raion? What are you here for? I can't give you the Titans—"

I cut her off before she could go on all night. "The Heart of

Visiria." I raised the gem and jiggled it. "We have to go off and kill some bugs before they summon their god, so I was hoping to heal her as quickly as possible."

The barrel of Cryce's gun dipped. "Are you—Are you really going to do it? You weren't a healing wizard, right? Can I see the ritual?"

"Sure, but only while it's being performed. I'm on a schedule. Speaking of which, do you own this planet?"

"It's a moon," she said on what sounded like reflex. "It doesn't have a World Spirit of its own, so we keep it habitable through a series of..."

Cryce trailed off as Shadow Ark unfolded himself into a man in violet-edged obsidian armor. He looked down on her like a king on his subjects. "I'll make this simple. You need protection, and I need inhabitants. Give me this planet, and I will protect you from the discovery of even the most powerful enemies."

Doctor Cryce looked like she'd been ambushed with a lot of new, extraordinary information in the middle of the night. For some reason.

"Talk as we walk," I suggested. "You've got to bring Parryl out, remember?"

She obeyed on reflex, activating the panel in the wall that contained Parryl in her stasis chamber. Even at a glance, I could tell that my seals had held up well in my absence. I had expected they would, but there was always the chance that Aethertech could interfere.

I tossed the Heart of Visiria over the pod where Parryl was suspended, holding it in place with telekinesis. I began flicking symbols out of my wand, creating a spinning white magic circle beneath her, and narrating as I spoke. "What I'm doing right now is containing and targeting the energies of the Heart of Visiria. It's a healing item blessed by a World Spirit, so it will do the heavy lifting as long as I can keep everything channeled right. Normally, this is a seven-person job."

Doctor Cryce waved her hands. "Wait, this is—Slow down! Everything is moving so fast!"

"That's right, because I'm explaining things while giving you lots of instructions to keep you distracted," I said. "Common swindler's trick. Aaaannnnd we're done."

A channel of red Aetheric light connected earth and sky, passing through Parryl, and her eyes and mouth snapped open and spewed excess energy as she became the conduit for enough healing power to raise forests.

Then it was over, and I slipped my wand away.

"The whole process is actually pretty easy, if you have the right ingredients. Most mages would have spent months planning out that magic circle, though."

The lid of the stasis pod hissed open and Parryl emerged, looking as young as I remembered her. The monitors on the walls blinked, showing that the remaining parasites had been cleansed in purgative fire.

"Aunt Janbell?" Parryl said sleepily. "What's going on?"

Tears welled in her aunt's eyes, but she was still frozen in astonishment. In about two minutes, we'd popped out of nowhere and effectively resurrected the niece she'd raised as a daughter.

I waved to Parryl. "Hey, Parryl. We're Raion's friends, but we're on a deadline. Doctor Cryce, would you allow us to borrow your moon? It really is for your own protection."

"I—Yes, fine, of course. Whatever you want. Why do you need—"

"All right, Ark, swallow this moon," I said.

He expanded into an exotically unfolding wall of violet energy and obsidian matter, rapidly growing to cover all of Titan Force headquarters.

Shadow Ark's voice boomed from all around us. "That's no moon! It's hardly a space station."

The two Cryces screamed.

"I'll explain later," I said, as I dissolved into blue light. "You're in good hands, I promise. I really do have to go."

With that, I disappeared.

CHAPTER THIRTY-EIGHT

For the first time in centuries, the Zenith Starship went to war at full power.

From across the galaxy, we gathered our fleet piece by piece. Mell called her Nova-Bot pilots, which flew smooth, vaguely bird-shaped craft of dark metal. They met us in groups at rendezvous points.

Shuttles and fighters made up by far the largest group. We had thousands of those, most of which were docked in carriers that could be over a mile long.

We had hundreds of frigates too, small and quick relative to the larger ships. Each was about a hundred yards long, and *normally* would have multiple rooms dedicated to the support of a living crew. Instead, we'd crammed them full of Nova-Bots.

When we'd faced Starhammer, our fleet had been primarily made up of those groups. The smaller ships, along with a handful of carriers and cruisers.

Mell had been hard at work since then.

When we entered the Visiri system, we had dozens of destroyers with us. Real warships, and the backbone of most fleets. They were dwarfed by our three battleships.

Each Zenith-craft had been assembled by Horizon's external fabricators. They were closer to mundane ships than *The Last Horizon* itself, but they still outperformed their everyday counterparts in every way that mattered.

Now that we were gathered, we had a fleet I'd stack against any in the galaxy. Which was great, because we were going up against world-eaters.

The Visiri system stretched out before us, infested by a buzzing hive of insects. Soldiers were a thick cloud, and every moon and planet in the system had at least one D'Niss burrowing into it.

Two of them were the survivors of the Seven Calamities. Sel'miroth, the subtle spellcaster and hypnotist who had broken through my mental defenses before, and Xarro'kesh. An ant with three heads, each the size of a dreadnought.

His magic would be a special pain, but at least he wasn't focused on us yet. He lifted limbs and heads to the heavens, directing the Aether.

Strangely, the giant bugs weren't the most eye-catching sight on our scanners. At least not to me. A golden disc of crawling alien symbols flickered in and out of reality, centered on Visiria's sun and stretching across the entire system.

A spell. A grand ritual to summon the Swarm-Queen, Esh'kinaar.

They'd certainly wasted no time.

Alarms blared as the attention of the insects shifted to us. Weapons of every shape and color streaked toward us.

"I said they would take days," I said. "Clearly, they think they can do it faster. Let's prove them wrong." I leaned back in my chair. "Shyrax, you have command."

"Target is marked," the Commander said. "We begin."

We started with a giant worm, which wrapped jealously around an icy planetoid at the edge of the system as though squeezing a fruit. A brief flash of Subspace and our micro-dive ended, leaving us flying straight into its looming mouth.

This wasn't one of the Calamities. An "ordinary" D'Niss, to the extent that there could be such a thing. Zyn'tharak, the Crawling Plague.

Its psychic scream warped the Aether around our ship, but the last time I had faced down a mental attack from a D'Niss, I'd been in an unshielded cruiser. Being in the Zenith Starship was...very different.

Horizon was swollen with power and protected by the greatest magical wards of the Zenith Era. I felt nothing but a distant, external anger.

At the same time, Zyn'tharak deployed all its defenses. Flocks of worms almost as long as Horizon, winged and undulating through space, flew toward us. They spat plasma balls that splattered on our crimson shields.

All I saw was Parryl's face as they tore her apart.

In a past life, but that didn't mean I couldn't take revenge in this one.

"Raion, clean this up," I ordered.

"Aye, Captain!"

He was barely patched up, with bandages slapped haphazardly all over him. Visiria was his home planet, and he'd been there only a day before. Mere hours later, it was crawling with bugs. Raion was likely dying inside.

But, as he would say, at least we were there to save them.

Crimson lasers and sweeps of plasma slashed from us, trailing scarlet flame. The Dance of a Burning World blazed across hundreds of miles of space as our Knight channeled his power through our short-range weapons.

We were far ahead of our ships, cutting recklessly into the insectoid soldiers like a scarlet star.

Minions weren't the only weapons of the D'Niss. The psychic assault continued—though it was fruitless—and spells bent the Aether into ominous, squirming curses that looked like living monsters made of nightmares. They opened slavering maws to swallow us.

No matter how good Horizon's static defenses, they would fall to a sustained magical assault.

If I wasn't onboard.

I combined my magic with Horizon's and targeted the center of the curses with a seal. Though my own curse magic was still locked away, I knew the theory better than anyone, which made the task easy.

Working on such a scope wasn't. The D'Niss generated enough curses to plague an entire star system, but guiding that magic took my concentration.

Meanwhile, the planet-eating insect released its superior soldiers. These were thick, armored worms that resembled battlecruisers more than anything biological, and they unleashed clusters of magically accelerated shell that functioned as missiles.

They were thousands and tens of thousands of miles out, which was where our Sword came into play.

Sola didn't say anything or wait for orders as she unloaded on the new wave. Missiles and bullets streaked out, lighting up like emerald comets, as long-range plasma cannons melted smaller targets.

I was still facing down the curses when I heard Mell shout into her transmitter, "What are you doing? Get over here!"

A Subspace warp bloomed open behind us, a multicolored rose in the center of space. It spewed smooth ships of dark metal that shone blue-green between the plates.

Normally, that Subspace route would be suicide. Running straight into one of the D'Niss was only slightly safer than surfacing in range of a black hole.

But *The Last Horizon* was stabbing through the worm's defenses, cutting them like the edge of a force-blade. We left a wedge of clear space behind it, and our ships poured into it.

The great worm Zyn'tharak refocused its attention onto the newcomers, leveraging its full psychic might. The Nova-Bot pilots never even noticed.

"Form up," Shyrax ordered. "Prepare to receive support."

Moments later, golden light erupted from *The Last Horizon*, shimmering in a halo around each craft of our fleet, big or small. Shyrax's magic and her Aethertech gift, enhancing all aspects of the ships.

But one magical buff wasn't the end of her responsibilities, and she locked hands behind her back as she continued to give orders to our fleet. "Group C, tighten formation. Group B, watch reinforcements planetside. Group F, screen for B."

Commanding Nova-Bots wasn't much like ordering around living troops, but Shyrax had gotten the hang of things quickly. As she did everything.

While she was moving her pieces across the board, Omega chuckled in a half-dozen different voices. "Yes, yes, *this* is it! Catch me if you can!"

His Aethertech eye gleamed orange as he watched data I couldn't even perceive, taking us through a dizzying blur of motion. I had to watch the monitors and my own deployed eyes, or I would have been lost.

With the greater perspective, I saw what was happening. Zyn'tharak had intervened personally, slithering up to crush us with bulk that blacked out the sun and eclipsed the moon.

Omega was twisting and moving even as the scenery changed. He wove through the battle, evading debris and enemy fire easily, all the while moving for a steadily changing gap in the worm's massive body.

I wanted to enhance him with pathfinding magic, but I suspected it would only slow him down. The target he searched for would change and change, maybe many times in a second, but I could only set each spell for one target.

Horizon watched it all, seven-pointed eyes shining and her grin so wide it stretched the boundaries of her face.

Once all the curses were crushed, I spared a second to ask, "Having fun, Horizon?"

"AHAHAHAHAHAHA!"

"Glad to hear it. All crew, watch my target. Sola, Raion, we're punching through." I marked a point on the monitor, and it shone on the viewscreen as a circle of blue-green light.

I targeted the underside of the worm's head.

Everyone shifted seamlessly, in complete unison. Omega veered closer, Shyrax altered her orders to the fleet, and weapons of green and red re-targeted simultaneously.

At the same time, I chanted the Mirror of Silence.

To get a clear view of us, Zyn'tharak had to squirm around itself. When its head of gnashing teeth, large enough to shred entire colonies, cleared its own body, I released my spell.

"All ships fire," I ordered.

Black-and-white clones shimmered into existence and all of us released our full payload onto the monster. It was a barrage unlike anything I'd ever seen, even the artillery we'd unleashed onto the Iron King.

The entire system lit up as we poured a river of light through the D'Niss.

It resisted for a moment, pushing against the deadly current. Then we pierced through, the far side of its head erupting into gore.

The whole battle against that first D'Niss probably only took two or three minutes, but it felt twenty times longer. It *had* to be fast.

Even we couldn't face down a system full of D'Niss and two of the Seven Calamities if they turned all their attention to us at once. But the D'Niss were focused on their spell, and they'd never expected us to get on one of them so fast and kill them so quickly.

The Aetheric circle that covered the system flickered, now that one of the three casters was destroyed, and the triple-headed ant turned two of its heads toward us. The third remained tilted up at the spell.

"Defensive formations, Shyrax," I ordered. "Close us off and prepare for clones."

Shyrax issued a few sharp orders and the Nova-Bot ships closed around us in time for the Aether to flicker and twist into the form of six more of these giant ants, though each only had one head.

The copied Mirror of Silence ships faded back into nothing like bad Subline reception, but that left no gaps in our formation as Shyrax had anticipated that. I'd filled her in on the weaknesses of all the Seven Calamities, and she'd known I wouldn't win a battle of clone magic with this guy.

Any of the Seven Calamities was a battle that would have required all five Divine Titans at our best. All five Titans…or one Zenith Device.

"Raion, hit anything that gets too close. Sola, hit the marked target. Omega, get us closer."

I spent my attention fighting the spell, preventing the six extra ants from becoming twelve or twenty-four, which would be overwhelming even for us. Binding and sealing magic circles flashed all over the nearest planet, but most of that work I did with raw Aetheric manipulation.

It was a bit like preventing someone from putting together a puzzle by slapping the pieces out of their hands, but the ant had more hands than I did. Consumed as I was with preventing him from creating more copies, I couldn't work on dispelling the ones that existed.

Soldier ants emerged from Subspace on shimmering magical wings, a numberless swarm. Our own ships and Raion's weapons engaged them while Sola focused on the bigger target.

The instant its carapace began to crack, I called Omega's name.

Before I could tell him what I wanted, he responded. "My pleasure, Captain!"

Shadows flickered around us and the barest hint of Subspace shimmer, as Omega lent his unique diving technology to Horizon. We emerged behind the head of the wounded ant-clone.

We were out of formation, but that was indeed the order I had meant to give. Sola and Raion unloaded on the ant's head and it exploded into red-and-green flame.

The pressure I felt from wrestling the spell lessened. "Good job, Omega. Shyrax, mark the next target."

A turquoise circle appeared on a second clone, the one under the most pressure from our fleet. We flicked through shadow again and emerged next to it.

This time, it struck out with its limb, as fast as a missile. A missile long enough to stretch across a continent.

"Shields!" I shouted, and Raion shifted his attention fully to defense. I did the same, and protective sigils shimmered all around the red bubble defending us.

Even so, the strike rocked us. That was enough force to damage a planet, and by rights only the largest ships ever built could take a hit like that on the shield.

The entire ship shuddered, and I steadied myself with telekinesis. While we were still shaking, Raion called out, "Shields at sixty percent!

I was relieved that had taken less than half our shield stability. Even with my support, I'd expected worse.

Still, you can't take forty-percent hits all day. Another strike was coming in, not to mention the swarm of soldiers flowing up to cut us off and the other ant-clone that moved to flank us.

"Break that target," I ordered, and we sprayed the closest ant with viridian firepower. While it was reeling, I had enough leeway to conjure magic of my own.

With Horizon backing me up, we manifested eyes all around the D'Niss.

They responded by cloning their soldiers, launching a cloud of millions more ants, but between the barrage coming from our ships and the one coming from *The Last Horizon*, we were able to hold off the tide.

Meanwhile, our eyes released their powers. Beams of paralysis, petrification, hypnosis, and magical dissolution struck one of the ant-clones from a thousand angles.

It worked against our magic, popping eyes like balloons here and there, but its attention was weakened enough for us to cut through it.

At that point, the magical restriction stopping us from diving too deeply into Subspace loosened.

We hadn't engaged a dive yet because we would be leaving our fleet behind, undefended. Against two of the ant-clones, that meant losing our fleet entirely.

Against only one, they could hold off for a short while. Shyrax's orders reflected that, as the Nova-Bots gathered into a regimented cloud that covered each other from the barrage of the lesser ant-soldiers.

Now that they could last, I turned from my incantation long enough to order a dive. I didn't need to tell them the coordinates.

Another micro-dive—the fourth in only a few minutes, which would have been far too reckless without Omega's systems supporting the Subspace Drive—and we erupted back into real space over the heads of the real ant D'Niss.

"Sola, now's the time," I said.

She flipped up a case on her console, revealing a stick. She gripped it, sighted, and pulled the trigger.

A green blade of endless length appeared, like a bridge connecting *The Last Horizon* and the two closest heads of the D'Niss. The Worldslayer cannon pierced both of them like a needle, streaking off into space.

The third head screamed, finally breaking from its spellcasting. When it lost its concentration, the spell-circle surrounding the system shuddered once again. It was losing stability.

That warmed my heart, but it wasn't time to hold back.

"Finish it, then regroup," I said.

The last head of the ant D'Niss couldn't stand up against our focused firepower. We'd have to wait for our fleet to catch up before we moved on to the shimmering moth, but we had bought plenty of time for that. Two-thirds of the summoning spell's casters had been interrupted and slain.

If Sel'miroth turned her attention away to prepare for us, that meant giving up the war to win the battle.

Victory was already ours.

Alazar, the Perfected Mage, gazed at the ancient scrying mirror on the wall. It served him like a monitor, projecting the state of the Aether many systems away.

The ritual of the D'Niss blazed like a supernova, though the blue light that clashed with it was only slightly dimmer.

Varic Vallenar's magic was extraordinary. He had been stretched beyond the Aetheric limits of any human. With the support of *The Last Horizon,* he and his crew would be a real threat to King Felrex.

And, of course, they had slipped out of the King's grasp once already. Punishment was in order.

The most senior Archmage among Alazar's Mage Corps stepped up to his side. "Sir, our preparations are ready, but we need your confirmation."

Alazar studied the symbols flickering around the mirror more closely. They needed his order not just so they had permission to cast. They needed Alazar to tell them if the threat was within their capacity to handle.

If they went through with this, they would be releasing the Swarm-Queen on the galaxy.

She was already in Alliance space. They had to be sure they could take care of her before she reached Karoshan planets. The others were expendable.

Alazar read the Aether and took a moment to enjoy what he saw. "This is well within our expectations. If the Swarm-Queen was strong enough to threaten us, she would require more power to summon. Begin preliminary casting."

He turned and seized his staff, a ten-foot sliver of dragon's bone set with crystallized enhancement gems every foot or so. It was topped with a sharpened edge that he had often used as a spear.

The enchantment of this staff was "extension." With it in hand, he could cast across the galaxy if he needed to. And this target was much closer.

It was a shame, in a way. He would have liked to meet the late Varic Vallenar.

Karoshan voices cried out to the Aether as six mages began their chanting. When the time was right, he joined them.

Opening the door wide for the entrance of the Swarm-Queen.

CHAPTER THIRTY-NINE

As we defeated our fifth D'Niss, we still had two-thirds of our fleet left. I could feel the release of tension in the room, and Omega had already started complaining about how fast the fights had ended.

There was only one major enemy left, though the system was littered with billions of soldiers and spawn. Sel'miroth, the lone survivor of the Seven Calamities, flared her wings as she desperately tried to maintain a spell beyond what she could support.

Perhaps she *could* have succeeded if she had been unopposed.

But we were not her only enemy. She crouched over the blue planet of Visiria, much of her magic dedicated to an iridescent shield that blocked the attacks coming from the planet. Not the planetary defenses. The *planet*.

The World Spirit of Visiria had manifested itself above the celestial body it represented, and it was...*angry* was a mild term. It was the physical embodiment of pure fury.

At the best of times, Visiria isn't what you might call a reasonable spirit.

He took the form of a muscular Visiri warrior with skin the color of fresh blood. His form loomed over continents, his three eyes all burning like captured suns. He wore glistening bronze armor and clutched titanic thunderbolts in his fists.

Those fists were where he deviated from typical Visiri anatomy, as he had six of them. He hurled the bolts like javelins—lightning of red, green, blue, and white. Each a slightly different variation of the same spell, and each devastating.

Raion punched the air and cheered, though he winced at the motion. "Don't worry, Visiria! We're coming to help!"

Visiria didn't look like he wanted any help. By his expression, I'd say he wanted to eat Sel'miroth raw.

Shyrax and I were the only ones who didn't celebrate. We watched the twisting golden spell-circle that stretched overhead. The Aetheric symbols shook, not as steady as when they had been maintained by many D'Niss in concert. At any moment, they were supposed to start falling apart.

At any moment.

"The spell is too stable," I said, after a few seconds of observation. "Horizon, bring me my staff."

The crystal containing Eurias appeared next to my chair, and I melted the case away with a command to the protection crystal.

Raion frowned at me in concern. "Is Sel'miroth doing this on her own?"

"Something else is helping her. I can't tell if it's another caster or if she figured out an anchor, but the summoning is still active." The center of the magic circle had begun to shimmer with the faintest hint of a Subspace rainbow. "We need to break it. Now."

Sola turned from her console. "Do we have weapons for this?"

"I do," I said.

Eurias lay across my lap as I sat in the Captain's chair, magnifying my effect on the Aether through both the staff and *The Last Horizon*.

I don't recommend the experience.

Casting through Eurias is to emphasize power over control. Casting through the Zenith Starship expands my reach as well, but its primary benefit is that it allows Horizon to share the burden of spellcasting. That avoids some of the limitations on Eurias; for instance, while I'm sharing my magic with Horizon, I can switch spells. Which comes in handy.

But the staff, I can use without Horizon's help, and when I'm not aboard the ship at all. Different tools for different situations.

Using them together was agonizing.

Every syllable I spoke into the Aether echoed throughout the entire system. I was building a spell on an incomprehensible scale, but that meant I was almost completely giving up control. It was like using an industrial forklift to operate a wrist console.

The incantation took much longer than usual, and I had little control over the results of the spell, but I eventually released a huge seal. White symbols appeared, overlaid atop the golden ones involved in the summoning, and began to float upwards.

As my spell sank into that one, the Aether gave off sparks. Fireworks that would be visible all over the sector.

Mostly, those were nothing but visual indicators of the spell, but I did distantly worry that there would be side effects to casting on this scale that I couldn't predict.

Oh well. First, I'd have to stop the godlike queen of the psychic insects from invading reality.

For a few seconds, I thought the spell had worked perfectly. It certainly *looked* like it had.

Sel'miroth panicked, sending out a psychic trill of distress. Visiria gave a victory roar that shouldn't have passed through vacuum but, thanks to the Aether, did anyway. He struck out in a flurry of fists, punching holes in her rainbow wings.

Only a moment later, the D'Niss summoning spell rippled gold again.

The spell almost looked like real gold—the metal, not the color—dull and material, before it returned to the ethereal light I expected from Aetheric symbols.

That moment was enough to break my seal. Lights in *The Last Horizon* flickered and my staff screamed as the Aether around us trembled. Our power readings spiked and bottomed out for a few seconds each before stabilizing.

"I don't know magic," Mell said, "but it's my professional opinion that something is wrong."

Spellcasting that deeply is like being in a trance, and I came out gasping. "Shyrax! I need your help!"

Shyrax pulled her wand. "Who is it?"

I studied the circle, trying both to read the magic and to imagine who would still be out there interfering with me. The rain that Eurias conjured spattered on my face, not helping my concentration.

Had I missed another of the D'Niss? Was there some ancient cosmic dragon interfering with me? Had the entire Magic Tower decided to take its revenge?

There was only one person I knew whose magic was suitable for this and who might have the arrogance to think he could deal with Esh'kinaar when this was over. He couldn't wield the same might I could with Eurias and Horizon, but if he had a ritual circle...and if he was only supporting an existing spell...

"Alazar," I said.

Shyrax's eyes narrowed as she studied the scene, though her wand was already moving. "Unless he has access to resources I'm unaware of, he would have to spend half of the royal court's magical treasures for a ritual of this scale. I cannot imagine he would have enough left to handle the Swarm-Queen in the aftermath."

"We won't have to worry about that when we stop it." That wasn't entirely true—I would be very worried if I had to face a team of Perfected who had enough magical power to do battle with the Swarm-Queen.

I began the incantation again, returning to my trance of intense focus. This time, I had golden light on my side as well, because my Commander joined me.

White symbols of my seal appeared on the underside of the summoning spell, each surrounded by Shyrax's golden fire. Her magic was that of enhancement, amplification. She added the magic of dragons to my spell.

Together, we crashed against Alazar and what must have been an entire circle of Karoshan mages.

Once again, the D'Niss spell flashed like real gold, but this time my seal flared brighter. Clashing against magic like that is, in essence, wrestling for control of the Aether. Part of the process is about throwing weight around, leveraging your magical influence to its apex. A lot of it is about how to *use* that weight; I've wiped out spells much more powerful than my own by knowing where to press.

But a lot of it is like trying to win an argument.

From a certain perspective, all magic is convincing the Aether to do what you want. Wizards specialize in one magic at a time because the Aether starts to see them in a certain way, which makes them more effective at asking for that same thing in the future.

My staff made it so that I was asking, not just on my behalf, but on behalf of the dead world Eurias. Add on *The Last Horizon*—another World Spirit and, of course, a unique Zenith Device—and my status as the galaxy's only sevenfold mage, and my default position becomes very compelling.

That the Perfected Mage's spell held as long as it did was cause for great concern.

In theory, any spell with that much leverage behind it should have wiped out any mortal opposition. Eventually, my seal did shove the other aside, replacing the halo of gold with a ring of white that shone down on the worlds of the local star system.

But it held on a long time. Maybe too long.

Even with the spell gone, the sky still shimmered. Subspace bled through reality like water seeping through a sheet of paper.

Panting for breath, I had to abandon this spell and switch to another. I moved from a seal that locked out magic to one that shut down Subspace. Ordinarily, that would only take me a second. Even with Eurias, it wouldn't be too bad.

With Eurias and *The Last Horizon* combined, I had to slowly ramp down my incantations lest the spell continue on sheer momentum. It was like piloting a tubby cargo cruiser instead of a quick starfighter.

That cost me a precious minute, all while nauseating colors steadily bled through the darkness of the void.

Finally, I unmade my seal and started chanting again. White symbols flashed into the sky all around the perimeter. It would be close, but I thought I would make it.

Until I heard a sweet, soft, inhuman song. It felt like hearing crickets at sunset, like seeing fireflies in the darkness. The end of the day was here, and while it might be sad, it was best to embrace the coming of the night.

Sel'miroth gave her own cry of joy, looking up to see her mother descend. She reached out with all her legs and her shredded rainbow wings.

The World Spirit of Visiria tore her apart. The moment her attention was diverted, he leaped on her with all six hands and pulled her to pieces like a sadistic child playing.

The last of the Seven Calamities resonated through the Aether in a song of triumph. Sel'miroth had died knowing that she was victorious. Her mother was here.

Like a flower blooming down from the branch of a tree, the Swarm-Queen Esh'kinaar ascended into our dimension.

Her head slid through first, an origami structure of many shimmering colors. Four mandibles, beautiful razor-edged blades that looked like flower petals, vibrated as she sang.

A pair of her mantis-arms extended next, her carapace shimmering like spilled oil, followed by a second pair. Then her thorax, armed and armored in black-diamond plates.

Finally, her abdomen came last, which split along the back to reveal wings made of wispy rainbows. She sang triumph. She sang destruction.

And as she sang, my spell went out.

If you use the analogy of spells as arguments persuading the Aether, Esh'kinaar's entrance was the equivalent of screaming so loudly that no one can hear how great anyone's argument is.

She herself was an accomplished spellcaster, as I was sure we would see, but she had obviously determined that stopping me was better than tossing out magic of her own.

I didn't need to give any orders before the others targeted her.

Sola unloaded all the remaining missiles and Subspace torpedoes we'd managed to fabricate since our last volley, and she started tapping stranger weapons. The ones we rarely used because they were so esoteric or uncontrollable.

She launched packets of physically manifested data, chaos bombs, vibrational scramblers, and spell-clusters along with her more traditional weaponry.

Like the rest of the D'Niss, Esh'kinaar wasn't invincible. We had done battle with her in my previous life and almost defeated her. Even in real history, she'd been defeated once before.

In fact, despite our strikes covering only a negligible percentage of her carapace, she staggered back, flaring her wings to take up a defensive position behind the local sun.

Then she stopped singing and got serious.

With a rainbow flash, the Swarm-Queen glared at us. Her gaze was like weaponized Subspace, and—even though I knew not to look—I felt the twisting illogic of Subspace tearing the fundamental order of my mind apart.

Next time you're in Subspace...well, I can't recommend you look out the window. Keep those shutters on. But if you can do it safely, sneak a little peek while the shutters are going up.

It's hypnotic. It doesn't feel harmful, it feels fascinating, like you can *almost* see something amazing. Maybe if you only looked a little longer, you'd catch sight of something you've wanted to see your entire life.

At the same time, it's nauseating and disorienting. Your body rejects it.

Esh'kinaar's eyes took that sensation and added on a layer of existential confusion. For a moment, I didn't know who I was or what it meant to even be someone. I forgot language, forgot how to breathe, and forgot why breathing was important.

For me, that didn't last long. I snapped out of it quickly.

Only to realize that Eurias was still out.

Rain soaked my chair and ran down the sides, and I was covered in vines. Black clouds six inches over my head rolled with thunder.

I shoved my way through, tearing vines apart faster than they could grow back. Only then could I reach the blue crystal leaning against my chair, liquefying it with a touch and returning Eurias to its case.

Then I hurried to Shyrax. She was already struggling in place, jerking as though trying to wake from a nightmare.

She would be the next one to free herself, and she could help me wake the others. I grabbed her by the elbow and shouted her name, at which point she snapped out of the trance instantly.

"Shields," she advised me, and I sent a burst of telekinesis to Raion's console.

As Shyrax remembered from my briefing, the Swarm-Queen didn't release these mental attacks alone. She used them to soften us up for the kill.

The shield shone brightly around our ship before a blade struck us. I call it a blade, but it's really the product of something like a Combat Art. The Swarm-Queen slashed her razor-sharp arms, sending a crescent cut across the system.

It looked like a string of diamonds colliding with our shield, like the curved edge of a sword was clashing into us, but *just* the edge, as though that was the only part of the sword that existed.

Her cut sliced through our shield and slammed into our armor. The Knight console blared a warning. The ship shook violently at the impact; unconscious, Mell and Raion slid out of their seats and would have fallen had I not caught them with my levitation ring.

Maybe it was the impact, but Horizon woke on her own, flickering into holographic existence and looking around wide-eyed. *"What was that? Did she* scratch *me?"*

I grabbed Raion by the shoulders and shook him as I shouted, "Incoming!"

Raion stood straight up and staggered out of my telekinesis, shoving me aside instead of doing anything useful. In other circumstances, I would have stayed with him to help him shake off the D'Niss-induced Subspace madness, but there was another cut incoming.

Just in time, Horizon dipped us under the slash. It still took our shields down another few percent by passing by.

Even empowered, star-eating, psychic insect queens can't throw out those strikes like nothing. If she could, we'd have been finished immediately, because she would have slashed us fifty times in the first second.

But she'd launched four.

The first hit us, and while it only temporarily destabilized our shield and scratched our armor, the rest of the cut swept into our ships and destroyed or destabilized at least a dozen.

We evaded the other three, but despite Shyrax's instructions, our fleet wasn't so lucky.

Even though we'd managed to preserve almost two thousand ships from a battle against a group of high-ranking D'Niss, the Swarm-Queen's opening volley reduced them to fragments.

Roughly speaking, we had one damaged battleship, a handful of frigates, three limping cruisers, a squadron or two of fighters, and whichever of the Nova-Bots was scrappy enough to fly through the void on their own jetpacks. There might have been a few others in Subspace or scattered through the system, but nothing that would help us.

When I finally woke Mell—and she stopped panicking about where she was—she looked at the readouts and groaned.

"It's going to take me *forever* to rebuild all that."

If we made it out alive to worry about that, I'd count it a win. Shyrax had woken Sola, and I saved Omega for last. Horizon could pilot the ship, just not as well.

Light blazed to life in his Aethertech eye, and he shot straight up. His head turned fully around to face me. "Run or fight, Captain?"

"Run," I said immediately. "We are not in condition for this fight, and we need backup. If we leave now, we can inform the Galactic Union. The most effective weapon we have left is the Divine Titan, and Raion's in no shape to pilot. If we keep fighting her here, there's not much I can do besides keep her spells off us."

Esh'kinaar still hovered over and slightly behind the local

sun, close enough that without the correction from the cameras, I wouldn't have been able to make her out except as a dark spot against the star's radiance.

Her arms were posed defensively, wings spread as though to take flight at any second. She appeared to be sitting still, waiting for us to make a move, but I knew her better than that.

She was doing something, but we couldn't see what. I suspected she was spawning an army of soldiers where we couldn't see, or even laying eggs of a future D'Niss into the star.

It wasn't magical, or I would have noticed. Which was interesting in itself. Magic was perhaps her strongest tool, but she hadn't cast a spell since arriving. She had only disrupted mine and enhanced her own scream.

It seemed she had weighed her chances against us in a magical contest and decided to save her energy for defense.

"When we come back, we can win," I said confidently. "She's not sure she can handle our magic or she would have used her spells already. If we bring Horizon back with a Divine Titan and a Union fleet, she'll have no chance."

I waited for a response, and while four out of my five crew members acknowledged me, I didn't get the reaction I'd expected.

"Where did Raion go?" I asked. "I thought I'd have to convince him to retreat." He hadn't returned to his console. Not that we needed him now; we were already in the process of diving away.

"Don't be angry," Horizon said, *"but he went to go see Ark."*

I didn't need to ask why. My whole body ran with electric panic.

"Bring him back!"

"I can't. You'll have to—"

"Yes! Send me!"

I had to stop my Knight from doing something monumentally stupid.

CHAPTER FORTY

RAION ACHED AS he took the elevator up to the chest of the Red Divine Titan. Sunlight ran through its metal, veins of power corrupting its original design. He could feel the heat radiating from it, and the feelings radiating even more intensely.

The Titan was eager. Its time had come, and it knew that.

Four more Divine Titans waited in the chamber. Still, quiet, lifeless with no one to pilot them.

Raion looked back on them fondly as his elevator took him up. There would be a whole new generation of Titan Knights after this. Maybe they could even work with *The Last Horizon!*

He imagined his successors working alongside his friends and he beamed, though there was no one to see him.

The chest hatch of the Divine Titan opened as he reached the top, ready to accept him in. Raion was holding his key, but he hadn't needed to say the motto or even wait for danger. Usually, the Titan didn't respond except in extreme circumstances.

Although he supposed the current circumstances were pretty extreme.

"You're willing to help me already, huh?" Raion asked his oldest friend. He patted the side of the hatch. "Maybe we can work together after all."

Then he slid down the hatch and into the pilot's seat. A little awkwardly, thanks to his injuries. He groaned as he twisted to strap himself in.

As the hatch closed in front of him, he looked up to the sunlight-orange veins that ran across the ceiling. "Listen, I need to think if we're going to win."

Metal groaned sullenly around him.

"We should work together," Raion said firmly. "But…I know you can't help it. If we need to push farther, you can do what you need to do."

Raion wanted to survive this fight. Their adventures as the crew of the Zenith Starship had just begun!

But if only one person could solve this problem, it was him. It was the Knight's job to defend his crew with his life.

The power of the Divine Titan surrounded him, straining his body, and making him clench his jaw…but not overwhelming his mind .

"Thank you!" Raion said to his friend. "Now…one last time!"

Safety clamps holding the Titan in position hissed as they disengaged. At the far end of the chamber, the launch bay opened onto the fractured black-and-violet sky of Shadow Ark.

Then a tiny spot of blue appeared on the floor below.

He shouted something that Raion only heard a moment later, when it came through the speakers inside the Titan. *"Raion, stop! We can't fight her now!"*

Raion heard Varic's voice and tears welled up in all three eyes.

He imagined Varic in the uniform of a Titan Knight. He had to imagine—he'd only heard stories about Varic's career from one of his other, magical lives. But Raion's imagination was overlaid with all the others he'd ever seen wear that uniform.

The only one still fighting was him.

"I've had longer than anyone else," Raion said to Varic. He meant it to sound encouraging, but there wasn't much of his usual energy in the words. "Longer than I deserve. I'm grateful for the time I got."

Varic had his wand in his hand, and Raion suspected what was going through his mind. He couldn't stop a Divine Titan with magic, at least not without his staff, but he could slow Raion down.

Finally, Varic lowered his wand. *"All right, Raion, let's at least do this the smart way. Let me put the safety seals on you, and we can stay close enough to recall you if something happens."*

"I need to be at full power," Raion said. "And I can't let you get any closer. This is the Knight's job!"

Varic lifted his wand as though prepared to throw it. *"There is no* need *for this! We can come back!"*

"How many planets will die if we do?"

"That isn't our responsibility!"

"It's mine," Raion said. The Divine Titan gave a sharp squeal of impatience, and he agreed. He warmed up the forward thrusters, which kicked up enough wind that the protection field around Varic's amulet become visible.

Then he left behind the last words that he'd always planned. "Better to die for something than live for nothing."

"Don't die for something!" Varic shouted. "Live *for something!"*

"I did," Raion said. He grinned and pushed his controls forward.

As he rushed out into space to fight the last of the D'Niss, his Divine Titan screamed in metallic joy.

I watched Raion go in the Red Titan out of the launch bay, and I waited for the rush of despair that I'd felt last time. After all, I'd failed. I had let Raion die in the same way I'd let him last time.

But that despair didn't come.

Because, no matter what Raion thought, this wasn't over. There was no way I was letting this go like last time.

The launch bay doors stayed open, looking out onto the field of the moon of Delsin and a fragmented violet sky. We were still inside Shadow Ark, so it wasn't as though I could see the battle, and his Zenith Era technology maintained the atmosphere.

Still, to give myself time to think, I went to shut the doors. I marched across the launch bay, passing the Divine Titans as I moved for the door controls.

If this had been my ship, I could have closed them remotely, but instead I called Horizon as I talked. "Raion left in the Titan. Can you keep him inside Ark?"

"Of course not!" Horizon said proudly. *"It is not the role of the Zenith Devices to* prevent *people from acting like heroes!"*

"Heroes can *live,*" I shouted into the call, but I calmed myself down as I walked. "It's not my job to give my crew the most heroic deaths. Can you teleport Raion out of his Divine Titan?"

"Not without his consent."

That's what I expected, but there were sometimes workarounds for spell limitations like that. "Fine. Get Sola and Shyrax to draw up a battle plan. Us fighting with Raion in the Titan."

"With pleasure, Captain, but I would remind you that our *utility—as in, the two of us—will be limited in this conflict. The Swarm-Queen will keep our magic restricted to the ship."*

I knew that, but I didn't have a solution for it.

Or rather, I *did,* and my solution involved living to fight another day. But once again, Raion had settled on this.

I was close enough to activate the door with telekinesis, but the Aether was weak inside Shadow Ark, so I moved over to slap the bay doors closed with my hand.

The button was stuck. Irritated, I used telekinesis anyway.

Immediately, the launch bay shook as the doors began to slide closed again. I turned to walk back the other way—but hesitated as I heard another sound, alongside the shutting doors. A humming sound I recognized.

The light was suddenly bright blue.

When I turned around, the Blue Divine Titan shone eagerly. Awaiting its pilot.

"No way," I said aloud.

The Titan didn't respond, not like Raion's did, but I thought it looked suddenly smug.

Piloting a Divine Titan wasn't just a skill, like piloting a starship. It was a relationship between Knight and Titan, and it couldn't be one-sided. I knew this Divine Titan, but it didn't know me.

At least, it shouldn't.

"What's happening, Captain?" Horizon asked eagerly. *"Is it the Titan?"*

"Do you remember me?" I asked, looking up at the metal behemoth against the wall. In response, its chest plate hissed open, revealing the pilot's seat.

New options appeared to me by the second. If I had access to a Divine Titan, I could fight by Raion's side. More effectively than in *The Last Horizon*, given how Esh'kinaar could limit my magic. In the Blue Titan, I'd be able to push through her spell cancellation.

It was a weapon designed to defeat the D'Niss.

"Horizon, can you locate the key to the Blue Titan?" I asked.

Magic shimmered in midair, and the palm-sized badge fell into my hand.

"Thanks. Tell the crew what's happening and put Shyrax in charge. I'm going after Raion."

On my levitation ring, I floated up to the open cockpit. But as I was about to enter, Horizon cleared her throat in my ear.

"Aren't you forgetting something, Captain?"

Before I could ask what she was talking about, a pile of folded fabric fell onto the seat. A blue-and-white uniform.

I was tempted to toss it out of the Titan, but the clothes *would* improve my connection. And, no matter how you calculated time, it had been years since I'd last piloted a Divine Titan.

I pulled off my mantle. "How long have you had this suit ready?"

"Months, Captain. Months."

CHAPTER FORTY-ONE

When I emerged from Ark, I saw that Raion hadn't reached Esh'kinaar yet. Meaning that I didn't see an apocalyptic battle nearing the sun, which could only indicate that Raion was still in Subspace.

Now that my Subline connection improved, I started a call. "*The Last Horizon,* this is the Blue Titan, please respond."

A square popped up in the display in front of me. It was Mell, grinning around a toothpick. *"You wore the uniform! Sola lost the bet."*

Sola's face popped up next. *"I thought he had taste."*

"Common misconception," Omega said as he appeared in another square. *"Humans all taste about the same."* He glanced up and around himself as though looking around the box that contained him on my screen. *"Why are we all on separate feeds? We're in the same room."*

To demonstrate, he waved a hand behind Sola's head. She pointed a gun at it without looking.

"The Titan communication program is designed to call other Titans," Mell explained. *"They're individual Subline connections, so he's talking to us like we're fellow Knights."*

Omega stroked his short beard. *"Hmmm...How long would it take to fabricate an orange uniform, do you think?"*

I was letting them talk while I entered Subspace. Titans had great receivers for communication in Subspace—it was how the Titans themselves received the signals from their keys—but the transmissions from my side would be garbled until I returned to real space.

Finally, Shyrax entered the call and shut everyone down. *"We have Raion coming out of Subspace. He is engaging the enemy but will not accept our calls."*

"Stay on him," I said as clearly and loudly as possible.

Everyone flinched.

"Agh, don't talk from Subspace!" Mell protested, holding her ears.

Omega chuckled. *"I hear the voice of devils, and they sound like our Captain."*

"Seven seconds, Captain," Shyrax said. In the corner of her screen, I glimpsed shutters pouring over the forward viewport of *The Last Horizon,* so they were diving into Subspace.

Once they dove, I sent another transmission. "Better?"

Mell sighed in relief.

Horizon popped up on the screen, though I hadn't invited her to the call. Her horns stuck out of the box surrounding her, and she leaned her face far too close to the camera. *"I've told Raion that we're coming after him, Captain, but he didn't respond to me. And, of course, I didn't reveal that you're in a Titan."*

"Tell him!" I insisted. "It might get him to back off."

"Why would I spoil the surprise?"

Sola looked offscreen, checking a readout. *"Captain, we don't have many weapons left that can do anything to the enemy. I might be better off getting out and firing Worldslayer myself."*

"We'll hold that in reserve. How long until the ship's Worldslayer recharges?"

"An hour, and it would be safer to give it longer."

No sense in regret. It had made sense to deploy the weapon when we did; *stopping* the summoning had been our priority. If we had kept Horizon's Worldslayer in reserve for when we needed it, the fight would have taken much longer.

Of course, we'd ended up in the worst-case scenario anyway.

"There's still a way we can win," I said. "In the Blue Titan, I can use my magic for offense. Hit her with everything you have so Raion and I can secure the kill. And do it before we run out of power."

"We will play the distraction while the two of you strike the final blow," Shyrax said. *"I will take command. I have trained with the S'Dem Hajjar in the art of distraction."*

"I don't know who that is," Mell said, *"but I'm still not surprised."*

Instinct from another life was guiding me to check all my instruments as I spoke. "I never doubted you, Shyrax. Sola, prepare your Worldslayer. If we can make a window, I'll clone you and hit her with multiple shots. Omega, you still have my predictions of Esh'kinaar's patterns?"

"I lost them, but my best guess should be just as good."

"She'll trap us with plasma volleys from her wings when she feels overwhelmed. Do not evade. I'll hold that off so you can get Sola in position."

"We can't coordinate without Raion," Sola said.

That was a significant complication. We had to prepare our strategy without Raion, who was arguably the lynchpin of the whole thing.

"I'll get him to cooperate, but we have to assume he's operating on his standard tactics. Which means we prepare to follow him in through an army of soldiers. Ready to surface."

This had been a slow dive, especially for *The Last Horizon,* which could have covered intra-system distances in a handful of seconds. They had stayed in Subspace to coordinate with me, which would theoretically keep us on the same page.

Though I was sure that wouldn't last long after contact with the enemy.

"Ready, Captain," Shyrax confirmed.

Without further discussion, I triggered my Subspace Drive and emerged. While my external cameras showed me the view again, restoring themselves from Subspace shutdown, I glanced at my energy meter.

That dive had already taken four percent of my full power capacity. That wasn't so bad, as dives went, especially for one so short. The Skimmer Drives used in the Divine Titans were efficient over short distances compared to starships.

But in combat, they burned through energy fast. I would be missing that four percent soon, I was sure.

The cameras engaged as we fully emerged from Subspace, and I immediately threw myself into the controls, engaging reverse thrusters and spinning the Titan's staff in a circle.

I'd wanted a warm-up, considering how long it had been since I'd been in control of a Divine Titan, but Esh'kinaar wasn't considerate enough to oblige.

I'd surfaced in the middle of a swarm of shimmering locust soldiers, green insects the size of a starfighter who had smaller versions of the Swarm-Queen's rainbow wings. They were tougher than standard D'Niss soldiers, even projecting their version of a shield, and Esh'kinaar had been able to sow them around all the most probable Subspace entry points.

She could conjure millions of those in a handful of seconds. We called it "swarm magic," and I hated it.

Surfacing from Subspace into the middle of all those soldiers would have been even tougher if Raion hadn't passed through already.

My staff blasted through a few dozen soldiers, and I activated automated defense mechanisms. Panels on my mech's shoulders opened and released a swarm of thumb-sized missiles that sought different targets.

They were short-range weapons, on the scale of space combat, but they were warded to phase straight through magical shields. Hundreds of locusts exploded around me.

Only then did *The Last Horizon* surface, deliberately following me. I gripped my staff and pushed the Blue Titan forward, though we hadn't cleared everything out. The little ones could go to Horizon.

The rest of my crew was calling to each other, focusing on business now that the fight had begun, but I muted them as I sent out another call.

"Blue Knight entering the combat zone," I said. "You're going to hurt my feelings if you don't pick up, Red."

A second later, a square containing Raion's face popped up on my screen. All three of his eyes were wide. *"Varic?"* He gasped when he saw the view from inside the Blue Titan. *"It worked! I knew it would work! I told you!"*

Even while he talked, his eyes flicked with inhuman speed to the various controls surrounding him, and I tracked the Red Titan slicing through the D'Niss army as it approached the Swarm-Queen.

Who hunkered over the sun, motionless and watching.

Horizon cleared her throat, having un-muted herself somehow. *"Excuse me, Raion. He's wearing the uniform and everything. Please call him 'Blue.'"*

"Sorry, Blue!"

"Stop it, Horizon. Raion, I'm connecting you to the rest of the crew."

Audio returned as I linked the calls, and either Horizon had already allowed them to listen or she had relayed the conversation, because the crew reacted immediately.

"I thought you were calling him Red," Mell said.

Sola glared in Raion's direction. *"I hope you don't think you can get away from us, Red."*

"Call me Orange!" Omega shouted.

"The Red Knight is about to make contact," Shyrax said. *"Red, slow your approach until Blue is in place to cover you. Grant me access to your diagnostics so I can see your remaining energy. We will send you our plan."*

"Yes, Commander!" Raion looked like a totally different person than he had in the launch bay. It was like we'd injected him with a year's worth of energy, and he shone with the sunlight of the corrupted Divine Titan as though it was no extra burden at all.

Then his energy meter popped up and I saw he was on sixty-eight percent.

"Red, you're burning out too fast," I said. "Slow it down."

"I don't know if I can, Blue!"

Raion had reversed course on Shyrax's orders, but he couldn't disengage so easily. Soldiers swarmed around the sun in the millions, filling the void with missiles both material and magical. The Queen had taken over the remnants of the other armies, soldiers of many descriptions now cooperating perfectly under one mind.

Larger D'Niss-spawn had formed living firing platforms that were taking heavier shots at Raion. If he didn't shoot those down before the real fight, he would leave himself open to serious damage.

And the Swarm-Queen herself was about to act. Not only could I see her head turning in our direction, but I also felt her attention burning brighter than the radiant light of the local star. One of her four bladed arms unfolded, pulling back for a slash.

"Back off, Red," I said. "Let me take this one for a minute."

Divine Titans didn't have adaptive systems like Horizon did. They weren't Zenith Devices, after all. But there were a few similarities, one being that they were designed to magnify the abilities of the pilot.

The Blue Titan specifically was keyed to water elementalism, but its capacity had always exceeded my skill. There had been tricks I was sure the machine was capable of, but I didn't have the ability to try them.

Not in that life.

I switched off my microphone and spoke to the Aethertech mech around me. "Let's see what we can do."

I didn't hear any sort of response, but I would have sworn the Blue Divine Titan felt almost as eager as Raion's red one.

Through my staff, I conjured water, and oceans thundered from the Aether at my call. It was unnaturally blue, rushing out of nowhere and following the direction of my staff. Soldiers were swept up in the tide, crushed or torn apart by the tens of thousands.

Stronger than before, but in line with what I could have done in my previous life. The Titan could do better than that.

I conjured a few dozen eyes outside the Titan. That strained my concentration, but they gave me a broader view of the battlefield. With that view, I deployed my pulse-magnetic sword array.

Nine hilts shot out of a containment chamber on the Titan's back, igniting into blue force-blades. They flew away from me, moving in concert as they struck out at nine targets I designated.

Then I finished chanting the Mirror of Silence, and twenty-seven total swords flashed against the gunner platforms.

Once that weapon was deployed, I formed the water up into a shield in front of me, thick as a planet's crust.

Just in time to intercept the Swarm-Queen's slash. It carved into my water, but I had never stopped casting.

Seals appeared in layer after layer of the ocean. Her attack crashed through them, but it weakened every time.

And I was chanting a water spell into the Aether. Water elementalism didn't require verbal incantations, which was why it was so useful in the arena, but the words still had their uses.

Above the sun of the system, my water condensed tighter and tighter until it was a planet-sized spear pointed at the Swarm-Queen. She spread her rainbow wings and a shimmering shield appeared over her carapace.

The spell grew more and more focused, but Esh'kinaar used the same time to reinforce her defense. At that rate, it would be a stalemate.

I triggered the Blue Titan's resonance cannon.

Panels all over the Blue Titan's front popped open, and projectors in its eyes shone brightly. Magic circles engaged from all over the machine, resonating with the Aether. Aethertech and enchantments in the machine cascaded into one another, surrounding the Titan in a massive blue circle.

Sapphire light flooded out from the mech, whiting out my cameras as my entire Divine Titan became a single cannon.

I only got to see what happened thanks to the conjured eyes floating around the Titan, and the bright power of the weapon subverting the Aether meant that I still only saw it in fragments.

The light of the resonance cannon flooded through the spear of water, filling it like a flashlight shining into a crystal. Mystical light refracted in all directions, for a moment matching the sun below for brilliance.

The spell-weapons resonated, each reinforcing the other, and they shot into the Swarm-Queen at once.

She crossed two limbs in a block, the shield in front of her taking the attack as other, stranger magics worked on dismantling my spells. But it wasn't enough. The strongest attack the Blue Titan ever produced shoved through her defenses and crashed into her upper body.

Only when the spell cleared and my cameras came back on did I see what damage I had done.

Her outer shell was cracked and she reeled back, her mental wail prying at my concentration. The blade of one of her upper arms had been split completely off, spinning into space, and the other arm was cracked.

The only thing I had seen hit Esh'kinaar that hard was the five Titans working in concert.

Now that I wasn't pushing the Titan so hard, my force-blades returned, their clones having faded. The Subline calls reconnected one by one.

"What did you need my *weapons for?"* Sola asked.

Mell had pulled up holographic schematics of the Blue Divine Titan and was examining them while chewing on something. *"I can get that into a Nova-Bot, I know I can, but you'll have to help me with the magical bits."*

When the camera reconnected with Omega, I saw only a bit of his bare shoulder. He was hopping in place, presumably pulling on a pair of pants. Mell groaned and looked away while Sola rolled her eyes.

Shyrax reconnected, staring directly at Omega. *"Pilot, at your post."*

"Wait, I've almost…There!"

Omega pulled the last of the orange-and-white uniform up over his torso, slipping his arms in at the last second. It was, of course, the combat suit of the Titan Knights.

"Orange Knight, reporting for duty!" he announced as he dropped back into the pilot's seat.

"You look great!" Raion said. *"But I think we have a problem."*

The fact that Raion said that instead of rushing after the reeling enemy meant that he thought the same thing I did.

"Yeah," I responded, "she didn't move."

No matter how great my strongest attack was, it still required me to cast a planet-scale elemental spell and follow it up with an Aethertech cannon. Esh'kinaar should have been able to avoid it, at least partially.

That was a big reason to use the weapon at all: to force her away from her position. Any wounds I could inflict were an incidental bonus.

She'd been crouched over that sun since the beginning of the battle with the D'Niss. She was doing that for a reason, and I had wanted to disrupt whatever her plans were.

That she had stayed and taken the attack, and especially that she had reset her position afterwards and begun rebuilding her defenses, meant she had something to defend.

"Three possibilities," I said. "She's either laying a spawn army that she thinks can kill us, she's hatching a new D'Niss with abilities designed to kill us, or she's waiting for allies to show up. And kill us."

"We are restricted by the energy capacity of the Divine Titans," Shyrax noted.

"That's the problem. She knows Raion and I have limited time." My energy readout was already down to seventy percent, thanks to the cost of my resonance cannon. "She has to have a plan to turn the tables once she waits us out."

The Queen of Karosha straightened and placed hands on her controls. *"Then we have but one choice."*

"Yeah. Coordinate and hit her as hard as we can."

"Now that's *a plan!"* Omega cried. *"Why can't we have missions like this every day, Captain?"*

Raion gave him a thumbs-up.

"I'll work on that, Orange," I said. "For now, full speed ahead. Raion, take point. We're crashing through the trap."

CHAPTER FORTY-TWO

I FOLLOWED BEHIND as Raion tore through the ranks of the D'Niss soldiers, wishing we had the other three Titans with us.

Then again, no individual Divine Titans had ever been able to fight on the level Raion and I could.

Enhanced by the blood of the solar dragon, the Red Titan performed beyond anything it should have been capable of. Its sunlight-colored sword sliced apart swarms of a thousand insects that had joined their shields together, and Raion blasted through without slowing down. Orange-red wings spewed crystals of energy that wove between soldiers and deleted insects the size of cruisers.

Meanwhile, I covered him with titanic streams of water and calculated shots from the cannon on my Titan's left arm. Raion's Titan had power that the others never did, and I could use elemental magic beyond anything I had witnessed in my previous lives.

Even so, it would have been nice to have the others. Fire support from the Yellow Knight would have saved Raion energy, the speed and cloud-like weapons from the White Knight would have cleared out the armies without me having to bend my magic to it, and the Green Knight could have threatened Esh'kinaar directly.

Instead, *The Last Horizon* played all three of those roles.

Where clusters of soldiers managed to endure my magic on their shields, green plasma flowed through afterwards to tear them apart. When Raion's crystalline weapons missed their target by colliding with debris, Sola's didn't.

All the while, Mell analyzed the readings from the far side of the sun, which Esh'kinaar had shrouded with magic and her own titanic body.

"Hard to tell with the spell in the way," Mell said, *"but I'm pretty confident she's hiding one massive entity. I'm getting readings consistent with the birth of a solar dragon."*

"That comes from her spawning magic. It's a cocoon." The only question had been what was in it, which could technically still be up for debate. Just because it had the signature of one large creature didn't mean it *was* one.

"Evasion," Shyrax ordered, though Raion and I had already split away from one another.

Esh'kinaar may have been reinforcing her position, but she wasn't idle. Another volley of three slashes came at us, glistening diamond crescents projected by her equivalent of a Combat Art.

All three of us dodged, but the Swarm-Queen hadn't waited. She'd spread her wings and sprayed millions of rainbow-colored orbs into space. The ability I'd warned Omega about.

"Red, cover Horizon!" I called as I manipulated my water to do the same.

"Sola, now," Shyrax ordered.

This was the opportunity we'd been waiting for, though it wasn't ideal. Esh'kinaar had left herself vulnerable to leave us with no room to dodge, spawning these numberless attacks that would seek us of their own volition.

Ideally, we'd have been closer, and we wouldn't have been thrown off by the slashes. But she wasn't going to give us ideal conditions, so we had to take the chance we got.

As points of light like deadly stars streaked at us from every direction, I formed flowing water into a massive tunnel between *The Last Horizon* and the Swarm-Queen. Raion positioned his Titan above the tunnel's exit, already swinging his blade to strike down the enemy attacks before they reached us.

Meanwhile, a gray speck appeared over the falcon-like outline of *The Last Horizon*. Sola withdrew Worldslayer from her inventory, which I could see more clearly than I could Sola herself. The gun was a crackling collection of crimson razors that seemed to cut through existence itself.

Balls of light began to crash against my waves as Sola sighted down her weapon. *"I have a shot,"* she reported.

Esh'kinaar had stopped producing deadly balls of light and had returned to weaving her shield. But I was still chanting.

I stopped for a second to say, "Hold position," before I returned to the Mirror of Silence.

The Blue Titan's staff—as well as the mech itself—was designed to operate in conjunction with elemental magic. That didn't mean it *wouldn't* work for other kinds of magic, just that it wasn't ideal.

Through the staff, the enchantment expanded the scope of any spell cast. It was meant to draw more water than the caster could control on their own, and to enhance their control over that spell.

Which, of course, was equally helpful to the Mirror of Silence. I drew more copies of Sola than I would have been able to before, and the spell wasn't impossibly difficult to control.

Against the Iron King, I had duplicated half a dozen Solas with Worldslayer, but it had taken me several minutes of chanting to do so with the aid of Eurias. Both Sola herself and her weapon were significant to the Aether, making them difficult to clone.

Thanks to the mech-sized staff and the support of the Aethertech devices in the Titan, I could do it faster this time. But every second felt like our last as Raion slashed orbs from the sky, the Swarm-Queen wove new layers of defense, and deadly spheres of rainbow light crashed on the outside of the water tunnel.

Each successive attack pushed deeper into the tube of water, some even impacting on my own Titan's shield. I shook in my seat but kept my concentration.

"Five seconds to abort," Sola said. She was making a reasonable

judgment based on the pace of the attacks chewing through her defenses and the rate at which Esh'kinaar was adding shields.

In five seconds, Sola would die. She'd be forced to fire as she went down, which could result in our shot being wasted.

Fortunately, I only needed four seconds to finish the spell.

The instant the last syllable of the incantation was out of my mouth, I snapped, "Fire!"

As her finger tightened on the trigger, five colorless copies of Sola flashed into being around her. They were taking the same actions she was, squeezing their own Worldslayers.

Six bridges of light—one crimson and five gray—suddenly connected with the Swarm-Queen.

There was no waiting to see if they would work. Sola's shots passed all the way to the far side of Esh'kinaar's body, piercing her shield as easily as the rest of her. She was skewered in six different places, sending out a psychic scream that sounded like a mother whose children had stabbed her in the back.

At the same time, balls of light finally broke through my spell. They detonated against the Solas, obliterating them all and lighting the shields around *The Last Horizon*.

I leaned back in my seat wearily, checking the power readings on my Titan. Sixty-one percent. Not too bad, although casting a spell outside of water elementalism had been more draining on the mech's Aethertech than I had expected.

If I was going to keep using the Divine Titan, I would have to get Mell to look at it. She could repair and maintain most Aethertech, not only those which fell under the purview of her gift, but this was a humanoid robotic system. Her android gift should be very compatible with it.

Between the two of us, we might even be able to come up with some upgrades.

"Where are you going, Red?" I asked.

Raion had begun piloting his mech toward the falling body of the Swarm-Queen. There should be no need for that; she didn't have any ability to bring herself back to life.

"We can't let that cocoon hatch!" Raion declared.

"We won't, but it's better for us to check it out remotely," I said. "It's too risky to approach."

"Don't listen to him," Omega urged. *"What does he know? Go ahead and approach the alien magic. Do it, do it, do it!"*

"Thanks, Orange!"

"Shut up, Orange. Red, I don't know what's in that cocoon. The magic is only there for protection and nourishment, so it doesn't give me any hint of what's inside."

Pathfinding magic would only lead me to whatever was inside, which wasn't any help. We already knew *where* it was. To identify anything, I'd have to sit here and guess, crossing off possibilities with pathfinding spells one at a time. And the cocoon itself might interfere, making my spells even less useful.

"We can't sit here and wait until it's ready!" Raion declared. His Titan came to a stop, hovering between the Swarm-Queen's bleeding body and the cocoon she left behind.

Though I kept calling it a 'cocoon,' it looked more like a small, shimmering moon. Its exterior looked rigid and reflective, like a polished eggshell made of rainbow magic.

Many of Esh'kinaar's defensive spells had been poured into this, and in the Aether, it resembled a layered and complex fortress wall. Not only was it too thick to easily break, but fortresses could contain any number of tricks, traps, and hidden systems.

"Breaking it could release something that kills us," I said to the crew. "On the other hand, letting it hatch could produce something worse. What do we think?"

"Break it," Sola said. *"When the Iron Legion is making a new weapon, I don't wait to see what it is."*

"If it's a vote, I say we back off," Mell said. She hunched over in her seat as though expecting to be attacked. *"What? We don't know what's in there. It could be a giant bomb. Gathering more information can't hurt."*

"It can't hurt us," Raion pointed out. *"It could hurt others. We should take the challenge head-on!"*

Omega extended several tendrils of ooze that all sprouted eyes to glare off-screen. From the way Mell flinched, I assumed they were pointed at her. *"Are you asking if we should leave an unknown danger behind us, untested? Foolish, foolish."*

Horizon mirrored Omega almost exactly, producing eyes of magic out of nowhere to glare offscreen. Mell hunched deeper into her chair. *"My Pilot has the right instincts. Surely we cannot claim to have vanquished the enemy unless we have crushed her plans completely."*

"Engineer Mell gave us her analysis, and she is not speaking out of unfounded fear but out of prudence," Shyrax said. She looked down on Omega and Horizon. *"Anyone who pressures her to silence her judgment can remove themselves from my bridge."*

Horizon looked confused. *"But…it's my bridge."*

"I have spoken," Shyrax said. *"Nonetheless, I also must weigh my counsel against the Captain and the Engineer. Now is our best opportunity. Instead of deciding whether to strike, we should be discussing* how *to strike while exposing ourselves to minimal risk."*

Though I had been outvoted, I felt a rush of relief. I was torn between my fear of losing the crew and my fear of allowing a greater threat to plague the galaxy. At least now the decision was made.

With the matter decided, I turned my mind to accomplishing it safely. "In that case, Horizon and I will back off to a safe distance and begin analysis. Red, give it a weak hit."

Raion didn't need to be told twice. Sunset wings flared out and his force-blade glowed as he prepared the Dance of a Burning World.

I tossed seals around him as I retreated, protecting him from a potential backlash. It was hard to decide what to protect him from, since I couldn't be sure what spells were hidden in the cocoon, but I covered as broad a spectrum as I could.

Raion's 'light hit' was a lash of his Combat Art that rivaled a solar flare from the nearby star. It washed over the target and tore away a chunk of magic.

The destroyed section turned into a whip and lashed at Raion, but he deflected it easily. *"No problem, Blue! I can handle this!"*

"Agreed. Horizon, three torpedoes."

"Standby," Sola said. *"Launch countdown onscreen."*

After a three-second countdown, three torpedoes flew from Horizon. They flickered like green lights as they went in and out of Subspace, quickly impacting the cocoon.

More chunks flew off, but this time the energy was absorbed deeper into the shell.

Mell pushed her glasses up her nose as she leaned forward. *"I could use a wizard opinion, but that looked like it went to feed whatever's inside."*

"Agreed. Let me try magic."

My rush of water got the same response Raion's Combat Art had; I tore away a piece of the cocoon's outer layer, and the severed section turned into a whip that struck at me.

It wasn't as easy to defend against as Raion had made it look. My Divine Titan's performance wasn't as enhanced as his was, so I couldn't bat the attack aside. Then again, I was dealing with a magical effect, so I knew how to adapt immediately.

I blasted most of it apart with water and handled the rest with a seal.

"Aetheric attacks result in a backlash, but they work," I reported. The patches that Raion and I had removed remained gone, revealing deeper layers. "I think we can break through it. Red, what do you think?"

Raion looked like he had never been invited to anything better in his life. *"Let's show them our combined power, Blue!"*

"Copy, Titan Knights," Shyrax said. *"Horizon agrees. We'll cover you."*

Though we had killed millions of D'Niss soldiers, there were still many scattered around the closest planets. Horizon had been lashing out at them as a matter of course, and the remnants of our fleet even remained engaged with them in the far reaches of the system.

Horizon could keep them from bothering me and Raion as we attacked the cocoon, but it was also for the best that they remain out of range in case something especially nasty came out. In the worst scenario, they could grab me and Raion from our Titans to save our lives.

"Keep those teleporters hot, Horizon. Red, let's go."

Side by side, Raion and I engaged our Divine Titans at the same time.

Energetic wings of sapphire and sunset-stained ruby flared. Raion drew his force-blade back for a thrust, light collecting in it, as panels on my own mech opened. Conjured water from all around the sun pulled itself back together, gathering into another spear.

Blue and red Aethertech eyes flashed at once.

We released our attacks simultaneously, a shimmering lance of blue and a molten spear of burning sunlight striking the cocoon together.

The detonation as our attacks connected was enough to cause my external cameras to shake for a moment, and my energy supply went down to forty-four percent. When the light cleared, I saw the protective spell's retaliation coming for us.

It was like a rainbow wave rising up to drown us, or a mouth extending to swallow us whole. I quickly chanted while spinning my staff into Aetheric symbols, drawing water up into another barrier around us even as I enchanted it with sealing magic.

Raion supported my effort with his shield projector. Mine was at full power, but his had been enhanced like every other aspect of his Divine Titan. The sunlight-tinged red shield spread over both of us.

At that point, the wave of destructive energy crashed into us, and it didn't seem like this was just made up of the magic we'd torn away from the cocoon's exterior. It was as though the spell's entire structure was poured into this.

Which was good news, in some ways. We'd broken the cocoon.

On the other hand, we might be about to lose our Divine Titans as well. My water boiled away immediately, shredded by the alien magic of the D'Niss. My seals flared white, and I reinforced them with constant chanting as Raion's shield shone brighter.

The Aether was bending against me, leaning toward the force of the spell Esh'kinaar left behind. To some degree, she'd reinforced it by dying while chanting; it had been the last thing the Swarm-Queen focused on, so it had gained an extra measure of weight in the Aether.

I was feeling that weight, as I tried to keep my seals up while multicolored energy devoured me from every angle. No matter what I did, the spell crushed us in its iron grip.

Even Raion's shield crumbled and destabilized, leaving my own and the few remnants of my sealing magic. I chanted until the end, spinning my staff in careful patterns.

The spell slammed into us.

CHAPTER FORTY-THREE

ESH'KINAAR'S SPAWN MAGIC was a form of conjuration, a biological spell designed to make new versions of the D'Niss.

She could consume World Spirits by breaking them down and converting them to new creatures. When she turned that magic into a protective field, the result was insidious.

Her cocoon was wrapped with an insect queen's desire to protect her hive. Energy that could be absorbed and used for nourishment was absorbed directly, and anything else was turned against the attacker.

In other words, Raion and I were being digested.

When the spell hit us, the Blue Titan shone around me, but I instantly lost contact with the outside world. The mech glowed blue, its magic resistance engaged against the foreign energies, but I no longer had control. Nor any way to check on anyone else.

Not directly, anyway.

"Don't eject me, Horizon," I said into the silence. I wasn't sure she could hear me, and she couldn't transport me out of the Divine Titan without my assistance anyway, but I needed to handle this on my own.

I unstrapped myself from the pilot seat, pulled my wand, and continued casting.

All around me, I saw Aetheric symbols flashing like sparks in the darkness as the Titan's protective systems preserved me. I focused all my attention on helping them, tossing supportive seals in all directions.

It was five minutes before I felt the tide start to turn. The pressure on the Titan lightened, and my spells lasted a little longer. I'd weathered the worst of the storm, and it was only a matter of time before my mech came back online.

But the longer it took, the more I worried about Raion.

His Titan was more resilient than mine, and Horizon could pull him out. But he had no way of helping the Titan resist the magic. I could help, he couldn't. Which may prompt his Titan to start feeding on him like a parasite, as it had done before.

When the blue light faded inside my Titan and gave way to the light of consoles, I let out a breath in relief. But that breath caught when I saw the Red Titan in front of me.

It looked like it had bathed in acid. Plates all over were destroyed, revealing veins of molten sunlight or sparking Aethertech components within. Its left eye was missing entirely, showing arcane mechanical circuitry, and its left arm was skeletal.

Even the chest plate, behind which the pilot sat, had been largely dissolved. Aetheric symbols shone inside, enchantments exposed to the air.

Only a moment later, I finished my breath as Raion's concerned face popped up in a box on my screen. *"Blue! Answer me! Blue, are you okay?"*

"You should be able to see me by now, Red."

"That doesn't mean you're okay!"

I half-laughed, but I didn't have time to be too relieved. I turned my mech around—the Titan moved sluggishly as the computer informed me about damage to my primary thrusters—and I looked for the cocoon.

As expected, another D'Niss hung there. Its black carapace glistened in the starlight, and it folded itself in the fetal position.

Though it didn't move, I read deadly magic in the reflections of its shell. "Horizon, what can you tell me about that thing?"

Horizon herself appeared first, directing her multi-eyed glare at me instead of Mell this time. *"That thing? We were worried about* you! *Do you know what it would do to me if you died after asking me not to save you?"*

So she *had* heard me.

"Thanks for listening, Horizon. But I told you I was okay."

Mell appeared next. She had half a toothpick in her fingers. It looked like she'd bitten through it, and she was still pale. *"Captain—Blue, whatever—have you taken a look at your mech?"*

I hadn't, so I conjured an eyeball and used it to get a view of my own Divine Titan.

Throughout the cocoon's backlash, I had been more worried about Horizon than myself. I could read the wave of magic well enough, and besides, I was uniquely suited to defending against spells.

But I felt a thrill of too-late fear as I saw the state of the Blue Titan.

Both eyes were missing, and the head was little more than a mechanical skull. The staff was a lump of half-melted metal, and Aetheric symbols flickered from broken magic circles all over. Most of the armor's plates had been seared off, and overall the mech looked like a man whose skin had been melted away to reveal a mechanical body beneath.

"Ouch," I said. "Doctor Cryce isn't going to be happy with me."

"If I were her, I'd kill you," Mell agreed.

Horizon grabbed a camera and moved it so close that I could only see half her face. *"Worry about* my *happiness, Captain! Mine! My Engineer and I can help her rebuild the Divine Titan, but we can't rebuild you!"*

Mell looked me up and down while stroking her chin. *"I think I could."*

"Blue Knight withdrawing," I said. My power was down to twelve percent anyway, given what the Titan had poured into magic defense. "Tell Ark to open up. While I dock, brief me on what we know about the new D'Niss."

"Nonresponsive," Shyrax informed us. *"Scans are inconclusive, but given the state of your Titans, you should both withdraw."*

"I can still fight!" Raion declared.

"You're below twenty percent, and the time has come to retreat." Shyrax didn't tolerate argument, and her tone made that clear. *"Now that there is no cocoon, we will attack the target from a distance."*

I agreed, and I was about to say so when the entire Blue Titan shivered around me.

My head seemed to turn itself, forcing me to stare at the new, black D'Niss. It had begun to move.

One limb unfolded, revealing a gleaming, black blade. Only that glimpse, and I saw that its edge held a deadly enchantment. As powerful as anything I'd ever seen.

While the unsheathing of its blade was slow, its next motion was instant. The shell on its back cracked, revealing wings of shadow.

"Retreat!" I shouted.

In a flurry of shadow, the new monster vanished. I had only enough time to recognize a method of Subspace travel similar to Omega's when the light around me vanished.

Considering I was next to a sun, there was only one thing that could cause that. The D'Niss had reappeared right on top of me.

"Horizon!"

Before I'd finished calling her name, I was wrapped up in blue light and reappeared on the bridge of *The Last Horizon*. In time to see the giant insect slicing the Blue Divine Titan in half.

Now that it had unfolded itself and I could see its form clearly, my entire body shivered.

Esh'kinaar had given birth to a new Swarm-Queen.

This D'Niss looked like a clone of Esh'kinaar, but in shades of gleaming black rather than an alien rainbow. Its head was like an insectoid portal onto a dimension of darkness, not Subspace, and the edges of its four bladed arms drank light.

But more than its appearance, I was focused on its reflection in the Aether. There was no spawn magic in this Queen, for which I felt I should have been grateful. After her, there would be no more D'Niss to haunt the galaxy.

Instead, hers was the magic of death. The inevitable, unstoppable demise of all things.

When she screamed, her first cry in this universe struck us like a call for execution.

We were dazed by the cry, but Sola was more prepared than the rest of us. She wore her armor at her console, so she reacted immediately. She unloaded into the newborn Swarm-Queen, an emerald salvo that looked like it came from an entire fleet.

The first few shots impacted, but before I could see what they'd done to the alien carapace, the D'Niss vanished in another flurry of shadow.

And so did Raion.

A second later, black and red giants clashed over *The Last Horizon*. I staggered as the impact shook our ship, then I dropped into my captain's chair.

"Sola, what do we have that can hurt that thing?"

"Conventional weaponry can chip away at it eventually," Sola said. As she spoke, Raion and the Swarm-Queen traded blows, operating their Combat Arts to swing vast tides of crimson flame and deadly shadow all through the system.

Omega's eye flickered with superhuman speed to keep up as he manipulated the controls, unusually serious. For once, our Pilot was doing his job without comment.

"Without Raion aboard, our shields cannot take a direct hit," Shyrax reported. "Unless you can use your magic, Captain, we should retreat. We are unarmed and unprepared for this contest."

Mell pushed her glasses up and rubbed her nose. "It didn't go through the entire gestation process. It has to be weakened, right?"

"I believe this is *weakened,"* Horizon said. I agreed, but I didn't agree with the glee that lit her eyes as she said it.

"The best weapon we have left," I said, "is Raion. I have one last bet to make, and we have to make it fast. Twenty percent won't last in this fight. Sola, Omega, keep us alive. Shyrax, Mell, start rerouting power to the communications array. We need to reach as many Sublines as we can."

Raion clashed against the void-black D'Niss over and over again, and every time their swords met, he sank deeper into the battle.

Around him, the Red Divine Titan was having the time of its life. The veins of liquid sunlight running through it drilled into Raion, filling him with power and draining him at the same time. He felt adrift, drowning in a sea of energy.

Still, he maintained his consciousness. Barely. All he could feel was the rhythm of the Dance of a Burning World.

And the world was surely burning.

The slashes of his enemy's claws left a line behind, and while Raion was no wizard, he instinctively avoided the lines until they vanished. It was as though the D'Niss was breaking the world itself.

And the black energy that surrounded those blades was every bit as bad. It made Raion think of death.

The Dance of the Burning World required him to give himself over to the knowledge that everything was being destroyed around him all the time. It was the entropy of the universe, or so his mentor put it.

Raion thought of it as using negativity to a positive purpose. He knew the world was always falling apart. He could see it.

And if he could use the power of that destruction to prevent things from getting worse, well, that was the best thing he could do with his life.

The Divine Titan was crumbling around him, each exchange losing him another plate of armor. The more it did, the more it drew from him, and the more Raion's consciousness faded away.

And as it faded, he saw the constellation of friendship around him.

Varic was a burning sun nearby, his best friend from another life. He had drawn on that connection liberally to stay conscious, and though the relationship was strong, he had taken almost all he could from it.

When he saw that, Raion turned the rictus of his bared teeth into an actual grin. He had tried his best. He'd served *The Last Horizon* as its Knight until the very end.

The other members of the crew had been shouting at him from the beginning, but Raion had heard nothing of it. But as he sank deeper into the Divine Titan, losing his grasp on the world around him, for some reason their voices became clearer.

"How's our connection, Mell?" Varic asked.

"I don't know, but we're trying it! Raion! Stay awake!"

"My Knight!" Horizon shouted. *"Your contract is not done yet!"*

Raion agreed. His contract wouldn't be finished until he destroyed the enemy and left the others safe.

"Play it," Varic ordered.

Another voice came over the connection to Raion, then, a voice he remembered from his childhood. His brother.

"Raion, I'm sorry," Ryzer said. *"I don't...Worlds, I don't know what to say. They said to talk to you, but all I can think of is how sorry I am. I let you down. I need you to make it home so I can say it to you in person."*

As he spoke, the tiny spark that was their friendship grew a little brighter. A little easier to touch.

That small power brought some clarity to Raion's gaze. He pushed the Titan, taking back some of his control.

But not much. It was a nice boost, and a great memory to take with him when he left, but it wasn't enough to make a difference.

"Red Knight, are you listening to me, because you really shouldn't be piloting my Titan in that condition," a woman said in a rush.

Doctor Cryce.

"Having said that, I can't really stop you, can I? If you give up now, we don't have anyone else who can save the rest of us, so you really are the last line of defense between us and death. By the way, who was that Blue Knight? Was that you, Captain? What did you do to my T—"

"Oh no, we lost signal," Varic said.

Doctor Cryce's trust in Raion had always been one of the background stars of his constellation, but it had been buried beneath her own grief. This time, it shone through.

Raion touched it and more control returned to him. His third eye saw a little more of the giant insect's aura.

"Are you fighting alone again, Raion?" Javik Leed asked. His voice was scratchier than the Doctor's, stretched across more Sublines, but still clear enough. He sighed. *"You've got to stop doing that. Don't you have a new crew now? How do you think they're going to feel if you die?"*

The stars representing Raion's friendships weren't actually different colors. They weren't actually *any* colors, since they were nothing more than a representation of how Raion felt his connections. But he thought Javik's was yellow, and it grew that much brighter.

A second later, a green-tinged one shone as well.

A cough came through the Subline and somehow it sounded louder than anything Raion had heard thus far. Even the crash of battle.

"Can you hear me, Red?" Parryl asked.

The former Green Knight's voice was small and weak. Even more so than the last time he'd heard it, more than five years ago.

"Sorry I let you down," she said, and Raion shook his head even though she couldn't see him. He tried to speak, but he only made a choking sound. He still didn't have control over his own body.

"I wish I could be out there with you," Parryl went on. *"So don't lose until I can get there...Don't lose."*

Her star burned with flickering hope and steady faith.

The wings of the D'Niss spread and it struck with both of its upper claws at once.

Raion swept his force-blade in a circle, blocking with a shield of crimson flame. It didn't just block the attack. It sent a scarlet supernova flashing through space, brighter than the local sun.

The Red Divine Titan might have been on the verge of crumbling apart, but it burned brighter than ever. Rather than it drawing power from him, Raion shoved power into *it*. Power that he wasn't even sure he had.

"This is ridiculous!" Mell shouted. *"How does this work? After you win the fight, explain it to me!"*

Omega laughed wildly into the microphone. *"Go, fight, win! Don't let down your old friend, Orange!"*

"Stay alive," Sola said.

Raion moved his eyes to the monitors, where he saw Shyrax looking into the distance. *"I expect you back aboard* The Last Horizon *tomorrow, where we can discuss your performance. If you could fight at this level on the verge of death, you should be able to do it while healthy."*

Her trust in him was strong and steady.

Finally, Varic's voice came again. *"We've sent video of your fight into the galaxy as widely as we can. You have more friends than you think you do, Raion."*

Raion reached out to as many of the stars in his private constellation as he could, pulling on them as though drawing a deep breath.

They flared brighter. Thousands of them. Individually, they were weak, but there were far more than he could count.

Dark blades surrounded him, but the Divine Titan now flared like a red sun with his aura. The attacks of the D'Niss crashed into the energy around him and broke.

Raion woke entirely, gripping the controls. The orange-gold veins of the solar dragon's blood slowly transformed, turning a bright, burning red as his own power dwarfed that of the Divine Titan.

Then Raion slashed down as though he meant to burn through the world itself. A blade of flame passed through the D'Niss. And through most of the rest of the system.

A burning wall of fire sliced the Visiria system in half.

The D'Niss had thrown itself to the side, but it was still cleaved and burned at the same time. All the limbs on the right side of its body were missing, and its psychic scream was of equal parts rage and confusion.

Even so, Raion had put his whole being into that attack. He had nothing left, but everything wasn't enough. The monster was still alive.

It pulled its gleaming black blade back, and there was nothing Raion could do about it. But he was satisfied. He had really, truly, given everything he had.

"Absolute Burial," Varic said.

The remaining half of the new Swarm-Queen collapsed into a shining white ball, hovering in front of the Red Divine Titan.

Cheering came from the bridge of *The Last Horizon,* and Raion croaked out a question. "When...did you..."

"I needed you to weaken it first," Varic said. He had a barely visible smile, and his silver eyes twinkled. *"What? I couldn't leave it all to the power of friendship."*

EPILOGUE

As I sat in a chair in my room, Horizon sulked in front of me. Visibly. She had manifested herself in hologram form solely to demonstrate how upset she was.

"We could have kept it," Horizon said. Her crossed arms blocked my vision, and she kicked at my chair.

"I like it better in the center of a sun."

"You kept Starhammer!"

"We have Starhammer's creator onboard."

"Think of the magic you could have done with its body!"

"I have enough magic." Certainly, the corpse of a second-generation Swarm-Queen would have made great ritual material. And an almost infinite supply, given its size.

But I wouldn't sleep easy with its body around. Any chance of resurrection was too much.

"Then why can't we keep Esh'kinaar? We know for sure that she's dead!"

I pointed to the monitor on my wall, where a blinking red light approached the nearest star. "Too late now."

"Not yet! We can still call it back!"

"Yeah, but I don't want to. Besides, you got to keep a claw."

"I got to keep a shard *of a claw."* Floors below, in Horizon's sealed vault, two curved sections of razor-sharp carapace hung on the wall. They were crossed like a pair of swords, one black and one shimmering in many colors.

They were the largest pieces of Esh'kinaar and her heir that I had allowed Horizon to keep. Trophies to celebrate her victory, sure. A chance of world-eating monsters returning to existence, no.

"Last chance, Captain! We can call it off now! Maybe you want some time to think about it."

"No, I'm quite satisfied with the way things are going." The monitor showed the Subspace torpedoes impacting the star, and Horizon's pout turned into a glare.

"Destruction confirmed, Captain. You have successfully burned treasures worth half the galaxy so that you may rest more easily."

"One percent of the galaxy, at most. And we aren't done. I've been through this with the Iron King once already." Pathfinding spells confirmed that the two Swarm-Queen corpses no longer existed, cameras in the vault showed that the shards of their claws were still there, and I took a minute to glance through several carefully chosen eyes that I'd positioned around the impact site.

With all that, I breathed more easily. Unlike last time, I wasn't relying on *Moonfall*'s sensors but those of *The Last Horizon* with a Pilot aboard. Between those and my own spells, I was as certain as I could be that Esh'kinaar had been completely destroyed.

"To worry so much isn't very heroic of you, Captain. We defeated her once. We could do it again."

She was still sulking, and ordinarily I would have indulged her. At least to make her feel better. But with the immediate crisis past, I still had no sense that the world was any safer.

"What do you think the future holds for us, Horizon?"

She lifted her chin, her horns tilting back. *"Victory and glory, as long as we don't let* fear *make all our decisions for us."*

"I did everything I could think of to prevent the disasters I foresaw from coming true in this life. One failure, that's bad luck. Two is a coincidence. Three is a pattern."

In spite of her irritation, Horizon was looking more and more interested. *"I can only agree. But what do you plan to do about it, Captain?"*

"It's clear what the Aether is doing. It prepared me for the threats we would need to face. And the good news is, that means we know what we're up against."

I projected a list from my console onto the air in front of me. It was an old list, one I'd updated in light of recent events.

A list of five names. Three were crossed out: the Iron King, Starhammer, and Esh'kinaar.

"Only two enemies left," Horizon said. *"That's a little disappointing. Maybe my siblings will make them a better challenge."*

"That's not what I see." I looked at the remaining two names on the list. "The Aether didn't awaken all seven Zenith Devices and give me seven lives so we could face *five* enemies. Solstice and the Perfected aren't the last two obstacles remaining. They're the last two we know about."

Horizon's multicolored eyes sparkled. *"So how do we identify these unknown enemies, Captain?"*

"We cross off the two names we do know." I stood from my chair, settling my mantle around me. "Crew meeting tomorrow. I've had enough with waiting for enemies to strike first. We're taking the fight to Fathom."

Horizon clapped and jumped up and down. *"Well said, Captain, well said! And next time, we won't have to throw anything into a sun."*

I hoped that was true. Solstice was the hardest of my enemies to root out, a specter with no form. But we couldn't go to war with Karosha's Perfected while a hostile Galactic Union waited behind us.

The Aether had given me a chance to prepare. It was about time I got ahead of my enemies.

No matter who they were.

Benri Vallenar often worked late. In fact, he considered the rest of his life little but an extension of his work, so all his time was company time.

He dashed off his signature on a document, approving permission to extend manufacturing rights to a minor mechanical supply company in the Free Worlds. With the fall of the Advocates, many otherwise-independent companies were scrambling to join a major corporation, so everyone at Vallenar was scrambling to pick up as much as they could.

This was business as usual, though. He was sure there was about to be major news around the Visiria System, once the Subline caught up. More spotlight for *The Last Horizon,* and more scraps to pick up for the Corporation.

A light began to blink at the corner of his vision. An incoming call.

"Who's calling?" he asked, because it was easier to ask than to check on his own.

His processor's AI responded robotically. *"No one."*

Benri's heart rate quickened. "Accept the call."

"I apologize, but there is no call to answer."

Despite the words of his processor, the light stopped and he heard a soft click as his audio connected.

The voice that spoke into his head this time was smooth, cultured, a male voice he didn't recognize. It was as precise as an AI, though he suspected it wasn't one. *"Good evening, Mister Vallenar. I was disappointed to learn that you lost the Cannon."*

Benri dismissed his documents and leaned back in his chair, keeping the excitement from his voice. "I was expecting you to call earlier. Subline reception on Fathom must have gotten worse."

"There's been a lot to catch up on in the galaxy, these days. For the moment, however, you have my attention."

With a deep breath, Benri took a risk. "So am I talking to the Zenith Processor itself, or a host?"

"Well done, Mister Vallenar. I am indeed the World Spirit of the Zenith Processor. You learned quite a lot from examining my sisters, I see."

Benri drummed his fingers on the edge of his desk. "Consider that my application."

"Your son turned you down, did he? That's good to know. Well, you should know that the organization I represent is...quite averse to bringing in new members."

"Make an exception."

To Benri's relief, the Zenith Device chuckled. *"I think I will. Between the Iron King's high opinion of your magic, your connection to Horizon, and your own resources, I consider you highly qualified as an ally."*

Benri's breath released. "You won't regret it. I can meet you on Fathom in three days."

"We'll send someone for you. Though it may be presumptuous of me, allow me to be the first to say it: Welcome to Solstice, Mister Vallenar."

THE END

The adventures of
The Last Horizon continue in...

PILOT

THE LAST HORIZON

BOOK FOUR

AVAILABLE SOON!

(If you're flying through a star system with Subline access, tell your AI to visit **WillWight.com**)

SPACE BLOOPERS 3: REVELATIONS

Another voice came over the connection to Raion, then, a voice he remembered from his childhood. His brother.

"Raion, I'm sorry," Ryzer said. *"I don't...Worlds, I don't know what to say. They said to talk to you, but all I can think of is how sorry I am. I let you down. I need you to make it home so I can say it to you in person."*

"It's okay, Ryzer. I forgive you."

"No, I mean I need *you to make it home. I'm afraid of what your Captain will do to me if you don't."*

"Don't worry—"

"I fear for my safety. All I see at night are those burning silver eyes. I can't sleep! I can't eat! Please, just tell him how sorry I am!"

"Ryzer, it's all right," Raion assured him. "The Captain wouldn't hurt you. Right, Varic?"

Static came over the Subline a moment before Varic answered. *"Oh, never. Definitely. For sure. Ryzer, let's move to a private call, shall we?"*

The flame of friendship representing Ryzer flared brighter in Raion's mind. Almost as though his brother had started praying.

What a wonderful sign of friendship!

Kyri pulled her arm off.

"Wrong arm!" I shouted, but it was too late.

She screamed. I screamed. Blood sprayed everywhere.

Anyway, that's how she died.

After defeating the Swarm-Queen, Raion and I limped out of our Divine Titans and through the hangar. Even injured as he was, he supported me in my exhaustion.

"Whew," Raion said. "I can't believe we won."

"It was close, but at least we—"

"...without combining!"

"What?"

"Combining our Divine Titans. You know, the last resort. When things get really dire, we combine our mechs into a larger, stronger form! For the big enemies."

I staggered in place. "Raion, I've never heard of combining."

"You didn't know we could do that? Yeah, it's insanely powerful."

"Why didn't you tell me!? We could have *started* with that!"

"Oh, no, we'd never start with it! The fight would be over too fast."

I couldn't hurt Raion by punching him, but I tried.

"I'm glad we left the mission on Visiria to Omega!" Raion said, as our shuttle landed. "I trust him to get the Heart of Visiria and preserve our reputation!"

We left the shuttle to find a smoking crater where the Prime Coliseum once stood. Omega walked away from it, hands raised.

"Before you get all *mad,* let me first say that I had no choice."

I took a deep breath. "What happened, Omega?"

"You see, Captain, they told me that *The Last Horizon*'s reputation relied on my behavior. I *had* to challenge their greatest arena fighters, as representatives of their senators, or the ship's good name would suffer!"

"You shot them immediately, didn't you?"

"I shot them *immediately.*"

I turned to Raion. "You know, I've never asked: how did you get access to the power of friendship?"

His face turned serious. "It all goes back to my uncle. A mugger shot him, a mugger I could have stopped. 'If you want great responsibility,' my uncle said, 'you'll need great power to go with it.' Those were his last words."

"Never mind. For some reason I don't want to hear the rest of this."

"On the way home that night, I was bitten by a radioactive friend!"

Under our devastating barrage, the Swarm-Queen's cocoon cracked. It split apart, and *something* emerged. A river of brightly colored specks, pouring out into space. The river split into streams, targeting the nearby planets.

I choked down my horror. "Horizon, get me analysis. What is that stuff? Spores?"

"The substance has already reached Visiria, Captain. All over the planet, it appears to be…raining candy."

"What?"

"Yes, the cocoon was filled with candy."

"What kind?"

Horizon took in a deep breath, as though to deliver grave news. *"Candy corn."*

I gripped the controls of my Titan. "This monster must be stopped."

Bored, I flipped on the Subline and scanned for entertainment. The most popular broadcast on the closest planet was some kind of animated action show, so I projected it onto the screen in my quarters.

Colors flashed brightly as a theme song played.

"Welcome," the narrator cried, *"to the Adventures of Orange and Lemon, Citrus Crusaders!"*

A pair of characters dashed onto the screen. One, a bald woman with a flowing yellow cape and a bright 'L' on her chest. The other, a man with a beaming smile and a glowing orange Aethertech eye that matched his trench coat.

They reached each other and struck a pose.

"Crime won't pay with the Citrus Crusaders on the case! Orange and Lemon fly across the galaxy, seeking out the worst criminals and bringing them to justice! All fueled by Starpop Soda's new Double Citrus flavor! Starpop Soda: Embrace the Beast!"

Under his breath, the narrator muttered, *"Sponsored by the Vallenar Corporation."*

I turned the screen off.

WILL WIGHT is the *New York Times* and #1 Kindle best-selling author of the *Cradle* series, a space-fantasy series entitled *The Last Horizon*, and a handful of other books that he regularly forgets to mention. His true power is only unleashed during a full moon, when he transforms into a monstrous mongoose.

Will lives in Florida, lurking beneath the swamps to ambush prey. He graduated from the University of Central Florida, where he received a Master of Fine Arts in Creative Writing and a cursed coin of Spanish gold.

Visit his website at *WillWight.com* for eldritch incantations, book news, and a blessing of prosperity for your crops. If you believe you have experienced a sighting of Will Wight, please report it to the agents listening from your attic.

CREW DATA

THE CAPTAIN: VARIC VALLENAR

Human wizard with genetically modified silver hair and eyes. The only human capable of mastering seven different magic disciplines due to a ritual that gave him memories from several alternate lives. Doesn't like cheese.

THE KNIGHT: RAION RAITHE

Visiri fighter from an order of mech-piloting warriors known as the Titan Force. The last active member of that organization and the master of a legendary Combat Art. Fueled by the power of friendship, and can't handle scary movies.

THE SWORD: SOLA KALTER

Lichborn mercenary waging a one-woman war on the galactic force of cyborg zombies known as the Iron Legion. Wears a suit of Aethertech power armor that can be upgraded when she defeats powerful enemies. When killed, she returns to life from a magical flame. Enjoys bathing in deadly radiation.

THE PILOT: OMAL "OMEGA" ESCALON

Human vigilante/assassin extensively modified by Aethertech to give him the ability to teleport, shapeshift, regenerate, and melt into a puddle of dark grayish ooze. One eye is visibly artificial, glows orange, and can see into spectrums usually reserved for starship sensors. Had a pet dog when he was a child, and nothing tragic happened to it.

THE COMMANDER: QUEEN SHYRAX THE THIRD

Former queen of the planet Karosha before she was ousted in a coup. Currently gathering support for a rebellion. An expert Combat Artist, wizard, Aether Technician, tactician, marksman, pilot, programmer, botanist, and juggler.

THE ENGINEER: MELL D-ONE-TWENTY-FIVE

A human woman cloned from the DNA of four expert Aether Technicians. Has the gift for creating androids with a variety of functions and abilities, which she calls Nova-Bots. Her dentist told her to stop eating candy, but she refused.

THE ZENITH DEVICES

THE LAST HORIZON – THE ZENITH STARSHIP,

made to explore the galaxy. Borrows the power of six crew members, each of whom enhances the ship's systems in a different way.

SHADOW ARK – THE ZENITH COLONY,

made to contain and protect groups of people. Can take in entire planets, and its stealth and shielding capabilities grow stronger with more residents.

MORTAL EDICT – THE ZENITH CANNON,

made to combat alien threats. Its abilities are thus far unknown, but it requires a bearer with an Aethertech affinity for firearms.

VOID PRISM – THE ZENITH PROCESSOR,

a computer implant that enhances gifts, powers, and spells that affect the mind. Can interfere with lesser technology.

HALLOW DIVIDE – THE ZENITH BLADE,

a force-blade that enhances the power of the Combat Artist wielding it.

EMINENCE CORE – THE ZENITH ENGINE,

the ultimate energy-generating device. Further abilities are thus far unknown.

GENESIS VAULT – THE ZENITH CHAMBER,

a genetic modification machine in the care of the Perfected.

COMMON KNOWLEDGE OF THE GALAXY

The Five Major Species Humans, Karoshans, Visiri, Aethril, and Lichborn. There are many other intelligent mortals in the galaxy, but these are the most influential and widespread. Their origins are widely debated, but certain evidence suggests that all other intelligent species were originally humans modified through science and magic.

Of course, this is a human theory.

Karoshans With thick, leathery skin in a wide variety of colors and a towering height that averages at around ten feet, Karoshans maintain that they are the descendants of dragons. Their hair is made up of long, thick cables that naturally glow like strands of neon.

Karoshans are not only larger than humans but tend to be stronger and more magically gifted. They even produce more offspring and display a higher instance of Aethertech gifts. However, Karoshan Aether Technicians are never able to *create* Aethertech, only modify or enhance existing devices.

Also, while they have high average skill in both magic and Combat Arts, they tend to have a harder time reaching the heights of those fields.

The Perfected A group of Karoshans granted incredible abilities through genetic and magical engineering. They consider themselves superior to baseline Karoshans and believe that they should inherit the planet, but the process used to create them carries a high risk of death.

Visiri Red-skinned, three-eyed warriors with an innate pool of energy that can be used to enhance physical abilities, endure gunfire, shoot blasts from their hands, or even fly.

Historically, they tended to value warfare and combat ability more than the average species, but they have branched out into all other fields in recent centuries. They are natural Combat Artists, learning such techniques easily and getting better results out of them thanks to their energy reserves.

Aether Technicians and wizards are rare on their planet, and they tend toward more straightforward expressions of both Aethertech and magic, like shield projectors or elementalism.

Visiria is an ally to the Karoshan Empire. Together with a handful of other minor planets, they form the Karoshan Alliance, which was created to balance the influence of the Galactic Union.

Aethril A thin species of natural wizards with pale bluish skin and sparkling starlight hair. They have a connection to the Aether from the moment they are born, and even those who don't become wizards can still perform magic to some degree.

They are perfectly capable of developing Combat Artists and Aether Technicians, though their bodies are somewhat less durable than their peers. However, culturally they tend to celebrate magic the most.

Rather than an actual planet, their homeworld is a planet-sized tree nourished by the Aether. The advantages of this are unclear.

Lichborn The one major species indisputably known to descend from an altered group of humans, Lichborn were created using the Zenith Chamber. They were infused with magic to allow them to endure the most extreme environmental hazards, the process of which left them with gray skin and glowing green eyes.

They also tend to be unusually attractive by human standards, as their ancestors were custom-designed by humanity. Lichborn produce Aether Technicians and special Aethertech affinities at a high rate, and they have their fair share of wizards and Combat Artists as well.

Of course, they can't do it all. All their talents are influenced by the magic bound to their bloodline, meaning they have an excellent talent for fields like necromancy, genetic manipulation, and corrosive Combat Arts.

Their homeworld, Dornoth IV, is widely considered the worst inhabited planet in the galaxy. Its harsh, toxic conditions tend to be unpleasant even for Lichborn, and instantly lethal to humans.

Humans They're humans.

Aside from being the theoretical origin of all the other intelligent species in the galaxy, humanity is mostly known for their Aether Technicians. They produce the most Technicians and the best, so their home planet of Fathom is famous for its Aethertech exports. It is also the birthplace of the Zenith Devices.

Many of the major species also have difficulty reproducing with one another, with genetic technology required to viably produce a hybrid child. Human genes are widely compatible, making half-Visiri, half-Aethril, or half-Lichborn much more common when the other half is human.

Subspace A dimension of disorienting rainbow light considered to be "beneath" physical space. Diving into Subspace is required for interstellar travel, as physical distance can be easily skipped.

It's easier on the Subspace Drive to travel longer distances, as micro-dives can destabilize the engines and are inefficient in fuel consumption.

Subspace itself is poorly understood, but it is the home of indescribable creatures thought to come from beyond the universe. Fortunately, such monsters are rare. The more common danger comes from 'Subspace madness,' a condition that afflicts those who spend too long staring into the disorienting, colorful lights of the dimension.

If you stare long enough, you can almost hear something calling your name...

Subline An interplanetary information-sharing network in which data is transmitted through Subspace.

Most major planets, colonies, and organizations have a Subline, though there is no unified galactic Subline due to the difficulties of long-distance Subspace transmission.

The Aether An unseen force that flows through this universe and the source of all magic. Mysterious and beyond mortal comprehension, but it always responds to certain principles, allowing for the casting of spells.

The Aether is thicker in some areas and weaker in others, resulting in an increase or decrease in the power of spells. In certain zones, magic might even be completely unusable, though the Aether tends to balance itself over time.

Aethertech Technological devices with capabilities beyond normal science. People capable of making Aethertech are called Aether Technicians, who were usually researchers, scientists, engineers, or craftsmen gifted with the ability to break the limits of their mundane discipline.

A Technician's 'gift' determines what they can make. Some Technicians have a gift for Subspace Drives, while others might be able to create life-support systems or advanced materials. Depending on the gift, Technicians can bend certain limitations of the creation process; perhaps they can make ten remote controls though they only have the materials for nine, or perhaps they can substitute common metals for rare minerals.

Aethertech is divided into several grades.

Low-grade – The device is comparable to the best of mundane technology but has a few minor advantages, like being more durable, lighter weight, or smaller.

Middle-grade – The device is better than the best mundane technology, with major functions that can't be replicated otherwise, like a small breathing mask that creates breathable air from energy or a processor that connects to the Subline regardless of range.

High-grade – A creation is considered high-grade Aethertech when it has impossible functions that would normally require several middle-grade machines working together. Giant mechs capable of doing battle with monstrous aliens, gates that teleport people through Subspace without requiring a ship, and factories that produce Subspace Drives for a fraction of the normal cost are all high-grade Aethertech.

Masterwork – Not a separate grade of its own, but rather a designation for the best high-grade Aethertech. Sometimes called 'top-grade.' Masterworks are rare creations that even the best Technicians can only make a handful of times in their lives. Making one is what separates an expert Aether Technician from a master.

Combat Arts A method of magic that long ago branched off to become its own field, Combat Arts are methods of movement that invoke the Aether to produce supernatural effects.

In short, magical martial arts.

Since performing a specific technique is comparable to a wizard chanting a spell, simply performing the movements is not enough. A layperson could imitate the motions of a master Combat Artist and accomplish none of the flashy Aetheric effects.

Each Combat Art requires a specific mindset, philosophy, or set of actions to function correctly. Some mandate that their practitioners endure a year of training in the snow, climb a certain mountain blindfolded, or simply live by a particular mantra or code. Often, there are several such requirements that work in tandem.

The more a Combat Artist fulfills their requirements and practices their Art, the more powerfully they can call upon the Aether.

WILL WIGHT is the *New York Times* and #1 Kindle best-selling author of the *Cradle* series, a space-fantasy series entitled *The Last Horizon*, and a handful of other books that he regularly forgets to mention. His true power is only unleashed during a full moon, when he transforms into a monstrous mongoose.

Will lives in Florida, lurking beneath the swamps to ambush prey. He graduated from the University of Central Florida, where he received a Master of Fine Arts in Creative Writing and a cursed coin of Spanish gold.

Visit his website at *WillWight.com* for eldritch incantations, book news, and a blessing of prosperity for your crops. If you believe you have experienced a sighting of Will Wight, please report it to the agents listening from your attic.

HIDDEN
GNOME
PUBLISHING